DEATH BY INFERIOR DESIGN

The Domestic Bliss Mysteries
of LESLIE CAINE

Death by Inferior Design
False Premises
Manor of Death
Killed by Clutter

a domestic
bliss mystery

KILLED
BY
CLUTTER

Leslie Caine

A DELL BOOK

KILLED BY CLUTTER
A Dell Book / March 2007

Published by
Bantam Dell
A Division of Random House, Inc.
New York, New York

This is a work of fiction. Names, characters, places, and incidents either are the product of the author's imagination or are used fictitiously. Any resemblance to actual persons, living or dead, events, or locales is entirely coincidental.

Dell is a registered trademark of Random House, Inc., and the colophon is a trademark of Random House, Inc.

ISBN: 978-0-440-33598-6

Printed in the United States of America
Published simultaneously in Canada

www.bantamdell.com

OPM   10 9 8 7 6 5 4 3

To Claudia Mills

Like Wilbur's Charlotte, you are a great writer and a great friend. Thank you for all the wise counsel you've given me as both over the years.

acknowledgments

Many thanks to my family and friends and the fine people at Bantam Dell, and especially to the wonderful women in my critique groups. I don't know what I'd do without you, but it's a good bet I would be both a lesser person and unpublished. An especially hearty thank-you goes out to the astonishingly talented and generous Julie Thornton of Thornton Designs, and to Bill and Debbie Shaub.

KILLED
BY
CLUTTER

chapter 1

helen Walker scowled at me from her perch on the mottled pink polyester love seat. While fidgeting with the messy bun of powder white hair that sat lopsided atop her head like a shredded pillow, she declared, "You never should have come here, Miss Gilbert. You are not wanted. I am perfectly comfortable living out here in my garage!"

"Even so, now that I'm here, why don't we just take a quick look at—"

"Come off it, Aunt Helen!" Stephanie Miller interrupted. She stood with her sturdy arms akimbo. "Be reasonable, for once!"

Helen narrowed her eyes at her niece, then smiled lovingly at the calico cat that hopped onto the cushion beside her. A second cat, a beautiful smoky gray longhair, let out a rumbling protest from its hiding spot under the car. "I am always reasonable," Helen replied. "I am simply unwilling to roll over and play dead on your behalf, Stephanie."

I hid my smile as Stephanie clicked her tongue and glared at her brother, lurking behind us. "Say something, Peter!"

Just last Friday, the two attractive and well-dressed forty-something siblings had strolled into my interior-design office and hired me on Helen Walker's behalf. At the time, they'd said nothing about their "eccentric and willful aunt" (Peter's description) having moved into her attached two-car garage, only that "the woman is the worst pack rat you'd ever want to meet. Assuming anyone would actually *want* to meet a hideous pack rat in the first place." (Stephanie's words.)

The deep scowl returned to Helen's delicate features as she shifted her focus to her nephew. "You're kowtowing to your sister about my house, Peter?"

"Aunt Helen," Peter began with a sigh and a hangdog demeanor, "we're only trying to do our best to watch out for your interests." He peered over his sister's shoulder, allowing Stephanie to be human Scotchgard against whatever vitriol his diminutive seventy-five-year-old aunt might hurl his way. "Miss Gilbert here has come highly recommended, and is an excellent decorator, who trained in Manhattan at—"

"I do not need help with my decorations! Christmas is three months away!"

"Peter misspoke." Stephanie sniffed. "Erin's not here to deck the halls and hang mistletoe, Aunt Helen. Erin Gilbert is an interior *designer*. She's going to resolve your clutter catastrophe. Furthermore, Peter and I have already hired her. So there's no need to discuss whether you think you need her or not. You *do*, and here she is."

"*What* clutter?" Helen spread her arms to indicate this carless half of her two-port garage. "As you can see for yourself, there isn't a speck of clutter here."

That was true and quite curious for the World's Biggest Pack Rat, as her niece had dubbed her. I had yet to judge the situation for myself; when we'd arrived, fifteen minutes earlier, Helen had responded to the doorbell by opening the garage door, gesturing for us to come hither, and then had used a remote control to shut the door behind us as though we had driven—and parked—an invisible Buick. Although a few garagelike items lined the unfinished, tar-papered wall behind Helen's white four-door sedan, this second carport was spotless. It held just the love seat, a large electric blue suitcase, a beige two-feet-by-three-feet space heater, and a brass floor lamp, circa 1970 Montgomery Ward. These last two items were plugged into an extension cord that snaked across the concrete floor.

"Given time, the clutter will follow you out here, too," Peter told her meekly. "Or rather, it *would*, if you were to refuse to accept Miss Gilbert's services."

The older woman's face lit up. "I can do that? I can refuse to let her in?"

"No." Stephanie bristled, firing another glare at her brother. "You *can't*. It's a done deal. She's been prepaid. Like one of those phone cards at the supermarket. Which you're always buying and then losing in your messy house."

"Oh, I'm not all that disorganized," Helen replied.

"Yes, you are. Ever since Mother died, you've been living in your own little world."

All warmth instantly drained from Helen's expression. She stopped stroking her cat and began to wring her pale hands. At our introductory meeting, Peter had explained to me that Lois Miller—his and Stephanie's mother—had moved into her sister's house two years ago after the death of their father. Lois herself had died just three months ago.

Stephanie grimaced as she scanned the surroundings and added under her breath, "Your own little world encompassing the *garage*, as it turns out."

Peter dared to step forward far enough to touch an arm of the pink love seat. "Didn't this couch used to be in the living room? How did you move it out here?"

"Teddy helped me. Earlier this morning."

"Teddy?" Stephanie shrieked. "My God! Now that Mother died, is *he* hitting on *you*?"

Helen narrowed her eyes, but replied evenly, "I get to choose my own friends, Stephanie. Even if I apparently *don't* get to choose my own living quarters."

"Ms. Walker," I interposed, "my hunch is that your nephew and niece are unhappy at the notion of having their beloved aunt living in a garage. They're worried you're not comfortable out here."

"Precisely," Stephanie agreed stiffly. "So, let's go inside now, Aunt Helen, and show Erin just what she's dealing with." Her singsong tone was so patronizing that, even though she was acting as my advocate, my teeth were instantly on edge.

With surprising quickness, Helen rose and blocked our path to the door. "No, Stephanie. I'm not staying out here while you lead a full battalion through *my* home!"

Unable to suppress a smile at the notion of being termed "a full battalion," I cheerfully suggested, "How about just you and I go take a quick look, in that case?"

Helen pursed her lips and sized me up from head to foot. At five nine, I was considerably taller than she was. Despite Colorado's typical warm, dry September weather, this morning I'd chosen to wear a conservative and sophisticated baby blue skirt suit and pearls; my guess was that, otherwise, she might mistakenly assume that, at twenty-eight, I was too young to understand the sentimental value she placed on a lifetime's accumulation of personal possessions.

Though she didn't as much as smile, she finally nodded. "Peter, Stephanie, you two can wait out here." She gestured at the sofa, where the calico cat was now sprawled and licking a front paw. "Make yourselves at home."

"In a *garage*?" her niece huffed.

"Unless you'd rather wait on the driveway," Helen shot back in saccharine tones. She opened the door a crack, and the gray cat emerged from beneath the car and dashed ahead of us, emitting a *rr-r-rr* the entire time, not unlike a child squealing as he tries to avoid being touched in a game of tag.

Stephanie harrumphed again and looked at Peter, who let his hands flop to his sides in spineless surrender. With their matching dark hair and eyes and patrician features, it was obvious that the two were siblings, but that was where all similarities ended. Strange to think that this retiring, diffident man was a lawyer. His sister, a real estate developer, had confidence to spare.

Helen ushered me past the heavy door and breathed a heavy sigh of relief as it shut behind us. For my part, although I'd certainly been forewarned, I had to stifle a gasp.

This room made the Crestview County dump look like a city park.

Judging from what was visible of the hexagonal brown linoleum flooring, we now stood in Helen's kitchen. Helen sidled ahead of me through a narrow aisle that cut through towering heaps of junk. Her tiny, elderly body was dwarfed by the precarious stacks that surrounded her. She had hoarded paper products of every imaginable ilk—towels, napkins, crumpled wrapping paper, newspapers, magazines, and flattened bags. Like the cherry atop a potentially lethal sundae, Helen had weighed down the paper piles with heavy objects—mostly clay flower pots—which were now just waiting to topple over and conk her on the head.

Other piles were built from discarded clothing, books, and myriad colored containers. Various items poked out from bulging cardboard boxes—the fuzzy turquoise leg of a stuffed toy, a stiff-with-dirt gardening glove with holes in its fingertips, an orange foam football, a bicycle tire pump.

A stack of used tires served as a gigantic vase for an arrangement of long-handled gardening tools, and I bit my lip as I watched Helen duck below the pointy metal tines of a rake. She must have recently emptied out the garage, only to stash its contents here. That could explain why she'd been so adamant about not allowing her relatives through the door. Now she turned to face me at what could only be termed a "clearing" in the chaos. "Welcome to my home, Erin."

With a forced smile, I said, "Thank you," and followed her. I paused to relocate the rake safely between two relatively sturdy stacks of newspapers, with my mother's words, "This could poke out someone's eye," emerging unbidden from my lips.

Judging from the glimpse of a window and sink afforded by a path to my left, we were roughly in the center of her kitchen. Ahead of me were the refrigerator and pantry. Heaven only knows what she stored in there. To our right was an entranceway to the rest of the house. Thankfully, I don't suffer from claustrophobia, or I'd have been racing in that direction.

Instead, my attention was drawn to a half-opened box near my feet. The box contained at least one truly stunning crystal candle holder, a fuzzy purple slipper festooned with a leering poodle head, and a veritable bushel of small items—from screws to what appeared to be dime-store party favors. If all of these boxes held similar contents, it could easily take an hour to go through each one.

"I suppose I should say 'Pardon the mess,' but that's such a cliché." I swore there was a twinkle in Helen's gray eyes.

"Fair enough." *So I'll spare you the cliché of saying: I love what you've done with the place.* The funny thing was that I actually *was* picking up on a wonderful and welcoming ambiance to this home. I'd already fallen in love with the place from the outside. Set back from the road and beneath a thick canopy of trees, the dormers of this charming bungalow had winked an invitation to me. The house had freshly painted ecru siding with periwinkle trim and shutters. (Who can resist real shutters?) Window boxes brimmed with pink begonias and scarlet geraniums. Outside the kitchen window, yellow and red rosebushes graced a white picket fence, which enclosed the meticulously cared-for sprawling lawn. It was absolutely unheard of to have this much acreage smack between the foothills of the Rockies and downtown Crestview.

Moreover, even though I could barely see the walls, I could sense there was warmth within them, and I loved the sensible layout of a classic two-story, dollhouse-style dwelling. My most valuable professional skill was my ability to see the lovely possibilities in any given space, no matter how unlovely its current appearance might be. (That skill seemed to work in reverse when it came to men, however.) This home was a stunning sterling silver vase, now blackened with tarnish, crying out to me to use some elbow grease and uncover its luster.

From somewhere deeper in the house, a cat's plaintive meow arose.

"Ella? It's all right," Helen called. "They'll be leaving soon."

"Ella is your gray cat, right?"

"Yes, and she gets upset easily. Ella doesn't much care for my relatives."

"And what's your calico's name?"

"Vator."

I chuckled. "Ella and Vator? How cute! I love cats. My cat's named Hildi. She's a black longhair with a white tip on her tail."

Helen crossed her spindly arms, which poked out of the oversized purple and magenta floral blouse that she'd tucked into her black Capris. "You know, Erin, I was just being crotchety toward you out there for my niece and nephew's sakes. You don't have to work so hard at getting me to like you."

"I sincerely love cats, Ms. Walker, and, believe it or not, I love your home, too."

Her skeptical expression melted, changing into a heart-warming smile. "Call me Helen. But there's a big problem here, so let's get right to the point." She waggled her finger at the garage door. "You don't want anything to do with those two characters, Erin. Furthermore, my house truly isn't all that bad."

Tact isn't necessarily one of my strong points, but an understatement was clearly in order here. "The thing is, Helen, you have so much open storage that the overall charm of your home is diminished."

Her brow furrowed. "Well, it's true the kitchen needs work. After all, I had to put the garage contents *someplace*. And I gave up cooking, anyway, after my sister Lois died. And the basement was already jam-packed. Plus, well, I guess the den is a problem."

"Oh?"

"When Lois first moved in, we decided to turn the den into a storage room. Neither of us much cared for watching TV anyway . . . though I suppose it would be nice someday to see if it's still in there."

"Helen, my first concern, which we both know your nephew and niece share, is that your home is a fire hazard. These papers are highly combustible." Afraid that the slightest shove could cause a disastrous domino effect, I brushed my fingertips cautiously on the edge of a wobbly stack of yellowing newspapers. "In case of a fire, they'll block your access to the windows and doors."

"Not really." She made a Vanna White gesture at the window. "There's also a path to the back door. You just have to bob and weave a little. Besides, I'm living in the *garage* now," she reminded me firmly.

"The problem with that is, in an electrical fire, the power will go out, and then the garage door won't open. You'd be forced to search in darkness for the manual release, and even if you found it, you'd need the strength to lift that heavy door."

"Maybe so. But I never use the stove anymore, just the microwave, and I'm very careful to keep everything clear of the heating ducts." She gave me a reassuring smile. "Truly, Erin. You can just give my nephew and niece their money back and turn down the job."

"I already promised them that I wouldn't let myself get discouraged too easily. And I very much want to accept this job." I had to swallow my strong urge to add in all earnestness: *This house* needs *me!*

"Oh, but you mustn't accept it." Helen grabbed my wrist and met my gaze with fear in her eyes. "You need to stay out of my house, Erin. For your own good. And mine."

"But why?"

She frowned, her gray eyes still searching mine. "The *real* reason I've moved into the garage is for my personal safety."

"Because of the fire hazard, you mean?"

She shook her head emphatically, causing a lock of pure white hair to unfurl from her bun. "Oh, it's far more serious than that, I'm afraid. Someone keeps breaking into my house!"

"You mean, you've had a burglar? More than one?" I asked in alarm.

"Even worse." Her anxious gaze held mine. "I know it sounds crazy, but just three months ago, someone broke into this house and murdered my sister! And now they're trying to kill me!"

chapter 2

your sister was . . . murdered?" I repeated, stunned. "Stephanie told me just three days ago that her mother died of natural causes."

"That's what she's chosen to believe," Helen retorted tearfully. "So does her brother. It's so much easier that way." She shivered, as though an icy draft had made its way through her mountainous stacks. "But Lois was killed by a bell pepper."

I had a bewildering image of a man-sized bright green pepper with Mickey Mouse arms and legs wielding a razor-sharp ax. "Pardon?" I stammered.

"Lois was deathly allergic to them."

"I didn't even realize there *was* such an allergy..."

"Oh, yes. Peppers can cause every bit as severe an allergic reaction as peanuts. My poor sister is proof of that fact."

"But, how could her eating a pepper have been murder?"

"The night it happened, she'd had a bad head cold, you see, so I made dinner for her. I was leaving town for a couple of days, and when I saw how sick she was, I offered to stay, but Lois insisted she'd be fine. The killer added bell peppers to the casserole I'd prepared." She lifted her palms as if to fend off anticipated protestations. "Oh, I know how crazy that sounds, Erin. But it's the only possible explanation. We never kept peppers in our kitchen, let alone cooked with them. It was the head cold, I'm sure, that masked the first symptoms, till it was too late."

Her story was far-fetched, but not impossible. I tried to recall if I'd read anything in the Crestview papers three months ago about a death from an allergic reaction. It did sound vaguely familiar. "Aren't there emergency injections you can keep on hand for people who have severe allergic reactions?"

"Epinephrine syringes," Helen said with a sad nod. "We kept them right in the top drawer over there." She pointed to the left of the refrigerator, but all her cabinets were blocked from view. "This happened *before* I cleared out the garage, mind you...when the kitchen counters and drawers were accessible." She sighed. "Back when I still enjoyed cooking. Because I had someone I loved to cook *for.*"

My heart ached for her. The knowledge that a meal she'd prepared had killed her sister must have been torturous.

It also explained why she'd buried her kitchen. Even so, Helen's current lifestyle was risky for her health. Judging by her baggy clothing, it was causing her to lose too much weight. Not to mention that she would be flattened if one of her heavier stacks tipped over on top of her.

"The killer must have temporarily removed all the syringes from Lois's purse and kitchen drawer, though they were back by the time the police investigated," she informed me. "Otherwise Lois would have given herself a lifesaving injection." Her eyes misted, but she kept her voice steady. "She was at the base of the stairs when Peter found her...the next morning. She was obviously trying to get to the syringe she kept upstairs in her nightstand."

"How terrible! I'm so sorry, Helen."

"If only I hadn't left town, my poor sister might still be alive. Now nobody believes me, and I'm forced to match wits with her killer all on my own."

"What do the police say about her cause of death?"

"Oh, they treat me like a doddering old fool. All three times I spoke to them about Lois, they patted my hand and sent me on my way. Police officers seem to assume when your hair loses its color, your mind's gone, too."

I wondered if my friend Linda, who was a police officer, had heard about Helen's chilling theory. Linda, I was certain, wouldn't have been condescending. I decided to ask her about Helen the next time we got together. "But why do you think someone wants to kill *you*?"

"I don't know *why*, but I have warning signs on —"

Someone pounded on the door to the garage, and Stephanie called, "Are you about finished in there, Aunt Helen?"

"Not yet." Helen brushed past me, and I assumed she

was going to let her niece and nephew inside, but instead she threw the lock. She squeezed past me a second time, then crooked her finger at me. "Come on. Let me show you my proof."

Proof? She threaded her way to the back door, pointed to the top corner, and flattened herself against the door so I could maneuver close enough to see. "I tape a strand of my hair across the opening." Sure enough, tape was fastened on the trim and on the upper corner of the door. "If you look carefully, you'll see that a hair is snapped in two. Ever since Lois's murder, every time I leave home, I make certain that the hair is intact. I've got another one taped to the front door, and I always put a third one on the door from the garage. Whenever a door opens, the hair breaks. Six times in a row, I came home, and the hair was snapped in two. Had to keep plucking out more hairs. I'm going to go bald at this rate!"

"That's a clever alarm system." *Albeit wacky.* It could explain why her hairdo was so unruly.

"Oh, it's not original. Read about the trick in *1984.* The book, that is, not the year. As I was saying, the last several times I've gone out, I've come home to find the strands broken on the front or back doors, but never once on the door between the house and the garage. That's how I know I'm safe in my garage. Plus, if anyone tries to attack me *there*, I'll run right over the punk."

Someone rapped on the garage door again, much softer this time. "Aunt Helen?"

"Just two minutes, Peter."

Stephanie hollered, "If you're taking Erin on a tour, why is your voice still coming from the kitchen?"

"Ventriloquism," her aunt shouted. Quietly she said to

me, as she squeezed past me to head toward the main alley, "My garage guests are getting restless. We'd better shake a leg, Erin. Like I said, the only other room besides the kitchen that's really bad is in the back."

"The den?" I asked as I once again followed her.

"Yes. And let's not even look at the basement." She tapped an unadorned door near the kitchen entranceway.

Helen allowed me quick peeks into the small dining room and the bathroom, and we wove our way through the living room. These rooms were furnished in mass-produced items, unexceptional but functional. I automatically redesigned these spaces in spectacular fashion, adding color to the bone white walls and pizzazz to the furnishings, then tried to shut off my mental before-and-after camera; my role here, I reminded myself, was exclusively to get rid of Helen's mountainous hoardings.

Compared to the kitchen, the other rooms were livable but would rank as a clutter disaster by most standards; nary a flat surface could be seen because of the mishmash of *things*. Next to me, the spindly legs of an end table strained to support a ceramic cow, a wooden ladle, a deck of cards, a lamp with heavy terra-cotta base, a dozen books, a small loom, and a rusty motor of some kind. Balanced atop that messy pile was a candy dish filled with coins, peanuts, and little black wrinkled things that I dearly hoped were raisins.

Despite this avalanche of possessions, the bones of this house were marvelous, and the construction was rock solid. With its ornate trim and arched doorways, the house appeared to have been built in the fifties or earlier. "This wasn't the home you and your sister grew up in, was it?"

"Oh, no. I'm older than the house, actually."

"When did you buy this place, if you don't mind my asking?"

"Oh, well, I once owned quite a bit of stock in a start-up company that hit it big. Cashed that in some forty years ago, when real estate prices were a fraction of what they are now. The original owners were selling it themselves and took a shine to me." She primped at her lopsided bun and added proudly, "Even though they had better offers than mine, *I* was the only one who thought to promise them that I would never allow this property lot to be parceled out into condos. Also that I'd never let the house be bulldozed in favor of some sprawling, soulless monstrosity. Like those ones Stephanie's company keeps erecting. They specialize in enormous megahomes that can entertain a hundred partyers at a time. Heaven forbid you prefer to curl up in a corner with a good book, or sit and chat with a couple of good friends. For *that*, it's like trying to get snuggly in a cavernous museum."

It was true that this home was nothing like a "cavernous museum." A museum *warehouse* after an earthquake, perhaps. "I can see why preserving this place was so important to the original owners. It would have been a crime to tear it down. The home has such natural integrity and grace."

She grinned, pleased. "It does, doesn't it?"

"Which is not to say that a small addition wouldn't work wonders," I said with unbridled enthusiasm. "A workroom extending out back from the kitchen would solve most of your problems. We'd give it oodles of built-in cabinets, and skylights for natural lighting. Judging by your luscious flower beds, it's clear that you're a master gardener, so it could be a combination greenhouse and a…" I stopped myself, remembering belatedly the limited scope of this assignment. "Just something to think about for the future," I concluded lamely.

"Wow," she murmured. "A workroom. That really *is* tempting. Hmm. Maybe for once my niece knew what she was talking about when she said it was worth throwing money away on a designer."

"I'd like to think so." *Not counting the part about throwing money away.* "If nothing else, we can restore enough order to your household so that you'll feel cozy and safe here once more. It must be nerve-racking to have all these massive stacks everywhere you look. You can't ever see who or what else is in the room with you."

To my surprise, she agreed. "You might have a point there. I didn't always use to live like this, you know, Erin. Things only got really out of control when Lois moved in with me."

This woman had clearly amassed decades' worth of accumulations, but it wasn't the time to argue with her. She led me to the staircase but stopped abruptly and said, "Go on up. I'm staying down here. I don't ever go upstairs anymore. Just… be careful on the steps. You never know if they were booby-trapped during the latest break-in."

As with shutters, I had a thing for staircases, and this one was utterly adorable with its wonderful white-painted ball-finial banisters and understated trim. Suitably cautioned, I climbed the steps, which, except for their having been treated like ascending storage surfaces on both sides, were perfectly safe and solid.

I surveyed the two bedrooms and bathroom. For all of Helen's "booby trap" warnings, the construction of this house was sublime; not as much as a creak or loose nail among the wide-plank pine floorboards. The bedrooms, however, were dusty, and held three times the appropriate bric-a-brac. At second glance, Helen's large, taupe-painted room was actually overstuffed five times over. Even so, underneath it all, the spaces were really charming with their attic-style slant to the ceilings and dormers on the windows.

Evidenced by the many photographs of Stephanie and Peter at various ages, the smaller bedroom had been their mother Lois's. The room was Pepto-Bismol pink, and the fabrics were rose-patterned and edged with frilly lace. A key job requirement is to put my own tastes aside and un-cover the beauty within my clients' tastes, so, given the chance, I would have muted the elements—steered her toward dusty rose, which can be wonderfully neutral, and gently suggested that less is more with regard to lace and frill. Yet Lois or her husband had had an excellent artistic eye behind the camera lens; an especially evocative pho-tograph of young Stephanie and Peter on a hammock and framed in a rough-hewn, gray-painted frame caught my eye. Then-towheaded Stephanie was laughing as though she hadn't a care in the world, her arm possessively across her brother's chest, pulling him back against her. Peter wore a gap-toothed grin, but his eyes were wide and his fists clenched the edge of the hammock.

Helen was pacing by the foot of the staircase. "The bedrooms upstairs are wonderful," I told her as I de-scended. "Really cozy and inviting."

"True. But with all the break-ins, it's not worth it to me to risk going up there."

"Who else has the key to your house?"

"Oh, lots of people. Lois was so trusting, bless her heart, she gave them out like they were candy from a Pez dispenser."

Speaking of which, my gaze fell on a collection of at least thirty of the colorful candy dispensers in a shoe box on the second step. "First thing we need to do, then, is change all your locks."

"No, that's out of the question. I'm trying to get rid of clutter, not to add to it."

"But changing your locks won't—"

"Of course it would! I'd have a whole other set of door locks for the house. You don't actually expect me to discard a full set of perfectly good locks, do you?"

"I'll take them with me, so you—"

"No, no, Erin! If we change the locks, I'll be forever finding old keys that no longer work and getting them confused with the new keys... locking myself out, and so forth. Next thing you know, I'll get frustrated and feel I'll have to change the locks a second time. Then I'll have a *third* set of locks lying around in my house and even *more* keys that don't work. And I really *will* turn into a doddering old fool who can't even let herself into her own home." She shuddered and squeezed her eyes shut. "It's just better to keep that whole Pandora's box shut tight... with its existing lock."

Taken aback, I gazed at her for a moment. Before I could reply, however, the doorbell rang. Helen groaned. "That's going to be Rachel from across the street." Helen flung the door open, but kept her hand on the knob and gripped the door trim with her other hand. "This isn't a good time, Rachel," she said firmly.

A tall, pretty woman in her late fifties with short, honey

blond hair peered at me over Helen's shoulder and cried, "So it's true! You have an interior designer in here! I can tell by how well she's dressed. She has that professional aura that just says loud and clear: 'Appearance is everything.'"

I automatically glanced down at my pale blue skirt suit, thinking that if that was truly what I was projecting to most people, I'd change outfits in a New York minute; appearance *isn't* everything; *quality* is everything.

Treating Helen's outstretched arm as though it were a turnstile, the woman stepped inside, uninvited. "I'm Rachel Schwartz. I live in the Georgian colonial directly across the street."

Too offended by her shabby treatment of Helen to be more than marginally cordial, I didn't return her smile. "Erin Gilbert."

"Yes, I know. I saw your name on the minivan parked at the curb. Well, your *last* name is printed there, at any rate. I assumed the Gilbert portion of 'Interiors by Gilbert' was your last name. So I looked you up in the yellow pages." Rachel Schwartz studied my features as though committing them to memory. "Are you aware that there's a Sullivan Designs in town? So that together you'd be"— she paused dramatically—"Gilbert and Sullivan?"

She had just named my biggest rival—a talented, hunky man with whom I shared a tempestuous relationship. I replied dryly, "Steve Sullivan and I laugh about that all the time."

Helen cleared her throat. "As I said, Rachel, this isn't a good time. Go home!"

"Oh, I will," Rachel tittered, beaming at Helen. "Just

dropping by for a moment. I've come in response to the note that you put in my mailbox."

"A personal visit was hardly necessary, Rachel. Especially considering that the note was addressed to *Jack*, not to you."

The garage door, meanwhile, was rumbling open; the sound reverberated in the adjacent wall. Helen cast a nervous glance in that direction. So did I, worried that the tremor might start an avalanche of stacked newspapers.

"Maybe so, but I also wanted to introduce myself to your designer...always such invaluable people to befriend." Rachel winked at me, seemingly oblivious to the fact that my first impression of her wasn't one of chummy camaraderie. "And to let you know while I was here that Jack's going to be in Denver most of the day, but he'll be free tomorrow morning."

"Thank you," Helen said evenly, then gestured for her to avail herself of the wide-open front door.

"I'll drop by tomorrow, with Jack." Rachel gave me a big smile. "Nice meeting you, Erin Gilbert." She stepped onto the front porch and waved at Stephanie and Peter, who were now marching up the redbrick walkway. "Good morning, Stephanie. I noticed your Mercedes in the driveway."

"Yes, I know," Stephanie retorted. "I saw you watching us through your front window. Using your binoculars, just like always."

Rachel harrumphed and swept down the steps. "I was watching my *bird feeder*, not spying on you!"

Stephanie ignored the remark, brushed past her, and said to Helen, "Can we come in now, or are you going to leave a bowl of water and some kibble out here for us instead?"

"I'm sorry, Stephanie, Peter. I got distracted. Do come in, my dears. Let's all take seats."

Stephanie was still fuming. She gave me a furious glare, then headed straight for the kitchen.

Helen continued in vain, "Please don't look in the—"

"Oh, my God!" her niece cried. "I *knew* you were hiding something. Peter, come see the kitchen!"

"I'll take your word for it that it's bad." He took a seat on the bentwood rocking chair while I moved a pair of boxes, plus an armful of clothing, then claimed the beige recliner. Helen edged her way around the jam-packed coffee table and cleared off the Naugahyde lounge chair. This, judging from the wear marks in the area rug, had recently taken the place of the pink love seat now in the garage.

While Stephanie returned to the living room in a huff, Helen explained to me, "As you probably already gleaned, Rachel is a compulsive busybody. She actually came over to find out who you are. Her husband, Jack, on the other hand, is a wonderful, generous man...a retired electrician, and I need to hire him to install a doorbell in the garage."

Stephanie eschewed taking a seat herself, but stood gripping the top of Peter's rocker. I imagined she would chuck him out of the seat if he said anything she found disagreeable, and from the way Peter balanced himself, I think he feared the same thing. "*Well*, Aunt Helen?" she demanded. "Are you ready to let Erin begin her job?"

Helen folded her hands in her lap and closed her eyes

for a moment. "Even though I still have severe reservations about permitting strangers to handle my personal belongings"—she gestured at our surroundings—"I have to admit my lifestyle isn't working. So, since I've been living in a sow's ear lately, I might as well turn it into a silk purse."

"Huh?" Peter asked, confused. "Does that mean you're letting Erin work here . . . or in the garage?"

Helen nodded, apparently resolute now that she'd made her decision. "Both. Erin is going to help me get the place decluttered."

"Excellent." He settled back in his seat.

Stephanie shifted her piercing gaze to me. "How soon will we be seeing some results?"

"We'll create an action plan right now, if Helen is okay with that." Helen nodded at me in agreement. "I hope to get started tomorrow morning."

"Excellent," Peter said again, giving me a thin smile.

"What kind of 'action plan'?" Stephanie demanded.

"First off, Helen and I will need to agree on what I can and cannot remove from the premises."

"That's easy enough," Helen said. "All I ask is that you don't throw away anything I collect or use for scrapbooking."

"That's never going to work," Stephanie interjected brusquely. "Erin needs to get rid of *all* the old newspapers and magazines, Aunt Helen. She can't indulge you in the very hobbies which led to your pack-rat ways."

"I've been scrapbooking for fifty years. Way back before it became so popular that the word became a verb. I'm certainly not going to stop now."

Spinning the conversation, I said, "You've kept scrapbooks for the last fifty years? That is so terrific!"

"Thank you. I can remember the least little detail of my loved ones' lives this way. Drives everyone else nuts, though. Some people prefer to remember things however it best suits them."

Stephanie groaned. Then she said, "On that note, Peter and I have to leave. I'm already late for an appointment with a builder."

Her well-trained brother dutifully shot to his feet.

"Walk us to my car, Erin, so we can talk shop." Stephanie flashed a smile in her aunt's direction. "I'll drop by tomorrow and check on the progress." This sounded to me like a threat.

Peter hugged his aunt good-bye and asked if there was anything he could do for her before he left, which she obviously appreciated. I left on his heels, saying, "I'll be back in a minute, Helen."

"Certainly, Erin. Just come right on in whenever you're ready." Vator trotted up the driveway and purred as he brushed past me into the house.

"Oh, sure," Stephanie grumbled even before I'd closed the door behind us. "Treat the *designer* like a beloved old friend, but shut your own *niece* in the garage."

"I warned you my aunt was eccentric," Peter told me as we made the short walk down the driveway to Stephanie's Mercedes.

"An epic understatement," his sister countered, pressing the unlock button on her key chain with unnecessary force. "The woman clearly has incipient Alzheimer's. If not a full-blown case."

I protested, "She didn't seem all that—"

"She *is* delusional," Peter interrupted. "She just masks it reasonably well. Most of the time." He slipped into the passenger seat and shut his door.

"You made a tactical error already, Erin," Stephanie told me. "Aunt Helen claims *everything* is either a collectible or potential scrapbook material." She got behind the wheel.

"I'll make the best of it." I took a step back toward the house. "Maybe I'll see you here tomorrow."

"Count on it," she replied crisply, slipping designer sunglasses over her eyes.

I suppose she intended the remark as another threat, but I gave her a big smile, said, "Wonderful. See you then," and turned on a heel. My underlying mood, however, wasn't nearly as hopeful. Even setting aside concerns about Helen's alleged break-ins and how dangerously overstuffed her home was, her determination to keep the old locks had me deeply worried; convincing her to let go of the myriad useless items in this house was going to be really difficult. I silently repeated my standard mantra, "Confidence and optimism," as I followed Helen's instructions and reentered without knocking.

Flanked by piles of flattened Mylar balloons and yet more wrapping paper from Christmases past, Helen was seated at the black spinet piano, thumbing through a photo album. As I drew closer, I saw that this was no mere album, but rather an awesome display of photographs and memorabilia. Two pressed columbines graced diagonal corners of the page. Helen had picked up the lavender hues of the petals in the hand-painted borders of the pictures.

She wore such a beatific smile as she gazed down at the

pages that I decided not to interrupt her thoughts even to compliment her book. Her smile faded the moment she gently turned to the next page, however. She glared at an old photograph of a police officer. Mounted alongside the photograph were newspaper clippings. She slammed the book shut.

"Handsome man," I remarked, curious. "Of course, I'm a sucker for a man in a uniform."

"Aren't we all?" Helen replied under her breath.

"Who is he? A friend or relative?"

She wedged the scrapbook ankle-high into the stack. As she rose, she brushed her hands as if done with a dirty task and answered sadly, "That's the man who killed my sister."

chapter 3

our sister was killed by a *police officer?*"

She seemed to be taken aback by my question as she turned to face me. She gave my wrist a quick squeeze. "Oh, no, dear. I don't mean that he *literally* killed Lois himself. Much as I suspect the louse was *capable* of murder." She glanced down at the stacked albums. "That's George Miller in the picture, you see. My late brother-in-law."

I sighed with relief. With her tales of break-ins, be they real or imagined, it would have been terrible for her to believe that a police officer, of all people, had murdered her sister. "Your brother-in-law had already retired from the force before he passed away, right?"

"Before George died, yes. The phrase 'passed away' is too genteel for that stinker."

"What did George die of?" I asked cautiously, fairly certain I was going to hear another paranoid tale of murder.

"A heart attack. Two years ago."

Natural causes. *Thank goodness!* I inwardly chastised myself for being happy about hearing of a man's death. Then I asked in a somber voice, "George made your sister's life miserable, I take it?"

"You can say *that* again. Plus his reckless choices put poor Lois in the killer's path."

"How so?"

"Erin, I'm not going to get into all of that with you. You've got to dig through more than enough of my family baggage as it is. So let's get going on this 'action plan' of yours, shall we?"

"That sounds wise," I answered with a smile. I felt vindicated in my assessment of her. This wasn't a case of incipient Alzheimer's. This woman was as sharp as an upholstery tack.

She sat down on the padded piano bench and folded her hands in her lap. "I just hope whoever killed *George* is the same person who took my poor sister's life. That would mean George had at least sealed his *own* fate, along with Lois's."

I dropped into the recliner and massaged my suddenly aching temples. "But you said George died of a heart attack."

She wagged her finger at me. "Which was brought on by someone's messing with his medication."

Maybe Stephanie was right. Maybe this talk of bell peppers, medication, and break-ins was the paranoid rambling of an Alzheimer's sufferer after all. "But, Helen... wouldn't that be almost impossible? I think heart patients are carefully monitored, and their medication levels are checked regularly."

"Be that as it may, those pills he was taking at the end sure looked an awful lot like those little oblong mints that stores sell at cashier lines."

"Tic Tacs?"

"Precisely. Not the green or orange ones, though. I'm talking about the little white ones, which look like pills."

"But they don't *taste* like pills! There's no way anyone could unknowingly eat Tic Tacs in place of critical heart medication."

She gave me a blank stare, sighed, then brightened. "Enough of my family sagas. Let's talk about this plan of yours now, Erin. So where do we start?"

An hour later, I left Helen Walker's house with a better grasp of the staggering magnitude of the job ahead of me—and with the strong suspicion that her so-called "break-ins" were the product of her overheated imagination. I now felt the need to decompress in a relaxing, clutter-free space. I drove to my office in downtown Crestview. Although Helen had more or less consented to my "action plan," she'd been too concerned about the personnel involved to fully realize that we were going to be getting rid of lots and lots of her hoarded stuff. I have talented and reliable subcontractors whom I use regularly, but Helen would allow me to bring in only one "worker bee," insisting that she couldn't possibly handle more than one person at a time "pawing through" her personal belongings.

The short walk from my parking space to my redbrick office building was soul-cheering. There wasn't a cloud in the azure sky. The mountains in the background were stunning—the craggy rock faces took on the immortalized purple hue, a rich contrast to the dark patches of evergreens. I unlocked my office door and admired an even more inspiring sight: the elegant navy blue and royal red runner on the stairs that led to my loft-style workplace. The rug was secured to each step with old-fashioned brass fittings, which instantly evoked the image of climbing to the upper rooms of a Victorian mansion. I'd also replaced the painted pine handrail with carved oak, polished to a glossy sheen.

Recognizing that this was my first form of advertising for walk-in customers, I furnished my office lavishly and changed the decor frequently. The ambience this month was that of a refined English drawing room, with a pair of maroon and honey gold cushy overstuffed chairs facing my mahogany desk and its forest green Tiffany lamp. The mild aroma of lemon wax wafted through the air, mingling with the scent of eucalyptus leaves from a striking dried flower arrangement on the hammered-copper drum table in the far corner.

My seating area was arranged as a cozy living space nestled against the exposed redbrick wall. There, the oak-framed palladium windows revealed the glorious view of the Rockies. On a sea-grass area rug, maroon mohair slipper chairs flanked a sage tuxedo love seat, where I liked to sit with clients and page through my portfolio.

I'd only just settled into my plush leather desk chair with a sigh of pure contentment when I heard the downstairs door open. To my surprise, my visitor proved to be my archrival. Steve Sullivan looked disarmingly handsome and relaxed in a lime green polo shirt and jeans.

Our eyes met, and he gave me an annoyingly nonchalant "Hey, Gilbert."

Though my stomach clenched at seeing him, I forced a smile and said, "Hey, Sullivan. You're back."

"Yep."

"You were in California all this time?"

"Yeah. A little longer than I first anticipated."

"Bit of an understatement." As well as an outright lie. His trip, which Steve had originally said would take six days, had lasted seven weeks. We'd been trying unsuccessfully to schedule our first official date at the time. (Technically, it would have been our second date, but the first one hadn't gone well, so we'd mutually decided to wipe the slate clean.) Furthermore, a girlfriend of mine who worked in the same building as Sullivan had told me that he'd returned from California five days ago, which said more about his ambivalence toward me and our ever-gnarly relationship than words possibly could. "I take it your 'quick little job' must have turned into a not-so-quick, not-so-little one."

He nodded and rocked on his heels. "I'm getting some good connections established out there. One of these days, you should come with me, if you're interested in an occasional out-of-town job."

He dragged his hand through his stylishly disheveled light brown hair. The motion was a poker player's "tell": It betrayed the fact that he was uncomfortable. Join the club. Obviously, Sullivan too had been caught off guard by the kiss we'd shared two months earlier—hours before his abrupt departure westward. We'd exchanged several e-mails in the meantime; I'd even joked that he was clearly relocating to California rather than take me out to dinner. Our notes had progressed from chatty to shamelessly suggestive, and then without warning, suddenly stopped. Somewhere along the line, Steve Sullivan had obviously gotten cold feet.

So be it. We bickered compulsively whenever we were together. The smartest thing to do was for us to forget the kiss ever happened and go on with our lives.

And yet here I was, nervously fidgeting with my hair. The silence felt as awkward as a three-legged chair. I had to say something. Either that or start praying for a bolt of lightning to hit me. "Do you have any interesting new assignments?" I ventured.

"Nah. Just a wing of an office building east of town. You?"

"I started work on a pack rat's home this morning."

He grimaced. Pack rats are a major challenge in our profession.

"It's going to be rough, all right. I have to hire some muscle to help me clear the place out. The stacks of old newspapers and magazines alone weigh a ton."

"At least it's a good sign that he—or she—was willing to hire a designer."

"Actually, her niece and nephew hired me. They kind of forced me on her."

He raised an eyebrow. "Was the niece Stephanie Miller, by any chance? The real estate developer?"

"Yes," I replied, startled. "How did you know that?"

He hesitated, then claimed the nearest lounge chair facing my desk. "Tell you what, Gilbert. You need someone to tote and bail. Hire me. I'll work on the cheap— same wages you'd give to your regular muscleman."

"Why?" I'd gone from startled to suspicious.

"Things are slow, with my having been out of town. Plus, I'd like to get back on Stephanie's good side. She's a former client of mine. She got annoyed that I was out of town for longer than I'd anticipated, so she canceled an assignment we'd been discussing."

"What kind of assignment?" I wondered if he'd been offered the job at Helen's house before I had.

"I was supposed to design a game room for her. It's a lucrative job, which, as it turns out, is still up for grabs."

"Oh, I see." In other words, he planned to suck up to her while he was supposed to be taking work directives from me.

He leaned forward, forcing me to gaze directly into those dreamy hazel eyes of his. "If Stephanie does hire me for her rec room, I won't charge you for my work at her aunt's house. We'll consider it a trade-off for helping me to win the job back."

"Hmm. I don't know, Sullivan. Maybe she'd rather hire *me*. I'd be a fool to help you out at my own expense."

He squared his broad shoulders. "Hey. Fair's fair. Who do you think recommended you for her crazy aunt's place?"

"*You* gave Stephanie my name?"

"How else could I know who your client is?"

Maybe by listening to Stephanie talk about her aunt, the notorious pack rat. I decided not to press the point.

"Thank you. And Helen isn't crazy, by the way. She's just set in her ways. I like her."

"Glad to hear it. What do you say, Gilbert? I'll work hard . . . move mountains of junk at your beck and call."

It did solve my dilemma about hiring only one reliable "worker bee." And having Sullivan at my "beck and call" was the least the man owed me for sneaking back into town nearly a week ago. Not to mention for acting like we were now mere professional acquaintances. Heaven knows he deserved whatever grunt work I could dump on him.

"When you put it that way, it's irresistible. Fine. You can start by picking up the moving truck Stephanie rented for me." I pulled the receipt out of my drawer and jotted down Helen's address. When I looked up at him, he was watching me intently.

He cleared his throat as our eyes met. "Didn't mean to stare. But you look really hot today."

"*Hot?*" What a very un-Sullivan-like descriptor. Had he been conked on the head by a surfboard while he was in L.A.? Did he mean "hot" as in sexy, or as in sweating profusely? I actually *wasn't* perspiring, but then, my outfit was far from sexy; I was wearing a professional-businesswoman outfit, aimed to please a seventy-five-year-old woman.

"I thought about you a lot while I was gone, Erin. I think you'd have really liked the house I designed. It had this amazing deck, overlooking the Pacific Ocean. Sometimes I pictured you there, being caressed by the breeze, your auburn hair putting the colors of the sunset to shame."

Sullivan? Waxing poetic about me? Not even a substantial concussion could explain *that*. What the heck was he trying to pull this time? I'd been wrong earlier when appraising my reaction to the sight of him; that wasn't my stomach clenching: It was my heart—against the expectation of being broken.

He rose. For a panicked moment, I was certain he was going to round my desk and approach me. My pulse was racing. Through the lump in my throat, I managed somehow to ask evenly, "And how much were you thinking about me five days ago when you got back into town and couldn't be bothered to pick up the phone?"

He said nothing.

I handed him the receipt and Helen's address. "Meet me there at nine tomorrow morning."

He stared at the slips of paper, smirked at me, then turned on his heel and descended the stairs without another word.

chapter 4

How to tell when it's high time to rid your residence of clutter? When you can't find what you're looking for until you no longer need it.

—Audrey Munroe

"You look tired, my dear," Audrey, my beloved landlady, remarked as I sank into my favorite seat in the den—a blue and gold damask wingback. My seat perfectly fulfilled my desire to cuddle up in a megasoft chair with my cat and a steaming cup of mint tea. Although the wingback and the teacup were picture perfect, Hildi snubbed me in favor of the Sheridan in the corner. The white tip of her tail was flicking angrily at me. She'd no doubt detected the scent of Ella and Vator on me and felt betrayed.

I massaged a crick in my neck and glanced at Audrey. The pile of knitting on her lap was growing, dwarfing her petite, sixty-something frame. Audrey was expecting her first grandchild any day now. She had recently taken up this craft, intending to create booties and a baby blanket. First, however, she was "practicing" by producing a spring green scarf. "My day felt as long as that scarf you're knitting," I told her with a sigh.

"Dealing with difficult clients?"

"Oh, I guess you could say that." It was actually my encounter with Steve Sullivan that had taken the bounce out of my step, but there was no way I'd bring up his name. Never one to pull her punches, Audrey had informed me repeatedly that the two of us were "made for each other." I'd tried to point out how wildly off the mark that particular Cupid's arrow would be, but my landlady was also never one for listening to an opposing viewpoint. "I started working on a pack rat's house today, and it looks like we're going to have a major tug-of-war every time I try to get her to dispose of her . . . disposables."

Audrey looked up from her novel, which had been propped open on the oval mahogany coffee table. (The woman is so hyperactive that she routinely does at least two things at once.) "Clutter reduction. I love it! That is such a splendid topic for my show. It's almost a standby of mine, in fact, even though there are more than enough cable shows concerning clutter. It seems as though half the homeowners in America can never get the hang of clearing their homes of all the things they don't need."

"Said the pot to the kettle," I couldn't help but grumble. Granted, we were sitting in a cozy four-seat arrangement in front of the fireplace. But that was merely thanks to my ceaseless furniture arranging—

necessary due to Audrey's *equally* ceaseless tendency to use her house as a test tube for home-improvement experiments. She was forever testing out ideas for her local TV show: *Domestic Bliss with Audrey Munroe*. Even as we spoke, old hatboxes and leather trunks lined every wall. Audrey had acquired them for an excellent piece on how to jazz up old containers and use them as accent pieces. The episode had aired three months ago.

"My house isn't cluttered." Audrey sniffed. "It's merely imaginatively utilized with nonstandard spacing between items. As well as being a tad excessively furnished."

I had to laugh. "I'm impressed. That's the most creative description for clutter I've ever heard. You should help real estate agents come up with new terms besides 'fixer-uppers' for dilapidated houses, and 'charming bungalow' for dinky."

She shot a quick glare at me over her reading glasses, then flipped the page of her novel, blending the motion in with her incessantly moving knitting needles. "You know, Erin, just last week I had a closet organizer on the show. I have to say that—" She paused to peer at her needlework, cried, "Oh, shoot!" and started to undo her latest row, an action which she'd told me last night was termed *unknitting*.

"By a 'closet organizer,' do you mean the shelving, or the occupation?"

"Both, actually. But my point is that I would love it if you were to replicate that closet design you showed me for the master bedroom in north Crestview. You know—the one where you installed built-ins on the short wall at the end of the closet?"

"That worked out nicely," I muttered into my teacup, hoping to avoid the issue of the fact that I didn't want to appear on her show. Ever. I was extremely camera-shy, and her show taped at seven A.M., far too early for me to indulge in a sedative to relax me. Such as a martini. The design she was referring to had been to update a master bedroom that had been built before the advent of walk-in closets. My clients had to round a closet to get to their bathroom. The bedroom was too small for an armoire, and they were desperate for storage space. My solution was to salvage the wasted area at the end of the closet by installing six built-in drawers topped by a breakfront, which enclosed shelves for their linens.

"As the closet expert was saying on my show, in today's society, we've become possessed by our possessions. I'm just as guilty of it as the next person—of buying too much." She paused, eyed her ever-growing scarf, and added under her breath, "And of making too much. We get obsessed with holding on to all our excess belongings—with not letting anyone else take them from us. Yet, after a fire or a flood, victims are always grateful that they and their families are all right—because everything else was just...stuff."

"True, but it's nice to live comfortably, to surround yourself with nice things."

"Absolutely, but that's the key—to 'live comfortably' means to take *comfort* in your nice surroundings. Having too many possessions prevents that. When I find myself keeping some obscure item solely because I *might* want to use it someday, I ask myself: Am I going to be able to find this when the need arises? Because if not, there's no reason to keep it. There's great comfort in well-organized closets and storage areas."

"Yes, there is." I couldn't help but eye the hatbox-and-luggage display in the room, thinking that there was even *greater* comfort in having a well-organized den.

"Well, that's enough knitting practice," Audrey grumbled. "It's time for me to move on to my grandchild's booties and blanket. And, since I need to practice what I preach, I'll call a charity and schedule a pickup. We'll get rid of a few surplus items from this house." She sighed as she unfurled her knitting. "Starting with this scarf."

"No offense, Audrey, but the person who wants that scarf will have to have a neck like a giraffe. Have you measured it? I'm guessing that's about sixteen feet long."

She stretched it out along the floor, but stopped when Hildi raced toward her, twitching her black tail and pouncing on the scarf. "Sorry, Hildi," she chided gently. "I wasn't trying to beckon you to play with my yarn." Audrey looked up at me. "I did get a little carried away with all this green wool. Maybe the Jolly Green Giant is in the market for some new neckwear."

"He could probably use it. He spends all that time in freezers, hanging out with frozen vegetables."

Audrey laughed. She brandished her knitting needles as though they were carving utensils. "Well, Erin. Now that I've mastered scarf-making, it's *bootie time!*"

chapter 5

t he next morning, Steve Sullivan was waiting for me in the cab of a small rental truck when I arrived at Helen Walker's house. We exchanged our pat "hey" greetings and some small talk. But we didn't once look at each other as we walked to Helen's front door.

Sullivan commented on what a "nice place" it was from the outside. Although I kept the remark to myself, it struck me that, for all the amazing homes I'd been in since I'd moved to Crestview nearly three years ago, this was the house that best fit my own style and sense of scale. Much as I loved my home in Audrey Munroe's fabulous mansion, it was too large for me. Ironically, second-highest on my list of dream homes was Sullivan's, but I would allow myself to be dangled by my thumbs above open flames before anyone would ever drag that tidbit of information out of me.

I rang the doorbell and waited. "Just a minute," Helen soon called from inside.

In what I chose to take as an encouraging sign, she let us in through the front door, as opposed to the garage. With his typical suave manner when meeting new clients, Sullivan exuded charm and acted as if the ceiling-high stack of brown paper grocery bags by the front door was as common a sight as an umbrella stand.

Sullivan leapt at her offer of a fresh-brewed cup of coffee, and I was curious as to how she could manage such a feat. She'd told me she used her microwave exclusively. We followed her into the kitchen, where even Sullivan's stoic jaw dropped at her superstore-warehouse-run-amok interior. As we squished ourselves into the clearing, I spied an ancient-looking coffeemaker atop a Mount Everest of magazines.

"Erin? Is that you?" a vaguely familiar voice called from behind a wall of boxes.

"Stephanie?" I replied, hazarding an educated guess.

"Over here."

I followed her voice. Stephanie was sitting cross-legged on the floor, leaning against the back door, sipping a mug of coffee and reading a newspaper. "Brought an old coffeemaker over this morning. Thought I'd get filled in on current events back on"—she glanced at the header —"November sixth, 1987. Kind of uplifting, really. World events back then were every bit as frightful as they are today."

"Morning, Stephanie," Sullivan said, stepping beside me. We were all but wedged shoulder to shoulder. The close quarters, frankly, were making me edgy, but there was no place for me to escape, with Stephanie leaning against the back door.

Her smile spread from ear to ear. "Well, well, well. If it isn't Steve Sullivan. The world's most macho designer. You finally got bored with those West Coast babes?"

He gave her a sexy grin. "Started to miss the lovely ladies of Colorado, after a while. How are you, Steph? Great to see you."

Well, he was certainly wasting no time before sucking up to his former client. She had to be at least ten years older than he was, but her facial expression had suddenly turned downright coquettish.

"It's been so long, I was rather expecting to hear through the grapevine that you'd turned into a surfer dude and flown the coop for good."

"Not me. I'm strictly into mountains."

I dearly hoped that my eyes were playing tricks on me, and that I hadn't just seen him ogle Stephanie's breasts as he spoke!

"You picked the right house, then," she replied, gesturing at the piles and stacks surrounding us.

Helen produced Sullivan's cup of coffee—in a World's Greatest Dad coffee mug—and promptly excused herself to go "clean out Ella and Vator's litter boxes." I wound up holding Sullivan's cup for him while he gallantly assisted Stephanie to her feet. This time I saw clearly that he *did* give her body an appreciative once-over. Yeesh! Whatever had I been thinking when I'd let him kiss me like that two months ago?!

He was too focused on Stephanie to as much as look at me, let alone thank me for serving as his cup holder while he reclaimed the World's Greatest Dad mug. *World's Worst Egomaniac* would have been much more appropriate. "How's that rec room of yours coming along?" he asked, once again wasting no time on subtleties.

"Still waiting for the right man for the job." She gave him a sly smile. "Say, that gives me a good idea."

"Oh, yeah?" he said, taking a sip of coffee to play up his oh-so-cool routine.

"You two aren't booked solid right now, are you?" Stephanie looked at me, then back at Sullivan.

Sullivan and I exchanged confused glances. "You mean Gilbert and me? We're not partners, in any sense of the word."

The last phrase was hardly necessary—unless he felt he needed to make it crystal clear that we also weren't *sexual* partners. Our kiss truly had meant nothing to him. All his cute little e-mails must have been mere compulsive flirting. I glared at his coffee mug, willing it to read *World's Most Arrogant Bastard!*

"Oh, you aren't?" Stephanie replied. "When you showed up here together, I just assumed."

"No. He's just here to do the heavy lifting for me," I said.

"Maybe you'll nix this idea, then," Stephanie said, "but I'd like to hire you both to work as a team, to design my game room."

"Both of us?" Sullivan squared his shoulders. "You do understand that Sullivan Designs is fully autonomous, right, Steph? I'm just here as a favor to Erin. Plus I figured this'd be a great chance for you and me to get caught up again."

"Glad to hear you're not out of work and forced to schlepp for other designers, Steve. But I've felt for a while that the one thing lacking in your work is a woman's sensibilities."

"Huh," he said, covering his indignation by taking another loud sip of coffee. I, on the other hand, didn't bother to hide my grin.

"'Fraid so. Whereas Erin Gilbert here could stand to be a touch more imaginative in her designs...making them more on a par with your work."

"Ah," he said with a knowing nod. He clearly had no trouble agreeing with *my* having been handed the much more severe criticism.

"How did you come to that conclusion?" I asked, suppressing my umbrage as best I could; the last thing I wanted was to get on the wrong side of a powerful developer in this town. "I haven't even shown you any of my designs."

"It's what I gleaned from looking at the pictures of rooms on your Web site. They're all a tad too...predictable."

I held my tongue, but her statement contained more garbage than this kitchen.

"Whereas, as a team," she prattled on, "Gilbert and Sullivan would be without equal. And, as you can imagine, I have my new homeowners asking me for recommendations on designers all the time. I'd be happy to pass along your names. It sounds so cute, when you link them." She chuckled. "Face it...you two could make beautiful music together."

It was almost worth having to hear that insipid joke for the umpteenth time to watch Sullivan suppress a groan by noisily clearing his throat.

Helen appeared and exclaimed, "My goodness! Are you young folks still just standing here and gabbing?"

"We're discussing a business proposition, Aunt Helen. One that's going to work out great for all three of us, don't you think?"

Sullivan merely glowered at the steamy surface of his coffee. Damn it! Even though Stephanie was way off base in calling the fabulous designs on my Web site "predictable" (which could only mean that they were *predictably* stunning), the part about this being beneficial for Sullivan's and my careers was all too accurate. One of us was going to have to swallow some pride and say "Yes" first, and heaven knows I was the more emotionally mature.

"I agree," I said. Sullivan blinked at me in surprise. Once you've resolved to knock down a wall, there's no sense in stopping at the first peephole, so I continued, "Sullivan and I have worked on a couple of designs together, and I'm sure we can do one for you that will absolutely dazzle you."

"Wonderful!" Stephanie looked expectantly at him.

"Right." He took a swig of coffee and set down the cup. "Let us know when you'd like to start on your rec room, Steph, and Erin and I will be there."

"Tomorrow afternoon's fine by me. Whenever the two of you are ready. Anytime after three P.M., I can—" She broke off when her cell phone rang, answering in harried-businesswoman tones. She tugged fitfully on her dark hair as she listened. Within the next sixty seconds, she cursed colorfully a half dozen times, said a gruff good-bye to the three of us, and rushed off to handle a "crisis."

"You ready to get to work?" Sullivan asked me.

"Of course. I've just been waiting on you to finish your coffee."

Helen was peering at us, her arms crossed. I noticed the bun of her snow white hair was much neater than it had been yesterday. Maybe this meant she'd slept in her bedroom and had put up her hair while using the bathroom mirror, as opposed to the rearview mirror. I took a calming breath, buoyed myself with a silent "Confidence and optimism," and said, "Helen, as we discussed yesterday, the only way we're going to be able to do this job is to clear everything out of your house, then move back in only those items that you truly need."

"No."

"No?"

"That isn't the *only* way you can do this job; that's merely the *easiest* way. I need to give my personal okay before anything's removed from my house. I refuse to let you two load up that big truck out there and then dole out my own possessions to me."

"Um . . . actually, I wanted to first spread everything out on the lawn, *then* move them either into the truck or back into the house. Does that sound more appealing to you, by any chance?"

"No, I'm afraid it doesn't, Erin."

Somewhere in all this accumulated chaos a death knell was ringing for my chances of success in this assignment. "How 'bout we move things room by room into the garage, then?"

She shook her head obstinately. "Nothing leaves the

house till I've given it my okay. You can take away all the recyclable items, though—the cardboard, plastics, bottles, and bags. Everything except for the magazines and newspapers. Those I'll need to look through first."

"Helen, I'm sorry, but that just won't work," I said firmly. "If you have to examine every individual item before we remove it, we'll be here for a year."

"Oh, I didn't mean I would look through every single newspaper. I just don't want any periodicals from the fifties or sixties to be removed without my say-so."

I sighed, exasperated. "Okay, it's a start. At some point we absolutely *must* empty out everything in order to clean thoroughly and reorganize. But I guess if we have to, we can move things from room to room." I looked at Sullivan and found myself longing to take my frustrations out on him. He'd strung me along for two months, only to serve as my ersatz business partner upon his return. Even so, I couldn't mangle the sequence of events sufficiently to make Helen's pack rat ways his fault. "Let's get going."

Promising Helen once more that we'd remove "*only* recyclables," we started in on the kitchen. Helen told us that all of the periodicals that she'd wanted to keep were in her den, which allowed us to work quickly. Furthermore, Sullivan informed her that *all* of her hoarded scraps of paper and cardboard were recyclable. I, in turn, convinced her that old tires could be taken to a local dealer—which I think was the truth. In any case, I decided that my job was, after all, *interior* design, and she removed her lawn-care tools through the back door. In less than two hours, we had filled the truck and uncovered the dinette—an adorable hand-planed pine table and three captain's chairs—and Sullivan took off alone in the truck to drop off the first of what I hoped would be many loads.

Shortly after he'd departed, the doorbell rang and Helen grumbled, "That's probably Rachel Schwartz again. It's about time for her to arrive...and give me my daily dose of stress."

The moment Helen opened the door, Rachel swept through it, chattering a long-winded greeting. Rachel was closely followed by her husband, who set down his toolbox and a small bag of supplies to shake hands with me. Jack Schwartz was a nice-looking man, Helen's age, roughly twenty years older than his wife. He was medium height—an inch or so shorter than Rachel—with a bulbous nose, short-cropped white hair, and an affable smile. He greeted me warmly and mentioned how happy he was that I was "finally helping to put Helen's house back together again." The wording gave me an instant mental image of Humpty Dumpty, which wasn't far off the mark.

Interrupting our chat, Rachel deserted Helen and grabbed her husband's arm. "We're here to install the doorbell," she explained to me. "My, you look nice today." She was eyeing my khakis and dark-green knit top. "You've got that casual-elegant look going for you."

This being just the second time she'd ever seen me, it was an odd comment, but I simply replied, "Thank you, Rachel. So do you." She was wearing a light blue skirt suit and pearls, an outfit that looked disturbingly similar to the one she'd seen me wearing yesterday. Was the woman deliberately copying my wardrobe?

"Tell me, Helen," Jack asked, gently prying his arm free of his wife's grip, "do you want a separate doorbell outside your garage door, or do you just want to be able to hear the existing doorbell when you're in your garage?"

"Hmm. I don't know. I'm not sure which would be more practical...."

He picked up his toolbox and bag. "Let's go take a look at your garage, and I'll help you decide."

"I'll come, too," Rachel said.

"Don't be silly, Rachel," Jack snapped. "You can trust Helen and me to be out of your sight for just five minutes, can't you?" He forced a chuckle. His thinly disguised simmering anger brought back an unpleasant memory of the way my father spoke to my mother sometimes in the months leading to their divorce.

Rachel's cheeks flamed beet red, and she cast a painfully embarrassed glance at Helen and me. "Yes, darling, but you said I could help you, and that's what I want to do, Jack. Please?"

Helen pursed her lips for a moment, but then gestured for her to join them and said kindly, "I'd like to get Rachel's opinion on this, actually."

Rachel smiled gratefully, but the instant that Helen and Jack turned to head into the garage, an unmistakable expression of pure hatred flashed across her features.

chapter 6

Unexpectedly alone in the house, I indulged myself in a few moments of mental room makeovers—a designer's version of window shopping. Helen would never want a modern kitchen, complete with granite countertops, cherry cabinets, and stainless steel appliances. But with very little effort and expense, this kitchen could be marvelous; it was already so retro with its old appliances—back when the color choice was white or white—that it was even fashionable. I could paint the cabinets a stylish ivory and replace their boring knobs. With the limited wall space in this kitchen, we could go with a bright, fun color—tangerine, in this case—and give the room real pizzazz. The blah brown linoleum floors could be upgraded with two or three colorful rugs.

I peered into Helen's small dining room, now crowded with the boxes. This space cried out for wainscot: a simple bead-board—ivory—with a chair rail that we'd continue into the kitchen. And crown molding to add a dash of flair.

My Big Picture task was to create a nurturing environment for my client in which she could thrive and grow. For now, that meant merely disposing of that which didn't belong. I banished myself to Helen's pantry, but found myself running a mental inventory. On the shortest wall of shelves, she had three sandwich makers, four waffle irons, and two smaller-than-a-breadbox appliances with functions that I couldn't immediately identify. Judging by the thick coat of dust on the plastic bags that covered them, neither could Helen.

Someone tapped on the front door then opened it, and I rushed into the living room to see who was there. Sullivan leaned in and said with a sexy smile, "Your moving man's back."

"Come on in."

He entered, tentatively glanced around, and peered through the entranceway to the kitchen.

In answer to his unasked question, I reported, "Helen's in the garage, discussing the doorbell with the Schwartzes."

"The Schwartzes?"

"Her neighbors. The Georgian colonial across the street."

He gave an appreciative nod, then shifted his focus to

our surroundings. "Jeez. Underneath all the clutter, this house…"

"Oh, I know. This place is crying out to be a warm, cozy cottage. Helen would feel right at home in such a space if we could just isolate her hoardings to a work-room." Once again, the boring cabinet doors caught my eye. "I'm thinking of replacing the knobs with trans-lucent, sea mist green, cut-glass knobs on the kitchen cabinets."

"We'd have to first convince her that the hardware store kept her original knobs as trade-ins," Sullivan scoffed. "Sage walls?"

I shook my head. "Tangerine."

He grinned and said wistfully, "With hand-painted ce-ramic tiles on the backsplash."

"Yes! And complementary countertops . . . a maize, maybe. Or blue-gray."

We gazed in silence at our imaginary kitchen for a mo-ment. Then Sullivan grumbled, "If I move fast, I can get a couple armloads of newspapers from the sixties out of here before she notices."

"I don't want to betray her trust like that. Let's just fo-cus exclusively on the kitchen for today, and try to get an-other load dropped off to Eco-Cycle."

He gave his hair a quick rake, then he pulled some-thing out of his pocket. "What should I do with this?" He handed a slip of paper to me. I unfolded the sheet of his Sullivan Designs stationery. He'd written: *I'm sorry.* A man of few words.

"Gee, Sullivan." I smiled a little, in spite of myself. As much as the man infuriated me, he sure had a knack for catching me off guard. "I don't know what to say. I mean, this is just such ponderous reading material, it could take me a while to work my way through it." I handed the note back to him, and he returned it to the back pocket of his jeans.

"At least you didn't tell me to stick it where the sun don't shine." He gave me a shy, slightly crooked smile that had, no doubt, melted many a girl's heart. "For what it's worth, Gilbert, I—"

The doorbell rang, and I glanced through the screen door. A short, plump, white-haired woman waved and gave me a pleasant smile. "Good morning, dear. My name is Kay Livingston. I'm a friend of Helen's."

"Come on in, Kay."

The hinges squeaked as she let herself inside. "You must be Erin Gilbert, the designer. Helen was telling me all about you over the phone." She gave Sullivan a visual once-over and grinned. "She certainly didn't mention any young men, however."

"This is my assistant, Steve Sullivan."

Sullivan stiffened and cleared his throat, but didn't correct me.

"How nice for you! Gilbert and Sullivan? I absolutely love *Pirates of Penzance*."

"Different duo," Sullivan deadpanned.

Helen bustled through the inner garage door and greeted her friend with a hug, then introduced Kay to us, saying, "Kay and I have been friends longer than the two of you have been alive, put together. We met clear back in grade school in Denver. Then she and I, along with my sister, moved into an apartment together when we were in our twenties." She beamed at Kay. "That was a fun time, wasn't it?"

Kay glowered at Helen and replied, "For some of us, more than others." We shared an awkward silence until the garage door rumbled open. "Helen?" Kay looked perplexed. "Who's in your garage?"

"Jack Schwartz is installing a doorbell. So that I can hear the doorbell from the garage," she explained.

"A doorbell for the *garage*?" Kay held up her palms and said, "Actually, I don't *want* to know." She turned her attention to me. "One thing you absolutely *must* help Helen do, Erin, is to unbury her porcelain collections. She has a stunning set of Lladró figurines. Each one is of a dancer."

Helen groaned at her friend's instructions to me and said, "Erin and Steve are not going to be able to get much of anything done, till they get back to work."

"On that note," Sullivan said with a slight bow, "if you ladies will excuse me, I've got some more toting and lifting to do."

"It was nice meeting you, Mr. Sullivan."

"You, as well, Ms. Livingston."

He headed into the kitchen, and Kay squeezed my arm and whispered into my ear, "He is *so* handsome!" I gave her a noncommittal shrug—there was no denying the man's great looks—as she continued, "Helen's got a lot of truly beautiful things around. She just let the place go once Lois moved in with her. Lois was never much of a housekeeper and had a ton of curios herself, just not nearly the same quality as Helen's collections. Next thing you know, the house got out of hand."

"You can say that again," a woman's voice interjected. Rachel Schwartz was eavesdropping from the front porch. "Lois had no taste whatsoever," Rachel persisted. "She and George had let their own house go completely to seed."

Helen tried to cut her off, crying, "Rachel, I—"

Rachel merely raised her voice and prattled on through the screen door, "I always figured that was why Stephanie went into real estate. She wants to build nice new places to compensate for the—"

"Rachel!" Jack called from the garage door. "Just press the damn doorbell, would you please?"

"I'm on it, dear," she called back, rolling her eyes. She jabbed at the button as though she were typing Morse code, making the gong over our heads ring repeatedly. "Can you hear that?"

"Yes," he called back. "Stop pushing it, already!"

Sullivan came through the room, carrying a box full of jar lids, which quickly passed Helen's inspection. Rachel and Kay raced over to hold the door for him, both holding it open and then basking in his broad smile and his syrupy-sweet "Thank you, ladies."

Seconds later, Jack joined us, Rachel again latching on to his arm. "Helen," he said with a hint of exasperation, "I decided to install a remote doorbell ringer inside your garage. It will chime whenever anyone presses the front doorbell. It just plugs into an ordinary electric socket, so you can move it anyplace. I even set it up to play a tune for you."

"That sounds perfect, Jack. Thank you."

Although momentarily distracted by Sullivan's backside as he returned and walked past us once more, Rachel said, "But getting back to our discussion, Helen, you know just as well as I do that half the trouble with your sister's children never would—"

"It's time we got on home. Now!" Jack roared. He threw in a hasty "Bye," and all but dragged his wife out the door.

Turning to Helen, Kay said, "Wouldn't you think someone her age would have better things to do with her time than be such a busybody? All that woman ever does is stare out her windows and gossip!"

Helen merely frowned, but Rachel's behavior had raised my warning flags. Was it possible Helen's break-ins were real after all? Could Rachel be letting herself into Helen's house to poke around whenever Helen left her home? Curious if Helen shared my suspicions, I remarked, "Rachel's sure keeping a close watch on your house."

"She certainly is," Helen replied evenly.

Kay had the door duty to herself as Sullivan tried to come through a second time with another load for the truck. Helen blocked his path and made him lower the huge box to her eye level for inspection. This time she hemmed and hawed, before grudgingly allowing him to remove the jars.

As Kay shut the screen door behind him, she reached up and touched the tape fastened to the inside corner of the door frame. She gave me a sheepish glance and asked Helen, "Are you still having trouble with break-ins?"

"Yes," Helen said in a harsh whisper. "And Erin already knows about my security system...with the strands of hair. Just remember, Kay, you're the only one in our immediate circle who knows about it, so don't breathe a word to anyone!"

"You know how I pride myself on keeping secrets," Kay retorted. "I fully intend to take yours to the grave."

"Thank you, dear."

I studied Kay's placid features. If she in any way doubted that the break-ins were really happening, she was keeping her skepticism to herself.

As Sullivan returned once more, Kay remarked, "My, my. That young man is working so hard, it's exhausting just to watch! This is such an enormous job. Can I be of any help, Helen?"

"No, and much as I'd love to have you stay and chat, I really want to stay focused on working with Gilbert and Sullivan."

Kay grinned. "Far be it from me to slow you down, dear. I'll be going, then. It was a pleasure meeting you, Miss Gilbert. You too, Mr. Sullivan," she called into the kitchen.

"Take care, Ms. Livingston," came Sullivan's cheery reply.

She winked at me and called to Sullivan, "Love your work. Especially *The Mikado*."

"Yeah, thanks. I'm proud of that one, too," he shot back.

Helen walked her friend to her car, and Sullivan seized the opportunity to report to me that he was filling a box with extras from restaurants—condiment packets, straws, thousands of plastic utensils, and rinsed-out paper cups. "She's got enough junk like that to outfit her own fast-food chain. Just in case she disapproves, you'll need to distract her."

I nodded, thinking that although this didn't fit Helen's permitted category of "recyclables," we truly needed to dispose of them. I made a show of realigning yet more scrapbooks in the dining room as she returned, and Helen promptly rushed to my side. Meanwhile, Sullivan sneaked out the door. I muttered something about making sure the books didn't topple over and asked loudly, to cover for the squeaky door hinge, "By the way, Helen, have you ever asked Rachel if she's seen a prowler?"

"Of course not. That would be darned stupid of me. It would only serve to tip my hand. If it turns out Rachel's the one breaking into my home, she'd know I've got a system that alerts me."

"Do you have any reason to suspect her personally?"

"Well, of course." She put her hands on her hips and regarded me as though I'd just asked her what color she thought the sky was. "For one thing, there's the fact that she's never once said a thing about spying anyone entering my home in my absence. Yet she always knows about every single person who comes to my door when I'm here to let 'em in." Sullivan had eased himself back into the house and now tiptoed toward the kitchen. "Even as we speak, she's probably delighting in the way your assistant is making extra trips to the truck when he thinks I'm not looking."

Behind her, Sullivan froze. "Sorry, Helen," I said. "We're really just trying to move things along as quickly as possible, and to do that, you have to trust our judgment a little."

"That'd be easier if you weren't trying to pull the wool over my eyes."

"We won't do it again," Sullivan said, "I promise." He gave me a "Yikes" grimace and returned to the kitchen.

"We meant no harm, Helen. It was just things like leftover catsup packets that he took away."

"But . . . I *use* catsup, and there's no sense in—"

The doorbell rang again, and she grumbled, "What now?" I followed her back into the living room, and she swept open the door.

"Hello, Teddy." Helen's greeting held more exasperation than warmth. "This is a surprise."

"It is? I thought I told you I'd be stopping by." A slender elderly man with stooped shoulders bussed Helen's cheek, then beamed at me. He was wearing baggy pants and a plaid vest over his white button shirt. With his cherubic, dimpled, ruddy cheeks and bright blue eyes, he looked like a skinny overgrown elf. I returned his smile.

"This is Erin Gilbert. Erin, Theodore Frederickson."

"I'm an old friend of the family's," he explained, pumping my hand with a firm grip. He was hiding something behind his back. I hoped it wasn't anything for the house.

"It's nice to meet you, Mr. Frederickson."

"Everyone calls me Teddy."

He peered through the doorway into the kitchen, and Helen said, "That's Steve Sullivan. Mr. Sullivan? Meet Teddy Frederickson."

Teddy ducked into the kitchen for a moment to shake hands, then said, "Wow, Helen. These kids have made some terrific progress already! You can see some of your furniture, and all the way to the back door."

"I know," she replied. "It looks strange to me now. Empty, even."

"You'll get used to it. T'ain't like you need all the junk in here to weigh the place down and keep it from shooting up into outer space." He laughed and patted Helen on the back.

"No, I realize that," she said with a hint of irritation in her voice.

Teddy promptly stopped laughing, cleared his throat, and handed her a box of candy, clicking his heels in a pseudo-Hitler style. "These are for you, my dear."

"What's the occasion?" she asked as she accepted the box.

"A gift to celebrate your courage in allowing some changes to be made in your home."

"I don't have any problem with change, Teddy. Just so long as it's not for the worse."

"Won't know if change is good or bad till you try it on for a while!" Teddy said, again laughing. "They're first-rate chocolates. You're not allergic to chocolate, are you?"

"No, no," she said sadly, "Lois was the one with all the allergies in the family." She shook the box. "Aren't candy boxes normally shrink-wrapped?"

"Can you come here for a moment, Erin?" Steve called from the kitchen. I complied, and Sullivan showed me two cabinets jammed full with dusty, junky-looking cookware. With great effort, I extracted one of the pots. Both inside and outside were charred black. A five-year-old Cub Scout would consider this pot too grungy for a campout.

Both Helen and Teddy had followed me into the kitchen. "We should get rid of all these really beat-up pots and pans, Helen," I told her.

"But those are my backups. I might need them someday."

"What scenario will cause you to need four sets of 'backup' cookware?" I asked gently.

"What if the roof springs some leaks? Right while I'm preparing supper?"

Teddy guffawed. "You're afraid you'll have twenty or

thirty holes in your roof show up at the same time? What's your roof made out of? Swiss cheese?" He all but doubled over with hilarity.

Helen sighed, but turned to me and said, "Fine. Let's give my old pots to the needy."

"Good idea," Teddy declared. "We'll give 'em out according to which ones have the most holes in their roofs."

His last remark was voiced with such good humor that I had to laugh myself. Helen, however, thumped the box of candy on the counter, grabbed Teddy's arm, and started to escort him out. "Thank you for stopping by, Teddy, and for the candies. We're going to get back to work now."

"You sure I can't help? I can carry those pots and things to the truck—"

"That's a nice offer, but we can let the experts take care of everything. Erin and Steve know what they're doing."

Teddy said his reluctant good-byes and left. Helen promptly asked Sullivan and me, "Does either of you want a box of chocolate candy? I really don't care much for sweets. If Teddy wanted to impress me, he should've brought pretzels."

Not only did I love chocolate, but this gave me the chance to get an item out of her house; she was bound to get attached to the empty box someday. "Are you sure you don't want them yourself?"

"Oh, well, on second thought, maybe I do. I just hope they're fresh and won't break my jaw. Teddy probably bought these for my sister, Lois, months ago, before he learned she was allergic."

"She was allergic to chocolate *and* peppers?"

"Also peanuts and shellfish."

"Jeez," Sullivan muttered. "Last night I had Chinese

takeout. One of the dishes was shrimp with green peppers sautéed in peanut oil."

Helen glared at him, but he didn't notice.

We boxed up the worthless pots. As we worked, I worried about Teddy's gift to her; the chocolate could be tainted. But that was absurd; he wouldn't have given her poisoned candy in front of two witnesses. I asked Helen, "Stephanie implied that Teddy once dated your sister. Is that true?"

"Yes. They got reacquainted when he came to her husband George's funeral."

"Was the relationship serious?"

Helen nodded. "Teddy proposed to Lois, but she didn't want to get married again, or at least, not right away. He's a sweet man. And I think men are wonderful." She narrowed her eyes at Sullivan and added, "In general. *Husbands*, on the other hand, are problematic. They always seem to want their wives to mother them." With a wink, she added, "Although, that's the observation of a self-confirmed spinster." She rolled her eyes and repeated, "*Spinster*. Isn't that just the most sexist word you've ever heard?"

"I suppose it is, a little."

"It's worse than 'a little,' in my opinion. A man who never marries is a 'confirmed bachelor.' Whereas they make us unmarried women sound like *spiders*!"

Sullivan and I had appointments with separate clients in the afternoon, and we agreed to stop work at Helen's a little after one, with the truck still just two-thirds full with a second load. Our progress was bound to bog down as we continued to inch toward the items that were less obviously disposable. To pave the way for what was certain to be an emotionally challenging day for Helen, I announced that tomorrow we were going to move everything into the center of the floor and sort it into keep, toss, or sell piles.

Sullivan stretched his shoulder muscles as we made our way to my van and said, "I'm going to need a ride to the rental place to pick up my van."

"No problem." We had the truck leased for two weeks, which seemed like wishful thinking. Right now I could imagine myself having to wrench things away from Helen over the course of the next several months.

Sullivan moved the truck to an out-of-the-way overnight space around the corner from Helen's house. As we drove away in my van, he asked me to connect the dots from the snippets of conversation he'd overheard about break-ins. I filled him in on Helen's fears and suspicions. Then I sighed. "Even though her theory about her brother-in-law's death is a bit off the wall, I really don't agree with Stephanie and Peter about the Alzheimer's. As far as I can see, Helen's simply a little eccentric. Although I sure wish she'd listened to my suggestions about changing her locks."

"Wouldn't make any difference. It's not like anyone really *is* entering her house."

"What do you mean?"

"You don't seriously think she's taping hairs across the door openings each and every time she goes out, do you? Judging by the number of visitors she had today, those doors of hers are getting quite a workout. I bet she forgets about the hairs, opens her door for her cats or a guest, then later thinks, 'Oh, my! Somebody broke in!' Face it, Gilbert. Your client's a nutcase."

"Now you're making fun of my client?"

"No. I'm just saying I think your client's lonely and a little frightened being in the house by herself. So she's imagining things."

That was very possible, but his cockiness was annoying. "Or maybe her sister was murdered just like she says, and she's justifiably taking precautions."

"Come on, Gilbert! You really think there's a serial killer of harmless little old ladies running around? Whose weapon of choice is a bell pepper?"

"You know what, Sullivan? This is why Helen acts a little frosty toward you. She's smart enough to see right through your charming act and figure out how cynical you are."

"She's not 'frosty' toward me. She just doesn't jabber away at people the way you do."

"I don't jabber! Nobody has ever once accused me of jabbering!"

"Fine. I just meant that women tend to talk to other women a lot more freely than they do to men."

"Probably because *men* tend to use insulting terms such as 'jabbering' to describe women when we converse!"

"Hey! It was Helen who said we were 'gabbing' instead of working this morning!"

He had a point there. Sort of. I gritted my teeth and said nothing, but took a corner a little more sharply than I should have.

Sullivan retorted, "Furthermore, it's *not* an act! I *am* charming!"

"Not right now you're not." We'd reached the parking

lot of the rental place, and I pulled up to the curb. "See you tomorrow," I mumbled as he got out. And then I drove off instead of waiting to make sure he had his keys, thinking for the countless time that, without fail, Sullivan brought out the very worst in my personality.

To my disappointment, nobody was home when I arrived there at the end of my long day. Audrey was working late. The phone rang at about eight-thirty. It was a double ring, which meant that the call was for me. I answered.

"Erin?" The voice was elderly and trembling with fright.

"Yes. Helen, is something wrong?"

"I just got home from my scrapbooking session. I get together twice a week with friends to do our albums. Another hair has been snapped on the back door, so I'm in the garage again. It's the only safe place here!"

"I wish you'd reconsider putting new locks on the doors, Helen. I'm really certain we can make your house safe so that—"

"Wait! I haven't gotten the chance to tell you my problem yet. You're interrupting me!"

"I'm sorry," I said, truly contrite. The poor woman was scared out of her wits and here I was, bullying her. "Tell me what's wrong, Helen."

"The moment I saw that snapped hair, I got Ella to come join me in the garage, but Vator wouldn't come when I called. Then I heard this . . . this crash, and an instant later, the power went out in my house."

"Are the lights out in your neighbors' houses, too?"

"I don't know. The garage doesn't have any windows.

I'm calling from the cell phone my nephew and niece bought me to keep in my car for emergencies."

"So it's possible that somebody is in your house right now?"

"No, no! I haven't heard another sound after the crash. Vator must have knocked a lamp over, which tripped the circuit breaker."

"Why don't you call Stephanie or Peter, and—"

"But they could be the ones breaking into my house when I'm gone!"

"I thought you said nobody was there."

"I can't be certain!"

"Okay. Just in case then, Helen, I'll call the police right now and send them out there."

"No! Those people always treat me like a senile old fool! It's humiliating!" She took a ragged breath. Was she crying? "Please . . . help me."

I felt a pang of guilt. Helen was frightened and alone and deserved better. "I'll come out myself. I'll be there in ten minutes."

"Thank you!"

Although it took me a bit longer than ten minutes, I arrived at Helen's house, with a flashlight in hand. The power was on everywhere in the neighborhood, but her house was utterly dark. Without thinking, I pushed the button for the doorbell. When no one answered, I realized that, of course, doorbells don't function during power outages. I trotted over to the garage door and knocked.

"Erin?"

"Yes, Helen, it's me."

"I can't lift the door by myself with the power out. I'll let you in through the front door. It'll take a minute."

I waited, worrying that she'd trip over something and injure herself. After what felt like an hour, she swung open the front door. "Thank goodness, you're here!" she gushed and hugged me. She smelled of cinnamon. I could feel her trembling.

"Have you heard any more noises?"

"No, but I can hear Vator someplace in the house. I left poor Ella in the garage." She flicked on the tiny light in her key chain, and I turned on my flashlight. I sent the beam darting around the living room. The place looked eerie, crammed so full that anyone could be skulking behind a stack of boxes or a mound of old clothing.

"Everything seems pretty much the same as when I left the house a couple of hours ago," she said.

I deliberately left the front door wide open, taking advantage of the limited ambient light. I could indeed hear plaintive, muffled meows. "Sounds like Vator might be in the kitchen. Maybe she's gotten herself closed up in the pantry."

Helen stepped back and allowed me to lead the way. I walked up to the kitchen entranceway and stood still, listening. After a moment, I heard another meow. I said, "She's downstairs in the basement."

"That's impossible. I *never* go down there. That door's always shut." She held her ground, directly in front of the basement door. Vator cried again. The sound definitely came from the other side of the door.

"Oh, dear! Now I'm going to have to start taping a hair over this door, too!" She called, "I should have known!

Somebody's been going up and down those stairs, Erin. They keep making a path for themselves, no matter how much stuff I put on the steps to block them. We're coming, Vator!"

I opened the door.

Helen grabbed my arm. "Be careful, Erin! I can't imagine how my kitty got down there."

"Maybe Sullivan accidentally left the door cracked open this morning, and Vator's been trapped down there ever since."

"I guess that's possible. I can't remember when I saw her last. Vator? Come on, Vator. Come on upstairs, please."

Vator answered with another meow, but did not come running up the stairs through the darkness. I weighed calling the police, but other than the meows, the basement was silent. I urged Helen to stay put and started down the stairs myself.

As Helen had said, there was a clear path through junk piled on either side of the stairs. I grabbed hold of the railing and kept a firm grip on my flashlight as I made my way down a couple of steps. I started to get anxious. What if I tripped and fell? What would Helen do if I broke an ankle?

This basement was spooky and smelled musty. I would give my search for Vator thirty seconds or so, tops, then I'd call the police. Surprisingly, the boxes at either side of the open stairway were neatly stacked.

Wait! Was that running water I was hearing?

I shifted my light to the stairs below me once again. The beam reflected off the concrete surface. "Your basement floor is wet," I exclaimed in surprise.

"You mean it's flooded?" Helen cried. "It's never flooded

in the forty-plus years I've lived here." I heard a rustle as she started to follow me.

"It did rain for a few—"

I broke off and gasped as the beam from my flashlight fell on something lying motionless on Helen's basement floor.

"Go back upstairs, Helen!" I began to descend the stairs, staring at the horrible sight. Jack Schwartz was sprawled on his stomach in the inch-deep water.

chapter 7

refusing to believe my eyes, I called, "Jack?"

Helen gasped and sobbed, "Oh, no!" She hadn't gone upstairs like I'd asked. I turned and saw her wobble. I dropped my flashlight and rushed up to support her, then helped her sit down on the stair. "He's dead, isn't he?" she cried.

He was lying facedown in water, but maybe there was a chance he was still alive. "I'll check for a pulse. Stay right here."

Remembering a safety lecture from college about the danger of touching standing water in basements, I hesitated. The fuse had been tripped, though; there was no risk of electrocution. I slipped out of my shoes, made my way down the stairs, and stepped into the bone-chilling shallow water within the murky darkness.

I gasped and jumped at a hissing noise, panicking at the irrational fear that there was an electrical charge after all. It was just the cat. Vator was stranded on the peak of a mountain of boxes against the back wall, just beyond Jack's motionless body. In darkness relieved only by the ambient light from the window wells, her eyes glowed yellow.

Sloshing through the water, I crouched beside Jack. He wasn't breathing. I rolled him over onto his back. Just then, Vator leapt on top of him and sprang to the stairs, darting past Helen, who whimpered and repeated, "Is he dead?"

I couldn't see any blood on his face or wet clothes, yet one look at his frozen, glassy-eyed features had told me all that I didn't want to know. I checked in vain for a pulse. "Yes. We need to call nine-one-one."

I felt disoriented and thoroughly spooked. How could this have happened? Jack was a former electrician. He would have known not to step into water in a basement. Could he have had a heart attack? And what was he doing in Helen's cellar in the first place?

Helen was sobbing softly on the stairs above me. She seemed to be going into shock, and I wasn't going to be much use to her, fumbling around in the dark. I spotted my flashlight, which had landed on a thick, wet mat at the very base of the stairs. I fidgeted with the switch and felt relieved when its dull yellow light flickered back on.

My gaze promptly fell on an object wedged in the small gap between two stacks of boxes. My feet now numb with the cold, I waded closer and pointed my flashlight beam directly into the gap. An electric extension cord was immersed in the water.

"He was electrocuted," I muttered to myself in disbelief.

"Oh, dear Lord." Helen sobbed. "This was meant for me! It's a trap! Poor Jack died because of me!" She stumbled back up the stairs. I followed, retrieving my shoes, and finally realized that my cell phone was in the pocket of my khakis. "I'm calling nine-one-one," I told her as I grabbed my phone and dialed.

"This is all my fault!" She made her way to a chair at the kitchen table.

In the strained glow of my flashlight, her face was distorted with shadows. There was a gas lantern here someplace; I'd seen it in one of the boxes in the kitchen.

"A man's been killed," I said into the phone when the dispatcher answered. "My name is Erin Gilbert. I'm at . . . Helen? What's your address?"

"Twenty-six-seventy Violet Lane," she managed.

I repeated the address and said, "His name's Jack Schwartz. The neighbor from across the street. He died from an electric shock in the flooded basement. The power is out in the house."

Someone was knocking on the door, not loudly, but persistently. That couldn't be the police already; there'd been no sirens.

Helen was tugging on my arm, and I lost my grip and dropped my phone. "Erin? Can you take me back to my garage? Please?"

I fumbled with my phone but discovered I'd been disconnected. "Helen? You're trembling. Let's get you a blanket."

The front door creaked open. "Helen? It's Rachel."

My God. Her husband lay dead in the basement! "Stay there," I called to her. "I'm coming." Helen moaned softly and caught her breath, struggling to collect herself.

"Erin? Erin Gilbert?" Rachel persisted. "I thought I saw your van in the driveway. What on earth is going on in here?" she called.

"I came over to help Helen. Just a minute, Rachel. I'll be right there." I rested my hand on top of Helen's on the table and gave it a reassuring squeeze.

"I'm going back to the garage," she said, rising. "I knew I should have stayed in there—"

"Jack?" Rachel called. "Where are you?"

At this, Helen froze, then crumpled back into her seat. "Poor Jack," she whimpered, covering her face with her hands.

I made my way to the entrance of the living room. Rachel was standing near the front door, the beam of her flashlight darting about wildly. She shined the light directly in my face. "Where's Jack? Where's my husband? I need to talk to him."

I averted my eyes, feeling helpless. Should I tell her to sit down in this messy, pitch-black room while I broke the hideous news to her? "Rachel—"

"I know he's here. We saw a prowler running from here, and—"

"When? Just now?"

"No. Fifteen or twenty minutes ago. We knew Helen wasn't home from her scrapbook club yet. Jack came over to investigate."

"By himself? Didn't you call the police?" Maybe Helen was right! Somebody really *did* seem to be trying to kill her and had gotten the wrong victim!

"No, I couldn't. Jack had bolted outside, absolutely insisting on charging over here to investigate, even though I tried to stop him. I was afraid the police would mistake him for the prowler and shoot him! When he didn't come right back, I kept trying to call here, but nobody answered."

"That's because Helen's phone wouldn't have *rung*. Her power was out, and she has wireless phones." While I was speaking, I caught a whiff of smoke and glanced behind me anxiously. Judging by the scent and the flickering yellow-orange light, Helen must have lit the gas lantern in the kitchen.

"Nonsense! I heard it ringing on my end!" Rachel retorted.

"That's just a sound your own phone makes. It doesn't mean that the phone on—"

But Rachel had noticed the light from the kitchen. "Jack?" she called. Again, she swept her flashlight all around the room. "The power went off just after Helen drove into the garage, so I know he's here, checking the fuses and helping to fix Helen's power outage. Did something happen to her? Is there anything I can do?"

"No, Rachel. There's nothing you can do. The police are on their way. And it isn't Helen. She's fine . . ."

"So then where's . . . Wait. Are you trying to tell me something's happened to my Jack? But . . . that's crazy! The prowler had already *left*! We both saw someone run away. Someone wearing all-black clothes. And a ski cap. And Helen wasn't home yet, so . . . Jack was just going into an *empty* house!"

"There was a terrible accident . . . water in the basement . . ." I faltered.

Rachel gasped. "I have to see him. Jack?" she called frantically.

I grabbed her by the shoulders, afraid that she'd injure herself rushing down the dark stairs. "Rachel, Jack's dead," I told her gently. "I'm so sorry—"

"No!" She knocked my hands away. "You're *lying*! This is some kind of a sick *joke*!"

"I'm so sorry, Rachel." Helen's voice was full of sorrow. She'd come as far as the kitchen doorway.

"You're *sorry*?" Rachel shrieked. "Oh, my God! What's happened here? Did you think my Jack was a prowler? Did *you* kill my poor Jack? Where is he? Let me see him!" The flashlight dropped from her grasp, thudding to the floor, and she staggered back outside onto the porch. She seemed to be on the verge of fainting. I followed and grabbed her arm.

The police sirens were now wailing, turning the last corner directly ahead of us.

"Is there someone I can call for you, Rachel? Do you have a relative in the area who can come over?"

"Oh, dear Lord! The police! So . . . what you're saying is true? My husband is really *dead*? Jack!"

Two police cars pulled up alongside the curb. A female officer emerged from the first vehicle. She looked at Rachel and me. "Erin?"

"Linda," I exclaimed, so relieved to see that my friend Linda Delgardio was the responding officer that my eyes misted. I felt like hugging her.

"My husband's been killed!" Rachel shouted at Linda, wrenching free from my grasp with surprising strength. Then, just as Linda and her partner reached us, Rachel collapsed. Linda's partner, Officer Mansfield, managed to catch her before she toppled down the porch steps.

While the two officers from the second car tended to Rachel, Linda turned her attention to me. "This is a client's house?" she asked quietly.

"Yes." I turned. Helen was still standing by the kitchen doorway. "Helen? This is Officer Delgardio. Linda, this is Helen Walker. This is her house."

"I've lit a few candles," Helen told us. "And a camper's lantern."

"Helen called me when she heard a noise and her lights went out," I explained to Linda.

"Officer Mansfield is coming with me, Ms. Walker." Linda nodded to her partner to join us. Rachel Schwartz was now slumped on the top porch step, sobbing hysterically. Two officers were bent over her, trying to calm her.

Linda asked, "Can you show us where—"

"He's in the basement. Through that door." Helen pointed with a trembling finger. "He's my neighbor, Jack Schwartz. He came here while I was at a meeting of my scrapbooking club."

Linda donned disposable gloves and went into the basement. While we waited for her to return, Helen and I sat in the captain's chairs at the table. The propane lamp glowed, casting flickering, eerie shadows on the walls. Standing sentry over us from the corner of the kitchen, Officer Mansfield gathered basic information from Helen, which she supplied in a clear, surprisingly steady voice.

Minutes later, Linda joined us at the table and took over for her partner in questioning us while he went downstairs. When had we last seen Jack Schwartz alive, she asked us, which was the same time for both of us;

Helen hadn't seen Jack again since he'd left the house at midday upon installing the remote doorbell ringer.

Helen told Linda about Jack and Rachel's testy behavior during the doorbell installation, then skipped ahead. She'd come home tonight a half an hour early from her scrapbook session and heard "a strange noise" just as she'd stepped into the kitchen from the garage. Moments later, she said, the lights went out. Linda tried to get her to be more specific, but Helen began to wring her hands and rock herself. She would say only, "It was a thud and... maybe a buzz. I don't know. I thought a lamp had gotten knocked off a table." She hadn't noticed anything out of the ordinary and believed she was walking into an empty house.

When Officer Mansfield emerged from the basement, Linda held up a hand and said gently, "Excuse me," to Helen. "Mannie?" she said to her partner. "Why don't you take Erin's statement in the patrol car, while I finish speaking with Ms. Walker here?"

I rose, but Helen protested, "No! Please," and shook her head firmly. "I need Erin to stay with me."

The officers exchanged glances. "I'll check the whole premises now, if that's all right, ma'am," Mansfield asked Helen, who nodded.

"Be careful where you step," she warned. "You never know what you might find."

"How did Mr. Schwartz get into your house while you were gone, Ms. Walker?" Linda asked, as Mansfield exited through the garage door.

"My sister might have given him a key. Or the killer could have left the front door open. Assuming there's only one killer. Jack's the third victim."

"Pardon?"

"Two other people close to me have been murdered, Officer Delgardio," Helen said firmly. "Jack was the third. First someone switched my brother-in-law's medication with Tic Tacs, and he died of a heart attack. Then three months ago, somebody killed my sister with bell peppers. Now this. My basement was booby-trapped."

"You think your neighbor was murdered, Ms. Walker?"

"I'm certain of it! The killer flooded my basement and put my poor Vator inside to try to lure me to step into the electrified water." She shivered violently. "Instead, Jack fell for the bait. He must have come inside, heard poor, poor Vator crying downstairs, and waded into the water to get her down...."

"Do you know why someone might want to harm you?" Linda asked.

"Lots of reasons. To get my house away from me. I don't have any children, so everything I own will pass to my niece and nephew. Or maybe to get revenge on me for something. I've taught in public schools for many years and ruffled some feathers." She paused. "Though nothing that could lead anyone to hate me this much. But you read the papers. You're a policewoman. You know how crazy young people are these days. Or maybe..."

"Ms. Walker? Ma'am? What were you about to say?"

"Pardon? Oh, nothing. My mind...This has been so confusing. I don't know."

"When was the last time you went into your basement, prior to tonight?"

"I never go down there anymore, but I...set things down on the stairs sometimes. The last time I did that much was two or three days ago. And it wasn't flooded then. There's no way the minor rainstorm a couple of days back could have caused all that water down there."

I interjected, "I just don't know how or why an electrician would make such a careless mistake. Even in design school, instructors always warn students about standing water possibly carrying an electric current. That risk is surely drilled into electricians."

"There was a wood dowel, floating in the water at the base of the stairs," Linda said quietly. "If that was on a stair, Mr. Schwartz could have stepped on it and lost his balance, fallen into the water."

"I would never put a dowel on a stairway," Helen said firmly. "I may have lots of possessions, but I'm not an idiot! That was part of the trap. The killer probably set it on a step, hoping I'd trip and fall down and break my neck. *Then* get electrocuted for extra measure."

Mansfield came back through the kitchen, checked the pantry, and marched on through to the den, where I heard him mutter, "Whoa," no doubt in surprise at how jam-packed that room was. "I'm gonna check the upstairs," he called.

"This is all my fault," Helen moaned.

"Your neighbor's death?" Linda asked.

Helen nodded. Trembling, she started rocking herself on the chair, her arms wrapped tightly across her chest.

"Ms. Walker?"

She continued to rock herself without replying.

"Helen, are you all right?" I asked, heartsick at her suffering. "We've got to get you a blanket."

Linda rose. "Should I get one from upstairs, Ms. Walker?"

She didn't answer.

"I'll be right back," Linda told me. "Stay here with her, Erin."

I nodded grimly, as Linda used her flashlight to guide herself to the staircase.

"Helen, everything's going to be all right," I said gently.

She met my eyes. Hers were wet with tears. "There's only one way to stop this...."

"What are you talking about? How are you going to stop this?" I asked, bewildered.

"There's no other way to protect myself and everyone else. I have to do something."

"Helen—"

Someone pounded on the door, startling both of us, then the door opened, and an authoritative voice called, "Helen Walker? Detective O'Reilly. I'm in charge of the investigation."

I groaned. O'Reilly and I'd had more than one past run-in. O'Reilly was *always* the detective in charge whenever I was involved in a crisis. He was a tall, thirty-something, nondescript man with a cranky disposition, and he liked to intimidate me.

"The witnesses are in the kitchen," I heard Linda say. A moment later, she appeared in the doorway. I rose and grabbed a pink wool blanket from her and wrapped it around Helen's shoulders. O'Reilly followed Linda and glowered at both of us at the table, then bellowed at Linda, "What kind of procedure are you following here, Dell?"

"My partner is searching the house. Ms. Walker is quite upset, and—"

I heard Mansfield's footsteps as he headed down the stairs. It felt like my fault that Linda was getting chewed out by the detective. I rose. "Excuse me for a moment, Helen."

O'Reilly glared at me as I entered the living room. He shined his flashlight directly into my eyes. "You have quite the knack for finding dead bodies, Miss Gilbert."

There was no arguing with the statement, so for once I held my tongue. My cheeks felt aflame.

"Do you have an alibi?"

"I was home, alone, till Ms. Walker called me. Then I drove here."

"You just drove right here? Didn't think to suggest she call nine-one-one?"

"I *did* suggest that! I was going to call myself, but it sounded like her cat had simply knocked something over, and Helen was concerned that the police were just going to belittle her, like they have in the past."

"Mansfield, Delgardio, you need to escort Miss Gilbert out of here and get her statement. *Now.*"

"I'm on it," Linda said stiffly. I winced, knowing I'd gotten my friend in trouble with a superior.

"Check that," O'Reilly said, holding up a hand. "*I'll* interview her. You two get Ms. Walker's statement instead. There's been enough favoritism already."

He ushered me outside, opened the back door of his light-colored sedan for me, and got into the opposite side of the backseat. Wasting no time on niceties, he demanded, "What happened when you arrived?"

I intentionally went into as much excruciating detail as I could muster to describe the brief, dark journey from the driveway to Helen's basement steps. "You made your way through the house with just the light from your flashlight," O'Reilly said snidely. "Must have been a real challenge. She always keep her house like a pigsty?"

"That's why I was hired. I'm trying to help her straighten the place up. I was hired by her niece and..." I let my voice fade as I watched Mansfield round the car and bend to talk to O'Reilly.

"Something's come up during our interview of Ms. Walker," Mansfield told O'Reilly cryptically.

O'Reilly nodded. He turned to me. "You can go, Miss Gilbert. We've got your information if we have any more questions."

"Is Helen okay?" I asked Mansfield.

"Fine." But he said it with no conviction.

Not knowing what else to do, I waited in my van for the detective to leave so I could speak to Helen again. As the minutes dragged by, I saw Helen emerge from the front door. Detective O'Reilly had a grip on her arm, and they were walking slowly. I gasped as I realized she was in handcuffs.

I bolted out of my van and charged toward them. "Stop! What's happening? Where are you taking her?"

"The station house."

He helped Helen into the backseat of the patrol car without answering. He closed the car door behind her with a solid thud. She looked up at me. Her face was ghost white. Her lips quivered and her eyes were pleading. She was clearly scared half to death.

My eyes misted at the sight. "She's a seventy-five-year-old woman, for God's sake, and this is her home! Why is she in handcuffs?"

"No choice," O'Reilly growled at me. "She just confessed to the murder."

chapter 8

desperate to help Helen, but without a clue as to how I might do so, I followed the patrol cars to the police station, a modern-looking white-painted cement structure, now bathed in yellow-tinted light from the numerous lamps that surrounded it. I dashed inside and gave my name to the dispatcher and asked if I could speak to Linda Delgardio.

The dispatcher nodded and dialed, and I paced in front of her tall oak-veneered enclosure. She spoke quietly into the small mouthpiece of her headset, then relayed that it would be "a few minutes." I sank into a seat in the unimaginative lobby, furnished with bulky sectionals upholstered in durable-but-ultra-ugly blue-gray polyester. Pearl-gray fiberglass cubes, bolted to the floor, served as coffee tables. Whoever designed this space had to select furnishings that couldn't easily be picked up and hurled or smashed into sharp, weaponlike edges, not something that I ever had to take into consideration when planning my residential interiors. Considering the spate of violence that had enveloped me and my clients of late, though, maybe it was time for me to rethink that policy.

To bolster my spirits, I mentally redesigned the room around me, opting for a whimsical Lincoln Logs theme. By the time Linda emerged through the glass door, I'd turned the place into a toy fort, which may have been impractical, but was considerably more visually appealing than the existing design.

Linda gave me a kind smile and sat on the upholstered-chair-cum-tree-stump beside me. "I thought you'd probably show up here. Checking in on Helen Walker?"

I nodded. "I know she didn't kill Jack, Linda. The woman wouldn't hurt a fly. In fact, if a fly died in her house of natural causes, she'd probably dip it into preservatives and stash it in a shoe box."

Linda gave a weary shrug. "She confessed."

"Probably just to protect herself. She's certain that her life is in danger and that two of her relatives have been murdered. Now her neighbor stumbles into a trap she's convinced was set for her. She figures she's safer in jail. In her shoes, who wouldn't?"

"Even if that's true, Erin, it's also a crime to make a false confession. She's impeding a police investigation. That's obstruction of justice."

"Helen probably just became so desperate to get out of

her house, she figured a false confession was her safest recourse. She didn't stop to realize the full ramifications."

Linda sighed. Her pretty chocolate brown eyes met mine. "Erin, my hands are tied. O'Reilly is in charge of this investigation, not me. If he decides he wants to press the issue, frankly, there isn't a whole lot I can do about it."

"What's going on with Helen right now? Do you know where she is?"

She gave a quick glance at the dispatcher, then leaned closer to me. In a voice barely above a whisper, she replied, "Last I heard she'd clammed up . . . swore she won't say another word till her lawyer's present."

Just outside the wall of windows came the piercing shriek of brakes as a car pulled into a parking space at much too rapid a speed. The driver and her passenger emerged. I immediately recognized the imperious form of Stephanie Miller and her brother, Peter. I told Linda, "Here come Helen's niece and nephew. That was fast."

"Yeah," Linda said wearily. She rose.

Underneath the harsh lamps that illuminated the concrete slab by the entrance, Stephanie waited impatiently for Peter to catch up to her. The moment she strode through the door, she spotted me.

"Erin," she announced. "I'm glad you're here. I was going to call you to say that we might need you."

"How did you find out that—"

"Rachel Schwartz called us." Stephanie grimaced. "Quite the abrupt phone conversation, let me tell you. She identified herself, declared: 'Your crazy aunt murdered my husband, and the police are hauling her out of here in handcuffs,' then hung up."

"That's exactly what she told me, too," Peter interjected. "Got my attention in a hurry."

"I was in the car, on my way to pick up my brother in two seconds flat." Stephanie put her hands on her hips and eyed Linda skeptically. "Officer, where is my aunt, Helen Walker? My brother is an attorney and will serve as her lawyer. She needs legal counsel immediately."

"Did she call and request that you represent her?" Linda asked Peter.

"Yes," Stephanie replied irritably on her brother's behalf. "It's her legal right to have a lawyer present. Peter needs to be escorted to her side. Right now!"

"I'll have to verify that with Ms. Walker first." Linda took a step toward the door and said, "Excuse me for a moment."

"For 'a moment'? In other words, several minutes?" Stephanie taunted. "I don't want to sit out *here* in the meantime. Surely there's a more comfortable waiting room for members of families in a crisis! God knows we pay you people enough taxes."

"I can take you to one of the interrogation rooms, if you'd like," Linda offered, admirably controlling her temper, although Stephanie's bad manners had set my teeth on edge.

"No, thank you," Stephanie answered, plopping down beside me. She added under her breath, "At least this beats waiting in a garage." She glanced at the dispatcher, a pleasant-looking Hispanic woman, then muttered, "Sort of." Meanwhile, Peter began to pace, his hands buried deeply in his pockets, his head bent.

Could Stephanie have played a role in the murder? Or Peter? They would inherit Helen's property, when Helen passed away. "Has your aunt voiced suspicions to either of you about your parents' deaths?" I asked Stephanie quietly.

"She told you about that?" Peter asked, staring at me in surprise.

I said nothing.

He frowned. "You watch. This man's death is going to turn out to be the third time she's insisted an accidental death is something more sinister. Anytime anybody she knows dies, Aunt Helen cries 'murder.'"

"She's right this time, Peter," Stephanie asserted. "There's no way that basement could have flooded on its own. I saw it just last night, and it was bone dry."

"What were you doing in the basement?" he asked.

"Assessing the clutter problem. Why?"

He glowered at his sister, then said to me, "Even if Helen's right this time, there was no foul play in our parents' deaths." He resumed his pacing, then grumbled, "I need a cigarette." Waving off his sister's protests, he lit one.

The dispatcher leaned forward. "Sir? This is a public place. There's a no-smoking ordinance."

"Oh. Sorry." He took a deep drag, then snuffed out the cigarette and shoved it back into its pack.

Strange that a lawyer wasn't familiar with the smoking policy in his local police station. "Are you a criminal defense attorney?"

"No, I do family law...divorces, mostly. But I'm competent enough in criminal law to handle this nonsense." He sighed and dropped into a chair across from the fiberglass box of a table. "Seriously, Erin. Aunt Helen's way off base. Our father had a weak heart. Our mother hated my aunt's cooking. She must have chucked some of Helen's casserole down the garbage disposal to avoid hurting Aunt Helen's feelings, and then ordered Chinese takeout food, not realizing the main dish contained bell peppers."

Sullivan's earlier comment about his Chinese takeout containing three of the food types that Lois was deathly allergic to came back to me. Surely Chinese cuisine was the very last thing someone with those particular allergies would order. "Don't you know for certain?" I asked. "Were there takeout cartons in the house? If so, the police would have traced the order back to the restaurant. They'd verify what dish she'd eaten that contained bell peppers."

Peter didn't reply. Instead, he slouched further into his chair, like a turtle, drawing back into his protective shell.

I said, "Whether Helen's right or wrong to be suspicious about your parents' deaths, clearly, your aunt is so rattled right now that she thought she'd be safer in jail."

Stephanie shushed me. "Here comes some man in a cheap suit," she whispered. "Must be a detective."

I watched O'Reilly push open the glass door and approach us. Linda's partner followed him at a deferential distance. "Peter Miller?" the detective asked, but not before giving me a withering glare.

"Yes," he said, rising.

O'Reilly held the door and led Peter away, presumably to his aunt's side. Officer Mansfield, however, remained standing in the doorway. He said to Stephanie, "We need to ask you some questions, too, Ms. Walker."

She rose and said sharply, "The name is Miller. Stephanie Miller."

He held the door open and said, "Can you come with me, Ms. Miller?"

She sighed. "You might as well go home, Erin," she said, giving me a curiously hostile look. "It's going to be a long night. My brother and I will take over from here."

Despite Stephanie's parting words, I waited another thirty minutes before I finally gave up and drove home. I spent an anxious hour alone at home, pacing in Audrey's elegant showcase kitchen—one of the very few rooms in the house that Audrey kept pristine—until she finally arrived. Too traumatized to keep quiet even long enough for Audrey to get her customary glass of wine, I started to fill her in on the events of the day, and she took a seat at the black granite counter. She gasped when I mentioned Helen's full name.

"Is this woman petite like me, and in her seventies?" she asked. "Used to be a language arts teacher?"

"Yes. She lives in the—"

Audrey rose, grabbed her purse, and declared, "Come on, Erin. We've got to bust her out of jail. If it weren't for her, David could very well have wound up there himself."

"Was Helen Walker your son's teacher?"

"In ninth grade."

We got into my van. Audrey's BMW was much more luxurious than my wheels, but she preferred not to drive at night whenever possible. She was silent as I once again made my way to the station house. Eventually, too curious not to ask, I said, "David's an electrical engineer, right?"

"Yes. He's not all that avid a reader, then or now. Which

is part of why Helen's steadfast refusal to let him slip through the cracks was so remarkable. It wasn't like he wrote great essays in her class or anything. Fortunately, she saw something in David even so. She took him under her wing and mentored him. His father had died the summer before David started ninth grade. He was acting out... making horrendous choices... It was the one time in my life when, I have to admit, I found myself utterly over-whelmed. Simply put, I'm eternally indebted to Helen Walker. This is my chance to repay her for saving my son's life."

"Wow," I murmured, all the more determined now to help Helen out of her current predicament.

Minutes later, I pulled into the same parking space in front of the station that I'd used before. I glanced to either side as I shut off the engine. "Stephanie's car is gone."

"She's the bossy niece you were telling me about?"

"Yes. I hope that's good news—maybe she and her brother have already gotten Helen out."

Audrey flung open the passenger door, saying, "Either that, or poor Helen's trapped in there all alone." I hurried after Audrey, who was already halfway down the walkway to the station. I didn't bother to lock up; surely my vehicle was safe at a police station.

The same dispatcher was seated at the oak-veneered desk. I half expected her to greet me by name and tell me we had to stop meeting like this. Audrey strode up to the formidable-looking desk and announced, "My name is Audrey Munroe, and I'm here—"

The woman's eyes lit up. "I thought I recognized you! You're on the TV show on channel seven! *Domestic Bliss.* I *love* that show!"

Audrey brightened. "Thank you so much. I really need to speak to whoever is in charge of the murder investigation at Helen Walker's house."

I interjected, "It's probably not an actual *murder* investigation, Audrey. Just a suspicious death."

She gave me a look that clearly signaled my elucidations were not appreciated.

The dispatcher pushed a couple of buttons on her phone and spoke into her headset. Then she gushed to Audrey, "Someone will be right out, Ms. Munroe."

Minutes later, Detective O'Reilly emerged and muttered, "She's back," at the sight of me. He regarded Audrey for a long moment, then said, "Ah, Ms. Munroe. I'm Detective O'Reilly. We met a few months ago. Don't tell me that you, too, have a personal involvement in this matter."

"Yes. I'm a long-lost friend of Helen Walker's, and I need to know if I can post bail for her . . . whatever I can do that's necessary to allow her to leave here with me tonight."

He rocked on his heels. "There's no need for bail. She's recanted her story completely. It was obviously a fabrication. Implausible and full of contradictions."

"Then she can leave with us?" I asked.

"No. We've got her house cordoned off. It's a crime scene. Her niece is going to come get her."

"Is Stephanie on her way now?" I asked.

"No, but she's awaiting our phone call to come pick up her aunt."

"There's no need," Audrey said. "Helen can stay at my house for however long is necessary."

"Suit yourself," O'Reilly said, the self-satisfied smirk

back on his thin lips. "Once we make a determination on whether or not this was murder, we'll know for sure if we need to press charges."

O'Reilly ushered Audrey into the bowels of the building, no doubt to the detectives' quarters; I'd become all too familiar with this place in the past couple of years. Audrey was gone for an interminable length of time.

I was now too keyed up to pass the time with fictitious room designs. I merely sat in my chair, trying to identify the exact point at which my life had gotten so off-kilter. My calling is to harmonize people's living spaces. I believe with my heart and soul that the environment a person lives in is the most precious gift I can give. I'm honored to be able to create a place in which my clients can wake up every morning and just glow with happiness.

But something had gone dreadfully awry in order for me to repeatedly find myself in this godforsaken building. Somehow, as I'd tried to distance myself from the ugly and the banal in our surroundings, I'd managed to uncover extremely unlovely aspects of human behavior. I had let myself become involved in my clients' lives too quickly. And yet, if I had distanced myself and taken a less passionate role in the evolution of their homes, I wouldn't have been as good at my job. Did I really want to be the type of person who would have refused to come to Helen Walker's aid tonight?

Eventually, an officer I didn't know returned my landlady to the lobby, and Audrey told me that they'd be bringing Helen out in a minute. Linda led Helen toward us before Audrey even sat down. Although Helen looked drawn and exhausted, she straightened her shoulders, strode up to us, and said, "How are you, Ms. Munroe? And how's David?"

"He's wonderful, thank you. He and his wife live in Kansas City now. They're expecting my first grandchild. Any day now, in fact. We're all so excited."

"Of course you are! Their first baby? I'm so delighted to hear that! Please tell him I said hello and congratulations." She paused and wrung her parchmentlike hands, her gaze darting between Audrey and me. "But...what are you doing here?"

"Erin Gilbert is my tenant and a dear friend, and she told me about the death of your neighbor. I'm terribly sorry."

Helen pursed her lips, but did not reply. A shadow of something I couldn't identify—fear? regret?—moved in her eyes.

"Would you be so kind as to stay with us in my guest room? Just temporarily, of course?" Audrey asked her. "Or we could give you a ride to your niece's house, if you'd prefer."

"That's a very kind offer, Ms. Munroe, but..." Helen turned and searched Linda's eyes. "Is that really necessary? Can't I please go home?"

"We can't let you stay at your house yet, Ms. Walker," Linda replied. "I'm afraid we're still investigating, and it could take us a while."

"Good thing I called a friend to watch my cats, then." Helen forced a smile, then turned back toward Audrey. "In that case, I'd be delighted to come stay with you. Thank you. You're very kind."

"The pleasure's all mine. And please, call me Audrey." She took Helen's arm, and the two women left side by side, as if they were the best of friends. Linda glanced at me. I knew her well enough to know she had something to say to me, something she wanted said in private, so I lingered as Audrey and Helen left the building.

"Don't repeat this, Erin, but the crime scene investigators got the electricity turned back on. Things aren't adding up. You can easily hear when someone opens the garage door. From anyplace in the house. Including the basement."

"So you're wondering why Jack didn't come back up the stairs to let Helen know he was there, checking out the house after spotting a prowler? Maybe that's because the killer prevented him from doing so—by sneaking down the stairs after him and pushing him."

Linda shook her head. "The timing doesn't work. Once Helen recanted her bogus confession, she insisted that, just after she entered the kitchen from the garage, she heard a crash and the lights went out. Why didn't Mr. Schwartz *immediately* turn around at the sound of the garage door when she drove in?"

"Maybe he *did*, but the killer was standing on a stair above him, blocking his path. From the garage, Helen wouldn't have overheard them arguing or struggling, what with that noisy garage door closing behind her car."

"Then why was the victim found lying facedown, like he'd been shoved in the back?"

That gave me a momentary pause. "I don't know. Maybe he got twisted around a little. What are you suggesting? That Helen dragged Jack to the basement stairs and pushed him down them herself? O'Reilly just said that her confession was contradictory and full of holes!"

"It was. But if she'd given us a plausible story—that

she'd set a trap for him tonight, suggested he lead the way down the basement stairs, then gave him a quick shove—she'd be locked up by now."

Stunned into silence, I merely stared at Linda, my stomach knotting.

She narrowed her eyes as she watched Audrey help Helen into the van. "Helen Walker might not be quite the innocent she appears to be. Just don't be too trusting, Erin."

chapter 9

Linda Delgardio's warning about Helen kept running through my brain long after we'd returned home and helped Helen settle into the guest room. Despite the snuggly luxuries I'd selected for my bed—the soft and cradling foam topper for the mattress, the yummy Egyptian cotton sheets that were the softest fabric imaginable, and the silk-filled comforter with its magical lightness and warmth—sleep defied me.

Even the remotest possibility that a killer was occupying the room just on the other side of the wall was unsettling. I was grateful for my cat's company as she curled onto the pillow next to mine. There was a reasonable chance that she'd awaken me with a tail whap as she leapt from the bed if Helen were to sneak toward my bed to attack me. Not exactly as good as being guarded by a fiercely loyal Doberman, but it was something.

The overriding point, I struggled to remind myself, was that I knew in my heart Helen Walker was innocent. It could have happened precisely the way I'd suggested to Linda—that Jack fell sideways and twisted himself around in a vain attempt to break his fall. If so, Helen could be correct when she insisted that he'd died in a trap that had been set for her. She would have stepped unthinkingly into the electrified water to rescue her cat, but a retired electrician would never have been so rash.

Could it have been a simple accident? I believed Helen when she said that she wouldn't have left something like a loose dowel on a step. Nor would Jack have gone down a steep staircase without making sure he had a clear path. Also, he wouldn't have been heading downstairs if he'd heard Helen come home; he'd have immediately turned around, not lingered on the stairs only to trip just as Helen happened to enter the kitchen.

By my thinking, that added up to murder.

What if Jack had been the intended victim all along? It seemed to be common knowledge that his wife played neighborhood watchdog. Simple enough, then, for the killer to wait until Rachel was looking out a window, dash out Helen's front door, reenter through the back door, then wait for nosy Rachel to send Jack to investigate. Or was Rachel lying about Jack's having "charged" across the street of his own volition? Maybe she had set things up in the basement, then dragged Jack over to Helen's house to investigate a nonexistent burglar, and shoved him into the water.

I looked at the red-glowing numbers on my digital clock. Yikes! 3:34! I tried my best to distract my overwrought brain with a boring, pseudo mantra—words that rhyme with "hum"—and worked my way through the alphabet both backwards and forwards. Bum, come, dumb...

It felt as though I'd slept mere minutes when the morning alarm resounded like an air-raid siren. Determined to squeeze in some more sleep-time, I smacked the off button so hard my hand tingled. I lay back in bed, till my eyes popped open at the realization that I needed to call Steve Sullivan; he had to be told about the death at Helen's house or he'd arrive there this morning, unaware. Also, we were scheduled to begin work at Stephanie's house today, and she was so nasty to her aunt that she was a key suspect—on my list, at any rate, if not the police's.

Disturbingly, the notion of talking to Sullivan had given me a surge of eager anticipation. Was I so hooked on transforming clients' homes that I was now unconsciously expecting to perform a similar makeover on Steve Sullivan? Was I incapable of learning that the man was never going to magically transform into my Mr. Right?

Someone knocked so lightly that I wasn't sure the sound was actually coming from the other side of my door. I slipped out of bed and opened the door, Hildi's soft fur brushing against my bare shins as she trotted past me.

Helen gave me an apologetic smile. "Oh, good morning, Erin. I heard your alarm go off. I was just trying to see if you were awake and would mind if I took a shower."

I glanced at the clock. There was the possibility of even

this spacious house feeling very small very fast if Helen stayed here for long. "No, go right ahead." My first assignment of the day was supposed to be her house. "I have plenty of time this morning."

She thanked me, said she'd let me know when she was finished, and shuffled toward the bathroom. She'd borrowed a nightgown and robe from Audrey, which fit her perfectly, and she looked right at home.

I called Sullivan from my bedroom phone. His sleepy voice, I had to grudgingly admit, was annoyingly sexy; I truly seemed to be incapable of learning my lesson. We agreed to meet at a downtown coffee shop in forty-five minutes. I jabbed my heel into my shin to get my thoughts away from wondering if he slept in the buff, which he probably did, but was of no consequence to yours truly.

I felt a pang at the unbidden memory of our passionate kiss two months earlier. I was playing with dynamite by agreeing to work with him now. My twenty-ninth birthday was coming soon, and I'd already gotten the *Sex and the City* thing out of my system, thank God. Nowadays I wanted lifelong love or nothing. It was all too clear that Sullivan was *not* the love of my life, so he had to be nothing. It would be too cruel if the one person who most made me feel miserable about myself and brought out the very worst in my personality turned out to be my soul mate.

As a way to distract myself onto a safer and cheerier subject, I started to think about the design of the bathroom that Helen was now using. In lieu of paying rent, I redesigned Audrey's mansion. "My" bathroom was mired in the eighties with its blah beige tiles and yucky avocado linoleum floor. Audrey was atrocious at actually allowing me to enact my new designs elsewhere in her home, but she'd promised me a free hand in my bedroom and the adjoining bathroom. I was envisioning sparkle and pizzazz: hand-painted white and indigo porcelain tiles and polished brass fixtures, an above-the-counter porcelain bowl to emulate an antique washbasin on a mahogany vanity with carved cabriole legs, and a stone-and-tile steam shower with a rain-shower head and bright sea glass accents...

My stumbling block was that remodeling would mean putting my bathroom out of commission for weeks and sharing Audrey's. I shuddered at the memory of how Audrey had turned her bathtub into a terrarium when I'd first moved in; we'd shared my shower for two months, till she'd finally concurred that the terrarium was a mistake.

To her credit, Helen showered in record time and knocked on my door once more, then called, "It's your turn." I thanked her and dashed into the shower, emerged reasonably refreshed, and quickly dressed in an in-between outfit—casual slacks and blouse—not the Armani skirt suits I wore to impress clients, but not my paint-splatter clothes, either.

Both my housemates were in the kitchen. Helen was wearing powder blue drawstring Capris and a silver V-necked pullover that I recognized as Audrey's, and once again I was struck by the physical similarities between the two women. It was altogether too easy for me to picture Audrey in Helen's predicament—in her twilight years, scared that some deranged killer with a key to her house was making attempts on her life and had murdered a beloved neighbor in her own basement.

I declined Audrey's offer of breakfast and hurried to the

coffee shop where I'd agreed to meet Sullivan, having told him on the phone only that there'd been "trouble at Helen's house last night." I arrived first, and asked for his customary coffee order along with my hot chocolate. I'd just taken a seat at a table in the corner when he strolled through the door. He looked sexy and handsome, as always. The man was immune to bad hair days. Or bad complexion days. Life was so unfair!

"Thanks, Gilbert." He slipped into the chair across from me and pulled out his wallet.

I waved off his attempt to reimburse me. "I'm buying. I got you a tall latte."

"Great. Thanks." He blew on the surface of the steaming liquid. "So a neighbor died at Helen Walker's house last night, eh? What's the story?"

Startled, I asked, "How did you hear about it so soon?"

"When you said she had 'trouble' last night, I naturally imagined the worst...so I swung by her place on my way here. No offense, Gilbert, but you're something of a Typhoid Mary."

"Now, why would I take offense at that?" I snarled, glaring at him.

Sullivan blithely continued, "Yellow plastic police tape is strung across Helen's porch banisters. Then the news report on the radio said that a retired electrician had gotten electrocuted in a flooded basement. I put two and two together and figured it had to be Jack Schwartz."

"You figured right. Unfortunately. Sullivan, I think it's possible Helen has been correct all along. Someone's trying to kill her and make it look like an accident."

"What happened last night?"

"Helen called me when she heard a noise and her

lights went out. And...I found him at the base of the stairs. Jack's wife claims they'd seen someone dressed in black run off, so Jack went over to investigate."

"Odd that an electrician wouldn't know that water in a basement often carries a charge."

"No kidding. I'm thinking he was pushed into that water. Maybe the prowler that he and Rachel spotted leaving the house returned to grab a second load and shoved Jack down the stairs. In any case, since we can't work at Helen's house today, I'm hoping we can put in extra time at Stephanie's, and hopefully dig up some information to give to Linda Delgardio."

"You think Steph might be trying to bump off her own aunt?"

"It's possible. She'll inherit half of Helen's estate, and she'd have an extra-strong motive if she's secretly convinced that Helen killed her mom...that Helen deliberately put peppers into the casserole." I paused, deciding not to discuss Peter's confusing assertions that his mother had gotten the peppers from a Chinese takeout entrée. Sullivan was staring at me like I was nuts. "Why are you so incredulous? Are you too attracted to Stephanie to think she's capable of anything so heinous?"

"*Me?* Attracted to *Stephanie*?" He held up a palm. "Not my type. I mean, yeah, she's sort of pretty, but as soon as she opens her mouth...forget it. She's so brassy, she's part trumpet."

For some reason, this turn in our conversation was making me edgy. I focused on my cocoa and stirred it with extra vigor. "The way you were leering at her yesterday, you certainly seemed to find her *appealing*."

"I wasn't 'leering' at her, Gilbert. Give me a break!" In

gentler tones, he went on, "I *did* happen to notice she was wearing the same blouse I just got my mother for her birthday, which was a bit creepy." He paused. When I looked up from my cup, he was studying my face. He slowly grinned at me. "You're *jealous*. Huh. All's not lost, after all."

I clicked my tongue, but was too intrigued by his last phrase to leap to my own defense. Was I insane, or was Sullivan suggesting that he wanted to pick up where we'd left off before his California trip? It would be humiliating if I was wrong. And it would unquestionably lead to pain if I was right. I took a sip of cocoa before I replied, "I'm not jealous. I'm simply trying to find out if I can recruit you to help me do a little investigating at Stephanie's house. I'm arming myself with a digital camera, in case we turn up any evidence I can photograph."

"'Investigating?' Think your officer friend would be keen on that idea?"

"Linda won't like it, but I'm sure as hell not going to sit back and do nothing while someone's trying to kill Helen Walker. I did nothing when Helen told me two days ago that someone was breaking into her house. Now Jack Schwartz is dead."

He sipped his coffee thoughtfully. "Stephanie's not the sort to do her own dirty work. She prefers to throw money around . . . to hire someone else to do it for her. Maybe we can find some telltale financial reports, or something. She's inherited her aunt's pack-rat tendency when it comes to paperwork, and she's got a home office downstairs." He held my gaze and said, "Which, fortunately for us, is located right next to the rec room we'll be designing."

————

Having the ulterior motive of searching through my new client's personal papers was more than a little distracting, and I was off my game that afternoon as we met with Stephanie to discuss her rec room. My nerves forced me to let her and Sullivan do most of the talking. Once I had the sleuthing behind me, though, I'd be better able to pull my own weight. So far all I'd done was confirm Stephanie's ridiculous notion that, of the two of us, Sullivan had the more creative designs.

Stephanie had first hired him three years ago to redo her home in the wake of her divorce, and he'd done an amazing job. The main floor—all I'd seen of the house so far—was like strolling through the pages of *Architectural Digest*: astonishing attention to detail, every item the crème de la crème, from the magnificent Murano glass chandelier to the tiger-maple hardwood floors and the exquisite hand-knotted silk rugs. The living room in which we now sat was unmistakably a Sullivan creation. A lesser designer might have chosen some of these same exquisite furnishings, but wouldn't have so brilliantly captured the lines, tone, and texture of the stunning view through Stephanie's picture window. He'd made this space feel like a natural part of the glorious scenery.

My own design could well have been on a par with this one, however. Given enough time, I could probably even quibble with a selection or two. Then again, maybe not. This floral-pattern damask sofa was not only gorgeous, but incredibly comfortable. And since when did Sullivan select such perfect accent pillows? Not to mention the cashmere throw...

"Erin," Stephanie said with an arrogant smile during a rare pause in their banter, "you're being awfully quiet."

"I'm just in an observational mode right now." *And starting to develop an inferiority complex in the process.*

She nodded. "I'm sure last night's events were almost as traumatic for you as they were for me, but there's nothing quite like having it be within your own family."

Yes, and there's nothing quite like having discovered the corpse yourself, I retorted in silence.

"Well," she said, rising, "shall we take a look at the room?"

"Absolutely," I enthused, hopping to my feet to show that what I lacked in loquaciousness, I made up for in energy. My curiosity was eating me up, however. "I've got to say that I'm really impressed with this cashmere throw. What a gorgeous color!" I turned to Sullivan. "Where did you get it?"

Stephanie answered for him, "I'm not even sure where that came from originally. It's not as though I went to the store myself, after all. I brought in a second designer to accessorize Steve's room. As I said before, his work lacks the feminine touch."

I could read the tension in Sullivan's clenched jaw. No wonder Stephanie wanted us to combine our talents: apparently, I was here to dot Sullivan's *i*'s and cross his *t*'s. How very belittling. For both of us.

We descended a flight of stairs into the walkout basement. The irregularly shaped room at the bottom of the stairs was painted white and housed just a pool table and a wide-screen TV. Stephanie and Steve resumed their private conversation about her ideas and needs for the space, so familiar with each other that they could essentially speak in shorthand. They finally—and reluctantly, I thought—looked my way, and I asked, "Could Sullivan and I have a few minutes to gather our thoughts?"

"Oh. Certainly, Erin. You two discuss away. I'll be right upstairs if you have any questions."

"Thanks," we said simultaneously.

"Who'd she hire before to 'accessorize'?" I whispered the moment Stephanie was out of sight.

"Don't know," he murmured. "This was the first I heard about it. Told *me* she wanted to put on the finishing touches herself. I'd have froufroued up the place for her myself, if she'd been up-front with me."

I rolled my eyes, disagreeing as always with his tendency to consider any and all personal touches "froufrou," but we were too short on time to bicker. "Let's search the office."

At a glance, I took in the attractive room—heavy on the mahogany—with Sullivan's flawless, Zen-like style stamped all over it. Aha! *There* was a flaw! A gorgeous rosewood-inlay console was wasted along one wall. She needed to move that someplace front and center.

Rifling through her desk as Steve scanned the contents of the file cabinet, I soon located a folder with Helen's address on the tab. I opened it and skimmed the papers inside.

"Steve, look at this."

Selling her aunt's house with its two acres in downtown Crestview would net a million-dollar profit, provided the house was bulldozed and the lot parceled. As Sullivan scanned the information for himself, I balked at the thought that Stephanie's greed could motivate her to make attempts on her aunt's life; that would be so extreme and so heartless. Again, though, might Stephanie be capable of such a thing if she secretly blamed Helen for her mother's tragic death?

At the sound of footsteps on the stairs, Sullivan hastily shut the desk drawer, and I started blathering, "That's a good point, Steve, but this office space is quite... efficient."

Picking up on my diversion, Sullivan said, "Yeah. Probably makes more sense to keep the room dimensions intact."

"You're discussing moving the walls between the rec room and my office?" Stephanie asked.

"Just trying to be open to everything at this juncture," Sullivan replied without hesitation. The man was quite a smooth liar. *As if I hadn't already discovered as much about him all on my own.*

"Fine by me. Move as many walls in your imagination as you'd like. When it comes to the *actual* walls, though, I get the final say-so." She gave his arm a playful squeeze, which annoyed me to no end. The fact that I was annoyed only annoyed me all the more. "Anyway," she continued, "I didn't mean to interrupt your brainstorming. I simply realized I left my planner down here." She grabbed a leather-bound journal from the kneehole drawer. "By the way, Erin, I heard from the police last night that Aunt Helen is currently living at your home."

If she knew Helen was at my house, why had she waited this long to mention it? "Only for another day or two, until they let her go back home."

"If you're smart, you'll keep it limited to that. She used to drive my poor mother up a wall. That's why Mother had been so happy to get the house to herself for once.

Though that backfired, of course. If Helen had been home, she'd have been able to give Mother the epinephrine shot."

I asked, "Where was Helen the night Lois died?"

"She was at a book-scrappers' convention." I fought back a smile at the image that Stephanie's misspeak gave me—a batch of people getting together to throw away books—as she continued, "Ironically, I sent Helen there myself... paid for the registration and set everything up. I thought it would be good for them to separate for a while. They'd gotten to a point where they were constantly quarreling, and I was hoping to convince my mother to move in with me instead."

"You'd have had more than enough room, all right," Steve replied, and added casually, "although Helen's got an enormous lot, at least. That piece of property is probably worth a fortune on the open market."

Stephanie snorted. "Not while Helen's alive. She keeps saying I can sell the place over her dead body!" She blushed. "Not that I'd ever want to see that happen. All of her talk about attempts on her life is ludicrous. I don't for a minute believe her crazy theories about my parents' deaths being murder. And her neighbor's death was an accident. Aunt Helen forgot to turn off a water spigot in the backyard. She's paranoid."

"Well, Steph," Sullivan said pleasantly, "there's that famous quote from the wise men of Monty Python to consider—'Just because you're paranoid doesn't mean they're not out to get you.'"

I laughed. An instant later, I remembered myself, and felt guilty for finding humor in such a terribly stressful time for my client. Stephanie shot us both a withering glance, clutched her notebook to her chest, and left the room without another word.

Steve crossed his arms and regarded me. "You're a Monty Python fan?"

"Absolutely."

"Their humor is timeless, isn't it? Kind of like The Three Stooges."

"You're comparing The Three Stooges to Monty Python? Are you serious? That's like comparing Bozo to Bill Cosby."

He grinned and shrugged. "Just checking."

"Checking *what*? To see if I have any discerning judgment whatsoever?"

He chuckled. "I was just getting a *feel* for your sense of humor." He wiggled his eyebrows and added, "So to speak."

I said through a tight jaw, "In that case, let me just clue you in: I don't *ever* find double entendres amusing."

His eyes still merry despite my growing annoyance, Sullivan struck a theatrical pose and sang, " 'What, never?' "

The lyric was straight out of Gilbert and Sullivan's *H.M.S. Pinafore*, and his antics caught me so much by surprise that I laughed again. I replied in a deadpan, " 'Well, hardly ever.' "

He held my gaze and returned my smile, and I felt my cheeks burn crimson. An old adage claimed that the way to a man's heart was through his stomach, but the funny bone was most definitely the way into mine. Maybe Sullivan realized as much and was mocking me. That possibility sobered me. I snapped, "This is hardly an appropriate time to be clowning around. My client has been banished from her home because people are dropping dead all around her."

"Fine. I give you my solemn word . . . I'll never sing to you again."

"Fine."

Now if I could just make him promise never to make me laugh again, my heart might survive our working together after all.

chapter 10

We needed to finish up quickly before Stephanie became suspicious. I took digital photographs of the documents in Stephanie's file, then Sullivan and I went upstairs and bluffed our way through a generic, heavy-on-superlatives-light-on-content description of our initial thoughts for her room makeover. He and I privately set a time to get together and do the actual sketches and planning, then we left in our separate vehicles. I headed for a quiet side street and immediately pulled over. I called Linda Delgardio on my cell phone, and told her about the fortune Stephanie stood to gain if she were to get hold of her aunt's property.

Linda replied cautiously, "That's interesting. Though I have to ask how you happened to come across this document."

"She's a new client. And I was working in her office. Designing." True statements. If a trifle vague.

"And she just happened to leave an incriminating document out in the open for you to see?"

"Which I also photographed, as luck would have it," I replied, hoping my voice sounded breezy and guileless.

"My. That *is* lucky." She paused. Rather than risk trying to bluster my way through an additional explanation of my rifling through Stephanie's files, I eyed the poplar saplings in a nearby lawn; the owners were going to regret their choice of a quick-growing, short-lived tree. Plus, their front steps were dreadful; they looked like cinder blocks. The steps should have been curved, less steep, and much less angular.

I rolled my eyes, annoyed with myself. It was one thing to mentally redecorate to calm myself, but my stress level must be off the charts for me to be doing drive-by designs.

"While we're on the subject of your clients," Linda said at last, "we've removed the crime scene tape from Helen Walker's residence. Helen can move back home."

"Oh, good." I waited, hoping she'd announce with the next breath that Rachel Schwartz had confessed to her husband's murder. Helen didn't like her to begin with, so she would be the least traumatic suspect I could think of offhand. When Linda remained silent, I prodded, "So . . . does this mean you have a suspect in custody?"

" 'Fraid not. Turns out Jack Schwartz was hard of hearing. He might not have heard the garage door open after all."

"He *was*? He wasn't wearing a hearing aid when I met him, and I sure didn't pick up on any indications that he was partially deaf."

"He was, though. O'Reilly says hearing loss can throw off a person's balance, and he's decided it's likely that he just tripped. As for all the water in the basement, a tap near one of the window wells had been left running, and the window was open."

"Which further makes it look like *the killer* deliberately flooded the basement," I protested. "Cats never willingly wade through water, so for the flooding to be an accident, Vator had to have crossed the basement floor back when it was still dry. In any case, Helen always keeps the basement door shut. So how did the cat get in?"

"O'Reilly thinks she climbed in through the one window that was cracked open a couple of inches."

"But if all this water was pouring through the window well, Vator would have avoided that window like the plague! It's way more likely someone picked up the cat, carried her across the wet floor, and left her on the stack of boxes. Then, after getting to the dry stairs, he or she deliberately dropped the electric cord into the water. Don't you think?"

"Probably. But, be that as it may, we're calling this an accidental death, for the time being at least."

"What?!"

"We've got a new chief of police, and a whole lot of bureaucratic red tape to deal with right now, so unless we find any subsequent information . . . In any case, you didn't hear any of this from me, Erin, okay?"

I rubbed my forehead in annoyance, but for my friend's sake, replied jovially, "Hear *what*?"

"Is Ms. Walker doing all right?"

"I haven't seen her since first thing this morning. Audrey has the day off, so I'm guessing that the two of them have been taking a lengthy stroll down memory lane...exchanging stories about when Audrey's sons were in high school and Helen was teaching there."

"Were they friends back then?" She was speaking in her investigating-officer tones.

"More like allies. Helen was a major positive influence on Audrey's oldest son, when he was a troubled teen."

There was a pause. "So Audrey's opened her house to someone who taught her kid some twenty years ago, and you've spent all of, what? Twelve hours in the woman's company?"

If that. Wanting to voice my confidence in Helen, I replied, "Sometimes that's all it takes to get a good feel for a person's character."

"Or at least for the image they choose to project," she grumbled.

"You know, Linda, the loveliest colors imaginable look dull till you see them in sunlight."

"And the nastiest, most ruthless people you'd ever want to meet can seem as sweet and complacent as can be, till you get them under the spotlight and interrogate them."

"Thanks for sharing, girlfriend," I shot back sarcastically. "You really know how to brighten my day."

She laughed. "Take care, Erin. Talk to you soon."

Just as I'd started to pull away from the house with the unfortunate landscaping, my cell phone bleated. I pulled over once more and answered. It was Helen. "That nasty detective from last night called and said that I can move back home," she told me. "Can you please give me a ride?"

"Right now?"

"Yes. If you don't mind, Erin. I asked Audrey to drive me there, but she's stalling. She obviously isn't sure I should move back in and wants to discuss the matter with you."

I glanced at my watch. Thanks to my not working at Helen's house today, my schedule was light, and I had the next two hours free. In the background, I could hear Audrey's protestations over Helen's statement. I said to Helen, "Tell Audrey I'll be home in five minutes."

Helen had changed back into the clothes she'd been wearing last night. She was waiting by the door when I arrived. Audrey, on the other hand, dragged me into the kitchen to speak to me in private, then quietly asked, "Are you sure it's safe for her to go home so soon?"

"No, I'm not. But the police seem to think it is, and this is Helen's decision."

From the parlor, Helen called out, "I have excellent hearing. It's lovely of you to offer to let me stay on, Audrey, but I'd rather get back home to my cats and resettled in my own house."

Audrey ushered me back into the parlor. Firmly, she told Helen, "I fail to see how you can manage to feel all that 'settled' when you're terrified someone who's trying to kill you has a key to your house."

"Well, I know, dear, but I'm afraid this could be my one and only chance to move back home."

"Why do you say that?" I asked in alarm.

"I really don't want to go into this at length, but Stephanie has been trying to boot me out of my home, and she..." Helen's eyes filled with tears.

"Your niece is trying to kick you out of your house?" Audrey shrieked. "We have to stop her! I know lots of influential people in this town—"

"No, Audrey. I need to deal with my own family in my own way," Helen said. "Let me give returning to my house a try, and if I find myself quivering at each little creaking board, we'll reevaluate."

Audrey flashed her patient smile that indicated she was losing her patience. "Fine. I have some errands to run anyway, so I'll tag along, just to make sure I can't convince you to change your mind and stay a second day at *my* home."

After wrangling with some logistic challenges, we piled into Audrey's car, with me in the backseat. The two of them chattered away—the kind of mindless, nervous prattle that old friends might exchange on their way to a scheduled biopsy.

The tension dissipated a little when Audrey pulled into Helen's driveway. The home's exterior was as inviting as ever. Audrey praised Helen's house to the hilt as they climbed the front steps. When Helen let us inside, however, Audrey turned a little green around the gills as she eyed the various piles and stacks throughout the living room. For my part, I had to remind myself that we'd already come leaps and bounds from how the house had looked just three days earlier.

"Look at all the footprints in the carpet!" Helen exclaimed as she picked her way across the room. "A whole platoon of policemen must have marched through my house! Even the air smells different." She hugged her arms tight across her chest and added in a small voice, "It feels as though I've been violated. Someone was touching my things . . . setting a deadly trap. Poor Jack! He was such a decent person. A real sweetheart."

"Are you sure you wouldn't rather turn right around and go back to my house?" Audrey suggested gently.

Helen shook her head, her lips set firmly, but I got the impression that she didn't trust her voice just then. She glanced around as though trying to decide if she should sit down, but was uncomfortable with the notion. We followed her into the kitchen, now the neatest room in the house. (Although that wasn't saying much.) She eyed the closed basement door and forced a smile. "Ella and Vator should be here soon, and I'll feel better then. They're with Kay. I called her from the police station last night, and she fetched them for me. The house feels so empty without my little darlings."

There was an awkward pause. Then Audrey said with false cheer, "While we're waiting for your cats, how about taking us on a tour of your home?"

Helen shook her head. "Why don't you let Erin show you around? You'll like the upstairs. I don't go up there. Makes me too nervous."

"I really *would* like to see the second floor," Audrey told me. Her expression made it quite clear that she had an ulterior motive for wanting to go up there.

We climbed the stairs, and Audrey promptly shut the door to Lois's old room behind us. "My God, Erin," she whispered, grabbing my arm, "this place is closer to a messy storage shed than a person's home! Please tell me this isn't a visit from The Ghost of Christmas Future, giving me a peek at what my own house will be like, ten short years from now."

"You're not going to turn your home into a storage shed, Audrey. I won't allow you to, for one thing. And I'm remedying the situation at Helen's too, for that matter."

"You mean, it used to be *worse*?"

"Yes. I'm hoping that we'll make so much progress that we'll have the whole place livable in a couple of weeks." I sighed and looked around. "Let's take quick peeks in all her closets and make sure there are no more horrid surprises. I don't want to leave her to fend for herself till we know there's nobody hiding here."

We checked Lois's room and closet, looked in the bathroom, and went into Helen's room. We nearly set off an avalanche by opening her closet door. "For sure nobody's hiding in *this* closet," Audrey grumbled as we worked to pile the toppling mountain of clothes and shoe boxes back far enough into the closet to allow us to shut the door.

Afterward, we rejoined Helen in the kitchen. Taking a positive slant, Audrey said, "Your upstairs rooms have oodles of potential. Your house is so cozy and quaint. We really should check out the basement, though," she added, glancing at me, "just to make sure it's truly safe now."

"I won't go down there," Helen declared.

"You don't have to," I interjected hastily. "Audrey and I can investigate."

Instead of making a move to join me, Audrey said, "Can I make you some tea, Helen?"

Helen said, "No, thank you, dear," and sank into a seat at the kitchen table.

Not to be a baby, but I didn't particularly want to go

downstairs by myself, either. I stalled and said, "Your homeowner's insurance will probably cover the damage to your possessions in the basement. We need to sort through everything and see what can be salvaged, so—"

"Let's let that go," Helen interrupted. "Maybe in a couple of weeks I'll be up for the task, but right now, every item down there will only remind me of poor Jack."

"I understand." Although procrastinating was probably going to lead to even greater losses, as the mold and mildew took hold. Then again, her basement possessions were probably even less valuable than the four sets of rusted cookware that she'd hoarded in her kitchen. We really *should* check for prowlers, just to be cautious. For Audrey's ears, I hinted, "Maybe the status of your basement will be enlightening. I'd like to figure out how the police could possibly conclude that Jack's death was accidental."

"So would I!" Helen exclaimed. "The officer told me they found a ruptured hose in the yard with my fingerprints on the nozzle. It's true that I have a hose out there, but it was perfectly fine the last time I used it. The police claim the water came in through the window well...that the window was open. But I would *never* leave my water running. And I didn't open the window. Plus, I always keep the basement door shut, so how did Vator manage to get herself locked down there?"

"It's very peculiar, all right," I replied. Audrey took a seat at the table next to Helen. So much for having a partner in spelunking through a basement where I'd recently found a body. "I'll go take that look downstairs now," I grumbled.

I flicked on the light switch and picked my way down

the junk-free strip in the center of the steps. The place seemed a little less spooky with the overhead lights working, but the air smelled dank and musty—rife with wet cardboard, although the cement floor was now dry—and there was no other evidence of the lethal two inches of water in which Jack had died just last night.

The small square of soggy carpeting at the base of the stairs had been removed. The extension cord was also gone. The electrical socket was now visible between the boxes. A particularly large box right next to the socket formed a ledge a couple of feet from the bottom step. I whipped out my tape measure, extended it, and easily touched the ledge. The killer could have placed the cord on that ledge, flooded the basement, put Vator on top of a stack of boxes, then used a broom handle—or perhaps the infamous wooden dowel—to shove the cord off the ledge and into the water. I sidestepped along the perimeter of the small open area at the base of the stairs, unwilling to walk directly on the spot where Jack's body had lain.

I scanned the head-high stacks of boxes occupying most of the remaining floor space. The police had made an aisle to the window where the water had gotten in, supposedly from the busted hose. I examined the walls of boxes as I made my way through the aisle. Curiously, unlike any other boxes in the house, these had been labeled; each had a small letter and a number written on a corner.

I peered up at the nearest window well. A chunk had been broken out of the plastic cover. It looked as though someone had kicked it in. The window itself was open about four inches—wide enough for Vator to have squeezed through. From there, as long as you ignored the powerful feline aversion to getting wet, the cat might very well have leaped onto one stack of boxes after another, but refrained from jumping down when she spotted the water below her. Again, however, no way was that cat going to jump from the lawn into a flooded window well in the first place.

Just as I turned away, I heard a noise outside and whirled back around. I gasped at the sight of a pair of ankles framed by the window well. They were clad in support hose, and the accompanying pair of feet was clad in white soft-soled nurse shoes. A moment later, a face peered down through the Plexiglas well cover at me. Kay, too, gasped and drew back instantly, no doubt startled at unexpectedly seeing me staring up at her.

"Goodness, Erin!" she cried. "You gave me such a fright! What are you doing in Helen's basement?"

"Looking for storage space," I fibbed.

"And are you looking for the Holy Grail, while you're at it?" she said with a wobbly laugh.

"What are *you* doing in Helen's backyard?"

"Being nosey." She chuckled. "I'm going to come inside, rather than throw my neck out of whack by continuing to chat with you through this window."

"Sounds wise."

She was being more than pleasant, but my cynicism had kicked in full force. Kay Livingston's devotion to Helen could all be an act. She could very well have been double-checking the scene of her crime to ensure that all looked well in the daylight.

I emerged in the kitchen at the same moment that Kay knocked, rather than ring the doorbell. "Oh, Kay's here," Helen said, rising.

"Yes. I saw her through the basement window just now. She was in your backyard, peering into the window well."

Apparently unconcerned about her friend's snooping, Helen happily threw open the door and invited her inside. Two cat carriers were on the stoop, to either side of Kay.

Kay pulled Helen into a hug, saying, "As horrible as this is, thank God *you're* unharmed!"

"I do have to remember to be thankful for that much," Helen said sadly.

Helen introduced Kay to Audrey, then we brought the carriers inside and Helen cooed over her beloved pets. The two cats dashed past her with indignant meows the instant she'd opened the carrier doors. Ella darted underneath the vinyl lounge chair and Vator raced past Audrey and me into the kitchen. "Thank goodness the police allowed me a second phone call, so I could find someone to watch my cats. I can't thank you enough, Kay," Helen said.

"Well, they were perfectly wonderful house guests, not counting how hard it was to get them into their cages. I positively couldn't manage the feat on my own. A very nice policeman helped me last night, and I had to get Teddy to help me today. Both of us got scratches on our arms in the process."

"*Teddy* helped you?" Helen asked in obvious surprise.

Kay didn't answer. She was staring at Audrey as though mesmerized. Finally, she snapped her fingers and grinned. "Oh, my! I know who you are! You have that TV show: *Domestic Bliss with Audrey Munroe.*"

"That's right," Audrey said, beaming.

"I've been meaning to write to you and suggest that you

invite Helen on your show. She's unbelievably good at scrapbooking." Kay made her way over to the stack of albums. "Mind you, Helen's too modest for her own good, but let me show you a book or two." She handed Audrey the top book on the stack, but then bent down a little for a closer look at the labeled spines. "George Miller?" she read aloud. *Helen's late brother-in-law*, I remembered. She turned to face Helen. Kay's face had gone very pale. "I thought you told me you lost this one!"

"We've been uncovering all kinds of things lately." Helen's smile was sheepish.

Kay's jaw dropped.

Oblivious to the domestic drama surrounding her, Audrey had sunk onto the piano bench, with the scrapbook Kay had given her, and was oohing and ahhing as she flipped through the album. "That's a terrific suggestion, Kay," she exclaimed. "In fact, the timing is absolutely brilliant! A guest I'm supposed to tape tomorrow morning had a schedule conflict and canceled on me. Not to mention that I'd love to get into scrapbooking myself, now that my first grandchild is on the way. What do you say, Helen? Will you appear on my show to talk about scrapbooks?"

Helen was already shaking her head, but Audrey was never one to take no for an answer. She coaxed, "You'd be helping me out *immensely*. It's only a six-minute segment. All you'll have to do is answer my questions about your techniques and follow my lead. Please?"

"Oh, yes," Kay cried. She seemed to have regained her composure. "That would be so much fun, Helen! You'd be striking a blow for us over-seventy crowd, proving we still have talents to offer the world."

"That's being so grandiose. They're just picture albums. I'm hardly Joan of Arc."

"Granted, this won't qualify you for sainthood," Audrey said, rising and handing the scrapbook to Helen as though it were solid gold, "but you *would* be paving the way for our less courageous friend Erin, here. She's too scared of the camera to appear on my show."

Helen looked at me in surprise. Then, resolved, she said, "Okay, Audrey. I suppose I could manage. Erin, do you think you could please come with me and sit in the audience?"

"I'd really rather—"

"Please?" Helen insisted. "I'd feel better with you there."

Audrey was grinning at me, and I could see the wheels turning in her head; she was thinking she had just killed two birds with one stone. And maybe she had. I sighed. "Can I give you a ride, Helen?"

"Actually, Helen," Audrey quickly interjected, "you and I need to be in Denver about two hours in advance of the show. I could give you a ride, so that Erin can come later. Then she can give you a ride home right afterward."

Kay said, "You can give *me* a ride both ways, Erin."

We set times for our early departure, Kay deciding she'd take a bus to Helen's home at the crack of dawn so that she could help Helen get ready, but that she'd "only be in the way" at the studio, so she'd "keep Ella and Vator company" till I arrived.

Helen seemed to have become more comfortable in her house now that she had Kay's and her cats' company, and so I suspected that, like me, Audrey no longer felt guilty at leaving her there. On our way back home, Audrey released a sigh of satisfaction. "Well, Erin, that worked out quite nicely. Remember how much I was complaining to you about my guest canceling?"

"Yes, I sure do."

"It's like they say... 'Ask and thou shalt receive.'" She shot me a sideways glance. "Except when it comes to asking *you* to be on my show, that is. You might even be more stubborn than I am." She paused. "On second thought, the smart money's on me getting my way, sooner or later."

Too true, I mused to myself. If only the "smart money" were on the police realizing that Jack's death was indeed murder, so that Helen and everyone else could get through this unharmed.

chapter 11

Our memories are our most precious possessions. They comprise our lives, determine who we are. Scrapbooks are a marvelous means for preserving and honoring our most cherished memories.

—*Audrey Munroe*

DOMESTIC BLISS

"Do you have any plans tonight?" Audrey asked as I came trotting downstairs, having gotten off the phone in my room from chatting with a friend. (The friend had sympathized at gratifying length about my fear over Helen's staying alone in her house, and had agreed wholeheartedly that Steve Sullivan was impossible to deal with, which had made me feel immeasurably better.) I gave Audrey a wary look. She was jingling her car keys and was wearing a gray CU jogging suit, with the hood pulled up over her head. With her normally impeccable fashion sense—not to mention her strong distaste for jogging—this was akin to spotting the Queen of England in hot pants and a halter top.

"Just a Pilates class. Why? Did you want to join me?"

"Heavens, no. You can do that another night, though, can't you?"

"I suppose so. Is there something you want me to do with you?"

"I thought you'd never ask. I need you to come with me to a class in Westminster." She put on a pair of sunglasses, despite the fact that it was nearly sunset and we were indoors. "It starts in half an hour, so we've got to leave right now. I'll buy you dinner afterward. Let's go."

"Okay." I grabbed my purse and followed her out the door. "But is there a reason you're dressed like the Unabomber?"

"Of course."

I waited, but she didn't continue. "You don't want to be recognized?" I suggested.

"Precisely. You're driving. My vanity plates are a dead giveaway."

Her plates read DOMBLSS. I'd always thought that they could too easily be misinterpreted into "Dumb Lass" (by someone who couldn't spell the word *dumb*), but that was not the kind of observation I cared to share with Audrey. Mostly because she'd take my head off. She led the way to my van, which was parked near the front walkway. "Is this 'class' going to be something I can look back on someday with pride?" I asked. "Or should I put on a disguise, too?"

She clicked her tongue. "It's just research for my segment with Helen tomorrow. I've been woefully bad at staying up-to-date with scrapbooking techniques. It's embarrassing. Here I am, doing all these shows on arts and crafts, and Helen uses all these stenciling and embellishing techniques I've never even seen before. I'm taking a crash course, rather than risk making a fool of myself tomorrow."

"That's admirable. But, really, your show covers the gamut from makeup tips to designing koi ponds. It's not like the public at large expects you to be current on all arts and crafts at all times."

"True, but when it comes to hobbyists, scrapbooking is right up there with needlepoint these days. This would be like your attending a class on furniture placement, side by side with your prospective clients. Besides, I'd like to get an album started for David and his wife and the new arrival."

"Fine, Audrey. If it doesn't bother you wearing sunglasses indoors and a hood, it doesn't bother me to be seen with you. Even if it *does* make you totally stick out like a sore thumb . . . in a gray fleece Band-Aid."

"I'm claiming that I have allergies. And I'm dabbing blusher on my nose, and I'll sniffle a few times. Just remember that, for tonight, *no matter what*, my name is Alexandra Parker."

"Pleased to meet you, Alexandra. My name is Cleopatra, Queen of Denial."

We arrived at the shop in Westminster and joined two dozen other women, seated in workstations around four large tables in a brightly lit room. The air bore traces of the paint-and-paper scents unique to art studios, instantly transporting me to my college days at Parsons in Manhattan. Counters rimmed the room with various die-cutting presses and cutting boards, and the walls were decorated in primary-colored cutouts, all labeled to allow us to quickly locate the corresponding template.

Our instructor, a thirtyish former cheerleader sort, asked if we could each introduce ourselves to everyone and state why we were here, and started with Audrey. "My name is Alexandra Parker," my devious landlady declared smoothly, "and I have allergies, hence the sunglasses. I have my very first grandchild on the way, and I want to be prepared to immortalize the occasion in proper style."

"Wonderful!" the instructor gushed, then looked expectantly at me.

"My name is Erin, and I'm here to support my friend . . . Alex." Although her dark glasses dulled the effect, I was certain by the pursed lips that Audrey gave me a withering glare.

While the others were giving their introductions, Audrey produced a dozen photographs from her purse, all of them of her eldest son and his pregnant wife. She slid half of them to me and murmured, "Play along."

We listened as the instructor gave a lecture on the dos and don'ts of scrapbooking (do annotate your scrapbook pages; don't use products that are corrosive for photographs), and demonstrated how to use the various items in the kits in front of her. There was an impressive array of adhesives, pens, and cutting tools. The miniature paper trimmers were especially appealing, and I made a mental note to purchase one in the near future. While the instructor was talking, Audrey unobtrusively grabbed the products she needed and went to work. Not even five minutes into the task, she'd removed her dark glasses to select from the rainbow of colored paper, which included sparkling metallic and glittery sheets. The textures were impressive, with fuzzy mulberry papers for layering and sheer vellum for overlays to enhance the cardstock.

By the time our instructor was asking if we had any final questions and were ready to begin, Audrey was putting the final touches on a two-page spread that was almost at the astonishing level of Helen Walker's work. The instructor wandered over to Audrey, saying, "One of tonight's students has been hard at work already. Alexandra, did you want to ask me about some of the more advanced . . ." She froze as she looked at Audrey's imaginative display. "Oh, my gosh. I've never seen anyone do such a fabulous job!"

"Thank you."

"Wow!" the woman directly across from Audrey exclaimed as she stood to get a better view of Audrey's work. "Look, everybody!"

Drinking in the praise of our classmates, Audrey spent the next hour working side by side with the instructor on everyone else's layouts, especially mine. She was unwilling to accept the "competent but altogether too commonplace" presentation I was creating for her son's photos, and, infuriatingly, used it for a "don't" demonstration to our classmates.

By then, we'd gone into overtime and my stomach was growling, but still nobody was leaving; Audrey was firmly entrenched as Belle of the Bookers' Ball. Finally, the store manager appeared, and Audrey critiqued a presentation board that the instructor had been using. The manager offered her a job on the spot, and Audrey said she couldn't possibly accept, announcing, "I have a confession to make. I've come here incognito. I'm actually Audrey Munroe, of the television show *Domestic Bliss with Audrey Munroe.*"

"Oh, my gosh! Are you serious?" the instructor shrieked happily. "Is she *serious*?" she asked, turning to me for verification.

I shook my head sadly and gathered up Audrey's and my scrapbook pages. "It's time to go home now, Alexandra." In a stage whisper to the instructor and manager, I said, "The resemblance is remarkable, isn't it? But I've met Audrey Munroe. And, for one thing, she's a much snappier dresser."

chapter 12

early the next morning, Kay and I got stuck in a traffic jam on the Interstate and arrived at the studio in the nick of time. Helen was already onstage, seated next to Audrey in one of the lovely indigo Bergère guest chairs that I'd helped Audrey select for her show's pseudo–living room.

Kay and I whispered "Excuse me" a half dozen times as we made our way to the only two vacant seats— upholstered in rich red velvet—at the far wall. I was getting my bearings among the fifty or so auditorium-style-filled seats when Kay gasped, then elbowed me and pointed behind us. Rachel Schwartz stood at the back of the auditorium, just inside the doors. The usher was trying to convince her to leave with him quietly.

Rachel must have followed us here! She had somehow gotten past the ticket taker, and now she made a show of looking for the ticket stub in her purse.

My imagination ran wild as I worried about what she might do. Surely, though, if she had a handgun in her purse, she'd have produced it by now. The usher would be able to handle her, I hoped, though it was unfortunate that Rachel towered over the young man. Meanwhile, Audrey and Helen had launched into their staged conversation.

"—used bleach on ink before, of course," Audrey was saying by the time I relaxed enough to listen, "but never with these amazing results. The delicacy and accuracy is simply stunning. Let's move the camera in really close, so the television viewers can see how astonishing these details truly are." As the big screen above our heads in the studio showed us Helen's remarkable work, the oohs and ahhs were audible, and we all applauded.

"Stop this charade right this minute!"

Rachel was pushing her way past the usher to race down the aisle. "I taught those bleach-and-ink techniques to you!"

Her accusing finger was pointed straight at Helen. Helen, shading her eyes from the bright stage lights, looked up at Rachel in shock.

Rachel glared at Helen on the small stage with that same look of abject hatred that I'd seen flash across her features when Jack was installing the doorbell for Helen. Rachel swatted at the usher as he tried to get between her and the stage. "I showed you how to do it! You're taking credit for *my* signature techniques!"

"Balderdash!" Helen retorted. "I'm the one who taught those techniques to *you*, Rachel, and you know it!"

"That's not true! Helen Walker is a husband-stealer, a murderer, *and* a scrapbook plagiarist!"

A second usher rushed toward Rachel, and the two men grabbed her and dragged her back up the aisle and through the doors. The entire audience was murmuring and shifting uneasily in their seats. Audrey's theme music began to play, and a voice over the speaker system asked us to pardon the interruption and promised that the show would resume momentarily.

Kay turned to me. "What on earth was Rachel thinking? Good Lord! I hope they wring her neck!"

"No kidding." My heart was thumping, and I was relieved that Rachel hadn't become violent. "Her husband died the night before last. Yet here she's tailing us to Denver, just to harass Helen." That was quite the suspicious connection.

Kay frowned and fidgeted in her seat. "I never should have let her know where we were going. She was watching through her window this morning when Audrey picked up Helen. Rachel raced over right after they left to pump me for information. I never dreamed she'd do something like this, though." She shook her head and released a sigh, although the corners of her mouth were slightly upturned and there was a glint in her eye like a highly polished black onyx. "Poor Helen."

Below us on the stage, Audrey quietly conferred with her guest, presumably giving Helen the choice between delaying her segment or proceeding now. Helen kept nodding and saying, "I'm fine." Minutes later, Audrey began the show again as if nothing had happened, and the two women carried off their interview just fine, although immediately afterward, Helen asked if it would be all right if she left for home. Then she rose and scanned the audience for Kay and me—her transportation.

We shared an unspoken agreement not to risk mentioning Rachel's name until we were safely distanced from the TV station, but when I merged the van onto the Interstate to head north for Crestview, I said, "Helen, I'm so sorry about Rachel's outburst. I had no idea she was following us to the studio this morning."

"It's okay," she replied, mustering a tentative smile. "That was just her grief talking, I'm sure."

"That's magnanimous of you," Kay replied from behind me. She'd insisted on letting Helen have the front seat. "It's just a good thing that the show is taped. If that had been a live telecast, you'd have been well within your rights to sue her for slander. In fact, I'd have insisted."

Helen gave a slight shrug. "Well, she was right about the technique we were showing on camera not being my own private discovery. Remember how you and I experimented and discovered the right mix of bleach and ink together?"

"Yes, of course I remember. Though I have to admit that I was starting to wonder if *you* remembered."

"I'm sorry about that, Kay. I was just about to mention your name, when Rachel interrupted me. After the security guard had to escort her out of the studio and everything, I just didn't have the energy to go back into the whole topic a second time."

"Oh, it's no problem."

Kay's tone, though, didn't sound like it was "no problem." I glanced at her in the rearview mirror. She was glaring out the window. It wasn't my place to question a sixty-year friendship, and yet the hints of friction between the two women worried me. Helen had trusted Kay with the fact that she was monitoring whether or not her house had been surreptitiously entered in her absence. I couldn't help but wonder if Helen could be absolutely certain that *Kay* wasn't the culprit who'd been entering uninvited. After all, even though she was aware of Helen's monitoring system, Kay couldn't replace the telltale hairs and still get outside, except by darting beneath the garage door as it was shutting on her.

"You're a big scrapbooking hobbyist as well, Kay?" I asked.

She smiled at my reflection in the mirror. "I used to be. After a while, I realized there wasn't much point in keeping a record of everything. So few things actually happen to me. I don't have a family, and I retired more than a decade ago."

"What did you used to do for a living?"

"I worked in a bank. Again, nothing interesting ever happened. I dealt with more than a few cranky customers over the years, but no bank robbers."

"Kay's just being modest, Erin," Helen interjected with a chuckle. "She travels all the time. She belongs to a book group that goes all over the world."

"That's true. Every year we pick the setting of a book we've read where we most want to visit ourselves, and off we go."

"And so, every year she has some wonderful scrapbooks that she puts together for her whole club to enjoy."

Kay cleared her throat, and there was an awkward pause. "Actually, Helen, I must have forgotten to keep you up-to-date. Rachel Schwartz joined the group a few months ago, and she took over my position on the Keepsake Committee."

"Oh, Kay! Why? You loved that job! You originated it, even! Why did you let Rachel do that to you?"

"It was perfectly fine with me, Helen. I truly didn't mind in the least. I'm their oldest member by at least ten years. They all felt the scrapbook was taking up too much of my time and energy, and Rachel was dying to do it. They only had my best interests at heart."

"Your 'best interests at heart,'" Helen mocked. "Pish posh! People always claim they're acting for someone else's best interest, when they're really just rationalizing their own heartless acts."

I looked into the rearview mirror to gauge Kay's reaction to that. She was glaring at the back of Helen's head. Kay said through clenched teeth, "Yes, I guess you have a point there."

Our conversation during the rest of the drive home was forced. Although I had no idea what Kay was referring to, Helen had obviously hit a nerve when she'd mentioned "heartless acts," and we had to flounder to defuse the tension. As we pulled into Helen's driveway, the lovely flowerboxes and the spotless siding and cheerful trim made her home so inviting that it reminded me again how much potential this place had, buried beneath all those layers of possessions. I needed to get back to work. If Sullivan and I could somehow get the first floor de-cluttered in another four or five days, maybe by next week I could tackle her basement and inventory—as well as dispose of—everything that had been destroyed by the flood.

"Helen, could I do a quick survey of the main floor? Steve and I should be able to finish up the kitchen this afternoon, but I'd like to get a handle on tomorrow's goals as well."

"Oh, absolutely," Helen said, hopping down from my van with surprising agility. "In fact, why don't I make us all a nice lunch while you're doing that?"

"I'm so happy to hear that you're using your kitchen again," I replied. "And I'd love to, Helen, but my day is jam-packed with client appointments from here on out."

"I should get home soon, too," Kay said. "I can get a ride with Erin."

"Okay," Helen said, though I could feel her happiness fade. I had visions of her deciding then and there that she was never going to cook for anyone ever again, so she might as well rebury her kitchen. She unlocked the front door. "I wish I hadn't forgotten to take the garage door opener with me this morning. Now I'm not going to be able to tell if anyone broke in through the front door while I was gone."

To my surprise, the living room was much neater than it had been yesterday evening when I'd last seen it. Although the furnishings were still a hopeless mishmash— bentwood rocker, glass coffee table, nightstand-cum-end table, recliner, and pseudo-leather lounger—all the stacks of sundry items were gone. The piano and its bench had been cleared off and polished. The scrapbooks were still stored on the floor, but they'd at least been lined up along the walls instead of in piles.

Following me inside, Kay said, "I meant to mention on our drive down, Erin, how impressive your progress on this house has been."

"Much as I'd like to, I can't take any credit for this room. So far my work's been limited to the kitchen." I gave Helen a smile, which she didn't return. Uh-oh. Her lack of pride dimmed my hopes for my efforts to effect a permanent change in her living space. "Helen? Did you do all this yourself?"

She nodded. "Due to a bad case of insomnia. I was such a nervous wreck yesterday at the thought of doing Audrey's show that I cleaned this room when I should have been sleeping."

An unnerving thought occurred to me. "Where did you move everything?" *Don't say the kitchen! Anyplace but the—*

"Oh, it's all in the kitchen."

Damn! "We were going to move everything *out* of the kitchen and into another room, remember? So that we could get all your cabinets and pantry cleaned and reorganized." I couldn't completely hide my annoyance.

"Well, I know, but now the kitchen had the most available storage space, and . . . Oh, dear. I've made more work for you. Well, I'll just move my stuff back in here, then."

"No, please don't. That's counterproductive. We'll just start today by moving everything else out of the living room. This way we're at least halfway through with reorganizing your living room."

As I scanned the overstuffed entertainment unit and the long line of scrapbooks along the baseboards, I hoped that I wasn't underestimating the work that remained to be done in this space. Plus, at some point, I needed to get that sofa and floor lamp out of the garage and back in here. Along with putting a slipcover on the sofa. Come to think of it, I had to call Stephanie later today and ask that we rework the budget so as to allow me to bring in my paint crew. (Which, with Helen's objections to large numbers of "strangers" in her house, meant a "crew" of just one painter.) I had to have *some* fun here, by God, and nothing invigorates a room for less money than a fresh coat of paint. I could see a soothing sage in this room, a bright buttery yellow for the dining room, and maybe something daring for that disaster of a den—cornflower blue, perhaps.

Kay's attention had been drawn to Helen's photo albums again, and she made a beeline for the one marked "George Miller." She snatched it up and started paging through it, saying, "I never did look at this yesterday when I saw that you'd finally unearthed this one."

My suspicious nature still running amok, I wondered what she'd been doing while she was alone in this house, after Helen and Audrey left and before I arrived to pick her up. My hunch was that she'd pored through the album the instant Helen was gone.

Paging through the book, Kay said, "My, my, Helen! You've done such a great..." Her voice faded, and worry lines creased her forehead. "That's odd," she muttered as she flipped forward from the last page of the book.

"What?" Helen asked.

"Why are a third of the pages missing?"

"Pardon?"

"Well, take a look at it," Kay said. "This book is the one you put together on George's life and career accomplishments, but it doesn't even go up through 1960, when we all met George. It's all just things you pieced together from the photographs that Lois collected from his boyhood home."

Helen was clearly flustered, yet she said, "I was afraid something like this would happen. The binder had snapped open a long time ago, and the pages got scattered all around the house. I must have accidentally discarded them."

Kay studied her friend's features incredulously, and like her, I didn't believe a single word. "You don't discard *anything*," she said accusingly.

"I do now, though." Helen waggled her thumb at me. "It's either listen to Erin and do as she says or have to answer to Stephanie, my Nazi Niece."

"When you put it like that, I don't blame you. I'd sure opt for listening to Erin, too. That Stephanie is such a one-woman tank. And heaven help whoever gets in her way."

Helen sighed. "She can be difficult to deal with, but she means well."

Kay scoffed. "How do you know she 'means well'? What she *means* is to root you right out of house and home!"

Helen pursed her lips and continued to stare forlornly at the scrapbook in Kay's hands. She muttered, "Maybe so."

"We'll fix her wagon if she tries to give you the boot." Kay grinned at me. "Won't we, Erin?"

I merely offered a lame smile. I couldn't answer without insulting one of my clients, and this was a family matter. Besides, I didn't believe Kay's routine about only just now noticing the missing pages. Kay was either covering for the fact that she'd snooped earlier this morning, or she'd taken the pages herself. She seemed to have an old ax to grind, whereas Helen must have gotten so used to

Kay's occasional snipes over the years that they barely registered with her now.

Kay crammed the book back into its slot along the floor. Maybe there was an attractive bookcase in the den, which I could move into this room. If not, I could design one for her—one with surface spaces that could be pulled out to feature a couple of scrapbooks and Helen's beautiful layouts. Kay was saying, "Stephanie might have gone too far. If she was trying to scare you by flooding your basement, she's going to have to be stopped. She never would have intentionally killed anyone, but you have to suspect that maybe she sabotaged your cellar, and the whole thing backfired."

"I know my niece better than you do," Helen replied, her voice more worried than chastising. "I just can't believe she's completely evil."

As opposed to partially evil? Helen was drumming her fingers on her crossed arms, anxious about something that she clearly wanted to keep to herself.

"That's true," Kay murmured absently. "She's your niece, not mine, thank—" She stopped herself and turned to me. "Hadn't we better get going, Erin? My next-door neighbors are coming over today, and I was going to bake us some goodies." She gave Helen a quick hug. "I'm sorry to rush off. But you know how I hate to have a bare cupboard when friends visit. We'll have lunch soon. Tomorrow."

"That would be wonderful," Helen replied, but her smile lacked its usual warmth. She accompanied us as far as the porch and stood watching as we drove away. Kay waved back at her as though they would be separated for an eternity.

As we turned the corner, Kay sighed and settled back into her seat. "I wonder if they're going to arrest Rachel Schwartz for... harassment or trespassing, or something."

"I doubt the station executives will want to press charges. Especially once they learn she's a recent widow."

Though I felt a tinge of guilt at prying, this was an excellent chance to befriend Kay and get her to confide in me. "Rachel really seems to hate Helen. I saw Rachel give Helen the evil eye the other day, right before the... accident in Helen's basement."

Kay nodded. "The feeling's mutual. Although Helen's much too nice to sink anywhere near as low as Rachel does. But those two definitely bear grudges toward each other."

"Why?"

"Oh, greed, envy, lust, spitefulness. The usual."

"The usual? That's quite the heavy-duty list, wouldn't you say?"

"I suppose so, but then, Rachel and Helen lived across the street from one another for twenty years, and a lot of water's passed under their bridge."

"Such as?"

Kay sighed again. "Let's just say that, back in the day, Jack was *quite* the ladies' man."

Even in my peripheral vision, though, I detected a hint of a smile that made me think that this gossip wasn't exactly being dragged out of her. Jack's fondness for women could certainly explain Rachel's obvious unwillingness the other day to leave him and Helen alone, even for a moment. "Jack had a wandering eye?"

She nodded and muttered slyly, "If only his eye had

been the only part of his anatomy that wandered, Jack might still be alive."

"You think that Jack was killed because he was having an affair?"

"Indirectly."

"Are you saying you suspect his wife killed him?"

"Well . . . Rachel would be my first guess. Though that's all it is, of course. A pure guess. I'm thinking she either accidentally got the wrong victim by electrocuting her husband, or she got the right one, but cleverly made it look like Helen was the intended target." She leaned toward me and added in a conspiratorial voice, "It's *always* the spouse who's the prime suspect, you know."

"Is it?"

"Oh, yes. I watch cop shows all the time. But then again, I'm biased. Rachel is not one of my favorite people . . . which makes me feel torn. If she's innocent, the poor woman's just lost her husband, and here I am, speaking badly of her. The Bible teaches us that we're all God's children . . . but Rachel Schwartz is definitely not His best work."

Three hours later as scheduled, I returned to Helen's house to resume my job. No sign of Sullivan's van. She opened the door before I could ring the doorbell, and she was clearly flustered. Her bun, which had been immaculate this morning, was once again in disarray. She grabbed my arm and tugged me inside, shutting the door behind us. "Erin! I thought we'd all agreed that you were going to let me go through the newspapers in the den myself before you took any of them away."

"We did."

"But they're missing! The important stacks are, that is. The ones in the corner."

"I didn't touch the newspapers, and neither did Steve Sullivan. Neither of us has even ventured into your den, Helen." And, judging by the view through the French doors, it was surprising that she could *reach* the corner of the room, let alone look at the dates of the newspapers to determine some of them were missing.

"In that case, I've been burglarized!"

"You think somebody *stole* your old newspapers?"

"Along with those pages from my scrapbook. And there's no way I'll get any help from the police to recover my loss. They're not going to rush to investigate the theft of several pages of an old lady's scrapbook. Not to mention a bunch of old newspapers."

"The pages that Kay noticed were missing weren't merely lost, were they?"

She shook her head. "They were stolen. But don't tell Kay, please. She has a vested interest." Helen snatched up the scrapbook that Kay had been looking through to show me how abruptly it ended. "The killer ripped out all the pages from my scrapbook that were about Lois and George's courtship."

"Why would somebody want to take pages out of your scrapbook? Hadn't your album been here, untouched, for several years?"

"Yes, but that's one of the good things about clutter, Erin. Nobody but me knows where to begin to look for anything in it. When Kay first showed me that some pages were missing, I kept trying not to worry. I figured I'd simply redo them. That's why I've been keeping backup editions of the newspapers from the fifties and sixties safe and sound in my den. I already have duplicates of the snapshots." She added sadly, "I should have photocopied the letters, though."

I stood at the now-open doors to the den and looked at the narrow makeshift aisle. Helen had burrowed her way to the adjacent corner of the room. There, stacks of newspapers were at least five feet deep and equally high. "There's still so many papers here, though, Helen. How can you know for certain that some editions were... stolen?"

"Because they're arranged chronologically. The oldest ones are on the bottom and back against the wall. And there are certain dates that are fixed in my mind. Those are *missing*, Erin."

Knowing I needed to get rid of that gargantuan accumulation of newspapers, I seized the opportunity. "Helen, I'll make a deal with you. You write down each of the dates that are fixed in your head for me. Sullivan and I will find and save those papers for you. In exchange, you'll let us get rid of all the other papers."

"You're not listening to me, Erin! Those editions were stolen! Along with half my scrapbook! Probably by the killer, because he or she realized they were incriminating!"

"But old newspaper articles are public records. They're stored on microfiche at the library. And at the publisher's. It wouldn't do a killer any good just to get rid of your copies."

Helen started to protest, but I laid my hand on her shoulder. "Maybe whoever is breaking into your house has been looking through your papers but, unlike you, didn't know the precise dates to search for. If so, the stacks have been rifled through and are probably out of order."

The doorbell rang. "Rachel Schwartz surely isn't at my door today," Helen told me. "I suppose this will be Steve Sullivan. Our conversation will have to wait."

"It's okay. You can trust him."

She stopped and turned back. "But...I really don't want to air my dirty laundry to just anyone."

"He's not just anyone, he's my associate, and he's going to have to help me look through your newspaper stacks for the few editions that you're going to keep."

"I can only keep a few?" she asked in wide-eyed horror.

"Fourteen. Tops. But I'll cut out up to fifty articles for you, as long as you choose the specific papers."

The doorbell rang again.

"Fine," she snapped, swung open the door, and cut off his apology for being late to inform him: "Erin Gilbert is stubborn and unreasonable!"

"Ah, you're getting to know each other well, then," he quipped, but winked at me as he stepped inside. He was in casual attire today, jeans and a bright orange polo shirt. "What's up?"

"Change in plans for the day." Two hours ago, we'd spoken on the phone about my desire to complete the kitchen today and to remove the junk she'd shifted there from the living room. "We're going to work on the den. Someone's taken or moved some of Helen's important editions from her stash there."

"After stealing my scrapbook pages," she piped up. "The ones that concerned my sister and her husband's courtship and marriage. And all of his trial proceedings."

"What trial?" Sullivan and I asked simultaneously.

Claiming that it was a long story, she insisted that we all take seats in the living room before answering. I tried to ignore how uncomfortable her Naugahyde chair was and how awkward Sullivan looked on the bentwood rocker. I was so dying to perk up this seating arrangement that my knees were twitching with restless-leg syndrome. From her perch at the piano, with schoolteacher inflections to her voice, she began, "George Miller—my late brother-in-law—and my friend Teddy Frederickson were once partners in the Denver police force." She frowned. "Back then, Lois was a floorwalker at a department store. Unbeknownst to me at the time when Lois and I first met them, she had recently blown the whistle on a shoplifting operation. And, unbeknownst to *either* of us, the kingpins were George and Teddy, who sometimes moonlighted as security guards at the store."

"Were they stealing the stuff themselves, or deliberately looking the other way?" Sullivan asked.

"Probably both, but Teddy was the only one who was convicted of anything. George even got to keep his job, though he transferred to the Crestview police department. The reports about the trial were in the papers that have gone missing from my den."

"You and your sister remained friends with Teddy? Even after he got convicted?" Sullivan asked.

"Oh, no. Not at all. For all the years that George was still alive, Teddy stayed far away. Even so, he let it be widely known that he was innocent and that George had set him up. Then, at George's funeral, he reintroduced himself to Lois. He'd lost his own wife about nine months before, and he and Lois eventually started dating."

I couldn't completely suppress a grimace. "And now *you* two are dating?"

"No, no. I'm not an idiot, Erin, despite what my niece might think."

"I doubt she—"

Helen cut off my protests with a wave of her hand. She continued, "Though there's no proof, I've suspected Teddy all along in Lois's murder. And now in Jack's, too. I'm merely minding the old adage: Keep your friends close and your enemies closer. If Teddy killed George, I can at least understand his thirst for revenge, though I could never condone such a thing. But if he thinks I'll let him get away with my sister's murder, and then wait around like a duck in a pickle barrel for him to come after me, he's badly mistaken."

"Yet you accept a box of candy from him?"

"You didn't see me *eating* any of them, did you?"

"No, but you offered them to *me!*" I shot back.

"I was just being polite. I never would have let you actually *accept* my offer. Honestly, Erin. Someone's tampering with my casserole and poisoning Lois wasn't enough to scare you off of eating food that's been given to me?"

"But...you invited me and Kay to have lunch with you just today!"

"I was going to make a fresh salad, and maybe open a can of soup. It's pretty hard to sabotage that...for those of us without deathly allergies, at least."

"Getting back to the missing newspapers and scrapbook..." Sullivan was leaning forward as far as he dared in the rocker. "Do you think this has something to do with Jack's death?"

"Of course! It's not a coincidence that someone who

knew about the whole sorry saga of George would want me dead. Certainly he or she wouldn't want the police to find my personal records that can spell out the motive in black and white."

"Which is?" I prompted, baffled.

"Well, my goodness, Erin. If I knew that, I'd know who killed my sister, now, wouldn't I?"

I grimaced at her twisted logic, but decided not to argue. "What did your sister believe was her husband's role in this shoplifting scam?"

"We never talked about it. She asked me never to bring it up. But I'm certain that's because she knew he was guilty."

"We should really get to work," Sullivan said, staring through the den's French doors. "Helen, we have *got* to be able to haul your excess things out of the den. Or there's no way we'll be able to sort through the stacks of papers. You can't even move in that room."

"But I don't want you taking things away from me that I might need someday!"

"Better that than to be unable to access the things that you need *today*," I pointed out.

"We need to clear enough floor space in the kitchen again to let us carry things out through the garage," Sullivan said, striding toward the entranceway. "That'll make it a lot easier to load things into the truck."

I joined him and studied the kitchen, saying, "At least it's not as bad as it was. You can still see—" Then I gasped.

"Erin? What's the matter?" Helen asked. She followed my gaze and spotted the dead mouse curled on the kitchen counter. "Oh, dear. The poor little fellow. I hope this wasn't Ella or Vator's handiwork. But... they'd never leave such a thing there."

"No, I don't..." I let my voice fade. The candy box from Teddy was on the counter near the little cadaver. A ragged hole had been nibbled through one corner.

chapter 13

the next morning, Linda called me at my office and verified what we already suspected: The chocolates had been laced with arsenic. It wasn't enough poison to have killed a human being, but Linda agreed with me when I suggested that the killer might not have realized that.

"So, that proves it," I said. "Somebody *is* trying to kill Helen."

"Did she ever offer you some of her candy?"

"When Teddy Frederickson first gave it to her, she suggested that I take the whole box. Why?"

"She might have poisoned it herself."

"Jeez, Linda. Talk about looking on the dark side! So now you think my client is trying to kill me?"

"No. But maybe she's trying to make it look like someone was trying to kill *her*."

"Why? To keep everyone entertained?"

"To give her a plausible theory on how her neighbor wound up dead in her basement."

"Helen did *not* kill Jack, Linda. Even his wife swears he went over there to investigate a prowler."

"Granted. It's unlikely that Helen's guilty. But not impossible."

Exasperated, I thanked her for calling, then got back to work on my bookkeeping, never one of my favorite tasks. I was blessedly close to being finished when Peter interrupted me with an unexpected visit. His hangdog bearing and his large, slightly pudgy frame made me think of an overgrown teddy bear. He was wearing the same gray slacks as he'd worn on every previous occasion when we'd met. I was surprised to see him and greeted him warmly, but he merely gave me a wan smile in return.

"How's everything going at my aunt's house, Erin?" His eyes were averted, making it obvious that he really didn't care one iota what my answer was.

"Fine, thanks. Have a seat."

He sat down in my plush stuffed chair but remained tense, obviously ready to rise at a moment's notice and bolt from the room.

"What brings you here?" I asked when he said nothing.

"Stephanie told me that you and your assistant were working on her house, too." He paused. I repressed a grin at Sullivan's being termed "my assistant," and waited for him to continue. He cleared his throat and fidgeted with a cuff of his white Oxford shirt. "I'm not comfortable with that."

"With my working at Stephanie's? Why ever not?"

"It's not fair to me. Stephanie wants to win Aunt Helen over and convince her to cut me out of the will. She's only remodeling right now so she can give herself more excuses to see our aunt. This way, she can drop by anytime while you're at Aunt Helen's house and pretend she needs to consult with you. Now *she* gets to be there all the time, and I never am."

How ridiculously juvenile. Not to mention nonsensical; the man could go to his aunt's house whenever he wanted. Apparently the sibling rivalry between Peter and his sister was still going strong, even now that their parents were in their graves and they themselves were old enough to have grandchildren. Half jokingly, I suggested, "You can always counter that by hiring Steve Sullivan and me to work on *your* place."

He made a derisive noise. "My finances fell into the crapper a couple years back. Had to move into a condo. It'd be like hiring you people to design the interior of a doghouse." He crossed and then uncrossed his long, thick legs.

"Your law firm isn't doing well?"

He shook his head. "Seems like half of Crestview's population is made up of lawyers or therapists. I have my own practice...which hasn't been practicing much of anything lately."

"I'm sorry to hear that. But I already started the job at your sister's place, Peter, and it really doesn't affect the work that I'm doing for you at your aunt's home."

"All I'm asking is for you to keep in mind that Stephanie

and I have equal say-so in decisions. Don't let her tell you what to do with Helen's things. Many of them are rightfully mine." Now he was fidgeting with his collar and wouldn't meet my eyes. Did he realize how whiny and petty he sounded? "Um, we both inherited my mother's personal effects when she died, but we all agreed that things were just too . . . messy at Aunt Helen's house to sort through them yet."

"So you two actually hired me to help you divvy up your personal inheritance?"

"Well . . . that was part of it. Mostly it was just to help Aunt Helen."

It would have been nice if he'd explained this to me up-front. I waited a beat to make certain my annoyance wasn't reflected in my tone. "I'll be mindful of your concerns, Peter."

"Thank you." He gave me a crooked smile. "And, by the way, even though I'm practically broke, you don't need to worry about my reneging on my half of your fees. Stephanie would have my hide. Now I'd better go chase some ambulances. . . ." He rose.

"Thanks for stopping by."

"When are you going to be working at my aunt's house again?"

"Nine o'clock tomorrow morning."

"Maybe I'll stop by then . . . and lend a hand."

"Fine. That would be terrific. And perhaps I'll see you at the service later today." When he looked puzzled, I explained, "Jack Schwartz's funeral service."

"Oh, of course." He looked at his watch. "I . . . forgot that was today."

I'd probably just embarrassed him into attending the

funeral of the man who'd died in his aunt's house. We exchanged good-byes, and he shuffled down the stairs.

Although Audrey had never met Jack Schwartz, in a show of solidarity for Helen Walker, she insisted on coming with me to his funeral service. We wound up dressing in similar navy blue skirt suits, but I lacked the motivation to change outfits. We took her Mercedes, and I settled back into her comfy leather passenger seat. En route, she asked me if the police had any leads. I told her that, last I'd heard, they were still considering Jack's death an accident.

"In that case, it's a good thing Helen has you to do the Crestview P.D.'s job for them. So: Who are your prime suspects?"

Although the names Rachel Schwartz, Teddy Frederickson, and Peter Miller (now that I knew how desperate for money he was) instantly popped into my head, I answered, "Linda made it clear to me that they'd reopen the case if any new clues emerge. So I've promised myself that I'll merely pass along to her whatever information I stumble across."

She snorted and muttered, "Good luck with that."

I studied her face in profile, but her expression was inscrutable. "What do you mean?"

"You're a helpful, take-charge person with a big heart, Erin. And you're naturally driven by that conscience of yours. One way or another, you and I both know you're going to put yourself front and center in the search for the killer. You might as well make up business cards that list you as a full-time designer, part-time detective."

"We'll see about that. Maybe the police will make an arrest soon, and I can get back to designing interiors exclusively."

We arrived at the funeral home, and Audrey pulled into a space at breakneck speed. She shut off the engine, then reached over and patted my knee. "It's always best to keep one's hopes up, dear. But, in the meantime, who do you *think* did it?"

"I don't know, Audrey," I said a bit irritably. I got out of the car, hoping that would be the end of our inane discussion.

Audrey, however, wouldn't drop it. "Keep me posted," she insisted, as we started down the sidewalk. "Helen's my friend. And I intend to help you catch this monster in any way that I can."

I nodded at an elderly couple in front of us who had overheard Audrey's odd pronouncement and had turned to stare. I whispered, "That's a generous offer, Audrey, but, like I said, I'm strictly a designer, not a detective."

"Whatever. Just keep me in the loop."

There was no sense in continuing to press my point. We entered the small chapel, made our way down the center aisle, and slid into a blond-ash pew. The room was at least two-thirds full. Peter nodded a greeting to me from the far side of the room. Why wasn't he capitalizing on this chance to play for his aunt's attention? Stephanie didn't seem to be here, and Helen sat two rows ahead of us. Judging by the body language, she didn't know the persons seated to either side of her.

I couldn't help but wonder about the rumored affair between Helen and Jack. Was she mourning the loss of a lover right now?

"Hey, Gilbert," Steve said as he sat next to me.

"Hi," I said. "I didn't realize you were going to be here."

He was already smiling at Audrey and didn't reply. The two exchanged warm hellos, then he returned his attention to me. Quietly he said, "Seems like we've been to far too many of these sad gatherings, doesn't it?"

"Definitely." In the corner of my eye, I spotted Rachel coming down the aisle. I held my breath, praying the grieving widow wouldn't pitch a fit at Helen's presence. As she passed our aisle and glanced in Helen's direction, her step faltered. I braced myself for screaming. But although she started weeping audibly into her lace handkerchief, Rachel took her seat without incident.

The service was lengthy and depressing. Many of Jack's friends and former coworkers went to the microphone to talk about how much they'd miss him. He'd come from a large family in Nebraska, and afterward most of them stood in a long line by the entrance, with Rachel at the end of the line. Peter all but sprinted up to Helen to give her a hug. After speaking with her quietly, he ducked out a side door. Truth be told, I'd have preferred to sneak out, too. Wasn't every single one of us saying how sorry we were for their loss? In my case and Sullivan's, the truth was we'd met Jack only once, and that was hardly appropriate information to pass along to his bereaved family. Nevertheless, I dutifully gave my condolences to each family member, and slipped into such a monotonous pattern that I was startled to realize that, just ahead of me, Helen was now speaking to Rachel. I overheard her declare: "He was a wonderful man. I'm terribly sorry for your loss. I'll miss him."

"I'm sure of that much," Rachel replied in a Bryn Mawr accent she'd suddenly acquired, reminiscent of the eulogist's. "Now you'll have to actually *pay* someone to do your repair jobs."

At that, Audrey stepped out of the line behind me and rushed forward to grab Helen's arm. "Let's go, Helen." I stepped away to join them.

Rachel's eyes widened as she saw who was ushering Helen toward the door. She grabbed Helen's other arm. "No, please don't disappear so quickly, you two," she said to Audrey and me. "I want to apologize for my outburst at your show yesterday, Audrey. I had a bad reaction to the antidepressants my doctor gave me. And I also wanted to tell you that there's a gathering of Jack's family and friends at my house. Please come. You, too, Erin. And Steve. Or should I say, Gilbert and Sullivan?"

"I'm afraid I have to decline, Mrs. Schwartz," Sullivan replied.

"That's a shame." Her features turned cold as she turned again to Helen. "You should come, too, Helen."

"We'll be there," Audrey immediately replied. It took all my willpower not to turn to her in astonishment.

"Good. Please just go on ahead to the house whenever you'd like. I hired a full staff of caterers to be ready for early arrivals." She then turned to the man in the line behind Sullivan, drew him into a hug, and once again grew weepy.

I said a quick good-bye to Steve as he headed toward his car. Helen said, "I don't want to go to Rachel's house. She obviously only invited me because I was standing between a celebrity and a designer . . . two people she desperately wants to impress."

"Maybe so, but this will be an excellent opportunity to do some digging," Audrey countered.

"Digging?"

"Our Erin here is not only a premiere designer, but a self-made detective. Not that she likes to talk about it, but she solved a pair of murders that had the Crestview police completely baffled."

"That's not at all accurate," I attempted.

"True, but I was trying to be modest on your behalf." Audrey turned back to Helen, who was staring at me in surprise, and said, "It was actually *three* murders. So let's go look for clues at Rachel's house right now, and with any luck, we'll be able to leave before she even arrives."

"But Rachel wouldn't have had anything to do with Jack's murder," Helen protested.

"Don't be so quick to exonerate her," Audrey said sternly. "Don't forget the famous police motto: When in doubt, blame the spouse."

"I've never heard anyone say that," Helen replied. (She mustn't have heard Kay's whodunit theories.)

"Well, if it isn't an actual motto it should be." Audrey unlocked her Mercedes with the button on her key chain. "We'll head to your neighborhood, Helen. Then we'll wait for you outside Rachel's house. Let's hurry over there before she has the chance to tamper with any evidence."

Just how Audrey had gotten the notion that Rachel could possibly have "evidence" at her house after all this time was anyone's guess. Helen and I exchanged exasperated looks, but meekly took our places in our respective cars as commanded.

Minutes later, the three of us were ushered inside the home of the late lamented Jack Schwartz by a properly somber host and hostess in funeral attire. A middle-aged couple whom Helen informed us she knew from her scrapbooking club had beaten us there. Audrey soon pulled me away from our conversation to whisper in my ear, "Quick. Let's look around."

Quasi-amateur sleuth or not, how could I resist? I enjoyed seeing people's homes too much to decline. To Rachel's credit, her Georgian colonial house was lovely, although Sullivan would have termed it "froufrou." They'd obviously modernized the interior in the last few years, installing recessed lighting in the coved plaster ceilings. A cool palette had been used—sea-foam, sage, azure, salmon—with exquisite crown molding and built-in nooks and cubbies, where Rachel had focused task lighting to show off her porcelain pieces to best advantage. In a corner étagère she had an impressive collection that—unfortunately, in my opinion—comprised clowns. The rich colors and remarkable individual yarnlike strands of hair on the pieces made it obvious at a glance that the artist was Zampiva, whose *non*-clown figurines were more to my taste.

The next room we peered into, Rachel's library, boasted a second—and amazing—collection of figurines that instantly commanded my attention. With their delicate long limbs and pale coloring, these dancers were Lladró porcelain, true works of art that I found breathtaking.

I stared at the pieces so long that Audrey finally had to ask if I was all right. I whispered, "Kay told me the other day that Helen had a lovely collection of Lladró dancers. Isn't it odd that both Helen and Rachel would collect precisely the same type of figurines?"

"Let's get Helen in here for a close look." Audrey turned on a heel, tossing an "I'll be right back" over her shoulder as she did so.

True to her word, my landlady soon escorted Helen into the room. "Erin's discovered a porcelain collection that she thinks might actually belong to you," she declared without preamble.

Helen opened her mouth as if to protest, but the color drained from her face. She stared at the figurines as if in shock. "I couldn't stake my life on it, but yes. These two are either mine, or exact replicas, right down to the smallest of imperfections . . ."

I said firmly, "I'm going to ask Officer Delgardio to swing by. She needs to take a look at this."

"No, Erin. I'm too uncertain to make a formal accusation."

"This is a really rare collection, Helen, impossible to buy new. To have two of them on the very same street without—"

"What are you looking at?" said a voice behind us with a Bryn Mawr accent.

"We were just admiring your porcelain figurines, Rachel," Audrey said. "They're absolutely exquisite."

"Thank you. They're Lladró, of course."

"I had a very similar collection," Helen said through clenched teeth.

"Yes, I remember seeing it once, a long time ago. Before it got buried in your avalanche of junk. I think that's probably what inspired me to start collecting porcelain myself. I couldn't stand to see anything that precious treated so haphazardly."

"To each his own," Helen said.

"Indeed," Rachel sniffed. "Thank you for coming today, Helen. Jack would have been touched that you insisted on coming to pay your respects, in spite of everything. But then, I've always felt that my poor husband was much too nice for his own good. And look at what his kindness toward you got him . . . an early grave."

chapter 14

my thoughts remained on Helen and her delicate dancing figurines after we'd abruptly left Rachel's house. Rachel had just lost her husband and suspected Helen had killed him, so Rachel needed and deserved plenty of slack. Even so, I'd felt a fierce desire to throttle her. The nerve of her for criticizing Helen's housekeeping when all indications were that she'd stolen Helen's expensive porcelain!

Audrey dropped me off at my van, explaining that she planned to double back and "keep a watch over Helen for an hour or so." I had some free time and decided that, for my own illumination if nothing else, I needed to get a look at the newspaper articles that Helen claimed were now missing from her house. Besides, research was an excellent excuse for a field trip to the Crestview library. The building's distinctive architecture, and the picture windows that showcased the craggy peaks of the Rockies, never failed to bring me some much-needed serenity.

Once there, I took my time in the glorious walkway, which spanned Crestview Creek. I then lingered in the children's section, admiring the playful animal-shaped seats and primary-colored pillows, and finally climbed the spiral staircase above the fountain. On the second floor, my mood dimmed a little as I entered the dreary microfiche room with its bone white walls and gray-and-blue-flecked industrial-strength carpeting.

Although I'd yet to discover for certain whether or not some newspapers in Helen's den had been stolen or misplaced, she'd jotted down the approximate dates of Teddy's trial, and it was infinitely faster to scan the library microfiche rather than sort through Helen's daunting stacks. Within minutes I was able to find the articles about the shoplifting ring. As Helen had reported, the officers involved were George Miller and Teddy Frederickson, and there had been concern that both cops were possibly involved in the operation of the ring.

My cell phone rang, garnishing me irritated glances from three other patrons. I snatched it from my purse to shut it off, but when I saw that the caller was Steve Sullivan, I said a quiet hello, bending over and practically speaking into my purse in my effort to keep my voice hushed.

"Hey, Gilbert. We need to go over our plans for Stephanie's. Where you at?"

"If you mean physically as opposed to spiritually, I'm in the microfiche room at the Crestview library, ticking off everyone in the immediate vicinity by talking on my cell phone."

"What are you doing there? Reading back issues of *Martha Stewart Living*?"

"No. I'm doing some research into the murder."

In my irritation at him for the *MSL* remark, I'd spoken louder than intended, and a few heads turned my way. I winced. "You caught my attention," Sullivan said. "I'll be right there."

Ten minutes later, I sensed someone reading over my shoulder and turned to give Sullivan the evil eye. "That's kind of rude, you know. You can't even say hi?"

But he ignored me and tapped the middle of the screen. "This is odd. Somehow I had the impression that Lois Miller was the whistle-blower."

"Me, too. I'm certain that's what Helen said her sister's role was. But according to this article, Teddy stated that it was a ring comprising store employees, and that Lois Miller was their chief suspect."

"Jeez."

"And then when you read the later articles, it seems that Teddy's accusations against Lois were lies he told in an attempt to cover up his own guilt."

"Huh. Didn't you tell me that Lois dated Teddy after her husband died? And Helen's real chummy with him now?"

"Well, I guess they say forgiveness is divine," I muttered, glancing at my watch. I had to get going.

"Also could have been deadly, if Helen had eaten the box of poisoned chocolates Teddy gave her."

According to the crime lab tests, she'd merely have gotten sick from the chocolates, nor did we know whether they'd already been poisoned when Teddy gave them to her, but this wasn't the time or place to argue such points. We printed two copies of each of the articles and left together, Sullivan still reading the columns as he walked beside me through the lot. "Sounds to me like Teddy and Helen's brother-in-law, George, had quite a racket going, then tried to use Lois as the scapegoat when things got too hot."

"But George was vindicated, and even got to keep his job," I replied.

"Maybe he just had better-connected friends than Teddy. According to this article, George and Lois married after charges were already filed against him. Maybe clever George married Lois so she couldn't testify against him."

I snatched the photocopies away from him. "I'm giving these to Linda Delgardio, just in case they have anything to do with Jack's death."

"S'pose it's possible Helen's been right all along . . . that Teddy's gunning for her, after having killed Lois. Which I guess would mean he had a grudge against her because she testified against him, and held on to his grudge for forty years. Seems strange to wait all that time to get revenge, though. He's been out of prison for, what? Thirty years now?"

"It's up to Linda and her fellow officers to unravel his motives," I said over my shoulder as I headed toward my own van, parked kitty-corner to Sullivan's. "Right now, I just want the police to acknowledge that Jack's death was no accident. Till that happens, I'm going to worry that

Helen's liable to have a similar *accident* herself." I unlocked my doors.

"Hang on a sec. I have a mock-up of Stephanie's game room design in my van."

"Oh, good," I replied. "I've got one I did in *my* van."

"Dueling designs?" Sullivan scoffed. "Great. Let the games begin."

We retrieved our drawings and climbed into my van to study them. I was stunned. "These are all but identical."

"I know." He studied my features as if in awe. Was he floored that I'd managed to produce a design as good as his? He went back to studying my drawing in silence, and I returned to studying his. "The hanging Tiffany lamp over the pool table in your drawing looks larger than the one I chose," I remarked.

"More even illumination of the table that way," he muttered.

Our designs had turned that large, dull room into a sophisticated space with quiet elegance, where Stephanie could feel proud to entertain her wealthiest friends or potential clients, yet by sliding the pocket doors shut on the pool room and bar area, would be cozy and inviting enough for even her aunt to cuddle up in front of the fireplace with a good book and her cats.

We'd both sketched in a large spectacular wet bar with Juparana granite countertops, which feature a dazzling yellow, gold, and black pattern. We'd both chosen buffed sandstone columns to either side of the bar, and Turkish travertine tiles that would shadow the lines of the countertop where it met with the plush, warm Berber carpeting. Behind the bar, both designs were awash in the rich hues of cherry, from the lighted glass cabinets to the corner wine cellar. I'd designed a charming cappuccino nook into my wet-bar design, which I suspected Stephanie would love. With our primo choice of materials and the understated grace, she and her guests could easily imagine themselves having a glass of Chardonnay or a café latte at a charming little bistro in Paris.

We'd also both used tumbled-travertine tiles to serve as wainscoted walls, but Sullivan had added a granite drink rail to the wainscoting, which was a nice touch; I should have thought of it. In my mind's eye, I was envisioning a wheatlike color above the wainscoting, something full-spectrum and highly mixed that could be almost chameleonlike—changing hues according to the sunlight that would slant through Stephanie's French doors.

"We could put a cove in the ceiling over the pool table. Maybe install copper tiles," I said.

"Or even hand-troweled plaster, with pewter paint."

"Yes."

He gave me a crooked smile. "I like what you did with the space behind the wet bar. I'll incorporate that into my drawing, then we're good to go."

"I'll start on a presentation board." Then I said on an impulse, "Tell you what, Steve. Why don't we agree to extend our partnership to include splitting my salary for the job at Helen's down the middle?"

He cocked an eyebrow. "Why would you want to do that? I said I was willing to accept workman's wages. And to forgo my fee entirely if I got Stephanie's job."

"Yeah, but I probably wouldn't have gotten the assignment in the first place if you hadn't happened to be in

California when Stephanie was looking to hire you. And we're already splitting the earnings for Stephanie's place."

He shrugged. "Fine by me."

Although stung by his lack of gratitude for my generosity, I continued, "I also want to try to convince Stephanie and Peter to let me add an elaborate workroom in back of Helen's house. She's got plenty of land back there. I'm thinking of a long space with lots of windows and counters, and, of course, tons of cabinets for storage."

"Uh-huh," he said with a nod. His eyes were getting the faraway look that I recognized was from his mentally picturing my idea. "Sounds good." He rolled up my sketch and tucked it under his arm. "You never know. Maybe 'Sullivan and Gilbert' is meant to be, after all."

I was stunned at his parting words, but he left without waiting for my response.

An hour and a half after Sullivan and I parted company, I was hard at work in my office, trying to get my ideas on paper for my proposed new storage space at Helen's house. The door opened and an elderly male voice called, "You up there, Erin?"

Was that Teddy? "Yes, I'm here. Just up the stairs."

"Good! No sense in climbing a flight of stairs for nothing. It's Teddy Frederickson. And Helen, too. We'll be right there."

I shut the drawer that contained copies of the articles on the trial and checked hastily to make sure that there were no other embarrassing items in plain view. I'd left the second copy with the dispatcher to give to Linda whenever she returned to the station house.

The lank Teddy being much taller than Helen, he came into view first. When he beamed at me and said, "Hi, ho, Erin!" I returned the smile, but felt a pang of guilt. Despite my assurances to Audrey earlier at the funeral, I now truly *was* forming a list of suspects. Teddy Frederickson's name had moved into the very top spot.

A step behind him, Helen's cheeks were flushed, and she was grabbing the rail with both hands. Teddy reached back to help her, but she swatted his hand away.

"I need your help, Erin," Helen said.

"Of course. Anything. What can I do?"

She slipped into the stuffed chair in front of my desk, then Teddy took the seat beside her. She straightened the hem of her black funeral dress, before answering. "Teddy and I are setting a trap for Rachel."

"Oh, no," I moaned.

Teddy wagged a bony index finger at me. "We know Rachel's the person who has been breaking into Helen's house," he explained. "We think she's behind everything. All that nonsense about seeing a prowler. Give me a break! She set up her own husband to be fried!"

I winced. "Why would she do that?"

He spread his arms dramatically. "To off her husband, of course! It's the only explanation. Jack was no fool. He wouldn't have stepped into water in a basement like that; he'd have known he might get fried. So here's what I'm sure happened. She follows him across the street, see, and gives him a little push. *Zappo!*" He smacked his palms on my desktop. "No more pesky spouse!"

"The marriage had been in trouble for at least ten years," Helen added in a much less lurid tone. "They weren't getting along...they were fighting like cats and dogs."

"But they could have simply gotten a divorce. That's what most incompatible couples do."

"Rachel Schwartz is obviously more money-driven than most people," Teddy insisted. "Why divorce your spouse and split the assets when you can off him and keep it *all*?"

Helen frowned but added, "We do already know that she's stolen valuables from my home."

"Yet you weren't willing to tell the police that," I reminded her sharply.

"She told *me*, though," Teddy interjected. "Let's not forget that I'm a retired policeman."

"More or less," Helen muttered.

"The point is," Teddy said, leaning forward and gripping the edge of my desk, "I know how to catch her in the act, and when I do, I'll make a citizen's arrest."

"That's why I need your help, Erin," Helen said. "We need you as an impartial witness."

"For when things go down tonight," Teddy added eagerly.

"Wouldn't it make more sense to have an actual police officer there when you...spring the trap? So that you can make an *actual* arrest?"

Helen sighed. "I thought of that, too, dear. But the biggest concession Teddy was willing to make was to let you be there."

He chuckled and rose. "Come on, Erin! You're a young woman! Live it up a little. Take some risks! You don't actually think you have to worry about any of us being taken out by Rachel Schwartz, do you? Why, I'm a trained officer of the law! I could handle this with both hands tied behind my back!"

The phone rang, but I decided to let the machine get it. "Please, let's think this thing through for a minute."

Teddy lifted his palms in a gesture of resignation and reclaimed his seat.

"Helen," I pleaded, "I really don't think this is a good idea. You're talking about springing out at someone while they're in the midst of committing a serious crime. In the very household in which a man lost his life." I listened with half an ear as the machine picked up and continued, "There's no way you can—"

"Erin," the caller said, "it's Linda. I got the—"

I lunged at the receiver and shut off the machine just in the nick of time, before Linda could go on to mention the articles I'd given her. "Hi. I've got some people in my office. Can I call you back?"

"Uh, sure."

"Okay. Thanks. Bye." I hung up.

Helen was studying my face, her brow furrowed. She cast a furtive glance in Teddy's direction, and I got the impression that she might have deciphered the gist of what Linda wanted to discuss with me. All Helen said now, however, was: "So you won't come?"

I met her steady gaze. "Teddy's plan is really risky."

"You really think that Rachel Schwartz is going to break in to Helen's house, armed with an Uzi?" He chuckled.

"What if you're wrong? What if it *isn't* Rachel?"

"It is," Helen said firmly. "I'm certain. And as sorry as I feel for her losing her husband, that doesn't give her the right to steal my possessions. I'm determined to embarrass that woman and get her to give me my statuettes back! Will you come tonight?"

I grimaced. The smart thing to do was to call Linda right now and tell her about this whole silly scheme. Yet I also knew full well that I wasn't going to *do* the smart thing. Instead, I was going to indulge the childish part of me. And Mini Me didn't want to be denied the pleasure of catching Helen's burglar in the act and, perhaps, solving Jack's murder in the process. "Let me see if Steve Sullivan can join us, just for strength in numbers."

"Excellent!" Teddy sprang to his feet with renewed energy. "Helen's going to leave right on time, just like always, for her meeting. Then she'll drive around back, where I'll be waiting for her. We all need to be sure to park in a street behind the house and take the alley to her back door."

"Will do." I resisted a childish temptation to give a mock salute.

"We'll see you there! Eight P.M., sharp!"

Before she and Teddy could head down the stairs, I took the opportunity to show Helen my preliminary sketches of the addition I had in mind for her house. She loved them (as did Teddy), and after a brief game of phone tag with Peter, Stephanie, and Sullivan, I managed to make an appointment at Helen's house for the next morning, which was Saturday, for Sullivan and me to present my idea to them.

Anxious to discuss my wanting his help tonight in person, I ducked into Sullivan's office later that evening. His space bore a masculine, modern look—clean lines, all very chic and Zen-like in its red, smoky gray, and whisky tones. He was on the phone and gave me a crooked grin as he hung up. "What's up, Gilbert?"

"I needed to see if you can come to Helen's house in a couple hours. Are you doing anything tonight at eight?"

He cocked an eyebrow. "Of course I am. It's Friday... date night."

His statement hit me like a blast of bitter cold air. He was seeing somebody. Maybe they'd met in California. That could certainly explain why he'd suddenly cooled our relationship and crept back into town without a word. I forced a smile. "Right. Forgot it was a Friday. No biggie."

Sullivan was going to be off on some hot date tonight, while I was on my own, chaperoning senior citizens intent on playing cops and robbers—with real-life robbers! I turned and grabbed the doorknob.

"Why? Is this important?"

Not unless there's gunplay. "No, no. Teddy and Helen are just testing a silly theory."

"What theory?"

His phone chirped. Maybe that was his "date" calling. "Nothing worth changing your big plans for. Have a nice evening."

Feeling like a complete ass, I let myself out the door before he could stop me. If things fell apart at Helen's house, I could picture myself sitting at the police station afterward, being grilled by O'Reilly and having to admit, "Yes, Detective. Shrewd observation. I am indeed missing my nose. I cut it off tonight to spite my face. You see, I couldn't swallow my pride long enough to tell Mr. Stuffed-Shirt Sullivan that I needed him to postpone his tryst with some other woman and make sure that Helen's burglar could be overpowered."

At eight P.M. "sharp," I was still kicking myself as I walked from where I'd parked, having taken a circuitous route through the neighborhood to avoid being spotted by nosey Rachel. I never should have agreed to any of this.

Helen and Teddy greeted me at her back door, and Teddy told me, "You're just in time, Erin. I spotted Rachel peering out her window at the house, and you can bet she'll be on her way over here any minute now."

"Rachel knows I have a scrapbooking club tonight. Somebody always breaks into my house on Friday nights." I could see Helen smile even in the limited lighting. "This is so much fun," she told Teddy. "I feel like a kid again! I don't know why I didn't try this weeks ago."

"Maybe because common sense prevailed," I couldn't help but retort, although I had to admit that I, too, felt a giddy surge of excitement.

"Now we just wait in the dark," Teddy instructed.

We all took seats in the living room. I'd felt my way to the armchair across from the piano. It was fortunate that this space had been de-cluttered. Otherwise we might not have found chairs so easily. Let alone a hapless intruder.

"Teddy! What's that in your hand?" Helen cried a moment later.

"It's my old service revolver."

"But you promised that there—"

"Don't worry. It's not loaded."

"That's not good enough for me," she persisted.

"Me, either, Teddy. I'm putting a stop to this right this

second unless you put that thing far out of reach," I demanded. "There's a drawer in this end table beside me."

"The gun's not loaded!"

Helen said firmly, "You have till the count of three to do as Erin says, or we're both turning the lights on, and you're leaving my home."

"Fine. Your concerns are stupid, but it *is* your house, so I'm respecting your wishes."

"How come you still have your service revolver?" I asked as I slid the revolver safely into the drawer. "I thought you had to return those things when you left the force."

"It's not the actual weapon. It's a duplicate I purchased myself."

"Shush!" Helen chastised.

We tensed. There were footsteps on the porch. Entering via the front door? Granted, the only house with a view of the front door was Rachel's, but this still seemed awfully brazen.

A key scraped in the lock. My heart started pounding. The prowler unlocked the door and stepped inside.

With a triumphant "Ta dah!" Teddy flipped on the lights.

We gasped in surprise as our burglar stood there, dressed in black from head to toe, cowering in shock at this unexpected exposure.

It wasn't Rachel Schwartz.

It was Helen's nephew.

Peter.

chapter 15

W hat's going on?" Peter said, donning a look of pure innocence. He scanned all three of our faces, finally settling on Helen's steely gaze. "I was just stopping by to check on the house."

Teddy let out a derisive chuckle. "Come off it. You don't actually expect us to believe that, do you?"

Peter spread his arms and pleaded to his aunt, "I've been swinging by your house after I get off work, ever since your neighbor's death. I saw that all the lights were out. I wanted to make sure you weren't having any more trouble with prowlers."

"So you dressed up like one?" Teddy snorted with disbelief.

"I wore black for the funeral earlier today."

Using the trick I used frequently when picturing rooms, I closed my eyes, trying to picture Peter at the funeral; I'd only spotted him briefly, but I could recall that he had indeed been wearing a black shirt of some kind.

"A black turtleneck? Baloney!"

Peter ignored Teddy and continued, "I wanted to make sure there were no lethal booby traps in your house ... like the electrified water in your basement. I'm simply trying to protect you, Aunt Helen."

Teddy stepped between them. "Don't be looking to your aunt to bail you out of your jam, Mr. Miller. Why are you breaking into her house? Grand theft? Attempted murder? Either way, it's a federal offense."

Peter shot him a look of pure disdain. "My mom was living here just twelve weeks ago! And I'm not 'breaking into her house.' I have a *key*! Since when is using one's own house key to check in on an elderly relative a crime?"

"I'm not as elderly as all that, Peter," Helen said. "And I'm still sharp enough to recognize when somebody's trying to con me."

Pacing in front of Peter as though he fancied himself as some sort of cogitating Sherlockian, Teddy said, "Don't lie to us, son."

Peter's face was nearly purple with anger. "Don't you dare call me that! I am *not* your son, thank God! And I've got a lot more right to be here than you do, so stop acting like you're the man in charge of this household!"

"I'm just trying to get at the truth, and we all—"

"That's enough, Teddy." Helen rose from the piano

bench. "Thank you for your help, but I'll take it from here."

Teddy's jaw dropped. His bravura instantly drained from him. "What do you mean?"

"You can go home now. Erin's here. She can serve as mediator."

Teddy shifted his injured gaze to me for a moment. "But... *I'm* the one who's trained in interrogation techniques, Helen." He shook a fist at Peter. "This chump is obviously trying to play the nephew card to get away with stealing from you. Lois admitted to me that she let him practically bankrupt her. He—"

"Hey! Leave my mother out of this, or else!" Peter shouted.

Teddy jabbed a finger at him. "You're the one we caught breaking and entering, Petey boy! So you have no right to make threats!"

"Again, Teddy, *I have a key*! And *you're* the one who's trying to weasel his way into my family fortune!" The men squared off and were practically spitting in each other's faces.

"Time to go home, Teddy." Helen grabbed his arm and tried to tug him toward the door.

Glaring at Peter all the while, Teddy wrested his arm away from her grasp. "Fine, Helen. I'll do as asked. *I* am a gentleman. Unlike someone *else* I could mention."

Peter balled his fists, but held his tongue.

"Remember, I'm just a phone call away if you need me," he said gently to Helen. He went to the table beside me and retrieved his gun, which he jammed into his waistband. He focused a hateful glare at Peter and dragged his finger across his throat, then left through the kitchen, letting himself out through the back door.

Helen sighed. She shook her head, settled into the beige recliner that she'd recently unburied (in favor of re-burying the kitchen), and gestured for Peter to take her now-vacated position on the piano bench. "Sit down, Peter. Tell me what's really going on here."

He followed his aunt's directive and perched on the bench, looking as precarious and out-of-place as a rooster on a telephone wire. "I . . . like looking at my parents' old things in privacy. I know it's corny and nostalgic, but it helps me focus whenever I'm upset. So, to comfort my-self, I come here sometimes when I know you're not going to be around."

Helen rolled her eyes. "Cut the crap, Peter. I'm a re-tired high school teacher. I can spot malarkey a mile away."

He stared at his lap for a long moment. He had a bald spot near the center of his dark brown hair. He was turn-ing into a real nebbish—a pudgy middle-aged man who would steal from his own relatives rather than work hard. He mumbled, "None of this was my idea. It was Rachel's."

Evenly, Helen asked, "That's how she got my porcelain dancers? You stole them from me and gave them to her?"

He nodded, his eyes still averted.

"But why?"

He shrugged—the proverbial little boy with his hand caught in the cookie jar. "Rachel really wanted them. She convinced me you wouldn't even miss them."

"What was in it for you?" Helen asked.

I had a hunch that the porcelain was payment for Rachel's running surveillance on Helen's house while he stole Helen's collectibles, but this being a family matter, I held my tongue, opting to make myself as unobtrusive as possible.

Again he took a long time before answering. Then he sighed, the muscles in his jaw working. "The deal was: I gave Rachel part of . . . what I took, in exchange for notifying me when the coast was clear to enter and . . . remove items."

"I see. So you've been stealing from me for how long now?"

He finally looked up. "Hey, it's not *theft*, Aunt Helen. Everything I took already belongs to me. I inherited them from my mother."

Another lie. The porcelain figurines he'd given to Rachel belonged to Helen. Had he gone to all this trouble just to avoid having to share their parents' estate with his sister? Surely Stephanie would eventually notice if Lois's most valuable possessions had been removed from this house. Maybe Peter had counted on claiming that Helen had lost their mother's things, once Helen had passed away and could no longer defend herself.

Helen cleared her throat. She asked, "How long has this been going on?"

In a near whisper, he answered, "Ever since Mother's death."

Helen paled. After a moment, she asked quietly, "What exactly have you taken?"

He ran both palms over his hair. "In my defense, you haven't even *noticed* anything was gone. Meantime, that's how I've kept my private practice afloat. I've been making a tidy profit on eBay. You name it, some nut out there someplace will collect it."

"I *have* noticed, Peter, dear. And not everything you've taken belonged to your mother. As, I'm sure, you're very well aware."

"Sorry, Aunt Helen," he said meekly.

That was it? He was just going to shrug this off—concede his role as the ne'er-do-well nephew? Assume his despicable behavior would have no consequences? And was Helen too kindhearted to press him further? "What exactly have you taken?" I asked him, repeating Helen's unanswered question and breaking my resolve to keep quiet.

He fired a stay-out-of-this glare in my direction.

"Peter?" Helen prompted.

"I dunno. Not all that much, really." He shrugged. "I have it all written down, though. The list is back at my office."

The doorbell chimed. After a deep sigh of resignation, Helen called out, "Come in, Rachel."

Rachel leaned in the door, and with a sheepish smile, said, "Good evening, Helen." She held out a plate of what looked like a small cake, jauntily covered in magenta-tinted plastic wrap with a glittery silver bow atop. "I brought you a slice of crumb cake. As a peace offering."

"Crumb cake?" Helen scoffed. "You really had to dig deep for an excuse to come over this time, didn't you?"

"Pardon?"

Helen frowned and didn't reply. I explained on her behalf, "Peter's just told us about how he gave you Helen's porcelain figurines in exchange for your playing lookout person when Helen left her home. Such as she did *tonight*, when she pretended to leave for a meeting."

"What?! Why, I never!" she huffed.

"Drop the I'm-so-offended routine!" Peter snapped at her. "This was all *your* idea in the first place!"

Rachel gaped at him. "Peter Miller! How dare you tell such an outrageous, hateful lie! To think that, all this time, I've been on *your* side! You were the one who told me over and over again that—" Her eyes flew wide. "My God! You've been lying to me all along, haven't you, Peter? You've been making yourself out to be this big softy, cruelly orphaned, bullied by his domineering sister and his willful aunt, when—"

Peter leapt to his feet. "I never said anything of the kind! Aunt Helen, she's twisting *everything* around!"

"Rachel, please go home. Now." Helen's voice was quiet, yet resolute.

Her cheeks now almost as crimson as her lipstick, Rachel nodded. She set the festively wrapped cake on the small pedestal table near the door. "I am so, so sorry, Helen. Like I explained at Jack's funeral, my medication caused me to lose my head at the TV station. But I have no excuse now. I let myself get duped into helping your nephew take his things from your home without your consent. That's . . . unforgivable." She lifted her chin. "I'd told myself it was a win-win situation. Jack and I used to worry all the time that one of your enormous junk piles would topple, and you'd be crushed. But . . . that wasn't really why I did what I did. Truth be told, I was too tempted by Peter's offer of your porcelain to say no."

Peter stomped his foot. "It's the other way around, Aunt Helen! *I'm* the one who was too weak to resist *her* offer!"

Helen rubbed her forehead and murmured, "Oh, Peter . . ."

"Please don't be angry with me." Peter strode up to his

aunt and gripped her hands, which looked so tiny and fragile in his. "The only person I was really cheating was Stephanie. And I'll swear on my mother's grave that I wasn't here the night Jack Schwartz was killed. This had nothing to do with that. I'd never have risked hurting you, Aunt Helen. Never."

Helen extracted her hands. "I'm going to need to see an itemized list of everything you took from this house. For one thing, those dancer figurines were mine, not Lois's. They were given to me by a gentleman friend who had personal connections to the Spanish factory that made them. He gave me a figurine on our first date, and on our monthly anniversaries."

Rachel seemed to be on the verge of tears. "I'll bring them right back, Helen. The two that Peter took from you, I mean. I've had the other eight for years."

"Ever since you first saw mine," Helen snarled. "I know."

Rachel winced, and her eyes misted. "I deserved that. I've done a terrible thing. But I'm also terribly sorry." She took a ragged breath. "At least Jack didn't live to see this day...and learn just how selfish and greedy his wife could be."

Looking both stunned and touched, Helen said, "Heaven knows we're *all* capable of making poor choices, Rachel."

She gave Helen a grateful smile. Then she curled her lip with disgust as she peered at Peter and walked away. In a choked voice, she cried, "Enjoy your cake, Helen," as she left.

"Thank you," Helen called after her.

Peter wobbled but stood his ground, looking mortified

by Rachel's accusations. When Helen avoided his gaze, he turned sheepishly to me and said in a quiet voice, "It was *my* stuff. Mostly."

I had no reply.

"Aunt Helen, I…" He stopped and tried again. "I'm just so…I really didn't…" His shoulders sagged with defeat, and he stared at the greenish-gold rug below his feet. Finally Peter gave his aunt a hug around the shoulders and a kiss on the cheek, then let himself out, quietly closing the door behind them.

Peter's actions made no sense to me. If he merely needed his inheritance sooner rather than later, he could have asked his aunt to let him have what was rightfully his. And the porcelain that he'd freely given to Rachel was surely as valuable as anything he might otherwise have been forced to divvy up with his sister. "Helen? If some of the items Peter took were actually yours, you may want to consider pressing charges."

She shook her head. "No, Erin."

"I know it would be painful for you to report such a thing to the police, but your candies *were* poisoned, so somebody is playing for keeps."

"Peter had nothing to do with that. And he's my only nephew. I'm not turning him in to the police over this."

"Fine." I disagreed with the decision, but it was hers to make.

Tomorrow morning, Sullivan and I were scheduled to come here and present our new design to Stephanie, Helen…and Peter. That was bound to be more than a little awkward. "Should we postpone tomorrow's meeting with—"

"No, Erin. Peter, Stephanie, and I need to patch this

up right away. If I've learned anything in this life, it's that things only get worse when you let them fester."

I dearly wished that I wouldn't have to witness either the patching or the festering quite so soon. My vision happened to fall on the cake. "Maybe I should have the police analyze the cake, just in case."

"Before more mice are killed, you mean?" The phone rang. Suddenly looking both world-weary and old, she shuffled toward it. "Go ahead and take it, Erin. Although I very much doubt Rachel would be so brazen as to poison it." She smiled and winked at me, but that was an obvious—and heartrending—attempt to cover for her immense sorrow. "Well, Erin, provided the phone hasn't been rigged to explode when I pick up the receiver, I'll see you tomorrow."

I picked up the cake while she answered. She gave me the okay sign as she said a shaky: "Hello?" Then she turned her back to me. I took that as a sign that I should let myself out as she said, "Oh, hi, Stephanie. What a coincidence that you called. I was just...thinking of you."

The next morning, Linda called to inform me that she'd pulled in all kinds of favors to get the cake tested for poisons immediately, but it was "just plain cake." The phone rang a second time moments after I'd hung up. I assumed it would be Linda who'd forgotten to tell me something, but it was Sullivan. He told me that he was going to pick me up an hour earlier than planned; Stephanie had just now informed him that, before she could "'make an informed decision on whether or not to fund an addition at Aunt Helen's house,'" she needed to see our design for her game room. "Weird, eh?" he added.

She wants to grill me about what happened last night with her brother. This was a designer's biggest nightmare—getting caught between warring family members. If I wasn't careful, Stephanie was going to want to kill the messenger, as they say; we could get the boot from both of her assignments. Maybe I could circumvent matters simply by refusing to go. "I'm running a bit late, Sullivan. Why don't you show our design to Stephanie yourself? I'll catch up with you at Helen's house."

"No way. You've got our presentation board, remember?"

"Oh, right."

"So I'll be there in about forty-five minutes. You can be ready by then, can't you? Otherwise, just…come as you are. Okay?"

I told him I'd be ready, and we muttered our good-byes.

An hour later, Stephanie let us into the posh Turkish-tile foyer of her spectacular house and remained standing by the door as she asked to "see what you've got cooking so far."

With the three of us standing awkwardly near the door, she flipped through our presentation board and drawings. I persisted in pointing out the photographs of gorgeous wrought-iron bar stools we'd selected. "The pictures don't do justice to the cognac leather, Stephanie. Just wait until you touch them. They're buttery soft."

"And we're picking up the buffed sandstone in your window well to use in the stone columns to either side of the bar," Sullivan said. "Pulls the outside indoors."

"Looks good," she said, and handed them back to Sullivan.

Good? It was freaking brilliant! "Oh, and I wanted to show you this, too," I said, handing her the picture of an astonishing, tiny chandelier. "I happened across this the other day. I was thinking you could hang two of these fixtures on either side of the mirror in the downstairs powder room."

Her eyes lit up and she mouthed a silent *wow*.

"Each one of those glass pieces is beveled and hand-made. It'll be like giving the room diamond earrings. Aren't they spectacular?"

"Yes. Yes, they are, Erin." With obvious reluctance, she handed the photograph back to me.

"I was thinking that, when you're ready to spruce up that bathroom, we could do Bordeaux walls with a pewter wash, and a silver ceiling...maybe even turn that rosewood console you're not really utilizing in your office into a vanity...put a smoked-glass bowl on top and use a swan-like antiqued-bronze faucet."

"Oh, wow, Erin. That sounds—"

"It'll be so beautiful. It will feel almost like you're walking into a luscious, bejeweled plum."

"Yes. Precisely!" The woman was practically drooling!

I grinned, thrilled that my plan had worked and I'd distracted her from all possible ulterior motives for asking us here.

Sullivan, who had finished slipping our artwork back into the portfolio case, said, "Let's set our next appointment, Stephanie. We need to choose some of the accessories for your wet bar."

Instantly, the spell was broken. Stephanie was back to

being curt and bossy as we blocked out time on our schedules. Then she glanced at her watch. "Good. Our meeting didn't take long at all." She glared at me. "Now that we have some free time, Erin, what exactly did you catch Peter doing at Aunt Helen's house?"

Damn! In my peripheral vision, I could see Sullivan's eyes widen in surprise. I felt a pang of guilt. I'd neglected to tell him about last night, even though I'd known full well what Stephanie's true purpose was for asking us here. Was I subconsciously punishing him for not instantly canceling his date in order to be with me? "Pardon?" I said, stalling.

Her glare intensified. If she furrowed her brow any further, her beady eyes would be squeezed shut. "You heard me."

"How much did Peter or Helen tell you?" I asked her.

"Why don't you just answer my question, and let me worry about how much repetitive information I'm getting. All right?"

So much for my staying out of a family squabble. I sighed. "Your aunt and I discovered that he's been letting himself into her house and removing things. He said that everything he took belonged to his mother and was his rightful inheritance."

Every muscle in Stephanie's body tensed, and her cheeks turned almost scarlet, but she said only, "I see."

Sullivan and I exchanged glances. "I guess you'll want to postpone our meeting with the two of you and your aunt later this morning," he said to her. "So why don't we—"

"No. Today is perfect. If nothing else, that will allow me to see my darling brother in person. He won't have the guts to stay away from this particular shindig. He'd be too afraid Aunt Helen would cut him out of her will." She opened the door. "So I'll see you there at ten o'clock sharp. All rightee?"

"Maybe it'd be best if Steve and I came a few minutes late. We wouldn't want to interrupt a—"

"Be on time," she snapped. "It's all I can do to cram these frivolous meetings about Aunt Helen's house into my schedule as it is."

We left, Sullivan cracking me up as we drove away by saying, "You know what makes this career so terrific, Gilbert? The power! Our clients treat us like gods!"

"It *is* something of an ego trip."

"And next up, we get to go to a 'frivolous meeting.' On a Saturday morning, no less! Hoo, boy! Who wouldn't love *that*?"

Again, I laughed. I'd underestimated the man. He was being incredibly nice to let me off the hook; we both knew I should have warned him about a source of contention with our client.

He said in serious tones, "Since we have some time, let's go back to your office and fine-tune our presentation."

"I was just about to suggest that," I said happily, and beamed at him like a lovesick schoolgirl. *That*, of course, was as far from my actual state of mind as was humanly possible. It's just that it was so nice to discover that I could get along with Sullivan, after all.

He frowned, his mood suddenly darkening. "Good, 'cuz you need to fill me in on whatever happened at Helen's house last night. What the hell was Stephanie talking about?"

"So much for our getting along," I muttered to myself.

chapter 16

We're holding your presentation in the garage," Helen called to Sullivan and me a short time later, gesturing for us to hurry up her driveway. "We're just waiting on Stephanie."

"Be right there," I replied with a smile, although my expression changed to a grimace the instant she'd ducked back into the empty half of her garage. The lighting and ambiance were dreadful there; this would be a terrible setting for our presentation.

As we unloaded our easel and portfolio, Sullivan asked under his breath, "Think it'll work to bribe her with a five-percent discount if we can meet in the living room instead of the garage?"

"No, but we could give it a shot even so."

Peter was pacing in front of the pink polyester sofa when we entered the garage. I'd managed to forget the fact that he and Sullivan had never met. He dashed up to Steve to introduce himself, then shook his hand vigorously. His giddiness was probably due to his relief at having one person present who wasn't mad at him.

"Peter arrived early to apologize to me another dozen times," Helen said matter-of-factly to me. "And before you ask, we can't move this discussion into the house. I'm letting Ella and Vator have free run there, so that they don't get anxious at having a whole crowd in the joint."

Before we could make a countersuggestion, Stephanie's Mercedes pulled into the driveway. She emerged and swept toward us, her eyes locked on Peter. "There you are! You sniveling little worm! Isn't it bad enough that you all but bankrupted Mother? Now you have to try to do the same to Aunt Helen?"

"Morning, Sis-boom-bah," he said, in what I gathered was a pet name for his sister.

She put her hands on her hips and gave him a visual once-over. Casting a quick glance at Sullivan and me, she explained, "Bet he never told you that Mother had to bail him out of a financial jam a few years ago. She had to mortgage our childhood home to the hilt. That's why she had to move in with Helen. By the time we paid off all the creditors after her death, there wasn't a penny left."

Peter muttered, "So now you're trying to recoup your losses, at Aunt Helen's expense."

"That's a lie! I'm trying to protect my own interests, yes,

but Aunt Helen's as well. And you've been going through everything in her entire house, haven't you? That's why the boxes in the basement are so nicely labeled, isn't it? I'll bet you put *my* stuff on the very bottom, because you *knew* you were going to flood the place to try to kill her!"

"That's outrageous!" Peter shrieked. "How dare you accuse me of trying to murder Aunt Helen!"

"You—"

"Stop it, Stephanie, Peter," Helen demanded. "You're scaring the cats." The accuracy of the statement was highly doubtful, considering that Ella and Vator were nowhere in sight, but before Stephanie could call her on it, Helen said, "Peter, you can set up the folding chairs, if you please." She pressed the button on the wall and the door began its noisy descent. "Steve, right in front of the sofa is a fine spot for the easel."

Stephanie's jaw dropped. "We have to sit in the *garage*, Aunt Helen? *Again?*"

"It's the largest open space."

"But I saw your living room just last night! It's as close to neat as I've ever seen it, thanks to Gilbert and Sullivan!"

I wasn't willing to interrupt and admit that Helen had been the one to clear out her living room—at the expense of the kitchen. But Stephanie must have come over after her phone call to her aunt. So Stephanie had been deliberately pulling me into the middle earlier this morning by insisting that I tell her myself about her brother's transgressions.

Helen said to Stephanie, "Be that as it may, a man died in my house because of a booby trap. *This* is the only place I feel safe." She sat down on the closest chair, and

Peter quickly claimed the one beside her. He'd left the folding chair for Stephanie leaning against Helen's sedan.

"Why is that? Does the smell of gasoline and motor oil invoke a sense of security in you? Is it the car fumes? I'm sure we can get some spray cans of Eau de Garage for your living room so you can feel *safe* there, too. Meanwhile your houseguests can sit in relative comfort."

"Steph!" Peter said. "If she wants us in the garage, let's sit in the garage and get this over with."

With an exaggerated sigh, Stephanie grabbed her chair and thumped it down directly in front of her brother's, blocking his view of the easel. "This isn't going to help you, you realize, Peter. Aunt Helen knows you're taking her side because you're desperate to get back on her good side. It's going to take a lot more than—"

"Let's talk about room design now, shall we?" Helen cut in. "We can resume our delightful conversation after Erin and Steve leave."

The doorbell rang, the remote doorbell that Jack had installed, playing the first stanza of "Twinkle, Twinkle, Little Star." Helen promptly rose, pressed the button, and the double-wide garage door growled open once more.

"This is not exactly how I envisioned this presentation going," I whispered to Sullivan.

"We're in here, Rachel," Helen called. "Peter," she instructed, "set up another folding chair. This will be Rachel, too curious about all the commotion to stay away."

Sure enough, it was Rachel who ducked through the doorway. She scanned our faces, cleared her throat, and said, "There you are, Helen."

"Yes, and here you are, Rachel. Again." She punched the

button for the door, which began to shut behind Rachel, and she reclaimed her seat, turning her back on Rachel.

Rachel looked at Sullivan and me. "You're showing a new design for Helen's house?"

"Yes, or at least we hope to do so, eventually," I replied.

She returned her gaze to Helen, putting a hand over her heart. "Oh, Helen, I'm so relieved! I saw everyone arrive and was afraid you'd had some sort of emergency. I just wanted to make sure everything was okay. As I'm now so painfully aware, life can be quite fragile..."

"I'm fine, Rachel," Helen said in a monotone. "Thank you for your concern."

"Oh, dear. I've interrupted, haven't I? I'm a little jumpy, in the wake of my husband's death. But as long as I'm here...Stephanie? Did your aunt already tell you our good news?"

"Good news?" Stephanie scoffed. "No, I'd have remembered that."

"Your aunt and I have patched things up between us," Rachel announced. "Although the police have foolishly decided to write off poor Jack's death as an accident, I'm now quite certain it was the prowler who killed him."

"And by 'prowler,' you mean my brother, Peter?" Stephanie asked pointedly.

"I told you already, I was not *here* the night of the accident!" Peter yelled. "That must have been the killer who ran off, not me!"

"It wasn't Peter," Rachel echoed. "He's never worn a ski cap, and he usually wears his regular clothes when he enters the house. Furthermore, he never once came here without my first giving him the coast-is-clear phone call.

This was the real thing—an authentic prowler. My Jack died valiantly, trying to rescue Helen. As well as dear little Kitty Vator."

Stephanie chortled.

Rachel's cheeks colored to the same hue as the roses in her floral-print blouse. With hands on her hips, she demanded, "I beg your pardon? You find my husband's death *amusing*, do you?"

Still chuckling, Stephanie said, "Sorry, Rachel, but... come on. Save Helen from *what*? Aunt Helen wasn't even *here* at the time. So Jack was merely rescuing a cat from getting her paws wet."

"That is a cruel thing to say! You're going to sit there and make fun of my husband's death?"

"I didn't mean to be indelicate. I was merely—"

"*Indelicate?* You mocked the love of my life, who's been wrenched from this world!"

"Oh, please! Just how much sympathy do you expect me or anyone else in my family to show you? *You're* the one who plotted to steal from my family's estate!"

"Your brother's to blame for that, not me. Peter's the one who called me and convinced me to take part in it. Which I only did because I could see how desperate he was, having to protect his inheritance from the likes of you!"

Peter shouted at Rachel, "It was *your*—"

"Shut up!" Stephanie sprang to her feet and headed for the door to Helen's kitchen. "I've been patient long enough! Come on, Aunt Helen. We're moving into the house."

"No, Stephanie," Helen said, rising. "And, Rachel, this

is my garage, not yours, so if you don't care for the company—"

Stephanie raised her voice another notch. "As executor of my mother's estate, I need to take immediate possession of my mother's personal effects. Aunt Helen, I've reminded you on more than one occasion that my brother and I only agreed to *delay* allocating her personal effects. We did *not* agree to let you keep them indefinitely."

She took another step toward the house, but Helen blocked her path. "This isn't your property. Not yet, anyway. You have no right to make a demand like that!"

"Actually, Aunt Helen, she *does*," Peter said meekly. "There was no rider on Mother's will saying you could keep her possessions. She probably never envisioned her estate being combined with yours."

"And whose fault is that, Peter?" his sister snarled. "Our mother lived here for more than two years. You're a lawyer, for God's sake! You should have suggested she update her will."

"*You* should have, too!"

"I *did*! But she would only listen to *you*!" Stephanie glared down at Helen, who hadn't budged from her post at the door. "You won't let me leave through the front door? Fine. We'll do this your way, then." She punched the button for the garage-door opener. "Let's just let all the passersby see what a ridiculous old ninny you are... sitting out here with your guests in the *garage*."

"One of us is going to watch out for our aunt!" Peter shouted at his sister. "It's obviously going to have to be me!"

"Oh, get off your high horse, Peter!" Stephanie all but shoved Rachel out of her path as she headed for her car.

"You're not going to convince Aunt Helen to make you her sole beneficiary, no matter how you act now. So you can just drop the phony Prince Charming routine."

He faced his aunt. "I have *never* sought to be your sole beneficiary, Aunt Helen. Regardless of how much more I need the money than she does."

At the top of the driveway, Stephanie stopped, pivoted, and brushed past Rachel again—who was having a hard time suppressing a grin—as she walked up to Helen. Gently she said, "Aunt Helen, I apologize for my bluntness. And for my brother's simpering. But as the de facto head of this family, I'm going to have to insist that my mother's possessions be separated from yours immediately. Anything you two purchased in common, you can keep. I'm afraid this is the only way we can keep Peter from pilfering yet more belongings from your house."

"That's very noble of you, my dear, but since when did you care about someone removing *my* belongings?" Helen asked. "And do you really think your duties as 'head of this family' include trying to drive me out of my house and home?"

Stephanie was momentarily taken aback, but then shot back, "You aren't safe in your house with its wall-to-wall clutter. If the only way I can keep you safe is to force you to live in a retirement home, that's what I'm going to do. Because, yes, Aunt Helen, I *do* really think that's my duty."

A palpable tension hung in the air as we watched Stephanie leave. Finally Peter broke the silence, saying, "Again, Aunt Helen, I'm sorry for entering your house without your permission and removing some of Mother's things. Maybe I'll go now, while the door's open." He strode down the driveway.

"You know, Helen, all families are a little dysfunctional," Rachel said, patting her on the shoulder. "If there's a competency hearing, I'm willing to testify in court that I'll look out for you."

Helen chuckled. "Thanks, Rachel. The one thing we know about you is you're a good watchdog."

Rachel arched her eyebrow, but said, "I'll take that as a compliment."

"And so, in summary," Sullivan said in Helen's direction, "we're grateful that you allowed us to work on this project. We had a lot of fun designing it, and we're confident that you'll have even more fun as you enjoy your new sunny and spacious room. Any questions?"

I didn't dare look at him, for fear that I'd lose my composure and laugh.

Helen said, "Can I at least see your finished drawings?" she asked.

Sullivan and I exchanged glances. "Of course." He removed the black cover from the display board.

"Oh, my! This is wonderful!" Helen cried. "I'm so sorry Stephanie and Peter stormed off before they could see this. All that counter space and drawers . . . It's just so practical. It'll take me *years* to fill up that much storage space."

Music to any designer's ear, I inwardly grumbled.

"It's very nice," Rachel agreed with a nod.

"We're going to have to discuss the plans for real at a future time," Helen said, "but thank you both for doing those lovely drawings."

Rachel insisted on helping us to take down the easel, then further insisted on carrying it to the van. "Oh, that room you two designed is just so beautiful!" Rachel exclaimed, now that Helen was out of earshot. "Would it be terribly selfish of me to ask that you build one for me, too? At my house? I'd like it to be identical to Helen's...only bigger."

The rest of the morning, Sullivan and I worked quickly and efficiently in Helen's den—as well as a quick touch-up on her kitchen. We hauled two full truckloads away. Underneath the detritus in the den, the room had the potential for being a cheerful little retreat. There were charming built-in cabinets that hadn't seen the light of day in years, which featured loving extra touches like dental moldings, and medallions at the center of the cabinet-door panels. By all rights, this should have been the nicest room in the house—and very soon it would be once again.

Unfortunately, part of the reason things were going so well was that Helen had stopped battling to keep anything. All of the fight seemed to have gone out of her. When she told us without a second glance to donate the numerous bags of tattered men's clothing that had somehow wound up in her den, I asked if everything was all right.

"I'm fine. I'm just tired."

Searching for a happy subject matter as Sullivan and I were leaving, I said, "I meant to tell you again how impressed I was with the effects of the bleaching technique that you demonstrated on Audrey's show. In fact, I'm going to try using it on mat boards. I'm framing some pictures for a client."

"You do that much of the detail work on your clients' homes?"

"Sometimes. Wall hangings are such an important piece of an interior that I choose them myself...and sometimes do the framing."

"In that case, I have something for you."

I half expected her to give me a painting she'd squirreled away under her sink, but she returned with a jug of Clorox bleach. "Here. Take this. I only use it for my scrapbooking."

"Oh, there's no need for you to give me your supplies. We have plenty of Clorox in the laundry room at Audrey's."

"Keep this bottle in your office, then. *Someone* might as well get some use out of it."

Strange of me to be taking a client's bleach bottle, but maybe this was a breakthrough of sorts for her—a willingness to let go of her unnecessary possessions. That possibility made me smile. "Thanks, Helen. I'll use it right away."

At my office that afternoon, I'd planned to complete my bookkeeping, but couldn't resist trying my hand at Helen's bleach-and-ink technique first. I poured an inch or so of bleach into a bowl. The phone rang while I was still setting up. It was a client. A rather long-winded one. By the time I was finally able to begin painting, I wondered if the bleach had spoiled somehow. It definitely wasn't working right; instead of removing the color, the paint was pooling. Maybe Helen had diluted it.

I was getting a splitting headache, but was determined to utilize those same lovely ghosting techniques that

Helen had used. I heard the door open at the bottom of the staircase. Just that slight movement of my head as I looked away from the mat board made my vision swim. I needed to get out of here, get myself home and to bed before I got any worse.

I rose, feeling strangely light-headed. I had to lean on the desk as I rounded it. My visitor, I realized dimly, was Steve Sullivan. His cocky grin faded as our eyes met. He came toward me.

Sullivan hooked a finger under my chin and stared into my eyes. For a moment, I thought he was going to kiss me, but he furrowed his brow and said, "Hey, Gilbert. No offense, but you don't look so good."

"I don't feel so good either. I must be coming down with something." I dragged myself back over to my chair and slumped down behind my desk.

"What's this you're working on?" he asked.

"Oh, I'm trying to teach myself how to duplicate the ink-and-bleach techniques that Helen uses sometimes in her scrapbooks."

"Is this the bottle you got from Helen?" he asked, eyeing the liquid with suspicion. "Are you sure it's just bleach?"

"I thought so. Unless . . ." I struggled to my feet again.

"Jeez! Bet it's been mixed with ammonia. Poisonous fumes!" Sullivan grabbed a breath of air over his shoulder, then poured the liquid in the bowl back into its container. He capped it tight and lifted the bottle.

He put his arm around me and ushered me toward the stairs. "Let's get you outside for some fresh air . . . then to the hospital. And while we're at it, we'll take this so-called 'bleach' to the police station."

chapter 17

following our emergency room visit, Steve drove me to the police station. Detective O'Reilly sat across the table from me, drumming his fingers. He'd made it abundantly clear that he resented my having made his life more difficult by almost becoming a murder victim myself, pesky troublemaker that I was. I'd informed him that I felt ill from having inhaled toxic fumes but had gotten no sympathy.

With O'Reilly having lapsed into one of his annoying silences, I muttered, "I'm hoping there will be some tell-tale fingerprints on the doctored bottle. Of bleach."

O'Reilly scowled at me.

"Ironic that bleach is a household cleaner. And that now this bottle of a *cleaning* solution might have some dirty smudges on it that could be evidence. Not to mention the ammonia that was added to the bottle. Which is a second household cleaner. Death by cleaning." Still no reply. "It's almost amusing, when you think about it."

As if O'Reilly could ever be amused. I sighed. He no doubt intimidated suspects with his silences, but I wasn't guilty of anything and wanted to go home. Maybe some idle chatter would annoy him. "You know, I could do wonders with this room. Have you ever thought about hiring an interior designer to jazz up your workplace? I mean, sure, obviously this room is minimalist by function . . . the chrome-and-Formica table, the cheap chairs, the stark overhead lighting. But what's with the chalk white walls and nine-ninety-five-a-yard charcoal industrial carpet? The whole place is so . . . eighties. It might be really effective for you guys to establish a sharp contrast in this space . . . kind of like playing good cop/bad cop with the décor, you know? The officers could be in really nice posh chairs, and the wall behind them could be textured and painted a soothing sage green and illuminated with soft task lighting. That way your suspects will be thinking: I want to be on the nice half of the room. I want to change my ways and—"

"What I don't get, Ms. Gilbert, is why and how you always manage to land right smack in the middle of murder investigations. Do you go *looking* for murderers? Or is there something in your character that makes murderers seek you out?"

"That's something of a no-win question, Detective

O'Reilly. I'll have to let 'I don't know' suffice. Any other questions?"

"Do you have any containers of ammonia in your office building?"

Did he think I intentionally made myself sick? Maybe we should go back to the what-was-it-with-me-and-murderers questions. "Not that I'm aware of. In any case, I certainly did *not* contaminate the bleach myself." I pushed back my dreadful chair from the dreadful table. "Since the emergency room doctor already advised me to do so, I'm going to try to sleep off the flulike symptoms that the fumes gave me." I headed for the door. "If you have anything else you want to know, please ask me tomorrow."

"I do have one last item to discuss."

I clenched my teeth and turned to face him.

"Were you aware that Helen Walker was once arrested for attempted murder?"

Although I struggled to keep a bland expression on my face, my heart skipped a beat. I'm sure O'Reilly could see my shock. "No. When was this?"

"Four years ago. Her brother-in-law brought the charges against her, though he withdrew them later. Apparently she'd tried to suffocate him."

"That's . . . news to me." I left the room, heading straight for the exit with my thoughts in a whirl.

Steve Sullivan rose from his seat in the lobby. "You're still here?" I asked in surprise. "That was nice of you."

"Didn't want to leave you stranded," he replied with a shrug. "Got to admit, I was beginning to think I'd need to post bail."

"O'Reilly is never the speediest interrogator."

"You don't look any worse for the wear, so I take it he didn't resort to torture."

"No, but he acted like he wanted to strangle me throughout."

My head was still spinning with O'Reilly's words as we got into the car. Was he telling the truth? Could Helen really have tried to kill her brother-in-law? Linda Delgardio had once told me that police officers were allowed to lie to suspects and witnesses. They did so whenever they felt it best served their purposes.

"Are you clearheaded enough to drive your van?" Sullivan asked as we pulled out of the lot.

"Yeah, I'm fine. Please just drop me off at my office."

"I can run you home, and Audrey and I could come back and—"

"I'm fine," I snapped, recognizing on some level that my voice was harsher than I'd meant it to be. "Really. Thanks, but I've already taken your entire Saturday afternoon."

O'Reilly could have been blowing smoke at me. If any of the officers I'd ever met was prone to saying all kinds of vile, misleading things during an interrogation, O'Reilly was. Nevertheless, I needed to find out the truth about Helen. Audrey seemed to be really bonding with her. If she was capable of attempted murder...

No! It had to be a lie! Linda would have told me right away if Helen had once been arrested for attempted murder. And they'd have never let her go free that first night, after Jack's fatal "accident."

"Erin?" Sullivan said gruffly, interrupting my thoughts. We were nearing my office. "I'm following you home. I've got to head in that direction anyway."

"No. I'm going to be several minutes. I've got some files I have to update," I fibbed.

"The fumes might not even have dissipated yet!"

"It's been hours, now. They're not *that* toxic."

He pulled up in front of my door, hitting the brakes a little too hard. "Suit yourself."

I hesitated. "Thanks so much for helping me today. You . . . practically saved my life."

"Yeah. You're welcome." He wasn't even looking at me. "I gotta run, so . . ."

I fumbled with the latch on my seat belt and opened the door, blathering, "Okay, well, I'll see you at Helen's first thing Monday morning."

"See ya," he muttered without even a semblance of a smile. He zoomed off the instant I'd shut the passenger door.

He'd spent his Saturday afternoon taking me to the hospital and the police station, and in return I'd snapped at him and shooed him away. "It's official," I muttered to myself. "I'm the Wicked Witch of the West when it comes to Sullivan." I didn't have time to flog myself now. My life and my business were interwoven with Helen Walker; I had to prove or disprove O'Reilly's assertion as soon as possible.

I tossed out my bleach-and-ink experiment and went straight to my computer and accessed the Internet, searching on Helen Walker and George Miller's names as linked in the same article. Nothing. I couldn't ask Helen directly; she was probably innocent, and she'd be irreparably hurt by my questioning her. Stephanie would sooner bite my head off than verify a story like that. And, if it was true that Helen had tried to kill her father, Stephanie had all the more motive for wanting her aunt dead. Having been caught illicitly entering his aunt's house the other night, Peter, on the other hand, was in a very weak bargaining position.

If business was as bad as Peter claimed, maybe he'd be pinching pennies and staying home on a Saturday evening. I drove to his house, in a residential section at the outskirts of town. His street address was in a row of town homes. I parked in a visitor slot and headed along the sidewalk, spotting his shingle advertising the office hours of his family-law practice on his door. He had to be saving rent money by working out of his home.

I rang the doorbell, and when Peter called, "Come in," let myself in. He was obviously surprised to see me. His cheeks pinked up as he said, "Hello there, Erin. Did Aunt Helen send you for my inventory list of what I reclaimed from her house? I'm just making sure it's completely accurate before I hand it over."

"No, I just wanted to talk to you for a minute."

"Ah. Welcome to my home-slash-office. Like I say, not exactly rolling in the dough here."

"It's nice, though. Is this a two-bedroom place?"

"Yep. The spare room upstairs is my office."

I nodded, wondering if it would behoove me to give him some advice. The front entrance was into his living room, and if he wanted to make a better first impression on potential clients, he really should consider swapping the functions of the two rooms; he could easily convert this space into a comfortable professional-looking office.

"Have a seat, Erin."

I obliged and sat down on the sofa, which was upholstered in a comfortable and attractive maroon brocade.

"I've come from an interview at the police station. I think it's possible that a second attempt was made on your aunt's life."

"When? What happened?"

"Someone mixed ammonia with her bleach, which causes toxic fumes."

"My God. Is she all right?"

"She's fine. The police sent someone out to investigate. *I* was the one who wound up inhaling the fumes, but I'm okay, too...just a little under the weather." How to broach the subject of Helen's dislike for Peter's late father? "I wanted to ask you about your aunt's enemies."

"Enemies? She doesn't have any. Not as far as I know. I mean, sure, she can be a bit blunt, and that can upset people sometimes, but...she's just a harmless old lady, set in her ways."

"She and your mother were really close, right?"

"Two peas in a pod."

"Even though your mom had a husband and family, while Helen was unattached? Didn't that ever cause some friction?"

He shrugged. "Well, Aunt Helen and my dad were never especially...chummy. But nothing major."

"A police officer told me that charges were once filed in a domestic disturbance...three or four years ago."

"Oh, right. That was just an overreaction on Aunt Helen's part."

"What happened?"

"Dad didn't take to retirement real well. One night he and Mom got into an argument after he'd been drinking, and Mom was so mad she pushed his face into the sink when it was filled with water. Aunt Helen happened to be at the house, visiting my mom, and she misinterpreted everything and called the police. All three of them wound up at the station house."

"So *Helen* called the police on your *mom*?" I asked, incredulous.

He shrugged. "Well, I guess Mom almost managed to...drown my father, and Aunt Helen was afraid if she didn't call the police in to break everything up, my dad was going to retaliate. But, still, she overreacted. It was just a fight. My parents would never have hurt one another. I'm sure of it."

"Were you there at the time?"

"No, but I was the attorney of record for my mom... she'd called me for legal help. We got everything straightened out right away."

"So your *aunt* wouldn't have a police record because of that incident, surely?"

"Absolutely not. Neither did my mother. Or my father. No charges were filed. You can ask Aunt Helen if you don't believe me."

I rose. "Thanks, Peter. That clears everything up for me."

"What was this about? Did some cop tell you Aunt Helen had a record, or something? She doesn't."

"I figured as much. I'm sure the police are just digging hard to get at the truth."

He was staring at me in alarm. Before he could ask me more questions, I said, "Have you thought about turning your spare bedroom into a more personal space, such as a TV room, and converting this room into a cozy office? That could do wonders for the professional impression you make on walk-in clients."

He lifted his eyebrows. "Huh. That's not a bad idea."

———

After my freebie consult at Peter's, I had every intention of spending the rest of the day in bed, curled up with Hildi and a good book. When I entered our foyer, however, the first thing I saw was that the Scalamandre wallpaper for the accent wall at the foot of my bed had finally arrived. This particular design was so amazing—its colors so vibrant and the detail so exquisite—that it was like applying a floor-to-ceiling Van Gogh to one wall. Nothing was going to make me feel better faster than installing the glorious wallpaper. My heart sang at the very notion of the vision that would soon greet me when I opened my eyes every morning.

This marvelous old house with its high ceilings and impressive scale allowed me to take some liberties with my designs. I'd recently found a custom furniture builder whose painted surfaces were smooth as glass. My bedroom furniture was currently a veritable flower garden of color. My headboard and frame were cornflower blue, my dresser mint green, my nightstand sunflower yellow, and my mirror frame a cross between lavender and magenta. The link to pull the whole room together was my customized colors within the delectable wallpaper.

I hugged the rolls with unabashed glee and dashed upstairs, calling out a quick hello to Audrey, who was on the phone in the kitchen. I changed into cutoffs and an old hot pink T-shirt and flip-flops, then trotted downstairs and through the kitchen so that I could get my supplies from the basement.

Audrey was off the phone and standing by the stairs when I emerged. "Erin? Are you all right?"

"Just fine, Audrey. Thanks. My wallpaper's here!"

"I know, dear. I signed for it. But I got a disturbing call from your friend Mr. Sullivan just now."

"You did?" Even though I knew better, I found myself opting for the I'm-too-busy-to-talk diversion and began to measure the paste and water into my bucket, which was really stupid, because it meant I'd have to carry the mixture upstairs, as opposed to using water from the tap in my bathroom.

"Is it true that he had to take you to the ER for inhaling poisonous gas?"

"Kind of."

"Kind of? So that's only *partially* true. Which part isn't accurate?"

I poured my measured contents and commenced stirring with a paint stick. "Um, it was just fumes, so I doubt that would qualify as 'poisonous gas.' Plus, it wasn't much of a medical treatment...they just had me inhale some oxygen, ran some tests, and released me. There's nothing to worry about."

"I see," Audrey said, crossing her arms. "So the doctor suggested you go home and wallpaper your room?"

"She said to take it easy and get some rest...and wallpapering is easy for me and very restful." I snatched up the three-step aluminum ladder that I'd left by the door, stashed it under one arm, and grabbed my now-heavy paste bucket in the other hand. "Want to help?"

"I think I should. If you get dizzy and fall off the stepladder, I'll catch you. Alternatively, if I miss, I'll be there to call nine-one-one."

Although she let me carry the bucket and ladder, she grabbed my cutting tools and T square, and we went to my room. She helped me open the wallpaper and held it up to the wall, noting the marvelous color pattern. "Like you were telling me, this is truly going to be the glue that pulls all your pieces together in here, isn't it?" Audrey said.

"The furniture maker and I matched all the paint exactly to the wallpaper sample that I brought him." Pointing with my chin at my favorite chair, I continued, "And my jumping off point was that indigo settee, which I bought years ago in New York." I love to do that with my designs: pick my one favorite piece in the room to highlight, and choose my palette accordingly.

We moved my highboy and went to work. Audrey was proving to be a surprisingly good assistant, though she kept checking her watch. She also denied that she was checking the time—never a good sign where Audrey's concerned. Especially considering how easily she'd let me off the hook regarding my hospital visit. The fourth time I caught her in the act, I said, "You're sure you don't need to be someplace?"

"Must be a nervous habit I've acquired."

Hanging the last piece, I glanced out the window. "If I didn't know any better, I'd think that you were expecting a visitor. Steve Sullivan didn't say he was coming here, did he?"

"What makes you say that?"

"Experience. And the fact that I just spotted his van turning onto the street."

"That would be a good clue, all right," she replied.

The doorbell rang. I cocked an eyebrow.

"He's worried about you. That's the first sign, you know."

"The first sign of what? And please don't say love, because if anything, we've been drifting even farther apart since he got back into town."

"It's the first sign that he's a decent, caring person," Audrey declared as she descended the stairs to show Sullivan inside. I couldn't overhear their brief, quiet conversation, but he soon stood alone in my doorway and said, "Hey, Gilbert."

"Hi. It's nice of you to check in on me, and I'm sorry if I was a bit brusque with you earlier."

"That's okay." He scanned the room. "Whoa. This is a lot more colorful than I imagined your bedroom would be."

"You've been imagining my bedroom?" I couldn't help but tease.

He chuckled. "I'm taking the fifth on that question."

"What do you think? Too froufrou?"

"No, actually. I like it. It's inviting. Makes me want to take my shoes off and stay awhile."

"I . . . have no response to that remark, Sullivan."

"Want me to suggest one for you?" Although I'd gone back to smoothing the paper with my brush and couldn't see his expression, his sexy tone of voice was all too obvious. Unfortunately, my pulse started racing, my stomach clenched, and I could feel the typical flight-or-fight instincts kicking up in me already.

"Not really. As you've no doubt realized, I'm feeling much better. But thanks again for stopping by to check."

"No problem." He ignored my obvious hint to leave and plunked himself down at the foot of my bed. "Did the police say if they had any more leads as to who doctored up the bleach?"

"Not really." I stepped back to study my handiwork.

The wall was complete, the seams straight, the pattern matching up perfectly. There was no more delaying the inevitable. I turned and faced him. Damn! He looked so good. I averted my gaze. *What was he doing here?* "Don't you have another hot date tonight, Sullivan? After all, it's Saturday . . . date night number two."

He immediately glanced at his watch. In a blatant change of subject, he said, "I'm still not certain that Helen is innocent. I think you've allowed your affection for her to cloud your judgment."

So he *was* seeing somebody, but didn't want to discuss it with me. "Yeah? Well, that shows how wrong you are. I double-checked on her guilt just today."

"What do you mean?"

"I went to see Peter Miller after you dropped me off at my office. To ask about Helen."

"Why?"

"Detective O'Reilly implied that she might have been arrested before, for the attempted murder of her brother-in-law. But it was nonsense. Helen's sister, Lois, was the one who'd gotten into a bad fight with her husband, and Helen simply called the police."

"According to Peter? Have you called Linda to get the real story?"

I shook my head. "She'd never tell me. She's not about to give me insider information that could jeopardize the investigation."

He raked his fingers through his hair. "This is just plain dumb, Erin." He rose. "Quit working at Helen's house immediately. I'll take over the job."

"Why? What good would that do? Other than make

you feel like the knight in shining armor, ready to take over for the damsel in distress, I mean."

"For one thing, I would be much harder for a killer to overpower than you would be."

"Oh, yeah?" I flicked the brush, wet with wallpaper paste, at him. The paste splattered on his chest. "If that were a knife or a bullet fired from a gun, you'd be dead right now, you realize."

He stood with his arms spread wide, glaring at his shirt for several seconds. With a deep scowl, he shifted his furious expression toward me. "And *you'd* better realize that you just deliberately got glue on my favorite shirt."

"Sorry. I was just making a point that men and women are equally vulnerable to certain weapons. The paste washes right out, you know."

"Yes, I do know that. If that had been latex paint, *you* would be dead." He stormed down the stairs, grumbling, "See you Monday. *If* I feel like working with you."

Even though I'd had all day Sunday to gather strength from my stunning bedroom—the bright colors were utterly soul-cheering and the perfect antidote to the worst case of the blahs—it did nothing to assuage my guilt. I'd broken my own dubious record for childishness toward Sullivan.

By Monday morning, I felt so terrible about my behavior that I decided I owed it to him to pay the ultimate price. I was going to have to look him in the eyes and tell him the very truth that I'd fought so hard to withhold, even from myself: that I'd messed up his sexy-looking shirt so that he couldn't flirt with me one minute, then dash off to his date with some other woman the next. As I headed to Helen's house, my prayers went unanswered—not a single semitrailer crashed into me or flattened me on the sidewalk when I got out of my van.

Time passed at Helen's, and he still hadn't arrived. My agony only escalated. Even so, I kept working away on the den. Helen told me repeatedly how mortified she'd been when the police came to investigate the tainted bleach that had made me ill. Eventually she calmed down and said that she wanted to run to the grocery store, with me there to "keep an eye on the place ... and Ella and Vator." Though I didn't point this out to Helen, I *never* had the chance to keep an eye on Ella, who hid herself away the instant there was company. Vator, however, entered the room periodically to meow at me.

As I worked my way to the far corner of the room, I found a Raggedy Ann doll, still in its original box. That could very well be worth three grand or so. Too bad for Peter's thriving eBay business that he apparently overlooked this.

I heard a key scrape in the front door and went into the living room, feeling a bit on edge. It was Stephanie, who gave me a hundred-watt smile. "Hi, Erin. I've just dropped over to check on the progress you're making at sorting my mother's possessions from my aunt's."

"You have your own key, too, I see."

"Yes, but I've used mine for good"—she jingled a pair of keys on a plain ring cheerfully—"rather than evil. I'm here to return Peter's keys and my own. Without being asked. It's the very least we can do."

And in no way guaranteed that they hadn't both made

duplicates, I thought sourly. Nevertheless, I mustered a smile. "Thank you. I'm sure your aunt will appreciate the gesture."

She set the keys in the red plastic colander that had somehow found its way onto the smoked-glass coffee table. "I already apologized to my aunt for my unfortunate outburst in her garage on Saturday. I owe you one as well."

"Oh, that's all right. You're under a lot of stress."

"Yes, I am." She wandered over to the den. "So how's the work going?"

"I've been separating her easily resalable items from the rest, and I'm waiting for Helen to return so we can determine who owned what."

"Oh, look at this." She grabbed the Raggedy Ann doll. "I wonder if this is worth... This doll was my mother's. I remember her showing it to me in our house. I'd wanted her to take it out of the box, and she wouldn't, because she knew how much more valuable it was this way."

"It's unfortunate that she didn't have an item like that written into her will specifically. With your brother's legal training, I'm surprised that he didn't recommend she do so."

"As you've no doubt gathered, Peter isn't the brightest of lawyers. He barely passed law school. Took him three tries till he sneaked through his law boards." She gave me a magnanimous smile. "I'll help you sort these things."

"Thanks, although I should tell you that I already promised your aunt that nothing will be removed from the house until she's had the chance to inspect it."

She put her hands on her ample hips and clicked her

tongue. "What a stupid thing for you to promise. This is your best chance to get rid of this crap."

"You *did* give us a week to go through everything in the house and separate it into your mother's and your aunt's things, and it will take every minute of that time to complete the job."

"It certainly will, when you won't accept anyone's help!" She spun on a heel and banged out the door, grumbling, "It's a good thing I forced you to team up with *Steve*, who does things efficiently, or you'd be wasting your time and *my* money."

"Good riddance," I muttered to myself. If my home was plagued by the same visitors as Helen's, I too would consider moving into my garage.

Just as I'd gotten back to work, there was a familiar rap on the door—Kay's signature knock. I called, "Door's open. Come on in, Kay." As she closed the door behind her, I added, "Helen's at the store. I'm in the den."

She joined me, weaving her way around the piles and stacks. "How's the pillaging and pruning going?" She laughed at her own joke.

"Not good, actually. It's pretty impossible for me to get much of anything at all accomplished with Helen gone. I have no idea who owned what . . . Helen or Lois."

"Maybe I can give you some insights."

"Do you know which sister owned the Raggedy Ann doll, by any chance? Still in its original packing materials?"

"I can't swear to it, but I'm almost positive that was Helen's. Both sisters were given their own doll, but Lois took hers out of the box. Helen felt it would be redundant to have two identical dolls that they played with, so they kept that one as a backup."

I smiled to myself at the image of the young Helen Walker, specifying that she needed a "backup" Raggedy Ann doll. A future pack rat in the making, if ever there was one.

Kay was staring at the short stack of newspapers that I'd unearthed earlier; they were the ones with the significant time frames. I hadn't looked through them myself. She'd only narrowed them down to the year and the month. "Oh, my." Kay's jaw dropped as she opened the top edition. "I don't believe it. Helen told me her newspapers had been stolen."

"The stacks were just out of sequence. Helen will be delighted to discover that they weren't stolen after all."

"You found my wedding announcement, then."

"You were married?"

"Just engaged...never made it to the altar." She showed me the picture. There she was, beaming into the camera. She appeared to be in her early twenties, but it was her fiancé who'd captured my full attention. I stared at the familiar-looking face.

Kay had once been engaged to George Miller, Lois's late husband.

chapter 18

You ... were once engaged to George?" I asked.
Kay was looking longingly at the picture in
the paper, her eyes brimming with tears.
"Until he suddenly called off our engagement
and eloped with Lois." A small sob escaped. "That was the
worst time in my life. I'm sorry to get so emotional. This
photograph was the last thing I expected to see when I
came over here today."

No wonder she occasionally hinted at past troubles in
her relationship with Helen. "You must have felt so betrayed," I ventured.

She nodded. "I really don't want to talk about this, let alone remember the whole thing." She sniffled.

"Let me get you some tissues."

"Thank you, Erin." She dabbed at her eyes with her puffy cotton sleeve.

"I'll be right back." My thoughts promptly dipped into the dark side as I left the room; was it possible Kay could have killed Lois in revenge? And now be seeking to kill the sister of the woman who stole her fiancé more than forty years ago? Could Kay be that insane?

Finding anything in the now partially reburied kitchen was easier said than done. I remembered the drawer in which I'd last spotted some tissues and made my way over to it. I then dug my way through two pairs of men's black socks, a bikini top, a mister, a dozen minirecorder tapes, golf tees, corncob holders, and an empty harmonica case. Just when I finally located a somewhat crushed tissue box, I heard the screen door slam. I rushed to the doorway in time to see Kay drive away. Strange woman, but that didn't make her a killer. After all, her friendship with Helen had endured decades. There was no logical reason for her to wait all that time, and *then* become murderous over losing her man, after he was dead and gone.

Unless Kay was avenging *his* murder—if, for instance, Kay had become convinced that Lois had swapped George's heart medication with placebos.

Jeez! Why was I thinking this way? Kay was a nice little seventy-five-year-old woman! And she was Helen's best friend! I should do what my friend Linda Delgardio was always advising me: stick to designing *spaces* and not motives for someone to commit murder in them.

I went back to the newspapers and rifled through them.

A brief search verified my initial suspicion: the newspaper Kay had been reading was now missing. "Drat," I muttered. I had really wanted to give that edition to Helen so she could begin to re-create the missing pages from her scrapbook. Seeing that announcement had been so painful to Kay, though, maybe it was best if she did claim it for herself.

Something else was missing, too. Kay had just run off with a considerably bigger prize. The Raggedy Ann doll had vanished.

Helen finally returned from the store with three bags of groceries, which I helped her to carry in from the garage. "How's the work going, Erin?" she asked, while, upon my insistence, we put the items away.

"Okay, I guess, but Kay came over for a quick visit and . . . I'm pretty sure she took your Raggedy Ann doll with her."

To my astonishment, Helen said mildly, "She couldn't help herself, the poor dear."

"What do you mean?"

"Kay is a kleptomaniac. This has been going on for more than fifty years."

"Her . . . stealing things, you mean?"

"I'm afraid so. Kay runs off with my things periodically, and has for all this time. She feels guilty about it, though. She's well aware of the fact that I know about her compulsion. It's a tremendous annoyance at times, of course, but I look at it as a simple way for me to help her. My allowing her to take things from my house lets her resist the urge to steal from stores. And, eventually, I find them in Kay's home and take them back."

"But what about the shoplifting ring?" I blurted out.

"Pardon?"

"That Teddy and George were mixed up with at one point. Is there a connection with Kay?"

"That's all water underneath a very old bridge," Helen snapped, turning her back on me to stare at the contents of the refrigerator.

We worked in silence for a while; she'd purchased mostly healthy foods—fresh vegetables and fruits—as well as two jars of prunes and a host of vitamins, which I arbitrarily stuck in the pantry for her. I asked, "Kay was a friend of your sister's, too, right?"

"Oh, yes. Absolutely. The three of us were sharing an apartment at one point."

"Wasn't that...difficult? Lois's having a friend with a problem like that, when she was working in a department store?"

"We didn't know about her kleptomania at the time." Helen eased herself into a captain's chair. "And, yes, you're right. The confusion about who was behind the shoplifting did cause lots of strain among the three of us. Lois knew items from her store kept showing up in our apartment, and for a while she was certain it was me with the problem, so she kept sneaking the stolen merchandise back into the store. When we finally compared notes and realized that the thief was poor Kay, we confronted her, and she cried her eyes out, explaining her compulsion."

"And yet, here Kay was engaged to George Miller, a police officer."

"How did you know about that?"

"I located the edition that had run Kay and George's

engagement announcement." Helen's eyes instantly brightened, but dimmed again when I added, "Kay took that paper, too."

Helen fidgeted with her messy bun. "It was so ironic . . . a kleptomaniac engaged to a policeman. Then, of course, George decided he preferred Lois and dumped Kay. Which broke Kay's heart. But eventually, she accepted my sister's apology. Lois had tried very hard, for Kay's sake, not to fall for George, but 'true love' won out in the end. Much to everyone's misfortune."

"So . . . Kay *wasn't* actually involved in the shoplifting ring that led to charges being filed against George and Teddy?" I tried again, gently.

"Oh, she was. That's how Kay and George first met. George caught Kay in the act when he was on security duty at the store. But the major thefts took place later. Kay swore she never set foot in the store again; she'd promised George she wouldn't, in exchange for his letting her go scot-free."

Before I could formulate another question, Rachel came to the door and called hello to us through the screen door, letting herself in and striding into the kitchen. "I noticed Kay leaving a few minutes ago," she said to Helen. "She seemed terribly upset. Is everything all right?"

"Fine. Yes. It was probably just the dust, making her a bit sneezy."

"I never knew she had allergies."

"Well, then, apparently you've learned something today."

Rachel ignored Helen's tone and took a seat opposite her at the table, shoving the collection of junk between them aside with a careless sweep of her forearm. "Helen, I'm returning the porcelain dancers on one condition."

I exclaimed, "You're making *conditions* for the return of stolen property to its rightful owner?"

"I didn't mean that quite the way it sounded. I simply want you to actually *display* the pieces, Helen. They're too lovely to be hidden away, and maybe they'll bring some blessings on this house. Heaven knows the place needs it."

"Not that it's any of your business, Rachel, but I *am* planning on displaying my collection. In the den."

"The *den*? You mustn't be in much of a hurry to get them back." Rachel chuckled and said knowingly to me, "That you're even able to *enter* that room now is a minor miracle."

I glared at her. "Something's puzzling me about the events of the night your husband was killed."

"Join the club," she muttered. "Lots of things puzzle me about that night."

"Did your husband know you were the lookout so that Peter could sneak in here?"

"No. I would discreetly place a call to Peter's cell phone and hang up before he answered. If Jack happened to be there at the time and saw me, I would pretend that I misdialed, and I'd place another phone call to someone else."

"So did you signal Peter that the coast was clear that night?" I persisted.

"No. I couldn't."

"You couldn't?"

"That's right. Jack was really worried about Helen." Rachel cast a quick apologetic glance at Helen, but continued to speak about her as though she weren't in the room. "We were both afraid she was going over the deep end...you know, living in the garage, like she was. That night, instead of his usual activities—reading or tinkering with his projects in the basement—Jack took my usual surveillance spot in the window. When we saw someone duck out the door, at first I thought Peter must have gone on in without my okay. So I tried like the dickens to stop Jack from going over there himself. He refused to listen to me. I told him I was calling the police, but...I didn't, of course. I was so sure he was going over to an empty house, which Peter had only just left. I figured the worst thing that could happen to him was he'd slip and fall in the dark. So I called across the street to him to turn on Helen's lights. He did, and he gestured back at me from Helen's doorway to keep my voice down. That was the last time I ever saw him."

"Haven't you been saying all along that it *wasn't* Peter?" Helen asked.

"Yes, but for all I know, Peter could have taken on a partner and still been inside the house. I told the police as much."

"So you told the police about your conspiring with my nephew?"

"Saturday," Rachel confirmed matter-of-factly, "right after I witnessed all that bickering in your garage. I have nothing to hide. The police understood that Peter's only been taking things that he inherited, and if he chooses to give them away, that's his own business." She rose and peered at Helen. "I just hope I didn't horridly misjudge your nephew, Helen. I very much hope he didn't shove my Jack down those stairs after all."

Steve never arrived at Helen's house. I guess he'd really meant his parting comment about seeing me on Monday only *if* he felt like working with me. I was relieved, then, when he arrived at Stephanie's house for our appointment later that afternoon. I waited out front for him and said, "Steve, I want to apologize for—"

"Don't worry about it," he interrupted. "You didn't louse up my plans for the evening, and the paste came right out in the wash. Shirt's good as new."

"Oh, great. I'm glad to hear that."

"Yeah, so let's just forget it ever happened."

"But . . . I really think I at least owe you an explanation."

"Nah. You don't owe me a thing, Gilbert. Let's just drop it. Okay?"

I mustered a smile and echoed, "Okay," but had to squeeze the word past the lump in my throat. I could see by the lack of sparkle in his hazel eyes that he was over me. Splattering him with wallpaper paste had been the last straw. He'd no doubt fallen for the woman he was now seeing. He was now being the mature one and had decided to move on. What choice did I have but to do the same?

We shared an awkward silence as we waited on Stephanie's porch. Wrenching my thoughts toward a less painful pattern, I mulled over my conversation with Rachel; something niggled at me but wouldn't reveal itself in full color.

At last, Stephanie arrived, several minutes late. She wove a bit as she navigated her circular driveway and parked in the garage. She seemed a bit unsteady on her feet, too, as she swung open her door, and I asked, "Are you all right?"

"Oh, sure. Just got back from a power lunch."

I could smell alcohol on her breath. "I hope you're not planning on driving anywhere else." I felt Sullivan stiffen beside me, and when I glanced over, he was giving me the evil eye.

"Goody Two-shoes type, are you, Erin?" Stephanie scoffed.

"When it comes to drinking and driving, yes." Ignoring the heat of Sullivan's glare, I added, "No offense, Stephanie, but if forced to pick, we'd rather lose you as our client over my having voiced concerns about your sobriety than as a result of a fatal car accident. Wouldn't we, Steve?" I smiled sweetly at Sullivan.

"Absolutely."

Stephanie chuckled. "Don't worry. I'm working from home the rest of the day." But her smile faded as she stumbled on the small Berber area rug. Sullivan grabbed her arm to steady her. "Jeez. I guess I really did have a bit too much liquid with my lunch."

"Did you still want to go over our designs?" he asked.

She let out a bark of laughter. "Why not? I agree to *everything* when I'm loaded. Probably why my husband's and my marriage lasted as long as it did. So long as I was schnockered, we got along just fine." She laughed again as she wove her way to her chaise and plopped down. "So let's see those final plans. I'm bound to adore whatever you've done."

"In that case, maybe we can work up a contract for all your properties." The twinkle in Sullivan's eye let us both know he was joking. "You can hire Sullivan and Gilbert to design all the interiors of your show homes from here on out."

"Done."

"Would you like me to fix you some coffee?" I asked her.

"So I can be an alert drunk, you mean?" She waved off the suggestion. "Tell me again what the purpose of this meeting was?"

"We need you to make the final selection in the materials we're going to use for your wet bar."

"Materials. Good. Right. Let's face it . . . I'm a Material Girl." She laughed heartily.

"So for starters, we have the stone for the floor and the countertop narrowed down to six choices total, and we've brought samples."

"You decide for me. I trust you."

Sullivan and I exchanged glances. "If nothing else, we'll need you to break a tie vote," I told her, "and besides, this is your house. It has to be to your taste, not ours."

"Well, then, I guess we'll have to postpone our meeting after all. This is what comes when you've been burning the candle on both ends for as long as I have. But, as they say, you don't get to choose your family. I'm stuck with my crazy aunt and my no-account brother." She made a dismissive noise. "My dad was, frankly, something of a jerk. I know that's not politically correct, but he's kind of the one who got Peter off on the wrong foot."

"In what way?" I asked.

"Oh, Peter had this basic fatherly love thing going. He worshipped Dad and couldn't see that he was someone who always took the path of least resistance."

"I'm surprised Peter didn't follow in his footsteps, then, and become a police officer," I said.

"He would have, if Dad hadn't insisted that he couldn't

possibly handle the job. That he was too…unathletic, let's say."

I gave a quick glance at Sullivan, who was packing up our samples, clearly not happy. Stephanie's current loose-lips state could help me test my theory that Kay might have been seeking to avenge George's death. "That reminds me," I said, "has Helen ever discussed her suspicions about someone having swapped out your father's medication?"

"Yeah, right. Aunt Helen started seeing the boogeyman hours after my mother died."

"Meaning she grew paranoid?"

She nodded, with drunken exaggeration. "I immediately called my father's cardiologist to ask if such a thing was possible, and it wasn't. Dad had undergone a recent, thorough screening that included blood tests, and there was nothing wrong with his medication. He died because he stopped watching his waistline. Just like my brother's doing now."

We said our good-byes and left, Sullivan muttering, "Seems like we've got some unexpected time on our hands. Just as well. I've got to phone my client in California for some basic PR."

"I'm going to swing by Peter's house."

"Why?"

"Something that Stephanie said is bugging me."

"What?"

"She mentioned Peter's weight and his not being athletic. Which led me to thinking: Jack Schwartz could conceivably have been confused with him, but never with Helen."

I glanced at Stephanie's window as we headed away

from her circular drive. Stephanie stood there, but she stepped away when she spotted me. *Was she merely pretending to be drunk in order to feed me false information of some kind?*

Peter was seated at his desk, going over some papers that looked like legal documents, and I couldn't help but feel flattered and proud. He'd taken my suggestion of swapping his office furniture into this room, and it worked wonderfully. The effect was that of walking into a homey, personalized office space—extremely functional and efficient-looking, yet displaying an appealing lived-in familiarity and comfort within the room. I loved the way the wingchair—cream-colored with tiny black polka dots—and the burgundy brocade love seat could serve as either a conversation nook for consultations or for simply lounging with morning coffee. That area nicely balanced the oak desk and credenza in the opposite corner. Framed photographs and whimsical metallic figurines had been placed among his numerous law books. Those eye-catching personal items lightened his bookcases and kept them from being too ponderous. He enthusiastically insisted on showing me the upstairs as well, then asked what brought me out to his house again so soon.

"I had a conversation with Rachel Schwartz today, which, after I thought about for a while, really worried me."

"Oh?"

"Yes, you see, she mentioned that her husband had turned the lights on in Helen's house when he went there to investigate."

"So?"

"I strongly suspect that Jack was pushed into the water. If the killer was hiding near the basement stairs in wait for Helen, there's no way tiny Helen could have gotten confused for the tall, rather husky Jack Schwartz. Especially not in a well-lit house. But you're not all that much taller than Jack was."

"So you're saying the trap was set for me? That *I* was the intended victim?" He shook his head emphatically. "That's not possible, Erin. The only person who knew I was entering Helen's house to remove my mother's possessions was Rachel Schwartz."

"And when Rachel called you that night, did she give you any indication that something might be wrong at Helen's house?"

"Rachel never called me that night. Which meant that it *wasn't* safe for me to get in and out."

"So you didn't speak to Rachel at all?"

"No. Of course, even if she *had* called me, we wouldn't have spoken. She used to hang up after my phone rang once. I...didn't want to have to pay for the minutes on my cell. But I'd know it was her, because my cell phone had her number in its phone book, so we never had to actually speak to one another."

"I see." My thoughts raced. Rachel had told me the truth about how their signals were passed. It still would have been possible for Rachel to have killed her own husband. Which she might have wanted if she was uncontrollably jealous of Jack and Helen's relationship. Rachel could have gone over there with him to investigate her *own* false claim that she'd seen a prowler entering and then leaving the premises. She might have stayed a step or two behind him, shoved him into the water, and fled from the house when Helen had become anxious and returned to her garage.

As if he were reading my mind, Peter said, "Rachel might be lying about the lights being on, you know. She's definitely lying when she says I was the one who engineered this thing. She put *me* up to entering Aunt Helen's home in the first place. She claimed she wanted to hire me to write her and her husband's will ... made at least a half dozen appointments with me, only she'd always have some excuse for why Jack couldn't make it. Then she'd start talking about how bad it must have made me feel to know that my parents' possessions were being mistreated at my aunt's place—"

"You're sure nobody else knew you were sometimes entering your aunt's house in her absence?"

"I'm positive. There's no way I could have been the intended victim, thank God. Like I don't have enough to worry about without worrying that someone's trying to kill me."

I took a much needed respite from my work that night and went to dinner and a movie with some girlfriends. The phone was ringing as I stepped through the door. I recognized Helen's panicked "Erin?" instantly.

"Yes, what's wrong, Helen? Are you all right?"

"It's happening again!" She was sobbing too hard to speak.

"What is?"

"Somebody's in the house again!"

"Are the police there yet?"

"No, but they will be soon. Can you come over?"

"I'll be right there."

I drove as fast as I dared to Helen's house and found, to my horror, no signs of activity and not a single police car as I parked in the driveway. The garage door was open, and the dome light was on in her car. Helen was sitting in the front seat. I shut off my engine and charged into the garage, my pulse racing, terrified that she'd been killed herself.

She turned and saw me as I ran up to her. She opened her car door. She was ghost white.

"Helen. Are you all right?"

"I heard a strange noise in the basement. And a cry of pain. I just know it was a body hitting the floor. I just... was too scared to go down there."

"Why aren't the police here?"

"I couldn't call. If I confess a second time, they'll think I really am guilty. *Why does this keep happening?*"

I punched 911 into my cell phone, telling Helen, "I'm going to sit right here next to you. This time, we're making darn sure that if there *is* someone's body in your home, the police find it this time, not you or me."

She nodded, her lips nearly as white with fear as her cheeks.

Eleven minutes later, two policemen were pounding on Helen's front door, although Helen and I were sitting in a squad car with a third officer, who took Helen's statement. She'd once again insisted that I stay and keep her company, and the policeman was kind enough to oblige.

The other two went inside to investigate. One of the officers returned a couple of minutes later. He looked badly shaken.

"Ma'am, was your basement door ajar when you left home?"

"Definitely not," she immediately replied. "Was there another body down there?"

The cop made eye contact with the officer behind the wheel and said quietly, "I already called it in. Looks like homicide."

"Oh, dear. I knew it," Helen said sadly. "Who is it? What does the victim look like?"

"He still had his wallet, with his driver's license. Ma'am, do you know a Peter Miller?"

"Oh, my God! Oh, no. Not Peter!" She crumpled, sobbing.

I comforted her as best I could, as she wept on my shoulder. Swallowing the lump in my throat, I explained to the policeman, "Peter is her nephew."

"And you said before that you're her interior decorator?"

I nodded.

"She lives here alone, right?"

"Yes."

"Er, miss?" he asked me quietly. "Do you happen to know if she kept a harpoon on the premises?"

chapter 19

With Helen's countless possessions, her having a harpoon was a possibility, but I merely gaped at the officer's face as he peered at me; he was clearly shaken by the murder scene in Helen's basement.

"Did you say something about a harpoon?" Helen asked, struggling to collect herself.

"That's what the murder weapon looked like to me," he answered.

"Oh, I am such an idiot! I thought I'd gotten rid of that damned thing!"

"You had a harpoon in your house, ma'am?" He grabbed his notepad.

She nodded, still crying. "I'd forgotten all about it. I'd hidden it in the basement many years ago. It was a gift from a rather eccentric man I once dated. He'd recently moved to Alaska, and I guess he wanted to send me something to remind me of him."

"Was it loaded all this time?" the second officer behind the wheel turned to ask.

"Of course not. And I'd hidden the . . . spears, or whatever they're called, in a completely different location." She dabbed at her eyes and took a shaky breath. "If only I'd disposed of the dreadful thing! Poor Peter would still be alive."

A third officer emerged from the house and strode up to us. Bending, he said, "Ma'am? Miss Gilbert? We need to take you both down to the station house now."

Detective O'Reilly allowed Linda to interview me, while he took Helen's statement. I hoped he would tone down the aggressive mannerisms with Helen that he invariably used when grilling me. In sharp contrast, Linda was her wonderful, kind-but-thorough self during my interview. For once, I had little to be defensive about—I hadn't barged into the house and found the body myself. Linda gently acknowledged that she was "proud" that I'd shown some restraint.

Afterward I waited in a small dingy sitting area near the detectives' desks; it served mostly as a kitchenette, but there was an ugly green-and-brown-checkered sofa and a sagging matching chair—Salvation Army castoffs, perhaps.

Linda was occupying the nearest desk, keeping a loose eye on my whereabouts.

The moment I spotted Stephanie approaching, I stood. A uniformed officer lingered a deferential step behind her. Stephanie's complexion was blotchy; her eyes were bloodshot and red-rimmed. She looked to be in utter despair.

"Stephanie, I'm so terribly sorry for your loss."

She turned her face away and gestured for me to sit back down. "Has Aunt Helen confessed?" she asked, her voice husky with emotion. "Giving a bogus one again, I mean," she added in a half shout, peppered with a quick glare to the officer who'd accompanied her.

"I don't think so. Helen's still here. But I don't think she's making any bogus confession this time. She was devastated to find out it was your brother."

Stephanie sank into the chair and grimaced as she shuffled her weight. "This cushion's so lumpy it feels like it's stuffed with squirrel carcasses." She rifled through her purse through a forest of used tissues and availed herself of a clean one. She closed her eyes and took a couple of deep breaths, then gave me a nod. "Okay. So no confession. At least that much is good. Do the police know yet who did this?"

"No."

"Figures. Batch of incompetents." Even as she spoke, she was looking directly at the officer in our immediate vicinity, who must have been assigned to stick to Stephanie. He balled his fists.

Stephanie plucked at the crease in her linen slacks, centering it on her knee, then glanced at her watch and rose. "I'm taking my aunt home with me this time. I'd appreciate it if you'd leave. Right now."

"But I need to tell Helen that I'm—"

"I'll give her your regards," she snapped. The male officer and Linda Delgardio were now giving us their full attention.

"I promised her I'd wait for her. I can't just get up and leave when she's in the middle of being interrogated. She'll think I'm deserting her."

"No, Erin. You are my employee, and I'm telling you to leave my aunt alone."

"I'm not your employee; you're one of many clients who've contracted me to do a design job."

She gave me a "whatever" shrug.

This would probably prove to be professional suicide, but I could not allow myself to be bullied into abandoning my poor, sweet friend and client without so much as a word of encouragement. "I'm sorry, Stephanie. But I'll leave when *and* if your aunt wants me to."

Stephanie fired visual daggers at me. "Hiring you to work for me was one of the biggest mistakes of my life."

"You've had a terrible shock, Stephanie, and you're taking it out on me."

"With good reason!" she shouted. "Look around you! My brother is dead! You've somehow bonded yourself to my aunt, who's one step away from dementia! How do I know that you're not the cause of all of this? That you didn't assess my aunt's mental status and decide to take advantage of it?"

"Stephanie, all I can do is assure you from the bottom of my heart that I am not trying to insinuate myself into

Helen's life. She's a dear woman who's had horrific things happen to her, and I'm trying to help her stay on her feet."

"Really? Well, you'll have to forgive me if I don't take your word for that. Seeing as you and your landlady have turned your home into my *aunt's* home and made her one of the family, I guess we'll just have to see what the *courts* say about the whole thing."

"What do you mean?" I asked in alarm.

"I'm going to schedule a competency hearing for Aunt Helen. To protect her from you. I'll get myself appointed as her legal guardian. *That's* what I mean!" She whirled around to face the thirty-something policeman she'd just gotten through insulting. "Officer?"

"Yes, ma'am?" he said without smiling.

"Tell Helen Walker that her niece, Stephanie, is terribly sorry, but since her *decorator* has refused to leave, she felt forced to leave herself." She grimaced at me. "I absolutely can't *tolerate* the present company."

As she stormed off, Linda asked, "What was that all about?"

I was too stunned to answer immediately, but managed, "She's accusing me of cozying up to her aunt to get my hands on her fortune, or some such nonsense."

"People say all kinds of crazy things when they've suffered a loss. She's probably just taking out her pain on you."

"I know. But it still hurts."

She gave me a sympathetic smile.

"Which reminds me," I added, "has anyone double-checked the possibility that George Miller's medications were tampered with, years ago?"

Linda nodded. "I did. Spoke to his cardiologist a couple of days ago. His meds were fine. George Miller was not murdered."

"Did you tell Helen that?"

"Not yet."

"Is it all right if *I* do?"

"You're actually asking for my official permission to give a suspect information?"

"A *suspect?* You don't really believe that she fired a harpoon to kill her own nephew! She's a tiny, seventy-five-year-old woman! How do you imagine she could steady and shoot a weapon like that?"

Linda frowned, then sighed. "Go ahead and tell her what the cardiologist said. But, Erin, my warning about Ms. Walker still stands. We're not done testing the murder weapon, so we can't rule her out as a suspect. And neither can you."

Detective O'Reilly approached and said that Helen had been asking for me. "Come on," he said. "I'll take you to her."

Again, astonishingly, he made no snipes at me as he led the way to one of the interrogation rooms. My heart lurched at the sight of Helen, slumped in a plastic-and-chrome seat at the small wood-grain Formica table. She perked up when I said, "Helen?"

"Ms. Walker," O'Reilly told her, "you can leave now. We might need to contact you again tomorrow, so are you certain you'll be staying at the Crestview Inn?"

"Please don't do that, Helen," I interjected. "You can stay with Audrey and me again."

"No, thank you, Erin. My reservations at the hotel are all set." She turned her hooded, crestfallen gray eyes on

O'Reilly. "I'll be at the hotel until I'm allowed to move back home. Thank you, Officer."

"I wish you'd reconsider," I protested.

She shook her head. "Can you drive me there, Erin? My car is back at the house. I suppose an officer could take me, but..."

"I'll give you a ride." If I failed to convince her to change her mind, the hotel on Main Street and Opal wasn't far from Audrey's house. Audrey would no doubt charge over there herself tonight and pry Helen out of her room. "Let's get out of here, Helen."

O'Reilly was still standing in the doorway as I helped her to her feet. "Good evening, ladies," he said as he held the door for us. Neither of us replied.

We rode in silence. Hoping it would ease her mind, I said, "My friend, Officer Linda Delgardio, told me that your brother-in-law was being given the right dosage of medicine. They're absolutely certain that nobody tampered with his pills."

For a moment, she didn't reply, and I wondered if she'd heard me. Then she said, "I guess that's good news. But I can't decide. Is it a good thing that the one member of my family who actually *deserved* an early grave is the one who died of natural causes?"

Helen refused to let me accompany her to her room. She wouldn't even meet my gaze as the elevator doors closed while she stood there, clutching her bulging purse to her chest. My only consolation was the thought that Audrey would likely be more persuasive—and insistent—

than I was at convincing Helen to change her mind and stay here with us.

As I hurried along the slate walkway, my heart began to sink. The lamps set by the timer were the only ones glowing yellow in my house. Come to think of it, they'd been that way earlier, when I'd raced inside to answer the phone. I let myself in and called "Audrey?" hopefully.

No answer. There was a note on the pad on the table in the foyer that read:

> Erin—Guess what? I'm a grandmother! It's a
> GIRL! I'm catching a red-eye to Kansas City to see
> her. Back Thursday P.M. See you then!

At the bottom of the page, she'd sketched a little rattle with a bow on it and a happy face and a heart.

The next morning, I dragged myself to my office. I tried to work on my plans for a client's new family room, but my heart wasn't in it. I weighed calling Sullivan, but felt too depleted. At the sound of my door opening, I hoped that would be him, but to my disappointment I could tell by the slow footfalls that it was someone else. White hair soon came into view; for just an instant, I thought it was Helen, but it was Kay, looking grim.

"Erin, I need your help with Helen," she said without bothering to greet me.

"What's wrong? Have you spoken to her at the hotel?"

"Yes, and she's back at her house now."

"She *is*?"

Kay clicked her tongue and made a vague gesture,

clearly flustered. "I brought her there a few minutes ago. The police have the house cordoned off, of course, but they're letting her pack up some personal items in her garage. She plans to insist that they let her stay there."

"In her garage?"

Kay nodded. "If she promises not to enter the house itself."

"I'm sure the police won't allow her to do that." For one thing, she'd need access to her bathroom.

"I pleaded with her to move in with me for a while, but she refused. She is so stubborn! I'm scared to death at the notion of Helen living on her own in that house. Two people have died there! I even offered to move into her house temporarily, once the police are done investigating." She sighed. "All Helen said to me was that there was room for me in the front seat of the car, but that the backseat was taken."

"Oh, jeez."

"Do you think you could come with me? Help me try to talk her into accepting my offer? Please, Erin. Helen listens to you."

"I really don't think that—"

"Please, Erin," she urged again. "I can't stand thinking about her, all alone in her garage."

For that matter, neither could I. "Okay. I'll do my best."

Kay and I stared at Helen, who was ensconced on her dull, dirty pink sofa in the garage—precisely where she'd been sitting the day we'd first met. Officer Mansfield, Linda's partner, had been assigned to watch her and keep her away from the crime scene inside her home. He'd told me in hushed, concerned tones that Helen "seems to think she's moving into the garage," and asked if I was here to help "get her back into her hotel room." I'd said yes and requested a few minutes of privacy. He was now standing sentry at the base of the driveway.

"No, Kay," Helen said, crossing her arms. "I already told you! You're not moving in with me, and I'm not leaving. It's too dangerous. People have died, being mistaken for me. I won't let my best friend get killed in my place. I already lost my nephew that way!"

"Oh, honestly!" Kay exclaimed. "Do you think you're made of titanium, and everyone *else* is just flesh and blood?"

"You know, Helen," I interjected, "I'm not so sure that the killer was aiming for you in the first place. How could anybody have mistaken Peter for you last night?"

"Maybe the killer just shot the first person who came down the stairs," she replied with a weary shrug. "In any case, two times I've left my house, and two times someone has died. The only way I can prevent more killings is to hole myself up here and never leave home. That's what I intend to do."

"Even if the police allow you to stay here, which they won't," Kay began, "sooner or later, you'll *have* to leave your garage."

Helen pursed her lips and said nothing.

"Do you really think you wouldn't insist on my coming home with you, if our positions were reversed?" Kay asked.

"But they're *not* reversed. Nobody wants to kill *you*. Whereas it's become painfully obvious that half of my acquaintances want to do away with me."

"I certainly hope present company is excluded," Kay stated, her voice agitated.

Helen studied her. "I don't trust anybody right now."

"I beg your pardon. Are you saying you think *I'm* behind these horrific crimes?"

"No, Kay. I'm just saying that I need to be alone."

"You're being a stubborn old woman! You're determined to get yourself killed!"

"No, I'm simply trying to prevent anyone else from getting killed. By forbidding everyone from setting foot in my house. So please leave, both of you."

"Fine, Helen," Kay retorted through a tight jaw.

I gave a quick glance down the driveway, and sure enough, Mansfield was starting to make his way toward us, no doubt concerned about the raised voices. Just then, somebody in a dinged-up pickup truck that needed a new muffler pulled up alongside the driveway. He went over to the truck to talk to the driver instead.

"Oh, good grief!" Helen groaned. "Now *Teddy's* here!"

"Kay's right," I said quickly before she could get distracted by Teddy's arrival. "At least allow us to take you back to the hotel, if you won't stay with either of us."

"No, Erin. I've made up my mind."

I glanced behind me again. Teddy had gotten out of his truck and was shaking Mansfield's hand and patting him on the shoulder.

"Ahoy, there, everyone!" Teddy announced, making his way toward us in a peppy march, Mansfield now responding to a call on the radio attached to his uniform. Teddy seemed utterly unaware from Kay's and Helen's frowns how deeply upset both women were.

"Maybe *you* can talk some sense into her," Kay told

him, then stormed past him toward her car. "I've had enough!"

Good thing we'd driven separately.

Teddy gaped at Kay's retreating form for a moment, then turned his attention to Helen, resuming his cheerful demeanor. "Helen, your tragedy is all over the news, and I'm here to offer you my services."

"No. Go home, Teddy," Helen said.

He made a placating gesture with his palms. "Now, Helen, I understand why you're upset, but this is important. The police aren't going to be able to guard you, like I can, twenty-four-seven. And let's not forget, I'm a former police officer, and I bear arms."

"You were kicked *off* the force for good reason," she snarled. "Which reminds me, Teddy. Is that gun of yours legal? Considering you're a convicted felon? Should we ask the policeman standing right outside?"

"You're not yourself," Teddy sputtered. "I should have realized how upset you'd be. I just...wanted to help."

"I appreciate that, Teddy, but you're wrong. I *am* myself . . . a happy-to-be-independent woman. And I want things to stay that way. I don't need or want anybody's help."

Kay returned. She'd fetched the boxed Raggedy Ann doll out of her car, and now she listened to Helen's and Teddy's exchange. "Teddy, we have no choice but to honor our former friend's wishes."

"Leave, Teddy! Go home!" Helen demanded. "Leave me alone!"

He gave a sad nod, acknowledged his departure to me and Kay with a little wave, then slunk back to his pickup.

He said a few words to Mansfield, then started his noisy engine and drove away.

"Now you're being abusive to poor Teddy!" Kay scolded. "Here. I brought your doll back."

"You shouldn't have taken it in the first place."

"I needed it for comfort. I assumed you would understand." Kay set the box on the sofa. Then she regarded Helen coolly. "I have to say that it's starting to become quite clear to me why you have such mortal enemies."

Helen gasped. "Kay Livingston! That is the meanest thing anybody has ever said to me!"

Mansfield rushed into the garage at Helen's raised voice. "Is everything all right, ladies?"

"No!" Helen replied. "I need you to escort them off my property!"

"Kay, for now let's do what—"

"Well, Helen," Kay interrupted me, "then you probably don't need me to point out to you that had *you* minded your p's and q's with Jack Schwartz, he might never have come over here and gotten himself killed!"

Helen stared at her, slack-jawed. "How dare you!"

"Are you coming, Erin?" Kay asked in a frigid tone.

I looked at Mansfield. The poor man seemed completely unsure of what to do. I answered, "We can't just leave now."

"*I* can." Kay turned and started to head out again, then hesitated, marched back over to the sofa, snatched up the Raggedy Ann doll, and left.

chapter 20

a uniformed policeman who'd been investigating the crime scene entered the garage from the house and appeared to be surprised to see that we were still here. He gave Officer Mansfield a reproving stare, then said to Helen, "Ma'am? You have to leave the premises now."

"But why?" Helen asked. "There's no evidence in the garage, and I'm perfectly comfortable out here."

"Garage is off-limits, too," he declared. "You've been out here for more than an hour. You were only supposed to collect a few personal items, then leave. We'll let you know when you can return home."

"Helen," I pleaded, "Audrey will never forgive me if I allow you to check back into a hotel. You absolutely must come home with me."

She sighed, rocking herself in her perch at the edge of the pink love seat. "Well . . . I suppose if Audrey needs her guest room, I could always stay in *her* garage." She rose and turned toward the officer. "Can I at least take my car this time?" Mansfield, meanwhile, reentered Helen's house.

"Uh, sure. Fine."

I gave the officer my address and number, then, after a struggle to get Helen's engine to start, she and I caravaned to my house. We had a brief tug-of-war with her lightly packed electric blue suitcase. She reluctantly allowed me to carry it up the slate walkway for her, and I unlocked the door and held it open for her.

"Audrey isn't here?" Helen asked the moment she stepped inside the foyer.

"No, she's—"

"In Kansas City." She picked up the note that I'd left on the foyer table. "Oh! David and his wife had a little girl," she said happily. "How marvelous!" Then she turned and swept up her suitcase, which I'd momentarily set down on the marble floor. "I'm going back to the hotel, Erin. I'd feel like I'm taking advantage of Audrey's generosity by staying in her house a second time, when she doesn't even know I'm here."

"But it's my home, too."

"She's the actual owner, though, and she's already done so much for me . . . especially considering the two of us hadn't even spoken in more than ten years."

"But, Helen, she credits you with saving her son's life!"

Helen clicked her tongue. "Well, the woman's a television star. She's prone to being overly dramatic." She headed toward the door. "Thanks just the same, but really—"

"Then I'll call her right now and get you a direct invitation. I'm absolutely certain she—"

"Please, don't! I don't want you to cloud her family's joyous occasion with my troubles."

"She'd want to know, Helen. She'll be angry with me for not convincing you to stay, and for keeping her in the dark."

"Maybe so, but this is my life, and I get to make my own decisions. Up until Stephanie gets ahold of a good lawyer and declares me incompetent, that is."

Heartsick, I watched her shuffle back to her car; the bag that had seemed so insubstantial when I'd carried it appeared to be a heavy burden for her. She heaved it into her passenger seat. Without a glance behind her, she started her car and drove away.

The next morning, I was awakened by a phone call from Sullivan, who greeted me with: "Gilbert! What the hell did you say to Stephanie Miller?"

"Nothing!" I retorted automatically, discombobulated and needing to battle my way out of sleep fog. "Um, when?"

"The last time you saw her!"

"Oh, right. At the police station. The night before last." Once again, I'd done a woeful job of keeping my "partner" informed; yet another reason I should always work alone. "I ran into her under the worst possible circumstances. I was waiting for Helen, and it was immediately after her brother had been killed. Stephanie felt I was overstepping my bounds."

"Because you were acting like a member of the family, instead of their designer?" he asked snidely.

"Something like that," I shot back, livid. "You obviously agree with her."

"She called me up just now and fired us. She's furious with you, Gilbert. She doesn't want you to step in her house. Those were her exact words."

"Oh, jeez. I was hoping she'd calm down by now… realize that she's really upset over her loss, not at *me* for simply being kind to her aunt in her time of need."

"I might have managed to clear this up yesterday, if you'd bothered to tell me about her brother's murder, Gilbert! Instead I found out about Peter's murder on the ten o'clock news."

My thoughts immediately flashed to how hurt I'd been a couple of weeks ago when I found out through the grapevine that Sullivan was already back in town. "You're right. I should've called you. Though it's not like you're Walter Cronkite when it comes to keeping *me* informed."

He ignored that and snapped, "I'll keep our scheduled appointment with Stephanie by myself and see if I can do some damage control. I don't want to lose her as a client."

"Of course not," I said, my voice simmering. "Business first, at all cost."

"Exactly. Because I'm a businessman. I run my own company for a living. So I'm going to try and smooth over the rift between you two. You got a problem with that?"

"No," I said in a small voice, realizing he was completely in the right.

"Good!" He hung up on me.

I flopped back down and threw my arm over my eyes, feeling frustrated and miserable. Hildi picked up on my distress. She nestled against me, purring.

I went to my office and did my best to stay productive for the next couple of hours, but failed miserably. Steve was keeping what would have been our joint appointment at Stephanie's. As time passed with no word, I finally couldn't stand to wait any longer and called his cell phone. He growled, "Yeah?"

We both knew full well that his phone had displayed my name and number. "Hi, Steve. I was just wondering how things were going. Is Stephanie—"

"Can't say one way or the other. Is our working at Helen's this afternoon still on?"

"No. The house is cordoned off while the police hunt for evidence. Helen hasn't been able to move back in yet."

"Yeah, she has, Gilbert. Stephanie raised a ruckus with the police chief. They allowed Helen to move back to her place about an hour ago."

"That's news to me."

"Unless I hear otherwise, I'll meet you there at three. I gotta run." For the second time that morning, he hung up on me.

There was a nip in the air, a harbinger that autumn was imminent. Fall was achingly beautiful in Colorado, when the aspen leaves turn as bright yellow as the sun. The maples in our neighborhood display a brilliant array of orange and red colors against the brightest blue sky imaginable. The sight is totally breathtaking! Yet now the seasonal change meant that I had to get Helen out of her garage once and for all, before she caught pneumonia or her space heater started a fire.

I arrived ten minutes early at Helen's, hoping to beat Sullivan. He pulled in behind me just as I was emerging from my van. "What's the latest with Stephanie?" I asked when he finally joined me. "Am I off the job?"

"Not completely. She still wants your input ... just doesn't want to have to deal with you face-to-face. She and I are cool, though."

"Congratulations. You must feel great. Meanwhile, she wants me to work for her, but never actually see her!"

"Or speak to her." He gave me a smug grin. "Luckily, you've got me as an intermediary, so that's not going to be a problem."

I let out a bark of sarcastic laughter. "Maybe not for *you*, it isn't. But I accepted her job primarily because Stephanie's such a mover and shaker in Crestview real estate. She's never going to recommend me to anyone now. And all because I was trying to help out her aunt under hideous circumstances!"

He wisely held his tongue, and we made our way up Helen's brick walkway. We stepped around a box on the stoop that I assumed was items that Helen had put there herself, and I stabbed at the doorbell.

My confidence-and-optimism mantra was letting me down.

Helen gingerly opened the front door for us, as if ready to slam it shut again if we turned out to be murderous intruders. Her "Good afternoon" was cheerless. "What have you brought me?" she asked, glancing at the box at our feet.

"It was here when we arrived," Sullivan replied.

Keeping her screen door ajar against one ankle, she pulled open the box flaps and peered inside. Among the various items was the Raggedy Ann doll, still in its valuable box, which Kay had stolen.

"Oh, dear!" she cried.

"What is all this stuff?" Sullivan asked.

She turned her injured gaze to me. "Now I've lost my best friend! She won't even keep the things she stole from me!" She pursed her lips for a moment, then announced, "I'm sorry, Erin and Steve, but there's no point in your continuing to work on my house. I'm just going to let my niece ship me off to a nursing home." With a grunt of effort, she picked up the box.

Sullivan gave me a worried glance, as he stepped forward. "Let me carry that for you, Ms. Walker."

"No, thank you," she said firmly. She took a couple of wobbly steps inside, then kicked the door shut behind her.

Sullivan looked at me in surprise. "Kay was *stealing* from her?"

"Kay's a closet kleptomaniac, apparently. I'm sure I exacerbated the strain Kay's compulsion has put on their friendship by asking Helen about it the other day. She'll calm down and pull herself together soon, though."

He released a weary sigh. "Let's go."

"I'd rather give her a minute or two, then make sure she's all right. I don't want to give up on her this easily."

"She just slammed the door in our faces!"

"That was hardly a slam," I replied.

He spread his arms. "And yet here we are, stuck out on her front porch." He started down the walkway. "She's probably going to hole herself in her house for a day or two. Maybe longer. You're wasting your time."

After Sullivan had driven off in his macho hissy fit, I walked over to Helen's garage door and knocked on a panel. When she didn't answer, I counted to ten and knocked again. At last she opened the door to the garage and even mustered a smile as she stood with arms akimbo at the back of the garage near the opener button. "Come on in, Erin. I'm glad to see I was right."

"About what?" I stepped inside, noting that her floor lamp and space heater were missing.

"Oh, just that you're much more patient than your boyfriend is."

"Sullivan's not my boyfriend."

Once the door had completed its noisy descent, she said, "I'm beginning to suspect that I've misjudged things terribly, Erin."

"My relationship with Steve Sullivan, you mean?"

"Good heavens, no. That's none of my business." She turned on a heel, opened the door to her house, and set the catch so that it would remain wide open. "We're moving the love seat back into the living room." She grabbed one arm of the small sofa. "Don't worry. It's not too heavy for me."

Surprised but glad that she was finally moving out of her garage, I picked up my end, and we shuffled our way into the kitchen. "That's far enough, for now," she puffed when we'd cleared the doorway. We set down the love seat, and she dropped onto a cushion and fanned herself. "Whew! Don't tell anybody this, Erin, but I'm turning into an old lady."

I chuckled, but then chewed on my lip. Knowing Helen, she'd be happy to leave this ugly love seat in her kitchen.

Helen caught her breath, then sat up and patted the tops of her thighs twice as if resolved to stand up and take action. "I didn't want to let Steve Sullivan see what I'm about to show you. You're the only one I dare to trust. Lois was so secretive about it."

I swallowed hard. Her pronouncement felt more than a little ominous, considering that two people had died in this house in the past week.

The doorbell rang, and someone promptly opened Helen's front door. Looking perplexed and unnerved, Helen got to her feet just as a voice called, "Yoo-hoo. Helen?"

"Rachel! Why do you think it's okay to just let yourself into my house?" Helen cried indignantly. I followed her into the living room. There Rachel stood, holding the two porcelain figurines that she'd ignobly obtained from Helen.

"I'm sorry, Helen. Your door was unlocked. I thought I could just slip these inside." Even as she spoke, she took it upon herself to come fully inside and set the delicate figurines on top of the upright piano. "I also brought you this..." Ducking back outside, she returned with a lush flower arrangement of white chrysanthemums, baby's breath, and yellow daisies in a white basket, which she handed to Helen. "There's no need to thank me. I just feel so horrible about your poor nephew. I can't tell you how deeply I regret agreeing to go along with his plan."

Without so much as taking a step, Helen set the flowers on the green-gold rug. She was blinking back tears.

"Rachel? Was he still working with you on Monday night... the night he was killed?" I asked before I could stop myself. "Is that why he was here?"

"No, no, of course not," Rachel replied. "I hadn't spoken to him since his scheme to take things from Helen backfired. I have no idea what he thought he was doing, coming over here again."

Helen said evenly, "Rachel, I really—"

"I know," Rachel interrupted. "Now is not a good time. Sorry to have intruded. I'll let myself out." She left, but an instant later leaned through the doorway. "Erin? Don't forget to contact me about some design work, just as soon as this sordid ordeal has worked itself out, would you?" She gave Helen a benign smile. "Take care. Do let me know if there's anything I can do. I feel like we're soul sisters, now that we've both lost a loved one." She gave a little wiggly-fingers wave, then left for real.

Helen promptly stomped over to the door and threw the lock, saying, "At least Rachel's assault on my home was reasonably well timed, for once." She gestured for me to follow as she returned to the kitchen. She removed the love seat cushion she'd recently occupied and reached her spindly arm inside along the armrest. "I was afraid the police would find this, but they didn't. Lois kept it under lock and key, and you're the only person I can trust to give this to Stephanie for me. Since she and I are no longer on speaking terms."

Just as I was about to confess that I, too, was no longer

on speaking terms with her imperious niece, Helen extracted a white athletic sock, slightly soiled, from the lower recesses of the sofa. She reached into the sock and removed a glittering pink and gold object.

I found myself looking at a jewel-encrusted Fabergé imperial egg carved in rose quartz.

chapter 21

in mute dismay, I held out my hand, and she slipped the precious egg into my palm. My heart was thundering. This was all too strange. I'd had clients reveal some heirloom to me that they were hoping I'd say was worth a fortune, which had yet to be the case. This egg, however, might actually *be* worth a fortune.

Not trusting my voice, I cleared my throat before I asked, "How exactly did your sister get this?"

Helen returned the cushion to the sofa and reclaimed her seat before answering. "According to Lois, it was a gift from George. From twenty years back. I was always a bit incredulous, though. The man wasn't exactly generous.

And she never once displayed it while he was alive. Not even after he died."

"Did she tell you why not?"

"Because it wasn't to her taste ... too delicate and fussy-looking. Plus she hated the color pink."

"Lois? Hated pink?"

"I know. It's odd. George was the one who *really* hated pink. After he died and she moved in with me, she painted her bedroom pink ... out of defiance, or something. She said afterward, 'I just remembered something, Helen. I dislike this color every bit as much as George did.' She decided it wasn't worth the effort, though, to re-paint."

My attention was riveted to the glorious three-inch egg. I am not a jewelry expert by any means, but there's a tell-tale precision and clarity to real gems that's difficult to miss. The brilliant gold band that circled the egg contained twelve large, sparkling jewels, which looked un-nervingly like two-carat diamonds. The carving in the pedestal base was astonishingly elaborate. It resembled a bouquet of roses, each bud of which boasted a dazzling ruby red gemstone. The base was black, perhaps carved onyx, decorated with scrolls of gold.

What should I do? I didn't want to take a wild guess and exaggerate the monetary value of the piece. Nor did I want Helen to think she could be cavalier with it, and risk having Kay swipe it in their personal version of "Keep Away." "If these gemstones are real, Helen, this could be worth a whole lot of money."

"Oh, I very much doubt they're real. George would never have given Lois anything expensive ... if this was truly a gift from him. He was always giving her little things after they'd quarreled, but otherwise, she was lucky to get a birthday card from that man."

"Even if the jewels are fake, this *is* real gold surrounding it, Helen. And the craftsmanship is exquisite. If this is a knockoff, it's an expensive one. I'd be shocked if it was worth anything less than ten thousand dollars."

Worry lines creased her brow as she eyed the egg nestled in my palm. "Oh, dear. That's what I was afraid of. Lois had told me it was just gold paint, but I began to worry when I couldn't scrape it off with my thumbnail. What should I do now?"

Though it was probably my imagination, the piece started to feel heavy and hot in my hands. "The thing is, Helen...there's a big possibility that this is stolen property. We should take it straight to the police."

"No, Erin. There's no proof that this is valuable. Maybe it's just...a really thin coating of gold. A veneer. I'm going to continue to hope that this *is* just some knockoff bauble that George purchased legitimately. After one of their bigger spats."

Her tone of voice made it clear she was trying hard to convince herself. For my part, my suspicious brain mulled various troublesome possibilities of how George had acquired this "trinket." "Here's what we'll do then," I said. "I'll see what I can find out about missing Fabergé-like eggs. In the meantime, you should probably return this to your sofa and not mention a word about showing it to me." I studied her guileless expression. "Have you told anybody else about this?"

"No one. Lois asked me not to. Not even her own children know about it. She said it would only cause bickering in the family...that Stephanie would be especially angry at her for keeping it hidden away." She sighed as she gazed at the thing. "I told Lois at the time that this did look like something that Stephanie would want to own."

"Yes, it does," I said as noncommittally as possible.

A very real—and chilling—possibility was that the secret hadn't been kept all that well. That would explain why Peter had been breaking into Helen's house to "steal" his own possessions. If he knew about this egg, he knew, too, that it was stolen property, and that neither he nor Stephanie could legally inherit it. To make any money whatsoever for the egg, it would have to be fenced. Maybe he reasoned that his sister had far too much to lose to risk taking such an illegal action.

Peter could very well have paid the ultimate price for trying to keep the tiny masterpiece away from his sister's hands.

I stopped in at my office, fired up my computer, and did a search on "stolen Fabergé egg Colorado." Soon I was looking at an archived article from the *Crestview Sentinel* on "Famous Unsolved Crimes." There were two paragraphs about "a Fabergé egg stolen from a Crestview art museum." The egg had been custom-made in 1955 by the artisans at Fabergé for a Denver aristocrat who subsequently donated it to the museum. The article went on to state:

The jewel-encrusted rose-quartz egg has not surfaced since it was stolen on July 14, 1966, from the Crestview Art and History Museum. With the curiosity factor adding to its value, some experts have stated the egg could now be worth more than $200,000.

The article had been written three years earlier. The egg was probably worth more like a quarter of a million dollars by now. In some ways, its value was irrelevant, because it belonged to a museum. With my heart in my stomach, I drove straight to the museum and pulled up at the small white house that had once been a private residence but now bore a hand-carved wooden sign that read *Crestview Art & History Museum*.

Charlotte, my favorite curator, was on duty that day. She was a pleasant-looking middle-aged woman with a daughter who was studying design, but I was too thirsty for answers to exchange more than the briefest of pleasantries before explaining, "I'm curious about a Fabergé egg that was stolen from this museum many years ago."

She nodded. "We get asked about that particular incident quite a bit. Every now and then, the newspaper does a story on it. The whole thing occurred before my time here, though. It must be some forty years ago by now. Why are you asking?"

"Research for a client. I'll explain it all to you later... once I get some answers for her. Is there anybody I could talk to who was with the museum at the time?"

Charlotte hesitated, searched my eyes, then slowly replied, "There's the former curator. She comes in every once in a while, but I'm not sure how trustworthy her memory is, frankly. But maybe I can answer your questions."

"Do you have any idea how the theft occurred?"

"Sure do," she said with a nod. "That incident is a required case study for all employees. We're hoping to avoid a repeat of past mistakes, and so far, thank heavens, we haven't had a second theft."

"Not in forty years?"

"Well, not ones which involve anything of that magnitude. Of course, that incident was also the last time we ever *displayed* quite such a valuable, easily pocketed item. And we have a lot better security devices in effect now. Laser detectors, and so on."

"I'd imagine so. How was the burglary accomplished?"

"With assistance from the security guard."

"Who was arrested, I assume?"

"No. Questioned at great length. The security guard on duty that night had ties to the police department, which probably didn't help matters. Apparently there was never enough evidence to charge the guy."

"Was the security guard's name Teddy Frederickson or George Miller, by any chance?"

"I'd have to look in our old records to get you that information. Can I call you later?"

"Absolutely. I'd really appreciate it. Thanks." I gave her my cell phone number and left.

My thoughts were in a whirl. Why would George have given his wife hot merchandise, worth a small fortune? Was there any explanation at all for her having it that didn't sound nefarious? Could Lois possibly not have realized it was stolen property?

I had reached my office when my cell phone rang. When I answered, Charlotte identified herself and said, "I've got the security guard's name for you, Erin. You were right. It's George Miller."

chapter 22

the task of letting Helen know that she possessed stolen property was best done face-to-face. I drove straight to her house after getting off the phone with the curator. The moment Helen answered her door and saw me, she sighed. "Come in, Erin, and have a seat. I can see this isn't going to be good news."

"No, it isn't." A few items of clothing and an ancient-looking transistor radio had migrated back onto her piano bench. In fact, her whole living room was starting to get messy again. Her clutter apparently behaved like a flock of homing pigeons. I cleared a space and sat down while she took a seat on the bentwood rocker. "The egg is stolen property, Helen."

"Oh, dear..."

"It's from a museum in Crestview. Where your late brother-in-law once worked as the security guard. Obviously you can't let Stephanie have it. We'll return it to its rightful owners through the police."

"I'm going to have to report *another* crime to the police? My word. The Crestview police are going to think I'm Ma Barker. Isn't there some way we could simply... drop it off at the museum? You could distract them, while I stick the egg on a shelf."

I knew she wasn't serious. "Maybe we should get this thing over with now."

"I just hope they won't decide to lock me up. They probably consider me a career criminal." We rose and headed into the kitchen, where her natty sofa was still stranded. She dug behind the cushions and removed the Fabergé egg in its sock. "You'd better hang on to this for me while I get ready to go."

She'd stuck Rachel's bouquet, basket and all, in the sink, I noted, which was the only available surface, other than the pathways on the linoleum floor that Sullivan and I had created on Saturday. I eyed the sofa, wishing I could teleport it into the living room. Helen handed me the egg, complete with sock, plucked a plastic footstool from a messy heap of possessions underneath the table, grabbed a roll of tape from atop the cat food on the kitchen counter, and proceeded to tape a hair across the opening of the back door. Apparently, we would be leaving through the garage.

Unable to resist stealing another glance at the astounding work of art, I peered into the sock. The Fabergé egg was every bit as stunning as I'd remembered it to be. "Has this been hidden in your sofa ever since your sister passed away?"

"Oh, heavens no. It was in Lois's bedroom till I decided to move it into the couch."

"I thought you said she kept it under lock and key."

"And so she did, for years. According to Lois, she'd kept it in a safety deposit box at a bank until George died. I myself had never seen or heard a word about the egg until Lois moved in with me two years ago."

"And at that point, she took it out of the bank and hid it in her bedroom?"

"Yes. Lois had kept it under her bed, stuffed inside that old sock. When she died, I moved it into the couch."

"It's kind of hard to believe that your sister never realized that she was in possession of stolen property."

Helen gave me a sidelong glance as she squeezed past the sofa and into the living room, where she dragged the piano bench toward the front door. She retrieved a second roll of Scotch tape from the piano keyboard, then allowed me to carry the bench to the door. She climbed onto the bench as she plucked one of her hairs. "Lois put up with a bushel of grief. She always had to work hard at keeping George under control. He was always a little on the reckless side." She frowned as she taped the strand of hair into place. "George had a drinking problem."

"And a theft problem, too."

"She probably *did* know it was stolen," Helen admitted with a sigh. "She must have snatched it away from George and hid it. That would have been just like her . . . to try to hide everything away and pretend nobody was hurt, if she'd discovered that her husband was a thief."

"She wouldn't have anonymously returned it to the museum?"

Helen froze for a moment as if realizing that her suggested scenario didn't paint her sister in the best possible light. Then she sighed again and shook her head. "Her first priority would have been George and the kids." She gingerly stepped back down from the bench, ignoring my proffered helping hand. "Lois wouldn't have been willing to risk the authorities tracing it back to George. That would have sent him to jail, plus ruined their children's image of their father. Those would have been terrible prices to pay, as a consequence of her good deed."

I had to bite my tongue as I returned the bench to its rightful place, thinking that returning the egg wouldn't have been merely a "good deed" so much as not committing a federal offense herself, in the aftermath of her husband's. Lois must have read about the Fabergé egg theft in the papers when it first happened. She had been aiding a crime and harboring a criminal—her husband!

I eyed Helen's guileless features. Was her story plausible? She kept all of the local newspapers where the stories of the theft would surely have been thoroughly reported. Yet the most recent article on the egg was from three years back, and she hadn't even known Lois had the egg till *two* years ago, when Lois moved in with her.

Helen was turning in a slow three-sixty, scanning the room, and I saw a set of keys near the porcelain dancers on top of the piano. "Is this what you're looking for?" I asked, holding the keys aloft.

She snatched them from my grasp and started to lead the way to the garage. "It's like I always say: If your house is truly messy, you can hide almost anything indefinitely. I guess subconsciously I've known for two years now that Lois's egg was valuable. And that it could have been stolen. *And* that it could be the reason someone kept breaking into my house."

"Maybe her having the egg is why she was killed," I said. I had a hideous, chilling image of someone deliberately feeding Lois the fatal bell pepper and then withholding the epinephrine shot until she revealed the location of her precious treasure.

Helen must have had an equally hideous vision, because she turned at the door and gaped at me. "Oh, Erin! Perish the thought! That would mean my keeping my sister's secret inadvertently led to *three* deaths!"

"No, it doesn't," I said, rapidly backpedaling. "You couldn't have known any of this would happen—"

"Yes, Erin, I *could* have. I knew very well about my sister's blind spot regarding George. And, as I said before, I was worried that the silly little egg was what the burglar was really after . . . but I never said a single word to anyone about it!"

She looked so upset that I was kicking myself for blurting out my current theory about the motive behind her sister's death. Fortunately, Vator had pranced into the room, and Helen swept the cat up. She dropped into the sofa.

"But, Helen, it was *Peter* who'd been breaking into your house," I reminded her.

"And somebody shot him with a harpoon! And poisoned my chocolates! And used my kitty to set a cruel trap that killed Jack!" She began to rock herself while cradling her cat. "Maybe I was wrong. Maybe Peter *did* find out about the egg . . . and that's what he was looking for when he was killed! I could have prevented everything, including Lois's death, if I'd just insisted that she tell me the whole story. And then made her turn the blasted thing in to the police. I'm a terrible, terrible person, Erin!"

"No, you're not, Helen. We don't *know* that the Fabergé egg has anything to do with any of those tragic events. And even if it does, you've only behaved the way we all do. You heard a fishy story from your sister, and rather than provoke her into an unpleasant confrontation, you accepted her version as the truth."

She muttered into her calico's fur, "Yes, bully for me. I swept the whole thing under the rug. Or, more accurately, into the sofa."

Vator made a *rr-r-rr* noise, hopped off Helen's lap, and darted out of the kitchen.

Helen got unsteadily to her feet. "Let's go, Erin," she said, her eyes averted.

My thoughts were racing. If the valuable within the sock I carried was indeed the underlying cause of these murders, there had to be a way to identify the killer; he or she had to have known that the egg was hidden in this house. "You're absolutely certain you never told anyone about the Fabergé egg?"

"Positive." She opened the door to the garage. "And Lois would have kept that secret, too, believe me. She would have wanted to protect George's reputation, at all costs." She winced and added under her breath, "Although I'm quite certain Lois would have had no idea just how terribly high those *costs* were going to turn out to be."

Helen insisted on driving us, even though she once again had some trouble starting her car. I emptied my purse into all my pockets and slipped the egg and its protective sock into my purse. I held the purse on my lap, half wishing the gem-encrusted treasure would magically vanish. It felt as though my brain were on a spin cycle. Helen was telling me the complete truth; of that much I was certain. But I couldn't help but conclude that the deaths and sabotage *had* all been caused by the Fabergé egg. I started to concoct wild theories—that Stephanie and Peter knew about the egg, but also knew they wouldn't get enough money for it in an estate sale, and so they were vying against each other to find it and fence it for cash, setting booby traps along the way to off the competition. Or that admitted thieves Kay or Teddy had somehow learned about it, and that one of them was the guilty party. Maybe Rachel had an affair with George, and he told her about the stolen egg, so she killed her own husband and then her partner-in-crime, Peter, to get it.

My immediate concern, though, was Detective O'Reilly. As outrageous as the scenario was, he *could* conceivably charge Helen with willful possession of stolen property. I had to give the egg to Linda. Except there was no telling what Linda would do; she would instantly recognize its significance in the case and would probably be duty bound to turn it over to O'Reilly immediately. My best hope was that she'd be out and Mansfield in; her partner was a nice enough guy, but not the sharpest crayon in the box. As partners, they worked the same shift, though, so that was a long shot.

We arrived at the station house. Helen shut off the engine, but remained in her seat. She gripped her steering wheel with both hands. She was pale, and her gray eyes were wide with fright. "Everything's going to be fine," I assured her. "I'll explain why we came in, and you just need to answer their questions, simply and directly. Please don't speculate about how Lois got the egg, though. If they ask you that, tell them you don't know . . . which is the truth. Okay?"

"Oh, dear. You're thinking that they truly might arrest me on the spot, too." She was on the verge of tears. "I'd get a lawyer, except Peter was the only lawyer I knew personally."

"Let's just hope for the best and see how this goes, okay?"

I helped her from the car and ushered her inside the imposing cement structure. With my heart pounding and Helen cowering behind me, I approached the dispatcher at his oversized desk in the lobby. I gave him a nervous smile and said, "Hi. Is Officer Linda Delgardio or Officer Mansfield here?"

"Just a sec," he said, and spoke into his headset. A few moments later he said, "Officer Mansfield will be right out."

I felt like leaping for joy, but whispered to Helen, "This is good. We'll give Mansfield the egg, and maybe he'll let us leave right away."

Helen nodded, grim-faced, and sank into one of the drab, blue-gray seats. I was too tense to sit. Mansfield soon lumbered down the hallway toward us. While watching him through the glass door and plastering an inane smile on my face, I reached into my purse and grabbed the egg. My nerves were making me almost woozy. If my decision to bring Helen here with me led to her arrest, I'd want to drop dead on the spot.

We greeted one another, and I did a hot-potato thrust into his hand with the Fabergé egg, blathering, "We came to give you this. Helen didn't realize it at the time, but her sister had hidden it in her bedroom, and now we think it's stolen property from the Crestview Art and History Museum. A theft occurred there about forty years ago, when George Miller was the security guard."

"Er, let's go inside and have a seat for a minute," Mansfield said.

"Sure thing," I replied, but was inwardly cursing. He opened the door for us. I gave Helen what I hoped was a reassuring smile and took her arm. Mansfield ushered us toward the desk that I knew he and Linda shared with other on-duty uniformed officers. I held a chair for Helen, who sat down.

While Mansfield rounded his desk, Helen announced, "I think the Fabergé egg could be what my nephew, Peter, had really been searching for in my house when he was killed."

I cringed, but silently took a seat beside her in one of their omnipresent straight-backed chairs—slightly padded and upholstered in a coarse black and blue fabric.

"Were your nephew and Jack Schwartz friendly?" Mansfield asked.

Helen frowned a little, either at the question or the bad grammar. "No. I don't think they ever even met. But then again, I would never in a million years have guessed that Peter and Rachel Schwartz would form a partnership, so I'm obviously unreliable."

Please don't say another word, I silently willed, trying to catch Helen's eye.

Mansfield examined the egg, rotating it on its base in his hands, the gold and the jewels sparkling in the fluorescent light from above. "Wonder how much this thing is worth." He looked at me. "Got any idea?"

"Uh, well, I guess it's been speculated that it's worth more than two hundred K."

He widened his eyes, then set down the egg, gingerly. "Thanks for bringing it in."

"Can we go now, Officer?" Helen asked.

He continued to stare at the egg, not much larger than my fist but worth a fortune. "Yeah, just let me write you out a receipt." He scribbled something on a printed form, handed it to Helen, and said, "We'll be in touch."

Hallelujah! I thanked him and hurried Helen out of there before he could reconsider, or O'Reilly could happen to stroll by.

As we reached her car, Helen said, "I suppose I should feel relieved. But this is all so sad. Tomorrow's my nephew's funeral. I remember holding him, at the hospital, on the day he was born." A tear trickled down her cheek. "Now here I am, having outlived both his parents and him. Gone before their time. Maybe all because of a decorated pink stone, shaped like an egg."

Helen dried her eyes and drove us to her house in silence. When we pulled into her garage, she said, "Thanks, Erin. This whole thing is aging me rapidly. And I wasn't all that young to begin with."

"I'm so sorry, Helen. You've had more than your share of woes lately."

"I have to admit that I always suspected that George really was the thief in that shoplifting scam from years ago, not Teddy."

"You think George framed Teddy?"

"Oh, Teddy probably played a part, too. But George was undoubtedly the ringleader, with Teddy ultimately taking the fall."

"Teddy's always so cheerful. He seems to have gotten out of jail with a remarkable lack of bitterness."

"Yes. He told Lois and me that getting arrested for theft as a young man was the best thing that could have happened to him. Otherwise he thinks he'd have spiraled."

"Gone on to worse and worse crimes, you mean?"

"Yes. This way, though, he got his act together, wound up running a small carpet-cleaning company that became quite successful. He said at one point he had over a hundred employees."

My cynical side leapt to the thought that he might have stolen items from all those homes with dirty carpets, but it was hard to believe he'd have gotten away with such a thing year after year.

"Are you coming to Peter's funeral services tomorrow afternoon?" she asked me hopefully.

"Yes, I sure am," I said.

"I'll see you there, then," Helen said, opening the door to the kitchen. "Thank you, as always, for going so far above and beyond your decorating duties."

My eyes returned to that sofa. I was already late for my next appointment, but another minute of delay wouldn't make that much difference. "Speaking of decorating, let's just move this sofa into the living room really quick, all right?"

The next day was Peter's funeral. Ironic that Peter hadn't wanted to come to a funeral for Jack Schwartz. A week later, he had no choice but to attend this one.

As was the case with Jack Schwartz, lots of mourners were in attendance. That surprised me a little. Peter had struck me as a fairly solitary person, just a step or two from being a recluse. Steve Sullivan appeared at the small church but sat in the back. Now the man wouldn't even sit next to me. At least he lifted his chin in a silent greeting when I looked behind me and our eyes happened to meet. Maybe our rocky friendship was over for good, and our even rockier partnership would end the moment we completed Stephanie's game room.

Though battling her emotions throughout, Stephanie managed to deliver a touching eulogy that brought tears to my eyes several times and caused poor Helen to dissolve into wracking sobs. I found myself unable to listen closely to the proceedings and instead drew up my own list of suspects. All four of them were in attendance: Kay and Teddy arrived together, and although I couldn't tell for certain from my vantage point, I got the distinct impression that they were holding hands. With the unsolved-theft issue concerning the valuable egg, Teddy was now my prime suspect, with Rachel just a notch below him. Kay was next. Stephanie, despite her very obvious grief, also remained on my list.

There was a reception afterward in the church hall below us. I spotted Linda Delgardio in a corner of the room. She was watching Helen like a hawk. Helen, meanwhile, was surrounded by a group of people her age, mostly women, including the couple she'd introduced me to at Jack's service as fellow scrapbookers. Pleasantly surprised that neither I nor, to my knowledge, Helen had been fully interrogated about the Fabergé egg, I avoided meeting Linda's eyes. I turned and glanced in the opposite direction, intending to wander off that way, only to meet with Detective O'Reilly's stony glare. Both police officers were here? Were they operating surveillance on both me and Helen now? If so, they were watching the wrong folks!

I needed to leave before O'Reilly could corner me. I'd already paid my respects to Helen. Stephanie was standing alone near the exit. Our eyes met. Although she probably didn't want to speak to me, I approached her. "Stephanie, again, I'm so terribly sorry for your loss. It was touching to see that so many people came to your brother's service."

She snorted. "They're mostly the competition."

"Pardon?"

"Most of the so-called 'mourners' are in the real estate business like me and want to be seen at my brother's funeral." She gave me a visual once-over. "It was good of you to come, though, Erin, in spite of everything that's happened. And, by the way, I realize now that I overreacted. It's very obvious that you're *not* trying to wrangle your way into Aunt Helen's will. You're just the Goody Two-shoes type who has to come to everyone's aid in order to feel complete as a person."

I cleared my throat and tried to count to ten before responding, but made it only to two. "I think it'd be more accurate to say that your aunt is a dear, sweet person, and I came to her aid when she was scared half to death."

"Whatever. At any rate, Aunt Helen adores you, and Steve insists he wants you as a full partner on my rec room, so—"

"He does?" I blurted out in surprise.

She shrugged. "It surprised me, too, but I figure, it's no skin off my nose...I'm paying the same amount either way. Might as well get two designers for the price of one. So, if you can join Sullivan at my house in two hours to pick up where you left off, that'd be fine by me."

Strange that she was working on something as frivolous as her game room on the very day of her only sibling's funeral. "That's great. Thank you, Stephanie."

She gave me a tight-lipped nod and walked away. I scanned the room for Sullivan to thank him and soon found him chatting up a foursome of middle-aged women who seemed to be hanging on his every syllable. Just then I saw O'Reilly making his way across the room toward me. I left hastily.

Later that afternoon, I arrived early at Stephanie's house so that I could tell Sullivan I was fully back on the job. I waited in my van till I saw him drive up and walked up to him. He was still wearing the tailored black Italian suit with a navy pinstripe silk tie he'd worn to Peter's funeral, and he bore just a hint of either cologne or aftershave. He looked and smelled delicious, darn it. "Hi, Sullivan. I wanted to thank you."

"You're welcome. What'd I do?"

"Stephanie told me how you went to bat for me."

"Oh, yeah? In what respect?" He managed to affect a bored and mildly confused demeanor at once.

"That you told her you wanted my help designing her rec room, so she says I'm fully back on the job."

"Oh, good. Actually, though, I just told her I liked using you as a sounding board and getting your input. But it's great that she rehired you."

No need to accidentally give me the impression that he valued me. I said, "I think it'd be wise, under the circumstances, if you handled most of the client interaction with Stephanie, for the time being."

"Fine." He hesitated, then gave me a look that was awfully close to a sneer. "You're really going to let me do most of the talking?"

"Yes, I am."

"I'll believe that when I hear it," he muttered.

I sighed, but decided to get in a little practice by holding my tongue now. Sullivan rang the doorbell and, as Stephanie ushered us inside, he slipped into his ever-so-competent-designer routine. I allowed Sullivan to take the lead as he went through the final check with her to make certain we were ordering exactly what she wanted. He seemed to be taking my suggestion to handle the bulk of the interaction a little too much to heart; I had to struggle to catch the slightest glimpse of the samples.

I couldn't help but widen my eyes when I spotted the too-red hue of the paint. Not to mention the new fabric selection for the sectional.

Stephanie must have been watching my face just then. "You were expecting a more neutral color, Erin?" she asked immediately.

"You'd wanted apricot paint. Isn't this more . . . tangerine?" I tilted the display board in Sullivan's hands so that I could finally really see it. "Or tomato, even?"

"Yeah, but then she remembered she'd painted her den apricot, and she doesn't like to repeat room colors, so she opted for desert-sunrise red," Sullivan said crossly.

Desert-sunrise red? For a basement rec room? With a gold satin sectional? It would look like a honky-tonk barroom. Or a brothel! Was this a test? The moment I objected, was Sullivan going to laugh and announce, "I *knew* you couldn't keep your mouth shut, Gilbert"?

"Do you have a problem with the color scheme, Erin?" Stephanie asked.

Sullivan was glaring at me. "Uh, no, not at all," I lied. "Not so long as you're sure *you* like it."

She'd picked up on my doubtfulness. Worry lines creased her brow. "It is a bit radical, but I do really like the subdued red palette in my dining room."

"Which has those wonderful vaulted ceilings and palladium windows," I replied. "That's not going to be the case in your game room." Not to mention that reds are flattering to food and to complexions, but are dark and dingy in a basement.

Sullivan cleared his throat. "Shall we move on, Stephanie?"

"Erin?"

The woman was paying for my advice and experience; I couldn't just sit here and nod like a bobblehead doll. "Could we possibly take a quick look at the apricot walls in your library, then take a peek at the game room for comparison purposes?"

"Maybe that would be a good idea," she said, rising.

"Great." I grinned at Sullivan, but he was avoiding my eyes. "There's undoubtedly a compromise color we can select that will be right in between these hues." *Then we can rethink the fabric for the sectional!* She escorted me into her den, and I instantly fell in love with the Tuscan ambience of the thick, hand-applied texture on the walls and the cherry desk and cabinets. The palette, however, would have been all the more striking with a darker base color—at three hundred percent or so. "Lovely room," I said, my eye immediately drawn to the marble fireplace and the built-in shelves to either side, which were filled with books.

"You see how bright this room is?" our client asked derisively. "The walls look practically like plaster of paris. Apricot can get a little washed-out in the afternoon sun."

"Which it wouldn't be on your downstairs walls with your east-facing windows. If anything, you could consider reversing the paint selections in the two rooms...painting the rec room this color and using the desert-sunrise red in here."

"Gilbert, I don't—"

"Actually, Steve, that's a great idea." Stephanie was eyeing the walls triumphantly. "It won't cost me that much more to have the painters do this one extra room."

"True," he said, instantly donning a positive attitude, the first requirement of being a good designer. "Although there will be a lot of prep work. Removing the books alone will take a while."

As I surveyed the array of books on the nearest shelf, I grinned. "You have a lot of albums. Are you into scrapbooking, too, Stephanie?"

"Years ago, but it became too time-consuming for me."

Even as she spoke, I did a double-take. One of the binders was a different shade of brown from the others. The oddball album was vinyl and looked like a cheap imitation of the others, which were covered in matching, high-quality leather. "Can I take a quick peek at your work?" I started to remove the vinyl binder from the shelf.

"No, Erin! I'm paying you to design my rooms, not to nose into my private albums!"

"I'm sorry. I didn't mean to pry." Except I *did*, actually, and my curiosity was already driving me nuts; my glance at the edge of the book revealed that about a third of the pages were a slightly different size and shade than the first two thirds. Why would Stephanie keep one odd duck with mismatched pages among her set of albums?

Dutifully, I returned the scrapbook to its place, but now I was dying to find a way to examine its contents. While Sullivan and Stephanie chatted about the precise wall color for this room, I slipped my small tape measure from my pocket and set it on the shelf.

We went downstairs, and when Sullivan's interactions with Stephanie were in full creative rhythm, I feigned surprise at no longer having a tape measure, muttered that I must have "dropped it upstairs," and slipped away.

Back in the den, I grabbed the album, confident that Sullivan would realize that I needed him to keep Stephanie engaged. I flipped to the oddball pages. My vision fell on the photograph of George Miller in his police uniform I'd first seen at Helen's, complete with her unmistakable borders. Stephanie had the stolen pages from Helen's scrapbook!

I rifled through the remaining pages and came across three sheets of stationery that had been placed, unbound, in the album. My heart pounding, I scanned the opening and closing of the letter; it had been sent to "Hell's Bell" and signed "Love, Lolo." That had to be to Helen from Lois. The letter began:

I don't know how long I can continue to live a lie. George is such a hypocrite. I know he is a thief and a con man, and I can barely sleep at night, thinking about how much jeopardy he's put himself and his family—

"Hello, Erin. Thought I'd find you here." Stephanie's voice was chill.

Mortified, I jumped and foolishly tried to hide the letter behind my back.

"Finding some interesting reading in my private album?"

"I'm sorry, Stephanie. But...your aunt was extremely upset about the pages of her scrapbook disappearing. I couldn't stop myself from looking when I realized that you had them."

"I told Helen I'd be borrowing them. She must have forgotten."

"*Borrowing* them? By taking them out of her album and putting them in yours?"

"Yes, actually. They were dangerous, now that she had them out in the open. Most of her things never see the light of day, as you know."

"*Dangerous*? They're fifty-year-old photos and clippings."

"As well as a private letter, between my mother and Aunt Helen," Stephanie said. "I took the pages out of Helen's book, before Peter could stumble over them while you were clearing out her place. It would have broken his heart to learn the truth about our father...about his being a common thief."

"Whereas *you* already knew the truth about your father?"

"I found and read our mother's diary many years ago, and I destroyed it after she died. I didn't feel I had the right to destroy my mother's letter to Aunt Helen, though."

Sullivan appeared behind Stephanie. "What's the matter?" he asked, giving me the evil eye.

"Nothing. Your partner apparently fancies herself an amateur detective." She snatched the letter from my grasp, returned it to a place between the pages, and shoved the album back onto the shelf.

"We need to give that letter to the police," I said firmly.

She swept her hair back from her face. "It's got nothing whatsoever to do with my brother's murder."

"Even so. It's evidence that should be given to the police."

"No way," she snapped.

"Your brother's gone now, so your suppressing the truth won't protect him."

"And airing my family's dirty linen won't help *anybody*. Like I said, it has nothing to do with his murder."

It might, if the letter shows that you or Peter knew about the Fabergé egg that your father stole.

"That should be up to the police to determine, Stephanie."

"Fine, Erin, you've made your point, more or less. I'll give the letter to the authorities, on the ridiculously remote possibility that it actually gives those dim-witted policemen helpful information."

My cell phone rang. It was a client, but I lied and said to Stephanie, "I'm sorry. This call is urgent. I'll step outside and be right back."

I quickly handled my nonurgent scheduling change, then called Linda Delgardio. I told her about the letter and the missing pages from Helen's album. She was letting me have my say, so I launched into my theory that the killings could be tied to George Miller's theft of the Fabergé egg. She cut me off and said, "I'll be there as soon as I can."

I ducked back inside. Sullivan promptly informed me, "We're going with the apricot downstairs and are debating fabrics for the sectional." His gaze was more intense than strictly necessary, letting me know that the subject of the letter was closed.

The doorbell rang just as Stephanie, Sullivan, and I were wrapping up our meeting. Stephanie answered the door. It was Linda and Mansfield.

Stephanie plastered on a smile. "Good afternoon, Officers. Can I help you?"

Linda said, "We're following up on a report about your having possible evidence related to your brother's death, Ms. Miller."

"Oh, are you?" Stephanie's voice was calm. "Please come in."

"Miss Gilbert," her partner said with a nod. Linda was taking in the room.

"Erin," Stephanie said with saccharine sweetness, "I was going to bring the letter to the police myself."

"That really isn't something that can be done at your convenience," Linda told her. "I would think you'd want to help with our investigation of your brother's murder."

"Oh, I do. It's just that I'm afraid you'll misinterpret what's written. You see, Erin, the letter doesn't merely implicate my father, but Helen as well."

"I'm . . . stunned," I muttered. *And incredulous.*

"I'll show it to you, Officers. Come with me." She paused and turned toward Sullivan and me. "And, by the way, Erin and Steve," she added gently, "you're fired for good this time."

chapter **23**

It's possible to add little touches to personalize even a store-bought gift, by painting it the recipient's favorite color, for example, or making the card yourself.

—Audrey Munroe

DOMESTIC BLISS

Home alone in the wake of our curt dismissal from Stephanie's, I was desperate for distraction. Sullivan had cut off my explanations with a clipped: "I've got a client appointment to get to. Give me ninety minutes, then call me." That was one phone call I was in no hurry to place. In retrospect, I felt guilty. I'd jumped the gun by notifying the police, and I shouldn't have been reading Helen and Lois's private correspondence.

I paced in circles in Audrey's sparkling kitchen as Hildi watched me from the colorful braided rug by the back door. I just didn't feel up to calling a friend and going out. What I wanted to do was hear all about Audrey's new granddaughter for a while and not have to think about my own problems. Nor about how furious Sullivan was with me. Audrey hadn't called me, however, and I had no idea what time her flight was scheduled to arrive.

What would be best for me now was to do something for someone else, so that I could remind myself that I was a good person. One who screwed up from time to time. It suddenly hit me that, last month, before she'd allowed herself to get waylaid with teaching herself how to knit, Audrey had been busily creating a "keepsakes storage box" for her soon-to-arrive grandchild. I'd loved that idea—much more so than her twenty-foot-long green scarf—and hadn't wanted her to drop the project. Maybe I could help her pick up wherever she'd left off.

I trotted up the stairs and entered her bedroom, where I'd last seen her spiriting away the box and its materials. It felt intrusive to be in her bedroom alone, not that she'd mind, just that it wasn't something I normally did. I indulged myself with a deep breath of the warm air, redolent with Audrey-like aromas—her signature perfume mixed with her favorite potpourri. Her room boasted an eclectic blend of items from the many places she'd visited: a handwoven basket from Australia, painted gourds from Kenya, a miniature gondolier in handblown glass from Venice, a Shoji screen from China. The room was a bit busy to the eye, but every item held a sentimental memory for her, and just knowing that fact made me smile. Her color palette, like her possessions, was all over the map, but the furniture was consistent and elegant: mission-style oak antiques.

I quickly found the box—a sturdy, acid-free cardboard designed expressly for keepsakes—under her bed. It contained only the materials that Audrey was using to turn it into such a keepsake in its own right. As I'd remembered, she'd already completed two of the sides; I merely needed to duplicate the designs on their opposing sides.

I brought the project downstairs to the kitchen and began to work. Though it pained me to do so, I cut up yet more gorgeous patterns out of fabulous sections of Belgian lace and Scalamandre wallpaper, used the same types and sizes of dried pressed flowers, and copied the tiny hearts and other adorable designs that she'd embossed into origami paper. The task was mind-numbingly intricate, exactly what I needed. Working with tweezers, I placed each item on the sticky side of translucent sheets of paper, always mindful of the fact that the top surface would become the backside when I pressed the paper against the cardboard.

An hour or two later, I admired our joint handiwork and especially how, to my initial exasperation, Audrey had so carefully duplicated the exact pattern onto the one-inch sides of the lid, as well as on the hidden top inch of the box. Now that the work was complete, the extra effort felt worthwhile. The only unadorned surface was the top of the lid, but I wouldn't dare do that without her expressed consent and directives.

Minutes later, while I was pouring myself a cup of Stress Buster herbal tea, I heard the crunch of gravel as a car pulled into the separate garage. I rushed outside to help Audrey with her luggage.

After we'd exchanged hellos and hugged each other, and I'd asked and she'd answered the mandatory question about how her flights were, I struggled with her enormous suitcase—unlike Helen, she had no problem whatsoever with my carrying it for her, and it was jam-packed and boasted an airline tag warning that read: *Heavy. Bend your knees.* I puffed, "So tell me all about your grandchild!"

"Little Natalie Audrey Munroe? She's absolutely magnificent! Oh, Erin! Having a grandchild is even better than having children! It's so much less exhausting when you're not the one giving birth." She opened and held the door for me.

"And another important distinction is..." Her voice drifted off as she spotted the box on the counter. "What's all this?" she asked in happy awe. Beaming, she turned the box in a slow three-sixty, examining every fabulous inch.

"I completed the sides for you. But I didn't know what you wanted to do with the top, so I had to leave that blank for now."

"Thank you, Erin! It's like you're my personal team of elves, making all the shoes for me during the night!"

"Well, not really. You still have the exact same number of shoes in your closet. And I haven't given a moment's thought to starting dinner." Which reminded me: Sullivan should have been done with his meeting two hours ago, and I should have called him back.

But I had Audrey's tales of her grandchild's birth to hear. Surely that took precedence. I could easily stall for another hour. Maybe two, if I could trick Audrey into repeating herself.

"I'm putting a photograph of Natalie Audrey in the center of the box, and working out to the edges." She turned on a heel and started to head outside again.

"Where are you going?"

"I have absolutely *got* to go get my photographs developed. I'll be back soon. If you don't mind being an elf for one more minute, could you please take my suitcase up to my room? Thank you so much, dear!"

With that, she was gone, leaving me to hunt for a new diversion on my own.

chapter **24**

i sat glumly at the black granite Caledonia counter, still trying to psych myself up for calling Sullivan. And still failing. The phone rang as I was staring at it, which made me jump a little. The moment I picked up, Sullivan said, "Is there a good reason why you couldn't wait till tomorrow or so to turn Stephanie in to the cops?"

"She'd probably been hiding crucial evidence!" I cried, leaping to the defensive in spite of myself.

"Or maybe it was *private* and *personal* correspondence that had *nothing* to do with the murders!"

"Then why would she *steal* it from Helen's house?" I fired back.

"I don't know, but if it was 'crucial evidence' that incriminated her, why wouldn't she destroy it? Or turn it in to the cops, if it identified her brother's killer?"

"Maybe because she was more concerned with protecting her father's reputation than with actually finding her brother's killer!"

"Or maybe because she's telling the truth! Because it wasn't *evidence* to begin with! In any case, she *said* she was going to give the damned letter to the police, so why couldn't you have waited and given her the chance to follow through? Why did you have to alienate an important client?"

I had no response.

"I'm waiting."

"For what? I happened to spot her scrapbook and saw that she'd stolen information from the murder scene. So I took the action of a responsible citizen: I notified the police. If, in the process, I lost a lucrative assignment for the two of us, I'm really sorry, Sullivan. But I did what felt like the right thing to do." I rolled my eyes, disgusting myself with my own sanctimonious tone of voice. "And even if it was a mistake, it's over and done with, and I can't turn back the clock now."

The doorbell rang.

Saved by the bell. "I have to go. Somebody's at the door." I hung up and rushed into the foyer and swung open the door. It was Sullivan. His face was practically glowing red with anger.

"I hate cell phones," I muttered. "Come on in. Unless you'd rather I join you on the porch so all my neighbors can listen in while you yell at me."

He stepped inside and closed the door. "I can handle

the fact that you lost the account, Gilbert. What ticks me off is that you just do whatever you want without the slightest regard for the consequences."

"That is *so* not true!"

"We were partners on this job. We were supposed to be watching each other's backs, helping each other. You stumbled across this scrapbook evidence with me right there, but you didn't say one word about it. You simply barged ahead and called the police."

"Yes, I know. All of that happened just a couple of hours ago. I don't need a recap. And I did it because, in the heat of the moment, I was afraid our client would destroy the evidence if I didn't take action right away."

"Well, I haven't heard any breaking news about an arrest many thanks to your earth-shattering evidence. Have you? Oh, and Stephanie also fired us from working at Helen's house, so we're now out of *two* jobs."

I winced, but said quietly, "I think Helen will just assume our fees."

"There's a relief," he muttered sarcastically.

"Helen loved the workroom. She might hire us to do that. And maybe Rachel will hire us to put one on her house."

"Great. Till you turn *her* in for . . . What was it again? Oh, yeah. Stealing porcelain figurines. And, by the way, I only learned about *that* because I happened to be there when Stephanie asked you about her brother's getting caught red-handed."

"If I'm such a terrible—"

Someone opened the back door, and I realized that Audrey had returned. "I'm back early from One-Hour Photo," she announced, waltzing into the room. "And I brought pictures of the world's most beautiful baby!" She beamed at Sullivan. "Oh, hello, Steve. This is a pleasant surprise. Did Erin tell you that I've now officially become an utterly *grand* mother? I have photos to prove it!"

Turning on the charm, Sullivan beamed at Audrey. "No, she didn't. Congratulations! Let's see these photos of yours right away."

The three of us shared the sofa in the parlor, Sullivan and me flanking Audrey as she showed us scores of snapshots of her new granddaughter, Natalie Audrey Munroe. Many of the photographs looked identical to me, but clearly they were unique in the eyes of a proud grandparent.

Within the category of something new learned every day, it occurred to me that it was absolutely impossible to begrudge a man anything when he's cooing over baby pictures. Steve's entire visit might have ended happily, if only Audrey hadn't said, while rising to put away her photos, "I'm going to get started on my own scrapbook for little Natalie Audrey. Which reminds me: How are things going with Helen? Are you two almost finished with her house?"

Sullivan and I exchanged glances. His mood instantly darkened. "Not even close," he answered. "With her nephew's murder taking—"

"Stop!" Audrey said. She slowly turned to face me. "Erin, please tell me I misheard just now. Helen's nephew wasn't murdered while I was in Kansas City, was he?"

"I'm afraid so. In fact, Helen's niece must have wanted to get the memorial service over with immediately, so it was held at noon today."

"This murder took place in Helen's basement, too," Sullivan added.

"And where is she now?" Audrey asked me solemnly.

"She's back in her house. She insisted."

"That's insane! Two people, including her own nephew, were murdered there! Why is she still living there? Why isn't she in our guest room? At the very least, can't you suggest that her niece pay for some nice hotel for her aunt to live in for a few weeks until this monster is behind bars?"

"We're not exactly on Stephanie's good side, right now," I replied quietly.

"All Erin's doing," Sullivan grumbled.

"What about Helen's friend? Hasn't Kay offered Helen a place to stay?"

"They had a minor falling-out."

"All Erin's doing." Sullivan was enjoying this.

"Steve!" I cried. "Quit with the put-downs! I already apologized for the mess-up with Stephanie! Furthermore, Kay and Helen's troubles aren't really my fault."

"Except that they might not have argued if you'd never brought up the subject of Kay's thefts in the first place. But on that note, I'd better leave." Sullivan rose and turned on his full-wattage smile as he faced Audrey. "Congratulations again on the birth of your beautiful and adorable granddaughter, Audrey."

"Thank you, Steve."

He gave her a peck on the cheek, fired a parting glare my way, and left.

The instant the door closed on him, Audrey demanded, "Fill me in, Erin, starting from the night I left and ending at how things currently are with Helen. And don't leave out a thing."

A little more than an hour later, Audrey sought me out from my bedroom hideaway and announced, "Good news. I've figured out how to help undo whatever part of the squabble you caused by meddling in Kay and Helen's friendship."

"I didn't meddle, Audrey."

"I've invited them both over for dinner tonight."

"And they accepted?"

"Yes. They'll both arrive in an hour, so we've got to get cooking. Oh, and by the way, Helen doesn't know who else is coming yet. She sounded truly down in the dumps, so I didn't want to mention Kay's name. Once the two women get to talking on neutral grounds, they'll patch up their differences."

"So you're meddling in order to repair the rift that you think *my* meddling created?"

"If that's the way you choose to look at it. Frankly, though, to use an interior-design analogy, that's a bit like using a wide brush to paint with all gloomy colors."

I rubbed my forehead. "Okay, Audrey. We'll give this a try. And we'll hope that Kay's compulsive kleptomania doesn't extend to when she's at the homes of people she's only just met."

"She was more than delighted to accept my invitation. That's one of the benefits of being a local celebrity. Even people who barely know me think they do, having invited me into their homes every week via their television sets."

"That's nice, Audrey." I couldn't resist adding, "Although in Kay's case, the invitation has been accepted by a known shoplifter and possible murder suspect."

She grimaced. "True." She rose to head toward the kitchen. "Well," she said cheerfully, "as they say, nobody's perfect."

Half an hour later, Helen called and said that she was going to have to cancel, that she'd discovered her car was "on the fritz," and she'd had to have it towed to the repair shop.

"Where are you now?" I asked.

"At home. A mechanic dropped me off. They tried to give me a loaner car, but I hate driving cars I'm unfamiliar with."

Kay would be going right past Helen's house on the way here, but I said, "How about if I come pick you up right now, and I'll bring you home again afterward? Better yet, you can spend the night here. Or do I need to get Audrey on the phone to extend that invitation herself?"

"It would be lovely of you to come get me, but I'm going to have to pass on the invitation to stay overnight. Ella and Vator really hate being left home alone."

"You could always ask Rachel to drop in and check on them," I teased.

Helen chuckled. "She probably will drop in, whether I ask her to or not." She paused. "On second thought, yes, actually. I'd love to accept your lovely invitation. I'm nervous about staying here alone at night, now that I won't even have a working car."

"I'll be there in fifteen minutes."

Kay was searching for a parking space in front of my home right while we were. They emerged at the same time, and the two women stood staring at each other for a few awkward seconds. Then each started apologizing to the other.

"The fault is all mine," Kay insisted, a statement that I happened to agree with completely. "I was being silly... overemotional. I flew off the handle."

Helen said, "In retrospect, I could have reacted better myself—"

"I had to take a good long look at myself after I got home. I think it was just my envy that made me say such nasty things."

"Envy? Of what?"

"It was none of my business that you and Jack had an affair. The hard truth is that I really only objected because you and Lois were always winding up with the men."

"Maybe I should—" I began to say, embarrassed that they were having such a personal conversation right in front of me.

"Kay, none of that is true," Helen said. "It wasn't Jack and me who had an affair. It was Rachel and George."

I managed to avoid gasping, but just barely. Kay looked shocked and confused. "But... you confessed about it to me. You said you'd had this... dalliance with the neighbor you deeply regretted. And that was why you didn't like to be around Jack Schwartz anymore."

"Lois was there at the time and was eavesdropping. I had to say *something* she'd believe. I told you that story to protect Lois. It was a partial truth... Jack and I had long had a harmless little crush on each other. But he was married, so I never let things progress, even when I found out his wife was being unfaithful to him. Although *Rachel* has apparently never accepted that. She seems to want to believe that Jack and I had an affair, so she could excuse her own infidelities."

"So you kept the truth from your own sister about her husband's cheating ways?" Kay asked incredulously.

"Oh, Lois already knew. I simply spared her the pain of knowing that *I* knew what she was putting up with. And all for the sake of staying married to her despicable husband."

"'Despicable'?" She scoffed. "Oh, come now, Helen. George wasn't all that bad."

"Oh, yes he was, I'm afraid." Helen put her arm around Kay's shoulders, and the three of us began to slowly make our way toward the house. "You know, Kay, I've been thinking about this a lot lately. You've suppressed a lot of hurt and disappointment over my role in your breakup with George."

"That's not true. I've long since let bygones be bygones."

"Even if that was once true, it seems to me as though it no longer is. You've been making odd little comments to me for a full year now. Ever since Lois and Teddy started dating."

Kay sighed. "That did bring up some past hurts. I'm sorry. And once *you* and Teddy started dating, I . . . well, it got really painful for me."

"Teddy and I aren't dating, and I think he finally realizes as much. Furthermore, though I hate to speak ill of the dead, you should realize that George Miller was simply not the wonderful man that you thought he was. Not only was he unfaithful, but he was a crooked cop."

"Oh, that's nonsense! You've swallowed all those silly rumors that went around."

"I just recently had to return some expensive merchandise that he stole."

She blinked. "Maybe he couldn't help himself." Her cheeks turned crimson. "I...know what that's like, to have uncontrollable urges to take things that don't belong to you."

"This was different, Kay."

"It was grand larceny," I added as I held the front door for them. "A museum heist, actually."

"My goodness!"

Audrey swept into the foyer, all set to welcome her guests, but hesitated as Helen said to Kay, "He broke my sister's heart much worse than he'd broken yours. I deeply regret not having spoken up about my doubts about George while there was still time. If only I'd known he was that much of a scoundrel, maybe I could have prevented their eloping somehow."

Kay said bitterly, "But, of all people, you knew George and I were in love. Or rather, that I was in love with him. So did Lois. Even so, she ran off with him. And you helped Lois to win him away from me!"

"What could I do?" Helen pleaded. "She was my sister. She told me she was in love with him. She begged me for advice."

"Even though you knew he was engaged to your best friend." The bitterness was rife in Kay's accusation.

"As I already said, I regret what I did. But these are hardly forgotten 'bygones' now, are they?" Helen asked gently. "I'm sorry, Kay. From the bottom of my heart. You don't know how many times I've told myself that at least my best friend wasn't saddled with being married to my louse of a brother-in-law."

"Truth be told, part of me felt that way, too. You're right. I was too good for him." She chuckled. "Not to mention what a union between a kleptomaniac and a crooked cop would have produced." Kay finally looked around and took in our surroundings in the foyer. "Oh, my gosh. This room is lovely!"

"Welcome to my home," Audrey told them. "I'm so glad you could come. And that you've made such a good start on dinner conversation."

Audrey's dinner was fabulous. We began with a classic simple Mediterranean salad—virgin olive oil drizzled over juicy ripe Italian plum tomatoes with thick slices of mozzarella and fresh basil—then she served popovers, delicious roasted lamb marinated in garlic and rosemary, mashed potatoes, green beans, and lemon cake with ginger ice cream for desert. I considered for the zillionth time how fortunate I'd been to luck into living with the local domestic goddess herself. Afterward, Kay suddenly announced that she'd forgotten about her book club meeting tonight and simply had to catch the tail end. Helen insisted upon walking her to her car, and the two of them bustled outside.

After praising Audrey's cooking one final time, I started washing the dishes, which was hardly unpleasant duty for me—I loved the balance and feel of her china so much that even washing them was a pleasure. I told her, "Hosting a dinner party was such a nice thing for you to do. And it certainly seemed to do the trick. Helen and Kay are back to being the best of friends, and it was an enjoyable evening."

"Yes, it was. Odd, but enjoyable."

"I don't know about you, but my definition of odd has been changing over time. It all seemed pretty normal to me."

Audrey didn't reply. Curious, I turned. She was staring at the built-in cherry-and-granite-topped desk across the room.

"Erin? Have you seen my pearl-handled letter opener?"

chapter 25

just then, I heard the front door open and assumed Helen was letting herself back inside. I said to Audrey, "It was there on the desk the last time I saw it."

"Yes. I saw it there, too, as I was putting dinner on the table. I was hoping you'd moved it someplace."

I sighed. "No, but I know who took it."

Helen entered the kitchen. "Took *what*?"

"Nothing important," Audrey answered breezily. "I just misplaced my letter opener."

"Oh, no," Helen moaned. "So *that's* why Kay rushed

off. She'd pocketed your letter opener and felt too guilty to stick around. She can't help herself, Audrey."

"I realize that. You know, I've never met an actual kleptomaniac before," Audrey said cheerfully. "I wonder if I can work that subject matter into my show somehow."

That would be quite a segment: *Domestic Thievery with Audrey Munroe*, I mused.

Mid-afternoon the next day I drove Helen home. As I pulled into the driveway, Kay waved to us from Helen's front porch. A pair of large suitcases was beside her. "I asked Kay to feed Ella and Vator this morning," Helen explained. "But I certainly didn't expect her to be intent on moving in with me when I arrived."

The moment we joined Kay on the porch, she announced, "I packed up my bags, and this time I'm not taking no for an answer. You shouldn't be alone in this house, Helen."

"We'll discuss the matter further later," Helen said curtly, unlocking the door.

"Yoo-hoo," Rachel called, crossing the street. "Is everything all right?"

"Fine."

"The police were here looking for you a couple of times last night, Helen. Did they arrest you?"

"No. If they had, I'd be in jail," Helen said evenly.

"Rachel, mind your own business for once in your life," Kay snapped.

"You can't treat me like that, Kay! You have no right! For your information, this is Helen's house, not yours!"

Helen grabbed one of Kay's bags. "Kay is staying with

me for the time being. And I agree with her that you should leave."

"Fine." Rachel glared at both of them. "I know not to stay where I'm not wanted." Even so, she made no move to leave.

Kay stood staring at her. "It must have been hard on you when Lois moved in here, eh, Rachel? Being so close to the woman you betrayed."

Rachel's jaw dropped and she sputtered as though too shocked to form actual words. She stepped inside the door, and finally gathered her wits enough to cry, "I didn't betray *her*, I betrayed Jack. Lois's husband was the one who pursued me relentlessly. *He's* fully responsible for the betrayal of Lois." She wailed, "It's bad enough knowing that I have to bear the weight of what I did to my poor Jack, without having to think about Lois as well."

"That was a long time ago," Helen said, giving Kay a sharp glance.

Rachel burst into tears. "I'll never forgive myself for the affair, it's true. But I swear to you all, I am innocent of both of the murders in this house."

"Why should we believe you?" Kay asked.

"This is the end of our friendship, Helen! I'm never coming back. It's obvious that I'm not wanted." Rachel ran sobbing across the street.

"She'll be back tomorrow," Kay remarked.

"She calls our relationship a friendship?" Helen shook her head.

"My God," Kay said. "It really *was* Rachel and George who were fooling around. You were telling the truth."

"Of course I was. You didn't believe me?"

"I wanted to, but . . . it was just such a strange story. I

didn't understand why you'd lie and confess to a bogus affair."

"If I hadn't, I was afraid you'd figure out that it was Rachel and George. Lois would have felt humiliated."

"In any case, it's such a shame that Jack had such a dreadful wife. Whereas George and Rachel clearly deserved one another." Kay made a deliberate show of patting a lump in her jacket pocket, muttering, "I wonder what *this* is?" She pulled out Audrey's letter opener. "Goodness. I wonder how this got in there. I must have picked it up someplace and stuck it in my pocket, accidentally." She then removed her jacket and draped it over a pile of items on the piano bench, setting the letter opener on top. "Erin, why don't you show me the progress you're making in the den?"

Kay led the way through the French doors into the den. I watched in amusement as Helen promptly snatched up Audrey's letter opener and stuck it in my purse.

I said to Kay, "I'm hoping to have this room in—" At the sound of someone opening the front door, I stopped and pivoted.

"Ding-dong," Stephanie said, leaning in without ringing the bell. "Is it all right if I come in?"

"Yes," Helen said, but she was staring at her niece in surprise. Stephanie seemed barely able to stand upright. It wasn't even three o'clock in the afternoon, but she was obviously very drunk. Stephanie dropped into the love seat.

Finally noticing my presence, Stephanie snorted. "Hello there, Erin. Figures you'd be here. Are you homesteading? Trying to get yourself adopted, maybe?"

I didn't bother to respond.

Kay asked, "Are you all right, Stephanie?"

"Other than my being the last living member of my immediate family, yeah, sure. I'm just peachy."

"You've been drinking," Helen scolded. "Why are you driving in that condition?"

"I only had a couple glasses of wine."

"Oh, Stephanie," Helen said. "You're drunk. You were putting yourself and others at risk! Honestly! What do you think your parents would say to you, if they were here now?"

"They're not. And I've been an adult for a long time."

"You can't drown your sorrows with alcohol."

"Coulda fooled me. My sorrows *feel* like they've been drowned. I feel happier right now than I have in days."

"Pardon me for interfering, but as your—"

"Bull," Stephanie interrupted her aunt. "Why should now be any different than any other time? You were always criticizing me and my husband. You caused the marital strife between me and my husband! It led to the breakup of my marriage!"

"Name one time that I criticized your marriage!" Helen retorted.

Stephanie did her best to focus her gaze on her aunt. "You didn't, in so many words. But I could always tell what you were thinking."

"You're blaming me for the *thoughts* that you *assumed* I was having?"

"You killed my mother!" Stephanie stabbed a finger at her. "You sneaked those peppers into her food. Then you cowardly left town so you wouldn't have to watch her die."

"That's not true!"

With unmasked fury, Kay stepped between Helen and Stephanie. "Stephanie Miller, I don't care if you *are* drunk as a skunk, you have no right to say something so horrible to your aunt! Helen would never do anything like that! We all know how much she loved your mother!"

Stephanie held up her palms. "You're absolutely right, Kay. I take it all back. I didn't mean any of it. I was actually just testing you."

"Testing me?" Kay repeated indignantly.

"What are you talking about?" Helen demanded.

"I needed to see how Kay would react," Stephanie answered, slurring her words. "*She*'s the one I really suspect is the killer."

"Oh, please, Stephanie," Helen scolded. "You don't mean that! Do you think a couple of glasses of wine can turn you into James Bond?"

Kay retorted to Stephanie, "Of any of us, *you* are the likeliest suspect."

"You honestly think I would kill poor Peter? My own sad-sack brother?"

"You would if you felt you had no choice," Kay said. "Maybe he saw you kill Jack. Maybe he threatened to turn you in."

"And what possible motive would I have had for killing Jack Schwartz?" Stephanie narrowed her eyes at Kay. "*You*, on the other hand, always hated my mother for stealing my father from you."

"I admit," Kay conceded with a sigh, "that I *was* always jealous of Lois for stealing George away. But Helen recently helped me to realize that George wasn't exactly the perfect husband."

"Nor the perfect father," Stephanie said under her breath. "But the point now is: I didn't kill anybody."

"Neither did I," Kay stated.

A silent pall fell over the room. Finally Kay said, "It's time we talked about something happy, for a change." Kay grinned. "Teddy has been spending a lot of time with me lately, Helen."

"Oh?"

"Yes, indeed. So would you mind terribly if the two of us were to become a couple?"

Helen was momentarily nonplussed, but then she managed: "I like living alone, whereas Teddy obviously needs a wife. You two are a much better match than he and I ever would be. But . . . I think it would be really wise for you to wait a while, Kay. Things are so dangerous around here, and—"

"Aunt Helen's trying to warn you that you're probably getting romantically involved with a killer," Stephanie cut in with grim satisfaction.

Kay's jaw dropped. She sneered at Stephanie. "Now you're accusing Teddy of murder? Who's next—the Easter Bunny?"

"Teddy's bad news, Kay. He and my father got into lots of questionable situations. And sometimes made terrible decisions. Not to mention that Dad told me Teddy was the worst cop imaginable." Stephanie got unsteadily to her feet. "I'm going home now. Got to sleep this off."

"I'll drive you," I offered.

"*You?*" she mocked. "No way. You'll probably drive me straight off a cliff, if you get half a chance."

"I'll drive her," Kay said, grabbing her keys.

"I'll go, too, to keep you company," Helen said. "Just let me check things upstairs first." She eyed her staircase anxiously, and I realized that she was still afraid of climbing it alone.

"Can I help you get the guest room ready for Kay, Helen?" I suggested.

"Oh, yes, dear. That would be lovely. Thank you."

"We'll wait for you in the car." Kay steered Stephanie toward the door.

I carried Kay's bags as I led the way upstairs and opened the door. To my considerable surprise, the room was in livable condition. In fact, with just a bit of tweaking here and there, it would be lovely. "Wow, Helen! I'm so impressed! When were you doing this?"

"It wasn't me. Peter must have been moving Lois's things down into the basement the night he was killed. He probably felt he could search the room better that way."

My eye fell on an end table that had been cleared of debris. "What's this?" I asked. The tabletop featured a lovely decoupage.

"The table?"

"Yes, it's really unusual. Did you create the decoupage?"

"No, Lois did. She started working on that after George died and we combined our households. I'm quite certain that Stephanie will want to take possession of it immediately. I'll ask her. When she's sober."

I stared at the tabletop. "It has what looks like an old handwritten letter to your late brother-in-law."

"Oh, yes. It's a 'Dear George' letter."

"Is that your sister's handwriting?" I asked, pointing at the lettering. The angular print bore little resemblance to that in the letters I'd found at Stephanie's house. Most of the words were covered by a photograph.

"No," Helen said after studying the writing. "I don't recognize it."

"This is a major long shot, but I wonder if it's worth removing the varnish and the photograph to read the letter and its signature."

"So you want to remove the individual pieces from the decoupage? I don't know how comfortable I am with your doing that. What if you destroy the table?"

"I won't destroy the table. Although I'll have to try my best not to ruin any of the papers in the decoupage. I'll make up a new one for you, if that happens."

Helen hesitated. "Oh, dear, Erin, I don't know. Technically, because the table was her mother's, it belongs to Stephanie now. We should probably ask her permission first."

"I'd really rather not mention this to her. Just in case this letter proves to contain something significant."

"Why shouldn't I tell Stephanie? Do you think she's behind the murders?"

"I'm suspicious of everyone. Except you."

"That's nice, dear. Thank you." She paused. "I suppose it's a sign that your life truly isn't going well when you start thanking people for not suspecting that you're a murderer." She stared at the table, her brow furrowed. "All right. Go ahead and remove the decoupage. I suppose I should be trusting of your abilities. Just do the best you can putting the whole thing back together again afterward."

"I will. I've done this sort of thing before. Do you know where Lois kept her decoupage supplies?"

"She used to keep them in our bathroom, under the sink."

Helen left, and I went to work. Fortunately, Lois had used a "removable" varnish, which only required mineral spirits—also stashed under the bathroom sink—and lots of elbow grease to remove. After several minutes of careful archaeologist-like varnish removal, I was able to get my fingernails underneath the edges of the photograph of Stephanie and Peter that had been covering most of the letter. I carefully peeled off the picture, and found myself staring at a love letter.

chapter **26**

Dear George,

I'm so blown away by the gift! An actual Fabergé egg! It's all I've ever wanted in my life! You really DO love me! I know that one day soon we'll be together. We'll get out of our loveless marriages and be together for the rest of our lives. (And, my darling, your "bad ticker" is going to be just fine! It's just the stress! Once you're away from that shrew of a wife, your heart will mend!) Won't that be wonderful? We'll both finally be free!

I hope you'll think seriously about what I said last night. I know you're too kindhearted for your own

*good, but you'll only be hastening the inevitable. If
God had wanted her to live long, he wouldn't have
given her such lethal allergies. It pains me to think
that she hid this Work of Art from you and the world
for all these years. But, as you said yourself, that's
because you were destined to discover her safety
deposit box only after we'd met, so you could give it
to the One who was Meant to cherish it—ME!*

> *Your One and Only,*
> *Rachel*

I reread the letter three times, trying to decide if I believed it was authentic. Or had someone faked the whole thing and planted it here? Why hadn't Lois taken this straight to the police?

I silently answered my own questions, remembering Helen's take on her sister, how protective Lois had been about her husband's reputation for her children's sake. She had probably discovered the letter after his fatal heart attack. Lois would have realized that Rachel wanted her dead, and yet she'd obviously managed to get the egg away from Rachel's clutches. Then Lois had hidden it under her bed. How odd to think that such an obvious hiding place had eluded discovery.

Helen had said Lois decorated this table shortly after she'd moved in. By working the letter into a decoupage, she was probably keeping the letter hidden from her children's and Helen's sight, and yet preserved so that she could produce it if she needed it as evidence to protect herself from Rachel, who'd urged George in the letter to hasten "the inevitable," regarding Lois's life-threatening allergies.

I needed to take the letter to the police. Its wording certainly implicated Rachel Schwartz in Lois's murder. Which was not to say that the police would agree that she had, indeed, been murdered. It certainly convinced *me*. I could easily envision Rachel discovering "her" egg was missing, realizing the "thief" was Lois, and seeking revenge after George's weak heart gave out.

Too anxious to take the care that I should, I worked the letter free, and picked up the phone to call the police. No dial tone. I checked the connection, which was fine. Lois must have had a private phone line, which Helen canceled after her sister's death.

I went into Helen's bedroom, but she had no phone there; the phone jack behind the nightstand was unused. I trotted down the stairs to use my cell phone, bringing the letter with me.

Just as I reached the bottom step, Rachel let herself into the house through the front door.

"What are you doing here?" I asked, hiding the letter hastily behind my back.

The alarm that registered on her features spoke volumes: She'd gotten a glimpse of the letter and no doubt immediately recognized her own handwriting and stationery. "Oh, hi, Erin. Goodness! You startled me! I thought you'd left with Helen and Kay."

"No, and you really need to leave."

"I apologize for overreacting earlier. And, also, I wanted to take a quick look at her porcelain dancers. I feel so guilty about taking them from her that I thought I'd see if I could surprise her by giving her one of mine, that Jack bought me. I just need to be sure it wasn't a duplicate."

She was obviously lying. "I think it'd be best for you to leave," I said firmly.

She stepped toward me, wearing an odd little smile. "What's that you're hiding behind your back, Erin? It looks so much like my own handwriting."

"It's just something from Lois. I was going to show it to Helen and see if she wanted to keep it in her scrapbook."

The color drained from her face. "Oh, my God. You found the letter I wrote to George. Lois told me she'd found it among his things after he passed away. I've been trying to find it ever since." She took another step toward me, looking panic-stricken. "You have to give that to me, Erin."

I took a step back.

Dots of perspiration formed on her brow. "It's not what you think, you know. It doesn't prove anything, in any case. That letter doesn't prove a single thing, Erin."

We were both unarmed, but I was nearly thirty years younger than she was and had utter confidence that I was stronger with faster reflexes. I said with confidence, "It proves that you took the Fabergé egg from George. The one that he stole from the museum."

She shook her head. "He *gave* it to me. And Lois stole it out of my house."

"You were possessing stolen property."

"So was Lois! And I had it for a lot less time than she did! She kept it for something like forty years!"

"Is that why you killed her?"

"Of course not! She had an accidental allergic reaction. She died of natural causes." She was a lousy liar, unable to even meet my gaze.

"You used your key to sneak in to the house when Helen was gone, and you put green peppers into Lois's meal and removed the epinephrine needles from the drawer. Then you came back over here and covered up your crime."

"That's not true, Erin! I did no such thing! Not even the police think Lois was killed. She was an old lady with lethal allergies. She wasn't going to live long! That was three full months ago! You're going to wreck my life if you tell the police that! Haven't I suffered enough? I'm a recent widow!"

"After you killed Lois, though, you couldn't find the egg. So you manipulated Peter into searching for it. And somehow you wound up feeling that you had to kill both him and your own husband. Why? Were you scared that they'd put it all together and turn you in to the police?"

"No! Stop it, Erin! I'm not going to let you give that letter to the police! They'll put me in jail! And you can't prove any of that!"

She pivoted and raced over to the end table between the front door and the sofa, yanked the plug out of the socket for the table lamp, and picked up the lamp, baseball-bat style, just below its large shade. It was too awkward to make an imposing weapon. I'd have to be standing right next to her before she could hurt me with it. She unscrewed the finial holding the lampshade in place.

"Rachel, put the lamp—"

Just then, Teddy barged through the door. To my horror, he had his gun drawn. "Aha!" he cried triumphantly. "I knew I'd catch the burglar in the act!"

In an instant, Rachel whirled and clocked Teddy in the forehead with the lamp base. The gun exploded as he toppled backward. I instinctively threw my arm over my head and dived to the floor.

When I raised my head, my ears were ringing, and the air reeked with gun smoke. Teddy had dropped the gun. I scrambled to my feet just as Rachel picked it up. She pointed it straight at me.

"Stay right there, Erin," she said. "Or I'll shoot."

chapter 27

You," Rachel told Teddy, gesturing wildly with the gun, while keeping an eye on me. "Move away from the doorway."

"Ow," he moaned. He scooted over a few feet, and she kicked the door shut behind him.

Teddy's face was as pale as the white wall behind him. A trickle of blood was beginning to run down his cheek from where one of the corners of the lamp base had dug into his flesh.

He touched his wound with his fingertips and stared at the blood in horror. "I'm bleeding!"

In an instant, Rachel Schwartz had transformed into a

frightening and imposing adversary. She now looked every inch the tall, fit, athletic woman that she was. I could no longer assume that I could take her in a physical confrontation; I was younger, but she was ruthless and desperate. "Go stand next to Erin," she commanded. "Now!"

"I . . . can't," he protested, but he wobbled to his feet and staggered toward me nevertheless. In direct contrast to Rachel's newfound strength and power, Teddy was a clear liability.

"You can't win, Rachel." I spoke with more confidence than I felt. "There's no way for you to get away with holding us hostage. The neighbors will have heard the gunshot. Somebody's sure to have called the police already."

"You're right," she said coldly. "So I'm going to have to kill you both."

Teddy started to wail, "No, please, no!"

I desperately searched my peripheral vision for a weapon of any kind. Nothing! Just old clothing and pillows! Fifty tons of junk in this house at one point, and the only semihard objects within reach were my shoes! "Shooting us will only give the police more deaths to charge you with. They'll lock you away forever."

Teddy let out a little moan, then collapsed beside me.

Rachel sneered as she looked at his motionless body. "I'll frame *him*. Murder-suicide. I already set that up by poisoning the chocolates."

My heart was in my throat. My brain screamed at me to run. But turning my back would surely only make it easier for her to pull the trigger.

Her hands were trembling as she aimed at me. My forehead felt as damp as hers looked. Her eyes were wild.

"No, Rachel," I pleaded. "Don't put two more murders on your conscience."

Tears filled her eyes. "This is all Helen's fault! I still can't find my precious egg, thanks to her! And Lois couldn't tell me where she'd hidden it, kept calling Helen's name as she died. All she had to do was tell me where it was, and I'd have given her the emergency injection and saved her!"

My own eyes misted at how horrid a death Lois had endured. Though I held my tongue, I was sure Rachel would have let her die, rather than go to prison for attempted murder and surrender the egg in the process. Lois had probably realized as much.

"Helen made me kill my own poor husband!" she sobbed. "He wanted to *leave* me for her. It was only a matter of time. I couldn't kill her till I got my egg back, so I tried to frame her for Jack's murder. And that worthless Peter! He tried to cut me out! Thanks to you, he'd started to suspect that I killed his pathetic mother. And he wouldn't ever have given me the egg once he knew. Not that he could *find* it. That idiot couldn't find his own nose, let alone a priceless Fabergé egg!"

We both flinched as we heard Helen and Kay's voices on the walkway. I bit back a curse. Momentarily they would get ensnared in this, too.

"Time's run out," Rachel said. "Tell me right now, Erin! Where's my egg?"

I had to stall, give her some reason to keep us alive. "Helen hid it in her car."

The door opened. Rachel pivoted toward the entrance, gun raised. I yelled, "*Run*, Helen! Get the police!" Then I dived at Rachel's knees.

The weight of my body knocked us both to the floor. She lost her grip on the gun, which skittered across the square of oak parquet flooring in front of the door. I scrambled over her, reaching desperately for the gun.

She elbowed me in the face. The blow connected solidly with my cheekbone. I saw stars, but somehow grabbed her wrist, wrenching it back toward me. She shrieked in pain. We both lunged at the gun, but Helen grabbed it first.

Behind Helen, Kay edged her way inside, looking terrified. "What in the world..."

With a steady, two-fisted grip, Helen pointed the weapon at Rachel sprawled on the floor, panting and sobbing. I grabbed both of Rachel's wrists. "Someone get me a rope! Kay, Helen, I need something to bind her wrists."

"No," Rachel desperately moaned. "It was Teddy. And...and Erin's been helping him."

"Oh, baloney," Teddy said from behind me. He'd gotten to his feet. "I'll take the gun now," he told Helen, full of false bravado to the very last. "I've been *pretending* to have passed out. Just until I could make my move and rescue you. It's an advanced hand-to-hand combat technique."

"Kay," I wheezed, feeling as though the whole left side of my face had been kicked in by Rachel's blow, "call nine-one-one."

I realized just then that sirens in the distance were growing louder. "Never mind. They're on the way." Somebody in the neighborhood who'd heard the gunshot must have called.

Kay was staring at Teddy as if transfixed. "Oh, you poor thing," she told him. "What happened to your head?"

"Rachel clobbered me."

"You're bleeding pretty bad. We need a bandage to close the wound."

"Yeah, I, uh..." He touched his fingers to the blood. Then, just as two police cars pulled up to the curb, he fainted.

chapter 28

Whether you're choosing a silverware pattern or paint for your living room, it's often best to make a swift decision, rather than to agonize over every possibility. After all, very few decisions that we make are permanent, and where would you rather be: sitting on the fence or blissfully enjoying your surroundings?

—Audrey Munroe

Over the course of the next several days, the shiner that I'd gotten during my desperate struggle with Rachel faded to a yellowish green, which could be hidden beneath makeup. I'd heard from Linda that Rachel had given a full confession and was in jail, although Linda suspected that she and her lawyer were mounting some sort of "diminished capacity" defense strategy.

A day or two after the arrest, I'd been fine, feeling proud of my active role in getting Helen's tormentor put behind bars, and relieved that the whole ordeal was finished. I'd even brandished my facial bruises as though they were a badge of honor.

Then I'd lost my sparkle. This morning, I'd unexpectedly grown fearful as I entered a prospective client's house. The floor plan was similar to Helen's, and I'd gotten too jumpy to think straight when I came down the stairs and caught sight of their front door. In my mind's eye, I saw Rachel standing there with a handgun. Claiming I was feeling ill, I'd bolted from the house.

Now all I wanted to do was to stay curled up on the sage velvet sofa, clinging to Hildi on my lap. My cat had apparently taken such great pity on me that she didn't mind being held a little too close for her usual feline comfort level.

Audrey was in the wingback chair, knitting with limited success. I could feel her looking at me as if pained by the sight. "I'll be all right eventually, you know," I told her. "I just need to get my feet back under me. That'll happen sooner or later."

"Oh, I know. I'm vexed about these booties, not you. I figure if I can't knit booties, I can at least knit my brow."

She set her needles down, studied my features, and exclaimed with exasperation, "Doesn't that pun at least warrant a smile?"

I mustered a half smile. "Sorry. It was very clever."

She sighed. "You were right about this yarn, I'm afraid. I should have gotten the kind you recommended . . . the wool that was pink and blue." She'd insisted that making pink booties for a girl was "too predictable" and that she'd wanted her grandchild to "celebrate her masculine and feminine qualities equally." Or some such ilk. In any case, she was creating half pink and half blue booties.

"I thought you decided you wanted to be in charge

of when the colors changed yourself, instead of the yarn dictating the color."

"Yes, but now I'm driving myself nuts by changing back and forth... 'Make it pink, make it blue...' I'm spending as much time making knots as I am actually knitting."

"They're coming out just fine, though, as far as I can see."

She frowned. "By the time I finish, little Natalie Audrey's feet will have outgrown them. Didn't the pattern say that they could be made in half an hour?"

I'd printed a free pattern for her off the Internet. "Yes, but I'm sure the time difference is due to your switching colors. Maybe you should make one bootie solid pink and the other one blue."

She shook her head. "It'll look like her parents were color-blind. Or too lazy to find a matched pair." She glanced at her watch. *Uh-oh.*

"I'm worried about Helen," I said after a heavy pause.

"Helen's a survivor, if ever there was one. She'll probably outlive us both." A second glance at her watch.

"I don't see how she can continue to live in that house. Not after all the violence the place has had to absorb. These days I can barely even stand to walk into a home that reminds me of hers. I don't want to have to go there again."

"But you will, Erin. And you'll get that place whipped into shape and looking better than ever. Plus, now that Stephanie's finally realized that she's indebted to you for rescuing her aunt, you'll be getting lots of referrals."

Startled by Audrey's words, I sat up. "How did you hear about that? I only talked to her myself earlier this afternoon."

She retrieved her knitting and said, "Hmm? Oh, you must have mentioned it during dinner."

"Except I *didn't*."

I waited for a response, but she was pretending to be thoroughly absorbed in her handiwork. When she finally met my gaze she said, "I'm bringing a knitting expert onto my show tomorrow. You should really take up the hobby yourself, Erin. It's relaxing, and they're doing so much with yarns today. The textures! And the colors! Just remarkable."

"Why were you talking to Steve Sullivan today, Audrey?"

She peered over her reading glasses at me. "Oh, yes. *That's* where I heard about Stephanie. I spoke to Mr. Sullivan recently. He said to say hi to you, in fact."

"Did he?"

She looked at her watch again and got to her feet. "It's time for me to throw in the bootie and admit that the skein of pink and blue yarn would have been easier to work with. I'm going to leave you here to hold down the fort and run back to the store."

"That's quite a yarn, all right."

"Excuse me?"

"You're not the only one who can make up puns. You've been looking at your watch, and half the time when you do that, it means—" The doorbell rang. "Audrey! Is that going to be Steve Sullivan, yet again?"

She clicked her tongue and swept up her purse as she strolled toward the kitchen. "All right, yes. I mentioned that you've been down in the dumps the last couple of days. He said something about dropping by this evening, on his way home."

"I don't need you to act as my social planner, Audrey!"

"Obviously that's not true, or you wouldn't have been staring into space for the last couple of hours. Anyway, I really do need to skedaddle and get some more yarn, so you'll need to see to our houseguest. Or to our door-to-door salesman, as the case may be." She winked at me. "Have fun!" She let herself out the back door.

I sighed. Then I made my way into the foyer and pulled open the door. Steve was standing there, hands buried in the pockets of his jeans, managing to look as if he'd just stepped off the cover of *GQ*. "Sullivan."

"Gilbert."

"Come on in." I noted absently that Hildi had followed me into the foyer; Sullivan hated cats, so her presence was bound to make him keep his visit brief. "I already know you're here on an official mission from Audrey."

"What do you mean?" He shut the door behind him.

"Oh, she told me she went to see you today to . . ." My voice drifted off as I watched him kneel to greet my cat.

"Hi, Hildi," he said gently, scratching her behind the ears.

"I thought . . . Aren't you allergic to cats?"

"Yeah, but I was talking to my sister about it the other

day, and she told me that lots of times folks with allergies don't have much trouble with long-haired cats, like Hildi."

"You even remembered her name."

He chuckled as he stood up straight. "What's so surprising about that? You think I never listen to you?"

"Frankly . . . yes."

"Shows how badly you underestimate me, Gilbert."

Rather than ponder that possibility, I turned and led the way farther into the house, asking over my shoulder, "Want something to drink?"

"Sure. You got any beer?"

"I'll check." He followed me into the kitchen. My heart was doing its rapid-heartbeat thing again. Yeesh! I checked the fridge. No luck, but I spotted an open and particularly tasty bottle of white wine. "No, sorry. Wine?"

"No, thanks."

"I think I'll have a glass." *If I can pour without spilling it everywhere, that is.* I grabbed a white wineglass and poured a splash of the Chablis. "How 'bout something else, then? Cranberry juice? Ginger ale?"

"Water's fine. I just need something in case we have good cause to clink glasses."

"Why would we do that?" I set a small glass of water in front of him and took a sip of wine.

He grabbed his wallet out of his pocket and explained, "I was hoping you'd agree to a merger. So I printed up a couple sample business cards."

I nearly choked on my wine. "You're serious?"

"Stephanie even offered us a loan against future services rendered. She's feeling bad about all the grief she gave you in particular. I told her I doubted we'd need a loan, but that she can make it up to us with future referrals. We can reduce our overhead a lot by combining our offices…and we can stop competing over the same customers. You know as well as I do that we're the two best designers in town. What do you say, Gilbert?"

"I have to give you an answer right on the spot?"

"Sure. You've always been decisive. Why chicken out now?"

I furrowed my brow. "Let me see those business cards."

He handed me the pair of cards. They were simple and tasteful, with a nice font on an excellent-quality cardstock. Truth be told, I liked them better than my own business cards. The only difference between his two samples was that one listed our company name as "Gilbert & Sullivan Designs," and the other as "Sullivan & Gilbert Designs."

"I like this one," I replied, indicating the one marked Gilbert & Sullivan. "It's more memorable." Plus *my* name would be first.

"Yeah, but that's why I like the other one. Clients will still make the connection, but will realize our names really *are* Sullivan and Gilbert." Plus *his* name would be first, I inwardly grumbled.

"You agree to go with 'Gilbert and Sullivan,' and you've got a deal," I stated boldly.

He gave me a haughty sneer and shook his head. "You go with 'Sullivan and Gilbert,' and *you've* got a deal." He spread his arms. "It's not like you're doing me any favors here. I've been in Crestview longer. I have a bigger client base than you do."

Annoyed, I asked in a near shout, "Then why did you print up the other card? Just to harass me?" I took a big swig of wine, draining the glass.

"No. Thought I'd propose a fair method to choose the new name." He snatched both cards from my grasp and started changing their positions in his hand like a con man operating a shell game. He stopped and held them toward me. "Here you go, Gilbert. Pick a card. Any card. Whichever one you choose is the new name for our business."

"Fine. Seems juvenile, but, like you said, at least it's fair."

Our typical way of dealing with each other, I thought; I hadn't actually even agreed on a merger, and we most definitely hadn't "clinked glasses" to celebrate the venture. On the other hand, he had given Hildi an affectionate pat, so it's not like he was *all* bad, and he was so handsome. *Talented.* I'd meant to think *talented.* Too much wine swallowed too fast.

I let my hand hover above the card on the left and then the card on the right, watching his face for any telltale reactions. He was holding the bottom of both cards and could read them easily. But he gave me no clue, them smiled at me as our eyes met.

I returned the smile and pulled out the card on the left. "You sure?" he said. "I'll give you one more chance to change your mind."

I hesitated. He would only have said that if it was "Gilbert & Sullivan," because otherwise he could have held his tongue and had things his way. An instant later, though, it occurred to me that he would take immense pleasure in tricking me into keeping the "Sullivan & Gilbert" card.

"I think I'll take you up on that. Thanks, Sullivan." I grabbed the other card and gave him back my original selection. I wagged the new card triumphantly in front of his nose. "This is the official name of our business."

He lifted his water glass as I turned the card over. "Here's to our new enterprise," he said. "Cheers."

I looked down at the card to see "Sullivan & Gilbert" emblazoned on its surface. I grabbed the wine bottle and filled my glass. "I hate you, Sullivan."

He grinned and clinked his glass against mine. "I know . . . partner."

about the author

Leslie Caine was once taken hostage at gunpoint and finds that writing about crimes is infinitely more enjoyable than taking part in them. Leslie is a certified interior decorator and lives in Colorado with her husband, two teenage children, and a cocker spaniel.

If you enjoyed Leslie Caine's
KILLED BY CLUTTER, you won't want to miss
any of the *Domestic Bliss* mysteries.
Look for them at your favorite bookseller.

And read on for an exciting early look at the
next *Domestic Bliss* mystery, coming soon from
Bantam Books.

a domestic bliss mystery

FATAL FENG SHUI

Leslie Caine

Fatal Feng Shui

Coming Soon

chapter 1

"Confidence and optimism," I muttered as I made my way along the curving concrete walkway toward Shannon Dupree Young's front door.

"Pardon?" Steve Sullivan said.

"Nothing." My cheeks warmed; I hadn't realized I'd spoken aloud. We'd merged our interior design companies less than two months ago, and I'd have preferred not to have him discover my idiosyncrasies quite so soon. "That's the mantra I use whenever I get nervous."

"You're nervous about this job?"

I scanned his handsome features, expecting to see a wry grin to indicate he was being sarcastic. Things had grown steadily worse here in the six weeks since Shannon had signed on as our very first client. "A little. Aren't you?"

"Nah. What's there to worry about? Just a feud raging between neighbors, and our client on the verge of a nervous breakdown. That's par for the course for us."

He was being gracious by not pointing fingers. In the past year, my one-woman company, Designs by Gilbert, had experienced such bizarre problems with a few of its clients that I qualified for hazardous-duty pay. Sullivan Designs had somehow gotten dragged into the fray more than once.

On the east side of Shannon's original entranceway, the construction of her addition was behind schedule but was finally starting to take shape. We were about to enter the fun phase of remodeling. Normally, I'd have to hold myself back from racing to the door. My head would be filled with one magical, delectable possibility after another—rainbows of colors, astonishing materials and furnishings. For me, designing a space was nothing less than being able to make my client's dreams come true, and I enjoyed that joyous journey more than I could say.

This particular client's "dream" was turning out to be a nightmare, however. Thanks to the proverbial Neighbor from Hell—Pate Hamlin.

I turned and eyed his house. Shannon had called us, in hysterics, last night about that sprawling, fortresslike structure directly across the street. The protruding peak of the roof over its new porch was indeed pointing straight at this home—a feng shui no-no. "It's just that Shannon seemed so nice and rational at first," I explained to Sullivan. "I never imagined she'd wind up so paranoid . . . thinking her neighbor's architecture was putting her in physical danger."

During our phone conversation last night, Shannon had declared that this was "now officially a no-holds-barred feng shui war." She'd asked us to launch a counteroffensive against her neighbor's designer. That notion made me severely uncomfortable. Granted, during the monumentally rocky start to our relationship, Sullivan and I had waged many a battle, but I'd naively thought those days were behind me now that we'd joined forces.

" 'Everybody was feng shui fighting . . .' " Sullivan

sang to the tune of "Kung Foo Fighting" as he brushed past me.

"Very funny," I said, resisting a smile. Although neither of us was an expert in the art of feng shui, we weren't neophytes, either. We had a healthy respect for its ancient principles, which have more than stood the test of time. Feng shui was among the first schools of design—a beautiful philosophy of harmonizing one's home with its surroundings.

We climbed the steps to Shannon's front porch, which would soon be removed. In its place, we had a fabulous design for a cedar wraparound deck. Its rich wood and gorgeous geometric patterns would embrace both the new and the original entrances of this home. *Our* additions emphasized and augmented the home's best elements. Unlike her *neighbor's* slap-happy add-ons, which the architect had apparently drawn up while bouncing around in an old pickup truck. (My refusal to engage in a feng shui war did not, alas, morph me into the Mother Teresa of interior designers.)

"Oh, jeez," Sullivan said. I followed his gaze. Shannon had recently painted a red dragon on the center panel of her front door. While I was studying her intricate handiwork, Sullivan suddenly staggered forward, clutching at the center of his back. "Ow! Help me, Gilbert! I think I just got hit by a feng shui arrow!"

"Keep your voice down!" I pressed the doorbell to Shannon Young's house. "If she hears us making cracks about this, our first official job as 'Gilbert and Sullivan Designs' will end today."

"You mean"—he paused as Shannon threw open the door— "'Sullivan and Gilbert,'" he continued with a smile, deftly turning his correction of me into a greeting.

"I remember who you are," Shannon snapped. "Hurry up and get in here." She all but yanked us inside and shut the heavy door behind us. She seemed afraid that we would *literally* be shot if we stayed too long on her porch.

I had to regain my composure at her appearance. Shannon had always struck me as being wound far too tight, but now the thin, attractive, fortyish woman appeared to be on the verge of exploding. Her eyes were bloodshot and she puffed fiendishly on a cigarette. Her strawberry-blond, wavy hair was an unruly mess—a *Bride of Frankenstein* look. She was wearing her navy-blue artist's smock over a plum-colored jogging suit. Her feet were clad in mismatched sandals and white socks.

She looked at us expectantly. "Well? What are you going to *do* about this? You can see for yourself what that awful man is trying to pull!"

"With his front porch, you mean?" I was already dying to throw open a window. The air reeked of stale smoke.

"The eave of the roof over it! It's a triangle! And not just *any* triangle, mind you. This one's a *jutting* triangle! Pate Hamlin is deliberately aiming that sharp point right at me through my window! I haven't been able to work with that . . . that vile weapon, aimed straight at me!"

"We sympathize, Shannon," Sullivan said. "Anything he can do to you with his exterior design, we can undo with yours."

She put a hand on one hip and looked at him in disgust. "Are you deliberately trying to sound like Annie Oakley . . . 'Anything you can do, I can do better'? This is all just fun and games to you two, isn't it! You design a new entranceway to my house; he aims his roof right at the windows in my studio."

Calmly trying again, Sullivan began: "One possible solution would be—"

"My studio is where my creative yin forces are the strongest," she interrupted, gesturing at that doorway. Her art studio was adjacent to the stark foyer where we now stood. "I can't work anyplace else! What am I supposed to do? Build a fence out of fun house mirrors? How the hell will I get any work done with something like that, uglifying my environment?"

I gazed into her studio. Unlike this whitewashed, forlorn space, that room was so warm and airy with its log-cabin-like natural walls, the windows and skylights, the red terra cotta tile floor . . .

"Haven't you people ever worked for an artist before? Don't you know anything at all about creative inspiration? Artistic vision?"

The harsh words snapped me out of my reverie. "Of course we do, Shannon." My tone, I was proud to admit, sounded soothing and professional. "Steve's and my occupation also hinges on creative inspiration, and on our artistic vision."

Behind the outside wall of the current living room, two or three carpenters were making quite a racket as they worked to finish up the addition. I'm sure all that noise wasn't helping Shannon's mood or her "artistic vision," either.

She took a drag on her cigarette and lifted her chin as she blew out a cloud of smoke. "You're right. . . you're right. I'm so rattled, I don't even know what I'm saying." She grumbled, "Artist's temperament. Forgive me."

"That's totally understandable, Shannon," Sullivan said gently. Seemingly oblivious to his charm, she corkscrewed an already tangled section of hair around her index finger and glared at the checkerboard linoleum floor, which we'd soon be replacing with yummy wide-plank maple.

Although high-strung, Shannon was talented and successful. Her haunting modern oil paintings, with their bright primary colors and rich shadings, had struck a chord with people all around the world. She'd recently been profiled in several travel magazines, and more than one enthusiastic journalist had stated that Shannon Dupree—she signed her work with her maiden name—was doing for Crestview, Colorado, what R. C. Gorman had done for Santa Fe. She was also a relatively recent feng shui devotee, with all the boundless zeal of a new convert to a worthy cause.

"Our use of mirrors can be subtle, as we reflect the negative energy lines right back at him, Shannon," Sullivan continued. "We should be able to install one-way glass in your windows, though they're banned inside city limits. You'll be able to see out as though they were clear glass, but they're silver or gold mirrors on the other side."

While puffing on her cigarette, she nodded. "Erin already mentioned that idea last night over the phone."

I decided to pose the obvious question. "Have you tried talking to your neighbor about his porch roof?"

She chuckled. "*Talk*? To *Pate*?" She flicked her wrist at me. "Puh-lease. You've obviously never met the man. Trust me. I'm not a glutton for punishment."

"How about having your husband talk to him, then?" I asked. "Pate might be the macho type who does better with man-to-man conversations."

Michael Young was a talented chef whom my dear friend and landlady, Audrey Munroe, hosted periodically on her show. Lately he'd given me the impression that he was worried that his wife was slipping over the edge. Perhaps with good reason.

Shannon snorted. "Oh, that wouldn't do any good. Michael doesn't understand why I love this place so. He doesn't share my same family history. I inherited this house from my parents, long before Michael and I met. I told you about all this when I first hired you, remember? And how Pate was trying to force me to sell to him?" She cast a disparaging glance out her front window as she stubbed out her cigarette in a striking—if oversized and nonetheless overflowing—ceramic ashtray, undoubtedly yet another of her amazing creations. "You know, Pate isn't really even a feng shui practitioner," she scoffed. "The pompous phony just wants to use my belief system against me. He's trying to drive me so nuts that I'll sell just to get away from him. As if all those oversized, octagonal caps on his fence posts weren't bad enough! Now I've got a knife-point aimed at the window of my studio! At least it's out of line with my new entrance . . . and the storefront."

" '*Store*front' ?" Sullivan and I asked simultaneously.

"You wanted that space to be your new living room, didn't you?" Sullivan asked.

"Things have changed. Ang Chung said I'd be able to double my profits by setting up a gallery here."

Sullivan and I exchanged glances. In a New Age, college town like Crestview, we had several feng shui experts in the area. Ang Chung, however, had failed to impress either of us, and we'd been extremely disappointed to learn last month that Shannon had already hired him to work in tandem with us.

"Ang's advising you to sell your work from out of your house?" Sullivan asked.

"Absolutely. I can't control the feng shui environment of the galleries downtown like I can here. Some of them are just . . . all wrong. Those people are cutting *chi*s as if energy lines are sandwich meat! So I'm pulling all my pieces as soon as the remodel is finished. I'll market them myself. Ang says he can tell me exactly where to place each painting in my house so it'll fetch the highest price. He's charting out the most profitable alignment for my new showroom and guarantees I'll see a regular financial windfall." She frowned. "Just so long as the forces haven't been thrown off-kilter by outside energy fields. And now, thanks to Pate Hamlin, that's exactly what's happening!"

"But you're fifteen miles from downtown Crestview here," Sullivan pointed out, just a moment before I could raise the same objection. "You'll lose all the exposure from having your paintings in gallery windows along the pedestrian mall."

She shrugged. "That's what I was worried about, too, but Ang says his plan will prove to be more profitable for me this way."

"Have you gotten any second opinions on his readings, Shannon? There are lots of highly qualified feng shui consultants in Crestview, you know."

She narrowed her eyes at me as though I was spouting blasphemy. "That's part of what I'm paying you two to do. So far, the three of you are in perfect harmony. Ang *also* says a good start would be for us to install the mirrored windows. In every window in the house that faces Pate's monstrosity."

"That's what we'll do, then." Sullivan forced a smile. "We'll make it work."

"We can also do some creative things with your landscaping to ward off negative energy fields," I added.

"I know. Ang told me. He's outside with the contractor right now, showing him how to build the gazebo that we want. Ang's also a certified landscape artist, you know."

He must have gotten his certification out of the same Cracker Jack box that held his feng shui credentials.

She went into the studio, cranked open a window, and leaned outside. "David? Can you come in here, please?"

When she didn't return to the foyer, Sullivan and I migrated into the studio with her. "We'll turn your living room design into an art gallery, if you're sure that's what you want," I said.

"It *is*." Shannon fired up a new cigarette.

David Lewis, her contractor, let himself inside and gingerly entered the room. He had been hired from Sullivan's list of subcontractors instead of from my own. He was a tall, angular man with sandy-colored hair that seemed to be perpetually flecked with sawdust. He now had the beleaguered look of someone who'd taken a few too many directives from our hard-to-please, frenetic homeowner.

"Just like Ang and I predicted yesterday," Shannon declared, "Gilbert and Sullivan here have come up with the brilliant idea of one-way glass. You'll install them in every window with the slightest view of Jerk Face's monstrosity."

David shook his head. "We can't do that, Shannon. I already checked with the building inspectors. Crestview county doesn't allow one-way glass to be installed in private residences. They feel the sun reflecting on a mirrored surface doesn't . . . look good."

"But this *isn't* just a private residence. Some of the windows will be in the portion of my house that's used to create the source of my income."

He shook his head. "Doesn't matter. Mirrored glass is banned in residential neighborhoods, Shannon."

As though she was speaking to a simpleton, Shannon spread her arms and announced, "Then make them change the rules, David! Make it happen!"

"I'll . . . see what I can do. But there are going to be layers upon layers of red tape. It'll take several months to push a thing like that through."

She sneered at him. "You've got quite a no-can-do attitude, there. Maybe I should get a contractor with more clout."

"Clout's got nothing to do with anything."

"Oh, please! You don't think Pate Hamlin paid off city officials so they'd approve of all his ridiculous-looking additions? This has *everything* to do with clout! But just because Pate Hamlin is some kind of hot-shot multimillionaire doesn't give him the right to destroy my home! We're waging a counterattack, David. And you're either capable of going toe to toe with that bastard, or I'm replacing you with someone who can!"

"Shannon? Why is Pate so determined to buy your house in the first place?" Sullivan's question was an obvious attempt to defuse the tension; she'd told us why when she first hired us.

"He wants my land," she huffed. "I've got eight acres... more than he does. Plus I've got the better view of the Rockies." She took a long drag on her cigarette and narrowed her eyes at David. "Which reminds me. Have you talked to that foreman of yours yet? There's no way I'm going to allow you people to fraternize with the enemy, you know."

"Yeah, I did. You're sure it was *Duncan* you saw with Pate Hamlin?" David asked.

"I'm positive. The two of them were over here yesterday, sharing a beer and a laugh at my expense."

"Duncan swears he doesn't touch the stuff, Shannon. He's a recovering alcoholic."

"Maybe he was drinking soda, while Pate was drinking beer, then. That's not the point! I'm certain he took Pate on a guided tour of my home while I was out." She looked at Sullivan and me and cried, "I could smell that vile man's cologne throughout my entire house!"

Frankly, it was hard to believe a chain-smoker's sense of smell was all that keen. (Considering Shannon's temperament, that was an observation best kept to myself, however.)

David said, "My foreman swears he's never taken anyone inside your house."

"He's lying." She waved her lit cigarette in front of

David's face. "Which he probably gets from you. *You* told me the front construction would be complete by mid-October, and it's already November. Meanwhile, your work here is so shoddy, it's like you're getting paid to *sabotage* the construction."

He balled his fists and took a step toward her.

"Before we order the one-way glass, Shannon," I interjected hastily, "Steve and I will talk with Mr. Hamlin and his designer. Maybe we can call some sort of truce."

She rolled her eyes. "Suit yourself, but you'll be wasting your breath. Rebecca Berringer knows precisely what she's doing. She's a lot feng-shui-er a designer than you two are. In fact, she was my first choice, till I learned she was working for Pate. No offense. It was *Michael* who wanted us to hire you."

I was taken aback by this news but managed to murmur, "That was nice of him."

"Oh, well, he was just trying to suck up to Audrey Munroe." She took another anxious drag on her cigarette and puffed out the smoke. She looked a bit like a fire-breathing dragon. "He knows how close you and your landlady are. He wants more money for his appearances on her show. Though I've gotten to be friends with Audrey myself lately. We have a shared interest in preserving Crestview's character. Did she tell you about our committee?"

I shook my head, unable to focus on this turn in the conversation; David was still red-faced and tense. He glared at her with raw fury. "David," Sullivan said laying a hand on the man's shoulder, "let's take a look at your plans and see how things are coming along."

"Yeah. Sounds like a good idea."

"We'll be back soon, Shannon," I said and quietly closed the door behind us. I took some much-needed breaths of the crisp autumnal air.

My "confidence and optimism" mantra would be getting quite the workout. Now that we'd finished up some short-term jobs, we had more time to devote to Shannon's home. That, unfortunately, meant we'd spend more time with Ang Chung, whom we both suspected was either a flake or a con man. Meanwhile, Steve's contractor, David Lewis, had missed one completion deadline after another. Our brilliant client whom we'd been so ecstatic to land was turning into a whiny shrew before our eyes. I didn't even want to *think* about the personal ramifications of having to convince designer Rebecca Berringer, of all people, to cooperate with us; no ethical feng shui practitioner would have designed a porch roof like that in the first place.

As we rounded the house, Sullivan said quietly to David, "Shannon's something of a . . . crab at the moment. But she does have a point. The front's finally coming along, but you haven't even started on the back. What's the holdup?"

"Problem's with the new foreman I hired last week. Thought he'd work out better than he has so far. You'll see what I mean when you meet him."

Despite Shannon's mention of Ang Chung's having been outside with David, there was only one person behind the house. My jaw dropped when I spotted the huge lumberjack of a man working at the table saw with his back to us. The guy was a twin for my half brother. It couldn't actually *be* him, though. Taylor Duncan was only halfway through a year-long sentence in the county jail. The man turned.

"Taylor!" I cried.

He shut off his saw and removed his safety goggles. "Hey, sis," he said.